By Terry Pratchett

The Dark Side of the Sun • *Strata*
Good Omens (with Neil Gaiman)
The Long Earth (with Stephen Baxter)
The Long War (with Stephen Baxter)
The Long Mars (with Stephen Baxter)

For Young Adults
The Carpet People
The Bromeliad Trilogy: *Truckers* • *Diggers* • *Wings*
The Johnny Maxwell Trilogy: *Only You Can Save Mankind*
Johnny and the Dead • *Johnny and the Bomb*
The Unadulterated Cat (illustrated by Gray Jollife) • *Nation*

The Discworld® Books
The Color of Magic • *The Light Fantastic* • *Equal Rites*
Mort • *Sourcery* • *Wyrd Sisters* • *Pyramids*
Guards! Guards! • *Eric* (with Josh Kirby) • *Moving Pictures*
Reaper Man • *Witches Abroad* • *Small Gods*
Lords and Ladies • *Men at Arms* • *Soul Music* • *Feet of Clay*
Interesting Times • *Maskerade* • *Hogfather* • *Jingo*
The Last Continent • *Carpe Jugulum* • *The Fifth Elephant*
The Truth • *Thief of Time* • *Night Watch*
Monstrous Regiment • *Going Postal* • *Thud!*
Where's My Cow? (illustrated by Melvyn Grant)
Making Money • *Unseen Academicals* • *Snuff*

The Last Hero (illustrated by Paul Kidby)
The Art of Discworld (illustrated by Paul Kidby)
The Streets of Ankh-Morpork (with Stephen Briggs)
The Discworld Companion (with Stephen Briggs)
The Discworld Mapp (with Stephen Briggs)
The Wit and Wisdom of Discworld (with Stephen Briggs)
The Discworld Graphic Novels: *The Color of Magic*
The Light Fantastic
Turtle Recall (with Stephen Briggs)

For Young Adults
The Amazing Maurice and His Educated Rodents
The Wee Free Men • *A Hat Full of Sky*
Wintersmith • *I Shall Wear Midnight*
The Illustrated Wee Free Men (illustrated by Stephen Player)

Terry Pratchett

MAKING MONEY

A Novel of Discworld®

HARPER

An Imprint of HarperCollins Publishers

This is a work of fiction. Names, characters, places, and incidents are products of the author's imagination or are used fictitiously and are not to be construed as real. Any resemblance to actual events, locales, organizations, or persons, living or dead, is entirely coincidental.

HARPER

An Imprint of HarperCollins*Publishers*
195 Broadway
New York, New York 10007

Copyright © 2007 by Terry and Lyn Pratchett
Interior Ankh-Morpork design elements copyright © 2007 by Terry Pratchett and Bernard Pearson (a.k.a. The Cunning Artificer, www.discworldemporium.com)
Terry Pratchett® and Discworld® are registered trademarks.
ISBN 978-0-06-233499-2

First Harper premium printing: November 2014
First Harper mass market printing: October 2008
First Harper hardcover printing: October 2007

HarperCollins ® and Harper ® are registered trademarks of Harper-Collins Publishers.

Printed in the United States of America

Visit Harper paperbacks on the World Wide Web at
www.harpercollins.com

10 9 8 7 6 5 4 3 2

Author's Note

Hemlines as a measure of national crisis (page 78): The author will be forever grateful to the renowned military historian and strategist Sir Basil Liddell Hart for imparting this interesting observation to him in 1968. It may explain why the mini-skirt has, since the '60s, never really gone out of style.

Students of the history of computing will recognize in the Glooper a distant echo of the Phillips Economic Computer, built in 1949 by engineer turned economist Bill Phillips, which also made an impressive hydraulic model of the national economy. No Igors were involved, apparently. One of the early machines is on display in the Science Museum, London, and a dozen or so others are on display around the world, for the interested observer. And finally, as ever, the author is grateful to the British Heritage Joke Foundation for its work in ensuring that the fine old jokes never die . . .

CHAPTER 1

Waiting in darkness ❋ *A bargain sealed*
❋ *The hanging man* ❋ *Golem with a blue dress on*
❋ *Crime and punishment* ❋ *A chance to make real money*
❋ *The chain of goldish* ❋ *No unkindness to bears*
❋ *Mr. Bent keeps time*

THEY LAY IN the dark, guarding. There was no way of measuring the passage of time, nor any inclination to measure it. There was a time when they had not been here, and there would be a time, presumably, when they would, once more, not be here. They would be somewhere else. This time in between was immaterial.

But some had shattered and some, the younger ones, had gone silent.

The weight was increasing.

Something must be done.

One of them raised his mind in song.

❋ ❋ ❋

It was a hard bargain, but hard on whom? That was the question. And Mr. Blister the lawyer wasn't getting an answer. He would have liked an answer. When parties are interested in unprepossessing land, it might just pay for smaller parties to buy up any neighboring plots, just in case the party of the first part had heard something, possibly at a party.

But it was hard to see what there was to know.

He gave the woman on the other side of his desk a suitable concerned smile.

"You understand, Miss Dearheart, that this area is subject to dwarf mining law? That means all metals and metal ore are owned by the Low King of the dwarfs. You will have to pay him a considerable royalty on any that you remove. Not that there will be any, I'm bound to say. It is said to be sand and silt all the way down, and apparently it is a very long way down."

He waited for any kind of reaction from the woman opposite, but she just stared at him. Blue smoke from her cigarette spiraled toward the office ceiling.

"Then there is the matter of antiquities," said the lawyer, watching as much of her expression as could be seen through the haze. "The Low King has decreed that all jewelry, armor, ancient items classified as Devices, weaponry, pots, scrolls, bones extracted by you from the land in question will also be subject to a tax or confiscation."

Miss Dearheart paused as if to compare the litany

against an internal list, stubbed out her cigarette, and said, "Is there any reason to believe that there are any of those things there?"

"None whatsoever," said the lawyer, with a wry smile. "Everyone knows that we are dealing with a barren waste, but the king is insuring against 'what everyone knows' being wrong. It so often is."

"He is asking for a lot of money for a very short lease!"

"Which you are willing to pay. This makes dwarfs nervous, you see. It's very unusual for a dwarf to part with land, even for a few years. I gather he needs the money because of all this Koom Valley business."

"I'm paying the sum demanded!"

"Quite so, quite so. But I—"

"Will he honor the contract?"

"To the letter. That at least is certain. Dwarfs are sticklers in such matters. All you need to do is sign and, regrettably, pay."

Miss Dearheart reached into her bag and placed a thick sheet of paper on the table.

"This is a banker's note for five thousand dollars, drawn on the Royal Bank of Ankh-Morpork."

The lawyer smiled. "A name to trust," he said, and added, "traditionally, at least. Do sign where I've put the crosses, will you?"

He watched carefully as she signed, and she got the impression he was holding his breath.

"There," she said, pushing the contract across the desk.

"Perhaps you could assuage my curiosity, madam?" he said. "Since the ink is drying on the lease?"

Miss Dearheart looked around the room conspir-atorially, as if the heavy old bookcases concealed a multitude of ears.

"Can you keep a secret, Mr. Blister?"

"Oh, indeed, madam. Indeed!"

She looked around cautiously.

"Even so, this should be said quietly," she hissed.

He nodded hopefully, leaned forward, and for the first time in many years felt a woman's breath in his ear:

"*So can I,*" she said.

That was nearly three weeks ago . . .

SOME OF THE things you could learn up a drain-pipe at night were surprising. For example, people paid attention to small sounds—the click of a window catch, the clink of a lock pick—more than they did to big sounds, like a brick falling into the street or even (for this was, after all, Ankh-Morpork) a scream.

These were loud sounds, which were, therefore, public sounds, which, in turn, meant they were ev-eryone's problem and, therefore, not mine. But small sounds were nearby and suggested such things as stealth betrayed, and were, therefore, pressing and personal.

Therefore, he tried not to make little noises.

Below him, the coach yard of the Central Post Office buzzed like an overturned hive. They'd got the turntable working really well now. The overnight coaches were arriving and the new Überwald Flyer was gleaming in the lamplight. Everything was going right, which was, to the nighttime climber, why everything was going wrong.

The climber thrust a brick key into soft mortar, shifted his weight, moved his foo—

Damn pigeon! It flew up in panic, his *other* foot slipped, his fingers lost their grip on the drainpipe, and when the world had stopped churning, he was owing the postponement of his meeting with the distant cobbles to his hold on a brick key, which was, let's face it, nothing more than a long, flat nail with a T-piece grip.

And you can't bluff a wall, he thought. If you swing, you *might* get your hand and foot on the pipe, or the key might come out.

Oh . . . kay . . .

He had other keys and a small hammer. Could he knock one in without losing his grip on the other?

Above him, the pigeon joined its colleagues on a higher ledge.

The climber thrust the nail into the mortar with as much force as he dared, pulled the hammer out of his pocket, and, as the Flyer departed below with clattering and jingling, dealt the nail one massive blow.

It went in. He dropped the hammer, hoping the sound of its impact would be masked by the general bustle, and grabbed the new hold before it had hit the ground.

Oh . . . kay. And now I am . . . stuck?

The pipe was less than three feet away. Fine. This

would work. Move both hands onto the new hold, swing gently, get his left hand around the pipe, and he could drag himself across the gap. Then it would be just—

The pigeon was nervous. For pigeons, it's the default state of being. It chose this point to lighten the load.

Oh . . . kay. Correction: Two hands were now gripping the suddenly *very slippery* nail.

Damn.

And at this point, because nervousness runs through pigeons faster than a streaker through a convent, a gentle patter began.

There are times when "it does not get any better than this" does not spring to mind.

And then a voice from below said: "Who's up there?"

Thank you, hammer. They can't possibly see me, he thought. *People look up from the well-lit yard with their night vision in shreds. But so what? They know I'm here now.*

Oh . . . kay.

"All right, it's a fair cop, guv," he called down.

"A thief, eh?" said the voice below.

"Haven't touched a thing, guv. Could do with a hand up, guv."

"Are you Thieves' Guild? You're using their lingo."

"Not me, guv. I always use the word *guv*, guv."

He wasn't able to look down very easily now, but sounds below indicated that hostlers and off-duty coachmen were strolling over. That was not going to be helpful. Coachmen met most of their thieves out on lonely road, where the highwaymen seldom bothered to ask sissy questions like "Your money or your life?" When one was caught, justice and vengeance were happily combined by means of a handy length of lead pipe.

There was a muttering beneath him, and it appeared that a consensus had been reached.

"Right, Mister Post Office Robber," a cheery voice bellowed. "Here's what we're gonna do, okay? We're gonna go into the building, right, and lower you a rope. Can't say fairer'n that, right?"

"Right, guv."

It had been the wrong kind of cheery. It had been the cheery of the word *pal* in "You lookin' at me, pal?" The Guild of Thieves paid a twenty-dollar bounty fee for a nonaccredited thief brought in alive, and there were oh, so many ways of still being alive when you were dragged in and poured out on the floor.

He looked up. The window of the postmaster general's apartment was right above him.

Oh . . . kay.

His hands and arms were numb yet painful at the same time.

He heard the rattle of the big freight elevator inside the building, the thud of a hatch being slapped back, the footsteps across the roof, felt the rope hit his arm.

"Grab it or drop," said a voice, as he flailed to grasp it. "It's all the same in the long run." There was laughter in the dark.

The men heaved hard at the rope. The figure

dangled in the air, then kicked out and swung back. Glass shattered, just below the guttering, and the rope came up empty.

The rescue party turned to one another.

"All right, you two, front and back doors right now!" said a coachman who was faster on the uptake. "Head him off! Go down in the elevator! The rest of you, we'll squeeze him out, floor by floor!"

As they clattered back down the stairs and ran along the corridor, a man in a dressing gown poked his head out of one of the rooms, stared at them in amazement, and then snapped, "Who the hell are you lot? Go on, get after him!"

"Oh yeah? And who are you?" said a hostler, slowing down and glaring at him.

"He's Mr. Moist von Lipwick, he is!" said a coachman at the back. "He's the postmaster general!"

"Someone came crashing through the window, landed right between— I mean, nearly landed on me!" shouted the man in the dressing gown. "He ran off down the corridor! Ten dollars a man if you catch him! And it's Lipwig, actually!"

That would have restarted the stampede, but the hostler said, in a suspicious voice, "Here, say the word *guv*, will you?"

"What are you on about?" said the coachman.

"He doesn't half sound like that bloke," said the hostler. "*And* he's out of breath!"

"Are you stupid?" said the coachman. "He's the postmaster! He's got a bloody key! He's got *all* the keys! Why the hell would he want to break into his own post office?"

"I reckon we ought to take a look in that room," said the hostler.

"Really? Well, *I* reckon what Mr. Lipwig does to get out of breath in his own room is his own affair," said the coachman, giving Moist a huge wink. "An' I reckon ten dollars a man is running away from me 'cos of you being a tit. Sorry about this, sir," he said to Moist, "he's new and he ain't got no manners. We will now be leaving you, sir," he added, touching where he thought his forelock was, "with further apologies for any inconvenience which may have been caused. Now get cracking, you bastards!"

When they were out of sight, Moist went back into his room and carefully bolted the door behind him.

Well, at least he had *some* skills. That slight hint that there was a woman in his room had definitely swung it. Anyway, he *was* the postmaster general and he *did* have all the keys.

It was only an hour before dawn. He'd never get to sleep again. He might as well arise formally and enhance a reputation for keenness.

They might have shot him right off the wall, he thought, as he sorted out a shirt. They could have left him to hang there and taken bets on how long it'd be before he lost his grip; that would be the Ankh-Morpork way. It was just his good luck that they'd decided to give him a righteous smack or two before posting him through the guild's letter box. And luck came to those who left a space for it—

There was a heavy yet somehow still polite knock on the door.

"Are You Decent, Mr. Lipwig?" a voice boomed.

Regrettably, yes, thought Moist, but said aloud: "Come in, Gladys."

The floorboards creaked and furniture rattled on the other side of the room as Gladys entered.

Gladys was a golem, a clay man (or, for the sake of not having an argument, a clay woman) nearly seven feet tall. She—well, with a name like Gladys "it" was unthinkable and "he" just didn't do the job—wore a very large blue dress.

Moist shook his head. The whole silly business had been a matter of etiquette, really. Miss Maccalariat, who ruled the Post Office counters with a rod of steel and lungs of brass, had objected to a male golem cleaning the ladies' privies. How Miss Maccalariat had arrived at the conclusion that they were male by nature rather than custom was a fascinating mystery, but there was no profit in arguing with such as her.

And thus, with the addition of one extremely large cotton print dress, a golem became female enough for Miss Maccalariat.

The odd thing was that Gladys *was* female now, somehow. It wasn't just the dress. She tended to spend time around the counter girls, who seemed to accept her into the sisterhood despite the fact that she weighed half a ton. They even passed their fashion magazine on to her, although it was hard to imagine what winter skin-care tips would mean to someone a thousand years old, with eyes that glowed like holes into a furnace.

And now she was asking him if he was decent. How would she tell?

She'd brought him a cup of tea and the city edition of the *Times*, still damp from the press. Both were placed, with care, on the table.

And . . . oh gods, they'd printed his picture. His actual picture! Him and Vetinari and various notables last night, all looking up at the new chandelier! He'd managed to move slightly so that the picture blurred a little, but it was still the face that looked out at him from the shaving mirror every morning. All the way to Genua there were people who'd been duped, fooled, swindled, and cheated by that face. The only thing he hadn't done was hornswoggle, and that was only because he hadn't found out how to.

Okay, he did have the kind of all-purpose face that reminded you of lots of other faces, but it was a terrible thing to see it nailed down in print. Some people thought that pictures could steal your soul, but it was liberty that was on Moist's mind.

Moist von Lipwig, pillar of the community. Hah . . .

Something made him look closer. Who was that man behind him? He seemed to be staring over Moist's shoulder. Fat face, small beard which looked like Lord Vetinari's, but whereas the Patrician's was a goatee, the same style on that other man looked like the result of haphazard shaving. Someone from the bank, right? There'd been so many faces, so many hands to shake, and everyone wanted to get into the picture. The man looked hypnotized, but having your picture taken often did that to people. Just another guest at just another function . . .

And they'd only used the picture on page one because someone had decided that the main story, which was about another bank going bust and a mob of angry customers trying to hang the manager in the street, did not merit illustration. Did the editor have the common decency to print a picture of that and put a sparkle in everyone's day? Oh no, it had to be a picture of Moist von bloody Lipwig!

And the gods, once they've got a man against the ropes, can't resist one more thunderbolt. There, lower down the front page, was the headline "STAMP FORGER WILL HANG." They were going to execute Owlswick Jenkins. And for what? For murder? For being a notorious banker? No, just for knocking out a few hundred sheets of stamps. Quality work, too; the Watch would never have had a case if they hadn't burst into his attic and found half a dozen sheets of halfpenny reds hanging up to dry.

And Moist had testified, right there in the court. He'd had to. It was his civic duty. Forging stamps was held to be as bad as forging coins, and he couldn't dodge. He was the postmaster general, after all, a respected figure in the community. He'd have felt a tiny bit better if the man had sworn or glared at him, but he'd just stood in the dock, a little figure with a wispy beard, looking lost and bewildered.

He'd forged halfpenny stamps, he really had. It broke your heart, it really did. Oh, he'd done higher values too, but what kind of person takes all that trouble for half a penny? Owlswick Jenkins was, and now he was in one of the condemned cells down in the Tanty, with a few days to ponder on the nature of cruel fate before he was taken out to dance on air.

Been there, done that, Moist thought. It all went black—and then I got a whole new life. But I never thought being an upstanding citizen was going to be this bad.

"Er . . . thank you, Gladys," he said to the figure looming genteelly over him.

"You Have An Appointment Now With Lord Vetinari," said the golem.

"I'm sure I don't."

"There Are Two Guards Outside Who Are Sure You Do, Mr. Lipwig," Gladys rumbled.

Oh, Moist thought. One of *those* appointments.

"And the time of this appointment would be right now, would it?"

"Yes, Mr. Lipwig."

Moist grabbed his trousers, and some relic of his decent upbringing made him hesitate. He looked at the mountain of blue cotton in front of him.

"Do you mind?" he said.

Gladys turned away.

She's half a ton of clay, Moist thought glumly, as he struggled into his clothes. And insanity is catching.

He finished dressing and hurried down the back stairs and out into the coach yard that had so recently threatened to be his penultimate resting place. The Quirm Shuttle was pulling out, but he leaped up beside the coachman, gave the man a nod, and rode in splendor down Widdershins Broadway until he could jump down outside the palace's main entrance.

It would be nice, he reflected as he ran up the steps, if his lordship would entertain the idea that an appointment was something made by more than one person. But he was a tyrant, after all. They had to have *some* fun.

Drumknott, the Patrician's secretary, was waiting by the door of the Oblong Office, and quickly ushered him into the seat in front of his lordship's desk.

After nine seconds of industrious writing, Lord Vetinari looked up from his paperwork.

"Ah, Mr. Lipwig," he said. "Not in your golden suit?"

"It's being cleaned, sir."

"I trust the day goes well with you? Up until now, that is?"

Moist looked around, sorting hastily through the Post Office's recent little problems. Apart from Drumknott, who was standing by his master with an attitude of deferential alertness, they were alone.

"Look, I can explain," he said.

Lord Vetinari lifted an eyebrow with the care of one who, having found a piece of caterpillar in his salad, raises the rest of the lettuce.

"Pray do," he said, leaning back.

"We got a bit carried away," said Moist. "We were a bit too creative in our thinking. We encouraged mongooses to breed in the posting boxes to keep down the snakes . . ."

Lord Vetinari said nothing.

"Er . . . which, admittedly, we introduced into the letter boxes to reduce the numbers of toads . . ."

Lord Vetinari repeated himself.

"Er . . . which, it's true, staff put in the posting boxes to keep down the snails . . ."

Lord Vetinari remained unvocal.

"Er . . . These, I must in fairness point out, got into the boxes of their own accord, in order to eat the glue on the stamps," said Moist, aware that he was beginning to burble.

"Well, at least you were saved the trouble of having to introduce them yourselves," said Lord Vetinari cheerfully. "As you indicate, this may well have been a case where chilly logic should have been replaced by the common sense of, perhaps, the average chicken. But that is not the reason I asked you to come here today."

"If it's about the cabbage-flavored stamp glue—" Moist began.

Vetinari waved a hand. "An amusing incident," he said, "and I believe nobody actually died."

"Er . . . the Second-Issue 50p Stamp?" Moist ventured.

"The one they call 'The Lovers'?" said Vetinari. "The League of Decency did complain to me, yes, but—"

"Our artist didn't realize what he was sketching! He doesn't know much about agriculture! He thought the young couple were sowing seeds!"

"Ahem," said Vetinari. "But I understand that the offending affair can only be seen in any detail with quite a large magnifying glass, and so the offense, if such it be, is largely self-inflicted." He gave one of his slightly frightening little smiles. "I understand the few copies in circulation among the stamp collectors are affixed *to* a plain brown envelope." He looked at Moist's blank face, and sighed.

"Tell me, Mr. Lipwig, would you like to make some *real* money?"

Moist gave this some thought and then said, very carefully: "What will happen to me if I say yes?"

"You will start a new career of challenge and adventure, Mr. Lipwig."

Moist shifted uneasily. He didn't need to look around to know that, by now, someone would be standing by the door. Someone heavily but not grotesquely built, in a cheap black suit, and with absolutely no sense of humor.

"And, just for the sake of argument, what will happen if I say no?"

"You may walk out of that door over there, and the matter will not be raised again."

It was a door in a different wall. He had not come in by it.

"That door over there?" Moist stood up and pointed.

"Indeed so, Mr. Lipwig."

Moist turned to Drumknott. "May I borrow your pencil, Mr. Drumknott? Thank you."

He walked over to the door and opened it. Then he cupped one hand to his ear, theatrically, and dropped the pencil.

"Let's see how dee—"

Clik! The pencil bounced and rolled on some quite solid-looking floorboards. Moist picked it up and stared at it, and then walked slowly back to his chair.

"Didn't there used to be a deep pit full of spikes, down there?" he said.

"I can't imagine why you would think that," said Lord Vetinari.

"I'm sure there was," Moist insisted.

"Can you recall, Drumknott, why our Mr. Lipwig should think that there used to be a deep pit full of spikes behind that door?" said Vetinari.

"I can't imagine why he would think that, my lord," Drumknott murmured.

"I'm very happy at the Post Office, you know," said Moist, and realized that he sounded defensive.

"I'm sure you are. You make a superb postmaster general," said Vetinari. He turned to Drumknott. "Now I've finished this I'd better deal with the overnights from Genua," he said, and carefully folded the letter into an envelope.

"Yes, my lord," said Drumknott.

The tyrant of Ankh-Morpork bent to his work. Moist watched blankly as Vetinari took a small but heavy-looking box from a desk drawer, removed a stick of black sealing wax from it, and melted a small puddle of the wax onto the envelope with an air of absorption that Moist found infuriating.

"Is that all?" he said.

Vetinari looked up and appeared surprised to see him still there.

"Why, yes, Mr. Lipwig. You may go." He laid

aside the stick of wax and took a black signet ring out of the box.

"I mean, there's not some kind of problem, is there?"

"No, not at all. You have become an exemplary citizen, Mr. Lipwig," said Vetinari, carefully stamping a $\mathbb{V}$ into the cooling wax. "You rise each morning at eight, you are at your desk at thirty minutes past. You have turned the Post Office from a calamity into a smoothly running machine. You pay your taxes and a little bird tells me that you are tipped to be next year's chairman of the Merchants' Guild. Well *done*, Mr. Lipwig!"

Moist stood up to leave, but hesitated.

"What's wrong with being chairman of the Merchants' Guild, then?" he said.

With slow and ostentatious patience, Lord Vetinari slipped the ring back into its box and the box back into the drawer. "I beg your pardon, Mr. Lipwig?"

"It's just that you said it as though there was something wrong with it," said Moist.

"I don't believe I did," said Vetinari, looking up at his secretary. "Did I use a derogatory inflection, Drumknott?"

"No, my lord. You have often remarked that the traders and shopkeepers of the guild are the backbone of the city," said Drumknott, handing him a thick file.

"I shall get a very nearly gold chain," said Moist.

"He will get a very nearly gold chain, Drumknott," observed Vetinari, paying attention to a new letter.

"And what's so bad about that?" Moist demanded.

Vetinari looked up again with an expression of genuinely contrived puzzlement.

"Are you quite well, Mr. Lipwig? You appear to have something wrong with your hearing. Now run along, do. The Central Post Office opens in ten minutes and I'm sure you would wish, as ever, to set a good example to your staff."

When Moist had departed, the secretary quietly laid a folder in front of Vetinari.

It was labeled: ALBERT SPANGLER/MOIST VON LIPWIG.

"Thank you, Drumknott, but why?" he said.

"The death warrant on Albert Spangler is still extant, my lord," Drumknott murmured.

"Ah. I understand," said Lord Vetinari. "You think that I will point out to Mr. Lipwig that under his *nomme de felonie* of Albert Spangler he could still be hanged? You think that I might suggest to him that all I would need to do is inform the newspapers of my shock at finding that our honorable Mr. Lipwig is none other than the master thief, forger, and confidence trickster who over the years has stolen many hundreds of thousands of dollars, breaking banks and forcing honest businesses into penury? You think I will threaten to send in some of my most trusted clerks to audit the Post Office's accounts and, I am *certain*, uncover evidence of the most flagrant embezzlement? Do you think that they will find, for example, that the entirety of the Post Office pension fund has gone missing? You think I will express to the world my horror at how the wretch Lipwig escaped the hangman's noose with the aid of persons unknown? Do you think, in short, that I will explain to him how easily I can bring a man so low that his former friends will have to kneel down to spit on him? Is that what you assumed, Drumknott?"

The secretary stared up at the ceiling. His lips moved for twenty seconds or so, while Lord Vetinari got on with the paperwork.

Then he looked down and said: "Yes, my lord. That about covers it, I believe."

"Ah, but there is more than one way of racking a man, Drumknott."

"Face up or face down, my lord?"

"Thank you, Drumknott. I value your cultivated lack of imagination, as you know."

"Yes, sir. Thank you, sir."

"In fact, Drumknott, you get him to build his own rack, and let him turn the screw all by himself."

"I'm not sure I'm with you there, my lord."

Lord Vetinari laid his pen aside. "You have to consider the psychology of the individual, Drumknott. Everyone may be considered as a sort of lock, to which there is a key. I have great hopes for Mr. Lipwig in the coming skirmish. Even now, he still has the instincts of a criminal."

"How can you tell, my lord?"

"Oh, there are all sorts of little clues, Drumknott. But I think a most persuasive one is that he has just walked off with your pencil."

❊ ❊ ❊

HERE WERE MEETINGS. There were always meetings. And they were dull, which is part of the reason they were meetings. Dull likes company.

The Post Office wasn't going places anymore. It had gone to places. It had arrived at places. Now those places required staff, and staff rosters, and wages, and pensions, and building maintenance, and cleaning staff to come in at night, and collection schedules, and discipline, and investment, and on, and on . . .

Moist stared disconsolately at a letter from a Ms. Estressa Partleigh of the Campaign for Equal Heights. The Post Office, apparently, was not employing enough dwarfs. Moist had pointed out, very reasonably, he thought, that one-third of the staff were dwarfs. She had replied that this was not the point. The point was that since dwarfs were on average two-thirds the height of humans, the Post Office, as a responsible authority, should employ one and one-third dwarfs for every human employee. The Post Office must reach out to the dwarf community, said Ms. Partleigh.

Moist picked up the letter between his thumb and forefinger and dropped it on the floor. It's reach *down*, Ms. Partleigh, reach *down*.

There had also been something about core values.

He sighed. It had come to this. He was a responsible authority, and people could use terms like "core values" at him with impunity.

Nevertheless, Moist was prepared to believe that

there were people who found a quiet contentment in contemplating columns of figures. Their numbers did not include him.

It had been *weeks* since he'd last designed a stamp! And much longer since he'd had that tingle, that buzz, that feeling of flying that meant a scam was cooking gently and he was getting the better of someone who thought they were getting the better of him.

Everything was all so . . . worthy. And it was stifling.

Then he thought about this morning, and smiled. Okay, he'd got stuck, but the shadowy nighttime-climbing fraternity reckoned the Post Office to be particularly challenging. And he'd talked his way out of the problem. All in all, it was a win. For a while there, in between the moments of terror, he'd felt alive and flying.

A heavy tread in the corridor indicated that Gladys was on the way with his mid-morning tea. She entered with her head bent down to avoid the lintel and, with the skill of something massive yet possessed of incredible coordination, put the cup and saucer down without a ripple. She said: "Lord Vetinari's Carriage Is Waiting Outside, Sir."

Moist was sure there was more treble in Gladys's voice these days.

"But I saw him an hour ago! Waiting for what?" he said.

"You, Sir." Gladys dropped a curtsy, and when a golem drops a curtsy you can *hear* it.

Moist looked out of his window. A black coach

was outside the Post Office. The coachman was standing next to it, having a quiet smoke.

"Does he *say* I have an appointment?" he said.

"The Coachman Said He Was Told To Wait," said Gladys.

"Ha!"

Gladys curtsied again before she left.

When the door had shut behind her, Moist returned his attention to the pile of paperwork in his in tray. The top sheaf was headed "Minutes of the Meeting of the Traveling Post Offices Subcommittee," but they looked more like hours.

He picked up the mug of tea. On it was printed: **You Don't Have to Be Mad to Work Here But It Helps!** He stared at it, and then absentmindedly picked up a thick black pen and drew a comma between **Here** and **But**. He also crossed out the exclamation mark. He hated that exclamation mark, hated its manic, desperate cheeriness. It meant: You Don't Have to Be Mad to Work Here. *We'll* See to That!

He forced himself to read the Minutes, realizing that his eye was skipping whole paragraphs in self-defense.

Then he started on the District Offices' Weekly Reports. After that, the Accidents and Medical Committee sprawled its acres of words.

Occasionally, Moist would glance at the mug.

At twenty-nine minutes past eleven the alarm on his desk clock went *bing*. Moist got up, put his chair under the desk, walked to the door, counted to three, opened it, said "Hello, Tiddles" as the Post Office's antique cat padded in, counted to nineteen as the cat did its circuit of the room, said "Good-bye, Tiddles" as it plodded back into the corridor, shut the door, and went back to his desk.

You just opened the door for an elderly cat who's lost hold of the concept of walking around things, he told himself, as he rewound the alarm. *You do it every day. Do you think that's the action of a sane man? Okay, it's sad to see him standing for hours with his head up against a chair until someone moves it, but now you get up every day to move the chair for him. This is what honest work does to a person.*

Yes, but dishonest work nearly got me hanged! he protested.

So? Hanging only lasts a couple of minutes. The Pension Fund Committee lasts a lifetime! It's all so boring! You're trapped in chains of goldish!

Moist had ended up near the window. The coachman was eating a cookie. When he caught sight of Moist, he gave a friendly wave.

Moist almost jumped back from the window. He sat down hurriedly and countersigned FG/2 requisition forms for fifteen minutes straight. Then he went out into the corridor, which on its far side opened to the big hall, and looked down.

He'd promised to get the big chandeliers back, and now they both hung there, glittering like private star systems. The big, shiny counter gleamed in its polished splendor. There was the hum of purposeful and largely efficient activity.

He'd done it. It all worked. It was the Post Office. And it wasn't any fun anymore.

He went down into the sorting rooms, he dropped

into the postmen's locker room to have a convivial cup of tar-like tea, he wandered around the coach yard and got in the way of people who were trying to do their jobs, and last he plodded back to his office, bowed under the weight of the humdrum.

He just happened to glance out of the window, as anyone might.

The coachman was eating his lunch! His damn lunch! He had a little folding chair on the pavement, with his meal on a little folding table! It was a large pork pie and a bottle of beer! There was even a white tablecloth!

Moist went down the main stairs like a maddened tap dancer and ran out through the big double doors. In one crowded moment, as he hurried toward the coach, the meal, table, cloth, and chair were stowed in some unnoticeable compartment, and the man was standing by the invitingly open door.

"Look, what is this about?" Moist demanded, panting for breath. "I don't have all—"

"Ah, Mr. Lipwig," said Lord Vetinari's voice from within, "do step inside. Thank you, Houseman, Mrs. Lavish will be waiting. Hurry *up*, Mr. Lipwig, I am not going to eat you. I have just had an acceptable cheese sandwich."

What harm can it do to find out? It's a question that left bruises down the centuries, even more than "It can't hurt if I only take one" and "It's all right if you only do it standing up."

Moist climbed into the shadows. The door clicked behind him, and he turned suddenly.

"Oh, really," said Lord Vetinari. "It's just shut,

it isn't *locked*, Mr. Lipwig. Do compose yourself!"
Beside him, Drumknott sat primly with a large
leather satchel on his lap.

"What is it you want?" said Moist.

Lord Vetinari raised that eyebrow. "I? Nothing.
What do *you* want?"

"What?"

"Well, you got into my coach, Mr. Lipwig."

"Yes, but I was told it was outside!"

"And if you had been told it was black, would you
have found it necessary to do anything about it?
There is the door, Mr. Lipwig."

"But you've been parked out here all morning!"

"It is a public street, sir," said Lord Vetinari.
"Now sit *down*. Good."

The coach jerked into motion.

"You are restless, Mr. Lipwig," said Vetinari.
"You are careless of your safety. Life has lost its
flavor, has it not?"

Moist didn't reply.

"Let us talk about angels," said Lord Vetinari.

"Oh yes, I know that one," said Moist bitterly.
"I've heard that one. That's the one you got me with
after I was hanged—"

Vetinari raised an eyebrow. "Only *mostly* hanged,
I think you'll find. To within an inch of your life."

"Whatever! I was hanged! And the worst part of
that was finding out I only got two paragraphs in
the *Tanty Bugle*!* Two paragraphs, may I say, for a

---

*A periodical published throughout the Plains, noted for its coverage
of murder (preferably 'orrible) trials, prison escapes, and the world
that in general is surrounded by a chalk outline. Very popular.

life of ingenious, inventive, and strictly nonviolent crime? I could have been an example to youngsters! Page one got hogged by the Dyslectic Alphabet Killer, and he only managed A and W!"

"I confess the editor does appear to believe that it is not a proper crime unless someone is found in three alleys at once, but that is the price of a free press. And it suits us both, does it not, that Albert Spangler's passage from this world was . . . unmemorable?"

"Yes, but I wasn't expecting an afterlife like this! I have to do what I'm told for the rest of my life?"

"Correction, your new life. That is a crude summary, yes," said Vetinari. "Let me rephrase things, however. Ahead of you, Mr. Lipwig, is a life of respectable quiet contentment, of civic dignity, and, of course, in the fullness of time, a pension. Not to mention, of course, the proud goldish chain."

Moist winced at this. "And if I *don't* do what you say?"

"Hmm? Oh, you misunderstand me, Mr. Lipwig. That is what will happen to you if you decline my offer. If you accept it, you will survive on your wits against powerful and dangerous enemies, with every day presenting fresh challenges. Someone may even try to kill you."

"What? Why?"

"You annoy people. A hat goes with the job, incidentally."

"And this job makes real money?"

"Nothing but money, Mr. Lipwig. It is, in fact, that of master of the Royal Mint."

"What? Banging out pennies all day?"

"In short, yes. But it is traditionally attached to a senior post at the Royal Bank of Ankh-Morpork, which will occupy most of your attention. You can make money, as it were, in your spare time."

"A *banker? Me?*"

"Yes, Mr. Lipwig."

"But I don't know anything about running a bank!"

"Good. No preconceived ideas."

"I've *robbed* banks!"

"Capital! Just reverse your thinking," said Lord Vetinari, beaming. "The money should be on the *inside.*"

The coach slowed to a stop.

"What is this about?" said Moist. "Actually about?"

"When you took over the Post Office, Mr. Lipwig, it was a disgrace. Now it works quite efficiently. Efficiently enough to be boring, in fact. Why, a young man might find himself climbing by night, perhaps, or picking locks for the thrill of it, or even flirting with Extreme Sneezing. How are you finding the lock picks, by the way?"

It had been a poky little shop in a poky alley, and there had been no one in there but the little old lady who'd sold him the picks. He still didn't know exactly why he'd bought them. They were only geographically illegal, but it gave him a little thrill to know they were in his jacket. It was sad, like those businessmen who came to work in serious clothes but wore colorful ties in a mad, desperate attempt to show there was a free spirit in there somewhere.

*Oh gods, I've become one of them. But at least he
doesn't seem to know about the blackjack.*

"I'm not too bad," he said.

"And the blackjack? You, who have never struck
another man? You clamber on rooftops and pick the
locks on your own desks. You're like a caged animal,
dreaming of the jungle! I'd like to give you what you
long for. I'd like to throw you to the lions."

Moist began to protest, but Vetinari held up a
hand.

"You took our joke of a post office, Mr. Lipwig,
and made it a solemn undertaking. But the banks of
Ankh-Morpork, sir, are very serious indeed. They
are serious donkeys, Mr. Lipwig. There have been
too many failures. They're stuck in the mud, they
live in the past, they are hypnotized by class and
wealth, they think gold is important."

"Er . . . isn't it?"

"No. And thief and swindler that you are—
pardon me, once *were*—you know it, deep down.
For you, it was just a way of keeping score," said Vetinari. "What does gold know of true worth? Look
out of the window and tell me what you see."

"Um . . . a small, scruffy dog watching a man
taking a piss in an alley," said Moist. "Sorry, but you
chose the wrong time."

"Had I been taken *less literally*," said Lord Vetinari, giving him a Look, "you would have seen a
large, bustling city, full of ingenious people spinning wealth out of the common clay of the world.
They construct, build, carve, bake, cast, mold,
forge, and devise strange and inventive crimes. But

they keep their money in old socks. They trust their socks better than they trust banks. Coinage is in artificially short supply, which is why your postage stamps are now a de facto currency. Our serious banking system is a mess. A joke, in fact."

"It'll be a bigger joke if you put *me* in charge," said Moist.

Vetinari gave him a brief little smile. "Will it?" he said. "Well, we all need a chuckle sometimes."

The coachman opened the door, and they stepped out.

Why temples? thought Moist, as he looked up at the facade of the Royal Bank of Ankh-Morpork. Why do they always build banks to look like temples, despite the fact that several major religions (a) are canonically against what they do inside and (b) bank there?

He'd looked at it before, of course, but had never really bothered to *see* it until now. As temples of money went, this one wasn't bad. The architect at least knew how to design a decent column, and also knew when to stop. He had set his face like flint against any prospect of cherubs, although above the columns was a high-minded frieze showing something allegorical involving maidens and urns. Most of the urns and, Moist noticed, some of the young women, had birds nesting in them. An angry pigeon looked down at Moist from a stony bosom.

Moist had walked past the place many times. It never looked very busy. And behind it was the Royal Mint, which never showed any signs of life at all.

It would be hard to imagine an uglier building

that hadn't won a major architectural award. The Mint was a gaunt brick-and-stone block, its windows high, small, many, and barred, its doors protected by portcullises, its whole construction saying to the world: Don't Even Think About It.

Up until now Moist hadn't even thought about it. It was a mint. That sort of place held you upside down over a bucket and shook you hard before they let you out. They had guards and doors with spikes.

And Vetinari wanted to make him the boss of it. There was going to have to be a *huge* razor blade in a stick of cotton candy this big.

"Tell me, my lord," Moist said carefully, "what happened to the man who used to occupy the post?"

"I thought you would ask, so I looked it up. He died aged ninety, of a schism of the heart."

That didn't sound too bad, but Moist knew enough to probe further. "Anyone else died lately?"

"Sir Joshua Lavish, the chairman of the bank. He died six months ago in his own bed, aged eighty."

"A man can die in some very unpleasant ways in his own bed," Moist pointed out.

"So I believe," said Lord Vetinari. "In this case, however, it was in the arms of a young woman called Honey after a very large meal of deviled oysters. How unpleasant that was I suppose we shall never know."

"She was his wife? You said it was his own—"

"He had an apartment in the bank," said Lord Vetinari. "A traditional perk that was useful when he was"—here Vetinari paused for a fraction of a second—"working late. Mrs. Lavish was not present at the time."

"If he was a Sir, shouldn't she be a Lady?" said Moist.

"It is rather characteristic of Mrs. Lavish that she does not like being a Lady," said Lord Vetinari smoothly. "And I bow to her wishes."

"Did he often 'work' late?" said Moist, carefully quoting. *No lady, eh?* he thought.

"With astonishing regularity for his age, I understand," said Vetinari.

"Oh, really?" said Moist. "You know, I think I recall the obituary in the *Times*. But I don't remember any of *that* sort of detail."

"Yes, what *is* the press coming to, one wonders."

Vetinari turned and surveyed the building.

"Of the two, I prefer the honesty of the Mint," he said. "It growls at the world. The tax gatherers used to have the top two floors, which may help engender a certain worried feeling. What do you think, Mr. Lipwig?"

"What's that round thing I always see poking out of the roof?" said Moist. "It makes it look like a piggy bank with a big coin stuck in the slot!"

"Oddly enough, it did used to be known as the Bad Penny," said Vetinari. "It is a large treadmill that provides power for the coin stamping and so forth. Powered by prisoners once upon a time, when 'community service' wasn't just a word. Or even two. It was considered cruel and unusual punishment, however, which does rather suggest a lack of imagination. Shall we go in?"

"Look, sir, what is it you would want me to *do*?"

said Moist, as they climbed the marble steps. "I know a bit about banking, but how do I run a mint?"

Vetinari shrugged. "I have no idea. People turn handles, I assume. Someone tells them how often, and when to stop."

"And why will anyone want to kill me?"

"I couldn't say, Mr. Lipwig. But there was at least one attempt on your life when you were innocently delivering letters, so I expect your career in banking will be an exciting one."

They reached the top of the steps. An elderly man in what might have been the uniform of a general in one of the more unstable kinds of armies held open the door for them.

Lord Vetinari gestured for Moist to enter first.

"I'm just going to have a look around, all right?" said Moist, stumbling through the doorway. "I really haven't had time to think about this."

"That is understood," said Vetinari.

"I'm committing myself to nothing by it, right?"

"Nothing," said Vetinari. He strolled to a leather sofa and sat down, beckoning Moist to sit beside him. Drumknott, ever attentive, hovered behind them.

"The smell of banks is always pleasing, don't you think?" said Vetinari. "A mix of polish and ink and wealth."

"And ursery," said Moist.

"That would be cruelty to bears. You mean usury, I suspect. The churches don't seem to be so much against it these days. Incidentally, only the current chairman of the bank knows my intentions. To everyone else here today, you are merely carrying out a brief inspection on my behalf. It is just as well you are not wearing the famous gold suit."

There was a hush in the bank, mostly because the ceiling was so high that sounds were just lost, but partly because people lower their voices in the presence of large sums of money. Red velvet and brass were much in evidence. There were pictures everywhere, of serious men in frock coats. Sometimes footsteps echoed briefly on the white marble floor and were suddenly swallowed when their owner stepped onto an island of carpet. And the big desks were covered with sage-green leather. Ever since he was small, sage-green-leather-covered desks had been Wealth to Moist. Red leather? Pah! That was for parvenus and wannabes. Sage green meant that you'd got there, and that your ancestors got there too. It should be a little bit worn, for the best effect.

On the wall above the counter a big clock, supported by cherubs, ticked away. Lord Vetinari was having an effect on the bank. Staff were nudging one another and pointing with their expressions.

In truth, Moist realized, they were not a readily noticeable pair. Nature had blessed him with the ability to be a face in the background, even when he was standing only a few feet away. He wasn't ugly, he wasn't handsome, he was just so forgettable he sometimes surprised himself while shaving. And Vetinari wore black, not a forward color at all, but nevertheless his presence was like a lead weight on a rubber sheet. It distorted the space around it.

People didn't immediately see him, but they sensed his presence.

Now people were whispering into speaking tubes. The Patrician was here and no one was formally greeting him! There would be trouble!

"How is Miss Dearheart?" said Vetinari, apparently oblivious of the growing stir.

"She's away," said Moist bluntly.

"Ah, the Trust has located another buried golem, no doubt."

"Yes."

"Still trying to carry out orders given to it thousands of years ago?"

"Probably. It's out in the wilderness somewhere."

"She is indefatigable," said Vetinari happily. "Those people are resurrected from darkness to turn the wheels of commerce, for the general good. Just like you, Mr. Lipwig. She is doing the city a great service. And the Golem Trust, too."

"Yes," said Moist, letting the whole resurrection thing pass.

"But your tone says otherwise."

"Well . . ." Moist knew he was squirming, but squarm anyway. "She's always rushing off because they've traced another golem in some ancient sewer or something—"

"And not rushing off after you, as it were?"

"And she's been away for weeks on this one," said Moist, ignoring the comment because it was probably accurate, "and she won't tell me what it's about. She just says it's very important. Something new."

"I think she's mining," said Vetinari. He began to

tap his cane on the marble, slowly. It made a ringing sound. "I have heard that golems appear to be mining on dwarf land this side of Chimeria, near the coach road. Much to the interest of the dwarfs, I might add. The king leased the land to the Trust and wants to make certain he gets a look at what is dug up."

"Is she in trouble?"

"Miss Dearheart? No. Knowing her, the king of the dwarfs might be. She's a very . . . composed young lady, I've noticed."

"Hah! You don't know the half of it."

Moist made a mental note to send Adora Belle a message as soon as this was over. The whole situation with golems was heating up once more, what with the guilds complaining about them taking jobs. She was needed in the city—by the golems, obviously.

He became aware of a subtle noise. It came from below, and sounded very much like air bubbling through liquid, or maybe water being poured out of a bottle with the familiar *blomp-blomp* sound.

"Can you hear that?" he said.

"Yes."

"Do you know what it is?"

"The future of economical planning, I understand." Lord Vetinari looked if not worried then at least unaccustomedly puzzled.

"Something must have happened," he said. "Mr. Bent is normally oiling his way across the floor within seconds of my entrance. I hope nothing unamusing has happened to him."

A pair of big elevator doors opened at the far end

of the hall, and a man stepped through. For just a moment, probably unnoticed by anyone who had never had to read faces for a living, he was anxious and upset, but it passed with speed as he adjusted his cuffs and set his face in the warm, benevolent smile of someone who is about to take some money off you.

Mr. Bent was in every way smooth and uncreased. Moist had been expecting a traditional banker's frock coat, but instead there was a very well-cut black jacket above pinstripe trousers. Mr. Bent was also silent. His feet, soundless even on the marble, were unusually large for such a dapper man, but the shoes, black and polished, mirror-shiny, were very well made. Perhaps he wanted to show them off, because he walked like a dressage horse, lifting each foot very deliberately off the ground before setting it on the ground again. Apart from that incongruity, Mr. Bent had the air about him of one who stands quietly in a cupboard when not in use.

"Lord Vetinari, I am *so* sorry!" he began. "I'm afraid there was unfinished business—"

Lord Vetinari got to his feet. "Mr. Mavolio Bent, allow me to present Mr. Moist von Lipwig," he said. "Mr. Bent is the chief cashier here."

"Ah, the inventor of the revolutionary unsecured one-penny note?" said Bent, extending a thin hand. "Such audacity! I'm very pleased to meet you, Mr. Lipwig."

"One-penny note?" said Moist, mystified. Mr. Bent, despite his protestation, did not look pleased at all.

"Did you not listen to what I was saying?" said Vetinari. "Your *stamps*, Mr. Lipwig."

"A de facto currency," said Bent, and light dawned on Moist. Well, it was true, he knew it. He'd meant stamps to be stuck to letters, but people had decided, in their untutored way, that a penny stamp was nothing more than a very light, government-guaranteed penny and, moreover, *one that you could put on an envelope*. The advertising pages were full of businesses that had sprouted on the back of the beguilingly transferable postage stamps: "Learn The Uttermost Secrets Of The Cosmos! Send 8 penny stamps for booklet!" A lot of stamps wore out as currency without ever seeing the inside of a posting box.

Something in Bent's smile annoyed Moist, though. It was not quite as kind when seen close.

"What do you mean by 'unsecured'?" he said.

"How do you validate its claim to be worth a penny?"

"Er, if you stick it on a letter you get a penny's worth of travel?" said Moist. "I don't see what you're getting at—"

"Mr. Bent is one of those who believe in the pre-eminence of gold, Mr. Lipwig," said Vetinari. "I'm sure you'll get along exactly like a house on fire. I shall leave you now, and await your decision with, ah, *compound* interest. Come, Drumknott. Perhaps you will drop in to see me tomorrow, Mr. Lipwig?"

Moist and Bent watched them go. Then Bent glared at Moist. "I suppose I must show you around . . . sir," he said.

"I have a feeling that we haven't quite hit it off, Mr. Bent," said Moist.

Bent shrugged, an impressive maneuver on that gaunt frame. It was like watching an ironing board threatening to unfold.

"I know nothing to your discredit, Mr. Lipwig. But I believe the chairman and Lord Vetinari have a dangerous scheme in mind, and you are their cat's-paw, Mr. Lipwig, you are their implement."

"This would be the new chairman?"

"That is correct."

"I don't particularly want or intend to be an implement," said Moist.

"Good for you, sir. But events are eventuating—"

There was a crash of broken glass from below, and a faint, muffled voice shouted: "Damn! There goes the balance of payments!"

"Let's have that tour, shall we?" said Moist brightly. "Starting with what that was?"

"That abomination?" Bent gave a little shudder. "I think we should leave *that* until Hubert has cleaned up. Oh, will you look at that? It really is terrible . . ."

Mr. Bent strode across the floor until he was under the big, solemn clock. He glared at it as if it had mortally offended him, and snapped his fingers, but a junior clerk was already hurrying across the floor with a small stepladder. Mr. Bent mounted the steps, opened the clock, and moved the second hand forward by two seconds. The clock was slammed shut, the steps dismounted, and the accountant returned to Moist, adjusting his cuffs.

He looked Moist up and down. "It loses almost a minute a week. Am I the only person who finds this offensive? It would appear so, alas. Let's start with the gold, shall we?"

"Ooo, yes," said Moist. "Let's!"

CHAPTER 2

"**S**OMEHOW I WAS expecting something . . . bigger," said Moist, looking through the steel bars into the little room that held the gold. The metal, in open bags and boxes, gleamed dully in the torchlight.

"That is almost ten tons of gold," said Bent reproachfully. "It does not have to look big."

"But all the ingots and bags put together aren't much bigger than the desks out there!"

"It is very heavy, Mr. Lipwig. It is the one true

metal, pure and unsullied," said Bent. His left eye twitched. "It is the metal that never fell from grace."

"Really?" said Moist, checking that the door out of there was still open.

"And it is also the only basis of a sound financial system," Mr. Bent went on, while the torchlight reflected from the bullion and gilded his face. "There is Value! There is Worth! Without the anchor of gold, all would be chaos."

"Why?"

"Who would set the value of the dollar?"

"Our dollars are not pure gold, though, are they?"

"Aha, yes. Gold-colored, Mr. Lipwig," said Bent. "Less gold than seawater. Gold-ish. We adulterated our own currency! Infamy! There can be no greater crime!" His eye twitched again.

"Er . . . murder?" Moist ventured. Yep, the door was still open.

Mr. Bent waved a hand. "Murder only happens once," he said, "but when the trust in gold breaks down, chaos rules. But it had to be done. The abominable coins are, admittedly, only goldish, but they are at least a solid token of true gold in the reserves. In their wretchedness, they nevertheless acknowledge the primacy of gold and our independence from the machinations of government! We ourselves have more gold than any other bank in the city, and only I have a key to that door! And the manager has one too, of course," he added, very much as a grudging and unwelcome afterthought.

"I read somewhere that the coins represent a

promise to hand over a dollar's worth of gold," said Moist helpfully.

Mr. Bent steepled his hands in front of his face and turned his eyes upward, as though praying.

"In theory, yes," he said after a few moments. "I would prefer to say that it is a tacit understanding that we *will* honor our promise to exchange it for a dollar's worth of gold, provided we are not, in point of fact, asked to."

"So . . . it's not really a promise?"

"It certainly is, sir, in financial circles. It is, you see, about trust."

"You mean, trust us, we've got a big expensive building?"

"You jest, Mr. Lipwig, but there may be a grain of truth there." Bent sighed. "I can see you have a lot to learn, and at least you'll have me to teach you. And now, I think, you would like to see the Mint. People always like to see the Mint. It's twenty-seven minutes and thirty-six seconds past one, so they should have finished their lunch hour."

I T WAS A CAVERN. Moist was pleased about that, at least. A Mint should be lit by flames.

Its main hall was three stories high, and picked up some gray daylight from the rows of barred windows. And, in terms of primary architecture, that was it. Everything else was sheds.

Sheds were built onto the walls and even hung

like swallows' nests up near the ceiling, accessed by unsafe-looking wooden stairs. The uneven floor itself was a small village of sheds, placed any old how, no two alike, each one carefully roofed against the nonexistent prospect of rain. Wisps of smoke spiraled gently through the thick air. Against one wall a forge glowed, providing the dark orange glow that gave the place the right stygian atmosphere. The place looked like the after-death destination for people who had committed small and rather dull sins.

This was, however, just the background. What dominated the hall was the Bad Penny. The tread-mill was . . . strange.

Moist had seen treadmills before. There had been one in the Tanty, wherein inmates could invigorate their cardiovascular systems whether they wanted to or not. Moist had taken a turn or two before he worked out how to play the system. It had been a brute of a thing, cramped, heavy, and depressing. The Bad Penny was much larger but hardly seemed to be there at all. There was a metal rim that, from here, looked frighteningly thin. It was hard to see the spokes, until Moist realized that there were no spokes, just hundreds of thin wires.

"All right, I can see it must work, but—" he began, staring up at the huge gearbox.

"It works very well, I gather," said Bent. "They have a golem to power it when needed."

"But surely it should fall to bits!"

"Should it? I am not in a position to say, sir. Ah, here comes everyone . . ."

Figures were heading toward them from various sheds and from the door at the far end of the building. They walked slowly and deliberately and with one purpose, rather like the living dead.

In the end, Moist kept thinking of them as the Men of the Sheds. They weren't, all of them, that old, but even the young ones, most of them, appeared to have donned the mantle of middle age very early. Apparently, to get a job in the Mint, you had to wait until someone died; it was a case of Dead Men's Sheds. Illuminating the bright side, however, was the fact that when your prospective vacancy became available you got the job even if you were only slightly less dead than the previous incumbent.

The Men of the Sheds ran the linishing shed, the milling shed, the finishing shed, the foundry (two sheds), the security (one shed, but quite a big one), and the storage shed, which had a lock Moist could have opened with a sneeze. The other sheds were a mystery, but presumably had been built in case someone needed a shed in a hurry.

The Men of the Sheds had what passed within the sheds as names: Alf, Young Alf, Gobber, Boy Charlie, King Henry . . . but the one who was, as it were, the designated speaker to the world beyond the sheds, had a whole name.

"This is Mr. Shady the Eighteenth, Mr. Lipwig," said Bent. "Mr. Lipwig is . . . just visiting."

"The Eighteenth?" said Moist. "There are another seventeen of you?"

"Not anymore, sir," said Shady, grinning.

"Mr. Shady is the hereditary foreman, sir," Bent supplied.

"Hereditary foreman . . ." Moist repeated blankly.

"That's right, sir," said Shady. "Does Mr. Lipwig want to know the history, sir?"

"No," said Bent firmly.

"Yes," said Moist, seeing his firmly and raising him an emphatically.

"Oh it appears that he does," sighed Bent. Mr. Shady smiled.

It was a very full history, and took some telling. At one point Moist was sure it was time for an ice age. Words streamed past him like sleet but, like sleet, some stuck. The post of hereditary foreman had been created hundreds of years before, when the post of master of the Mint was a sinecure handed to a drinking pal of the current king or patrician, who used it as a piggy bank and did nothing more than turn up now and again with a big sack, a hangover, and a meaningful look. The foremanship was instituted because it was dimly realized that someone ought to be in charge and, if possible, sober.

"So you actually run it all?" said Moist quickly, to stem the flow of really interesting facts about money.

"That's right, sir. Pro tem. There hasn't been a master for a hundred years."

"So how do you get paid?"

There was a moment's silence, and then Mr. Shady said, like a man talking to a child: "This *is* a mint, sir."

"You make your own wages?"

"Who else is going to, sir? But it's all official, isn't that right, Mr. Bent? He gets all the dockets. We cut out the middleman, really."

"Well, at least you're in a profitable business," said Moist cheerfully. "I mean, you must be making money hand over fist!"

"We manage to break even sir, yes," said Shady, as if it was a close-run thing.

"Break even? You're a mint!" said Moist. "How can you not make a profit by making money?"

"Overheads, sir. There's overheads wherever you look."

"Even underfoot?"

"There too, sir," said Shady. "It's ruinous, sir, it really is. Y'see, it costs a ha'penny to make a farthin' an' nearly a penny to make a ha'penny. A penny comes in at a penny farthin'. Sixpences cost tuppence farthin', so we're in pocket there. Half a dollar cost seven pence. And it's only sixpence to make a dollar, a definite improvement, but that's 'cos we does 'em here. The real buggers are the mites, 'cos they're worth half a farthin' but cost sixpence 'cos it's fiddly work, bein' so small and have got that hole in the middle. The thrupenny bit, sir, we've only got a couple of people makin' those, a lot of work which runs out at seven pence. And don't ask me about the tupenny piece!"

"What about the tupenny piece?"

"I'm glad you asked me that, sir. Fine work, sir, tots up to seven and one one-sixteenth pence. And, yes, there's one-sixteenth of a penny, sir, the elim."

"I've never heard of it!"

"Well, no, sir, you wouldn't, a gentleman of class like yourself, but it has its place, sir, it has its place. Nice little thing, sir, lot of tiny detail, made by widow women according to tradition, costs a whole shilling 'cos the engraving is so fine. Takes the old girls days to do one, what with their eyesight and everything, but it makes 'em feel they're bein' useful."

"But a sixteenth of a penny? One quarter of a farthing? What can you buy with that?"

"You'd be amazed, sir, down some streets. A candle stub, a small potato that's only a bit green," said Shady. "Maybe a apple core that ain't been entirely et. And of course it's handy to drop in the charity box. It makes a clink."

And gold is the anchor, is it? Moist thought.

He looked around at the huge space. There were about a dozen people working there, if you included the golem, who Moist had learned to think of as part of a species to be treated as "human for a given value of human," and the pimply boy who made the tea, who he hadn't.

"You don't seem to need many people," he said.

"Ah, well, we only do the silver and gold—"

"Goldish," Mr. Bent intervened quickly.

"—Goldish coins here, you see. And unusual stuff, like medals. We make the blanks for the copper and brass, but the outworkers do the rest."

"Outworkers? A mint with *outworkers*?"

"That's right, sir. Like the widows. They work at home. Huh, you couldn't expect the old dears to totter in here, most of 'em'd need two sticks to get about!"

"The Mint . . . that is, the place that makes money . . . employs people who work at *home*? I mean, I know it's fashionable, but I mean . . . well, don't you think it's odd?"

"Gods bless you, sir, there are families out there who've been making a few coppers every evening for generations!" said Shady happily. "Dad doing the basic punching, Mum chasing and finishing, the kids cleanin' and polishin' . . . it's traditional. Our outworkers are like one big family."

"Okay, but what about security?"

"If they steal so much as a farthing they can be hanged," said Bent. "It counts as treason, you know."

"What kind of families are you used to?" said Moist, aghast.

"I must point out that no one ever has, though, because they're very loyal," said the foreman, glaring at Bent.

"It used to be a hand cut off, for a first offense," said Mr. Bent the family man.

"Do they make a lot of money?" said Moist, carefully getting between the two men. "I mean, in terms of wages?"

"About fifteen dollars a month. It's detailed work," said Shady. "Some of the old ladies don't get as much. We get a lot of bad elims."

Moist stared up at the Bad Penny. It rose up through the central well of the building and looked gossamer-frail for something so big. The lone golem plodding along inside had a slate hanging around its neck, which meant it was one of those that couldn't talk. Moist wondered if the Golem Trust knew about it. They had amazing ways of finding golems.

As he watched, the wheel swung gently to a halt. The silent golem stood still.

"Tell me," said Moist, "why bother with goldish coins? Why not just, well, make the dollars out of gold?"

"Very fast way to lose gold, sir!"

"Did you get a lot of clipping and sweating?"

"I'm surprised a gentleman like you knows them names, sir," said the foreman, taken aback.

"I take a keen interest in the criminal mind," said Moist, slightly faster than he'd intended. It was true. All you needed was a talent for introspection.

"Good for you, sir. Oh, yes, we've had them tricks and a lot more, oh *yes*! I swear we've seen 'em all. And painting an' plating an' plugging. Even recasting, sir, adulterated with copper, very neat. I swear, sir, there are people out there that will spend two days scheming and fiddling to make the amount of money they could earn by honest means in one day!"

"No! Really?"

"As I stand here, sir," said Shady. "And what kind o' sane mind does that?"

Well, mine, once upon a time, Moist thought. *It was more* fun. "I really don't know," he said.

"So the city council said the dollars were to be goldish, mostly navy brass, to tell you the truth, 'cos it shines up nice. Oh, they still forge, sir, but it's hard to get right and the Watch comes down heavily on 'em and at least no one's nicking the gold," said Shady. "Is that all, sir? Only we've got stuff to finish before our knocking-off time, you see, and if we stay late we have to make more money to pay our overtime, and if the lads is a bit tired we ends up earning the money faster'n we can make it, which leads to a bit of what I can only call a conundrum—"

"You mean that if you do overtime you have to do more overtime to pay for it?" said Moist, still pondering how illogical logical thinking can be if a big enough committee is doing it.

"That's right, sir," said Shady. "And down that road madness lies."

"It's a very short road," said Moist, nodding. "But one last thing, if I may. What do you do about security?"

Bent coughed. "The Mint is impossible to get into from outside the bank once it is locked, Mr. Lipwig. By arrangement with the Watch, off-duty officers patrol both buildings at night, with some of our own guards. They wear proper bank uniforms in here, of course, because the Watch is so shabby, but they ensure a professional approach, you understand."

Well, yes, thought Moist, who suspected that his experience of coppers was rather more in-depth than that of Bent. *The money is* probably *safe, but I bet you get through a hell of a lot of coffee and pens.*

"I was thinking about . . . during the day," he said. The Men of the Sheds were watching him with blank stares.

"Oh, *that,*" said Mr. Shady. "We do that ourselves. We take turns. Boy Charlie's the security this week. Show him your truncheon, Charlie."

One of the men pulled a large stick from inside his coat and shyly held it up.

"There used to be a badge, too, but it got lost," said Shady. "But that doesn't matter much 'cos we all know who he is. And when we're leaving, he's sure to remind us not to steal anything."

Silence followed.

"Well, that seems to cover it nicely," said Moist, rubbing his hands together. "Thank you, gentlemen!"

And they filed away, each man to his shed.

"Probably very little," said Mr. Bent, watching them go.

"Hmm?" said Moist.

"You were wondering how much money is walking out with them, I believe."

"Well, yes."

"Very little, I think. They say that after a while the money becomes just . . . stuff," said the chief cashier, leading the way back into the bank.

"It costs more than a penny to make a penny," Moist murmured. "Is it just me, or is that *wrong*?"

"But, you see, once you have made it, a penny keeps *on* being a penny," said Mr. Bent. "That's the magic of it."

"It is?" said Moist. "Look, it's a copper disc. What do you expect it to become?"

"In the course of a year, just about everything," said Mr. Bent smoothly. "It becomes some apples, part of a cart, a pair of shoelaces, some hay, an hour's occupancy of a theater seat. It may even become a

stamp and send a letter, Mr. Lipwig. It might be
spent three hundred times and yet—and this is the
good part—it is still one penny, ready and willing to
be spent again. It is not an apple, which will go bad.
Its worth is fixed and stable. It is not consumed."
Mr. Bent's eyes gleamed dangerously, and one of
them twitched. "And this is because it is ultimately
worth a tiny fraction of the everlasting gold!"

"But it's just a lump of metal. If we used apples
instead of coins, you could at least eat the apple,"
said Moist.

"Yes, but you can only eat it once. A penny is, as
it were, an everlasting apple."

"Which you can't eat. And you can plant an apple
tree."

"You can use money to make more money," said
Bent.

"Yes, but how do you make more gold? The alchemists can't, the dwarfs hang on to what they've
got, the Agateans won't let us have any. Why not
go on the silver standard? They do that in Bhang-
Bhangduc."

"I imagine they would, being foreign," said Bent.
"But silver blackens. Gold is the one untarnish-
able metal." And once again there was that tic: gold
clearly had a tight hold on the man. "Incidentally,
sir, I of course know that the depraved would clip
slivers of metal from a coin, but what is 'sweating'?"

"For the *really* depraved, I'm sorry to say," said
Moist. "You have a leather lining in your pocket,
you put your gold coins in there, and you, well, you

jingle them as often as you can. The gold dust builds up. Small profits but fairly safe, and some people just can't help wanting to jingle."

"I will treasure the image," said Bent gravely. "Have you seen enough, Mr. Lipwig?"

"Slightly too much for comfort, I think."

"Then let us go and meet the chairman."

M OIST FOLLOWED BENT's jerky walk up two flights of marble stairs and along a corridor. They halted in front of a pair of dark wooden doors and Mr. Bent knocked, not once, but with a sequence of taps that suggested a code. Then he pushed the door open, very carefully.

The chairman's office was large, and simply furnished with very expensive things. Bronze and brass were much in evidence. Probably the last remaining tree of some rare, exotic species had been hewn to make the chairman's desk, which was an object of desire and big enough to bury people in. It gleamed a deep, deep green, and spoke of power and probity. Moist assumed, as a matter of course, that it was lying.

There was a very small dog sitting in a brass in tray, but it was not until Bent said "Mr. Lipwig, madam chairman" that Moist realized that the desk also had a human occupant. The head of a very small, very elderly, gray-haired woman was peering over the top of it at him. Resting on the desk on either side of her, gleaming silver steel in this world of gold-colored things, were two loaded crossbows, fixed on little swivels. The lady's thin little hands were just drawing back from the stocks.

"Oh yes, how nice," she trilled. "I am Mrs. Lavish. Do take a seat, Mr. Lipwig."

He did so, as much out of the current field of the bows as possible, and the dog leaped down from the desk and onto his lap with happy, scrotum-crushing enthusiasm. ·

It was the smallest and ugliest dog Moist had ever seen. It resembled those goldfish with the huge bulging eyes that looked as though they were about to explode. Its nose, on the other hand, looked stoved in. It wheezed, and its legs were so bandy that it must sometimes trip over its own feet.

"That's Mr. Fusspot," said the old woman. "He doesn't normally take to people, Mr. Lipwig. I am impressed."

"Hello, Mr. Fusspot," said Moist. The dog gave a little yappy bark and then covered Moist's face in all that was best in dog slobber.

"He *likes* you, Mr. Lipwig," said Mrs. Lavish approvingly. "Can you guess at the breed?"

Moist had grown up with dogs and was pretty good at breeds, but with Mr. Fusspot there was no place to start. He plumped for honesty.

"All of them?" he suggested.

Mrs. Lavish laughed, and the laugh sounded at least sixty years younger than she was.

"Quite right! His mother was a spoon hound, very popular in royal palaces in the olden days. But she got out one night and there was an awful lot of barking and I fear Mr. Fusspot is the son of many fathers, poor thing."

Mr. Fusspot turned two soulful eyes on Moist, and his expression began to become a little strained.

"Bent, Mr. Fusspot is looking rather uncomfortable," said Mrs. Lavish. "Please take him for his little walk in the garden, will you? I really don't think the young clerks give him enough time."

A brief spell of thundery weather passed across the chief cashier's face, but he obediently took a red leash from a hook.

The little dog began to growl.

Bent also took down a pair of heavy leather gloves and deftly put them on. As the growling increased, he picked up the dog very carefully and held it under one arm. Without uttering a word, he left the room.

"Ah, so *you* are the famous postmaster general," said Mrs. Lavish. "The man in the golden suit, no less. But not this morning, I note. Come here, dear boy. Let me look at you in the light."

Moist advanced, and the old lady got awkwardly to her feet by means of a pair of ivory-handled walking sticks. Then she dropped one and grabbed Moist's chin. She stared intently at him, turning his head this way and that.

"Hmm," she said, stepping back. "It's as I thought . . ." The remaining walking stick caught Moist a whack across the back of the legs, scything him over like a straw. As he lay stunned on the thick carpet, Mrs. Lavish went on, triumphantly: "You're a thief, a trickster, a charlie artful, and an all-round bunco artist! Admit it!"

"I'm not!" Moist protested weakly.

"Liar, too," said Mrs. Lavish cheerfully. "And probably an impostor! Oh, don't waste that innocent look on me! I said you are a rogue, sir! I wouldn't trust you with a bucket of water if my knickers were on fire!"

Then she prodded Moist in the chest, hard. "Well, are you going to lie there all day?" she snapped. "Get up, man. I didn't say I didn't *like* you!"

Head spinning, Moist got cautiously to his feet.

"Give me your hand, Mr. Lipwig," said Mrs. Lavish. "Postmaster general? You are a work of art! Put it here!"

"What? Oh . . ." Moist grasped the old woman's hand. It was like shaking hands with cold parchment.

Mrs. Lavish laughed. "Ah, yes. Just like the forthright and reassuring grasp of my late husband. No honest man has a handshake as honest as that. How in the world has it taken you so long to find the financial sector?"

Moist looked around. They were alone, his calves were sore, and there was no fooling some people. What we have here, he told himself, is a Mk.1 Feisty Old Lady: turkey neck, embarrassing sense of humor, a gleeful pleasure in mild cruelty, direct way of speaking that flirts with rudeness and, more important, also flirts with flirting. Likes to think she's "no lady." Game for anything that doesn't carry the risk of falling over and with a look in her eye that says "I can do what I like, because I am old. And I have a soft spot for rascals." Old ladies like that were hard to fool, but there was no need to. He relaxed. Sometimes it was a sheer relief to drop the mask.

"I'm not an impostor, at least," he said. "Moist von Lipwig is my given name."

"Yes, I can't imagine that you would have had any choice in the matter," said Mrs. Lavish, heading back to her seat. "However, you seem to be fooling all of the people all of the time. Sit down, Mr. Lipwig. I shall not bite." This last was said with a look that transmitted: "But give me half a bottle of gin and five minutes to find my teeth and we shall see!" She indicated a chair next to her.

"What? I thought I was being dismissed!" said Moist, playing along.

"Really? Why?"

"For being all those things you said?"

"I didn't say I thought you were a bad person," said Mrs. Lavish. "And Mr. Fusspot likes you and he is a remarkably good judge of people. Besides, you've done wonders with our post office, just as Havelock says." Mrs. Lavish reached down beside her and pulled a large bottle of gin onto the desktop. "A drink, Mr. Lipwig?"

"Er . . . not at this time."

Mrs. Lavish sniffed. "I don't have much time, sir, but fortunately I have a lot of gin." Moist watched her pour a marginally sublethal measure into a tumbler.

"Do you have a young lady?" she asked, raising the glass.

"Yes."

"Does she know what you're like?"

"Yes. I keep telling her."

"Doesn't believe you, eh? Ah, such is the way of a woman in love," sighed Mrs. Lavish.

"I don't think it worries her, actually. She's not your average girl."

"Ah, and she sees your inner self? Or perhaps the carefully constructed inner self you keep around for people to find? People like you . . ." she paused and went on: ". . . people like *us* always keep at least one inner self for inquisitive visitors, don't we?"

Moist didn't rise to this. Talking to Mrs. Lavish was like standing in front of a magic mirror that stripped you to your marrow. He just said: "Most of the people she knows are golems."

"Oh? Great big clay men who are utterly trustworthy and don't have anything to declare in the trouser department? What does she see in *you*, Mr. Lipwig?" She prodded him with a finger like a cheese straw.

Moist's mouth dropped open.

"A contrast, I trust," said Mrs. Lavish, patting him on the arm. "And now Havelock has sent you here to tell me how to run my bank. You may call me Topsy."

"Well, I—" Tell her how to run her bank? It hadn't been put like *that*.

Topsy leaned forward. "I never minded about Honey, you know," she said, slightly lowering her voice. "Quite a nice girl, but thick as a yard of lard. She wasn't the first, either. Not by a long way. I was Joshua's mistress once myself."

"Really?" He knew he was going to hear it all, whether he wanted to or not.

"Oh, yes," said Mrs. Lavish. "People *understood* more then. It was all quite acceptable. I used to take tea with his wife once a month to sort out his schedule, and she always said she was glad to have him out from under her feet. Of course, a mistress was expected to be a woman of some accomplishment in those days." She sighed. "Now, of course, the ability to spin upside down around a pole seems to be sufficient."

"Standards are falling everywhere," said Moist. It was a pretty good bet. They always were.

"Banking is really rather similar," said Topsy, as though thinking aloud.

"Pardon?"

"I mean the mere physical end in view is going to be the same, but style should count for something, don't you think? There should be flair. There should be inventiveness. There should be an experience rather than a mere function. Havelock says you understand these things." She gave Moist a questioning look. "After all, you have made the Post Office an almost heroic enterprise, yes? People set their watches by the arrival of the Genua Express. They used to set their calendars!"

"The clacks still makes a loss," said Moist.

"A marvelously small one, while enriching the commonality of mankind in all sorts of ways, and I've no doubt that Havelock's tax men take their share of that. You have the gift of enthusing people, Mr. Lipwig."

"Well, I . . . well, I suppose I do," he managed.

"I know if you want to sell the sausage you have to know how to sell the sizzle."

"Well and good, well and good," said Topsy, "but I hope you know that however gifted you are as a sizzle salesman, sooner or later you must be able to *produce* the sausage, hmm?" She gave him a wink which would have got a younger woman jailed.

"Incidentally," she went on, "I recall hearing that the gods led you to the treasure trove that helped you to rebuild the Post Office. What really happened? You can tell Topsy."

He probably could, he decided, and noticed that although her hair was indeed thinning and almost white, it still held a pale trace of orange that hinted of more vivid reds in the past. "It was my stashed loot from years of swindling," he said.

Mrs. Lavish clapped her hands. "Wonderful! A sausage indeed! That is so . . . satisfying. Havelock has always had an instinct for people. He has plans for the city, you know."

"The Undertaking," said Moist. "Yes, I know."

"Underground streets and new docks and everything," said Topsy, "and for that a government needs money and money needs banks. Unfortunately, people have rather lost their faith in banks."

"Why?"

"Because we lost their money, usually. Mostly not on purpose. We have been badly buffeted in recent years. The crash of 88, the crash of 93, the crash of 98 . . . although that one was more of a ding. My late husband was a man who loaned unwisely, so we must carry bad debts and other results of questionable decisions. Now we're where little old ladies keep their money because they always have done and the nice young clerks are still polite and there's still a brass bowl by the door for their little dogs to drink out of. Could you do anything about this? The supply of old ladies is running out, as I'm well aware."

"Well, er, I may have a few ideas," said Moist. "But it's all still a bit of a shock. I don't really understand how banks work."

"You've never put money in a bank?"

"Not *in*, no."

"How do you *think* they work?"

"Well, you take rich people's money and lend it to suitable people at interest, and give as little as possible of the interest back."

"Yes, and what is a suitable person?"

"Someone who can prove they don't need the money?"

"Oh, you cynic. But you have got the general idea."

"No poor people, then?"

"Not in banks, Mr. Lipwig. No one with an income under a hundred and fifty dollars a year. That is why socks and mattresses were invented. My late husband always said that the only way to make money out of poor people is by keeping them poor. He was not, in his business life, a very nice man. Do you have any more questions?"

"How did you become the bank's chairman?" said Moist.

"Chairman *and* manager," said Topsy proudly. "Joshua liked to be in control.

"Oh, yes, didn't he just," she added, as if to herself. "And I am now both of them because of a little bit of ancient magic called 'being left fifty percent of the shares.'"

"I thought that bit of magic was fifty-one percent of the shares," said Moist. "Couldn't the other shareholders force—"

An inner door opened at the far side of the room and a tall woman in white entered, carrying a tray with its contents concealed by a cloth.

"It really is time for your medicine, Mrs. Lavish," she said.

"It does me no good at all, Sister!" snapped the old woman.

"Now, you know the doctor said no more alcohol," said the nurse. She looked accusingly at Moist. "She's to have no more alcohol," she repeated, on the apparent assumption that he had a few bottles on his person.

"Well I say no more doctor!" said Mrs. Lavish, winking conspiratorially at Moist. "My so-called stepchildren are paying for this, can you believe it? They're out to poison me! And they tell everyone I've gone mad—"

There was a knock at the door, less a request to enter than a declaration of intent. Mrs. Lavish moved with impressive speed and the bows were already swiveling when the door swung open.

Mr. Bent came in, with Mr. Fusspot under his arm, still growling.

"I said five times, Mr. Bent!" Mrs. Lavish yelled. "I might have shot Mr. Fusspot! Can't you count?"

"I do beg your pardon," said Bent, placing Mr. Fusspot carefully in the in tray. "And I *can* count."

"Who's a little fusspot then?" said Mrs. Lavish, as the little dog almost exploded with mad excitement at seeing someone he'd last seen at least ten minutes ago. "Has oo been a good boy? *Has* he been a good boy, Mr. Bent?"

"Yes, madam. Excessively." The venom of a snake ice cream could not have been chillier. "May I return to my duties now?"

"Mr. Bent thinks I don't know how to run a bank, doesn't he, Mr. Fusspot," Mrs. Lavish crooned to the dog. "He's a silly Mr. Bent, isn't he? Yes, Mr. Bent, you may go."

Moist recalled an old BhangBhangduc proverb: "When old ladies talk maliciously to their dog, that dog is lunch." It seemed amazingly appropriate at a time like this, and a time like this was not a good time to be around.

"Well, it's been nice meeting you, Mrs. Lavish," he said, standing up. "I shall . . . think things over."

"Has he been to see Hubert?" said Mrs. Lavish, apparently to the dog. "He must see Hubert before he goes. I think he is a little confused about finance. Take him to see Hubert, Mr. Bent. Hubert is so good at explaining."

"As you wish, madam," said Bent, glaring at Mr. Fusspot. "I'm certain that having heard Hubert explain the flow of money he will no longer be a little confused. Please follow me, Mr. Lipwig."

Bent was silent as they walked downstairs. He lifted his oversized feet with care, like a man walking across a floor strewn with pins.

"Mrs. Lavish is a jolly old stick, isn't she?" Moist ventured.

"I believe she is what is known as a 'character,' sir," said Bent somberly.

"A bit tiresome at times?"

"I will not comment, sir. Mrs. Lavish owns fifty-one percent of the shares in my bank."

His bank, Moist noted.

"That's strange," he said. "She just told me she owned only fifty percent."

"And the dog," said Bent. "The dog owns one share, a legacy from the late Sir Joshua, and Mrs. Lavish owns the dog. The late Sir Joshua had what I understand is called a puckish sense of humor, Mr. Lipwig."

And the dog owns a piece of the bank, thought Moist. What a jolly people the Lavishes are, indeed. "I can see that you might not find it very funny, Mr. Bent," he said.

"I am pleased to say I find nothing funny, sir," Bent replied as they reached the bottom of the stairs. "I have no sense of humor whatsoever. None at all. It has been proven by phrenology. I have Nichtlachen-Keinwortz syndrome, which for some curious reason is considered a lamentable affliction. I, on the other hand, consider it a gift. I am happy to say that I regard the sight of a fat man slipping on a banana skin as nothing more than an unfortunate accident that highlights the need for care in the disposal of household waste."

"Have you tried—" Moist began, but Bent held up a hand. "Please! I repeat, I do not regard it as a burden! And may I say it annoys me when people assume it is such! Do not feel impelled to try to make me laugh, sir! If I had no legs, would you try to make me run? I am quite happy, thank you!"

He paused by another pair of doors, calmed down a little, and gripped the handles.

"And now, perhaps, I should take this opportunity to show you where the . . . may I say *serious* work is done, Mr. Lipwig. This used to be called the counting house, but I prefer to think of it as"—he pulled at the doors, which swung open majestically —"my world."

It was impressive. And the first impression it gave Moist was: this is Hell on the day they couldn't find the matches.

He stared at the rows of bent backs, scribbling frantically. No one looked up.

"I will not have abacuses, Calculating Bones, or other inhuman devices under this roof, Mr. Lipwig," said Bent, leading the way down the central aisle. "The human brain *is* capable of infallibility in the world of numbers. Since we invented them, how should it be otherwise? We are rigorous here, rigorous—" In one swift movement Bent pulled a sheet of paper from the out tray of the nearest desk, scanned it briefly, and dropped it back again with a little grunt that signified either his approval that the clerk had got things right or his own disappointment that he had not found anything wrong.

The sheet had been crammed with calculations, and surely no mortal could have followed them at a glance. But Moist would not have bet a penny that Bent hadn't accounted for every line.

"Here in this room we are at the heart of the bank," said the chief cashier proudly.

"The heart," said Moist blankly.

"Here we calculate interest and charges and mortgages and costs and—everything, in fact. And we do not make mistakes."

"What, never?"

"Well, hardly ever. Oh, some individuals occasionally make an error," Bent conceded with distaste. "Fortunately, I check every calculation. No errors get past me, you may depend upon it. An error, sir, is worse than a sin, the reason being that a sin is often a matter of opinion or viewpoint or even of timing but an error is a fact and it cries out for correction. I see you are not sneering, Mr. Lipwig."

"I'm not? I mean, no. I'm not!" said Moist. Damn. He'd forgotten the ancient wisdom: take care, when you are closely observing, that you are not closely observed.

"But you are appalled, nevertheless," said Bent. "You use words, and I'm told you do it well, but words are soft and can be pummeled into different meanings by a skilled tongue. Numbers are hard. Oh, you can cheat with them but you cannot change their nature. Three is three. You cannot persuade it to be four, even if you give it a great big kiss." There was a very faint snigger from somewhere in the hall, but Mr. Bent apparently did not notice. "And they are not very forgiving. We work very hard here, at things that must be done," he said. "And this is where I sit, at the very center . . ."

They'd reached the big stepped dais in the center of the room. As they did so, a skinny woman in a white blouse and long black skirt edged respectfully past them and carefully placed a wad of paper in a tray that was already piled high. She glanced at Mr. Bent, who said, "Thank you, Miss Drapes." He was too busy pointing out the marvels of the dais, on which a semicircular desk of complex design had been mounted, to notice the expression that passed across her pale little face. But Moist did, and read a thousand words, probably written in her diary and never ever shown to anyone.

"Do you see?" said the chief cashier impatiently.

"Hmm?" said Moist, watching the woman scurry away.

"See here, you see?" said Bent, sitting down and pointing with what almost seemed like enthusiasm. "By means of these treadles I can move my desk to face anywhere in the room! It is the panopticon of my little world. Nothing is beyond my eye!" He pedaled furiously and the whole dais began to rumble around on its turntable. "And it can turn at two speeds, too, as you can see, because of this ingenious—"

"I can see that almost nothing is beyond your

eye," said Moist, as Miss Drapes sat down. "But I'm sorry to interrupt your work."

Bent glanced at the in tray and gave a little shrug.

"That pile? That will not take me long," he said, setting the hand brake and standing up. "Besides, I think it important that you see what we are really about at this point, because I must now take you to meet Hubert." He gave a little cough.

"Hubert is *not* what you're about?" Moist suggested, and then headed back to the main hall.

"I'm sure he means well," said Bent, leaving the words hanging in the air like a noose.

O̲UT IN THE hall a dignified hush prevailed. A few people were at the counters, an old lady watched her little dog drink from the brass bowl inside the door, and any words that were uttered were spoken in a suitably hushed voice. Moist was all for money, it was one of his favorite things, but it didn't have to be something you mentioned very quietly in case it woke up. If money talked in here, it whispered.

The chief cashier opened a small and not very grand door behind the stairs and half hidden by some potted plants.

"Please be careful, the floor is always wet here," he said, and led the way down some wide steps into the grandest cellar Moist had ever seen. Fine stone vaulting supported beautifully tiled ceilings, stretching away into the gloom. There were candles everywhere, and in the middle distance something was sparkling and filling the colonnaded space with a blue-white glow.

"This was the undercroft of the temple," said Bent, leading the way.

"Are you telling me this place doesn't just *look* like a temple?"

"It was built as a temple, yes, but never used as one."

"Really?" said Moist. "Which god?"

"None, as it turned out. One of the kings of Ankh commanded it to be built about nine hundred years ago," said Bent. "I suppose it was a case of speculative building. That is to say, he had no god in mind."

"He hoped one would turn up?"

"Exactly, sir."

"Like blue-tits?" said Moist, peering around. "This place was a kind of celestial bird box?"

Bent sighed. "You express yourself colorfully, Mr. Lipwig, but I suppose there is some truth there. It didn't work, anyway. Then it got used as storage in case of siege, became an indoor market, and so on, and then Jocatello La Vice got the place when the city defaulted on a loan. It is all in the official history. Isn't the fornication wonderful?"

After quite a lengthy pause, Moist ventured: "Is it?"

"Don't you think so? There's more here than anywhere else in the city, I'm told."

"Really?" said Moist, looking around nervously. "Er . . . do you have to come down here at some special time?"

"Well, during banking hours usually, but we let groups in by appointment."

"You know," said Moist, "I think this conversation has somehow got away from me . . ."

Bent waved vaguely at the ceiling.

"I refer to the wonderful vaulting," he said. "The word derives from *fornix*, meaning 'arch.'"

"Ah! Yes? Right!" said Moist. "You know, I wouldn't be surprised if not many people knew that."

And then Moist saw the Glooper, glowing among the arches.

CHAPTER 3

MOIST HAD SEEN glass being bent and blown, and marveled at the skill of the people who did it, marveled as only a man can marvel whose skill is only in bending words. Some of those geniuses had probably worked on this. But so had their counterparts from the hypothetical Other Side, glassblowers who had sold their souls to some molten god for the skill to blow glass into spirals and intersecting bottles and shapes that seemed to be quite close but some distance away at the same time. Water gurgled, sloshed, and, yes, glooped along glass tubing. There was a smell of salt.

Bent nudged Moist, pointed to an improbable wooden hatstand, and wordlessly handed him a long yellow oilskin coat and a matching rain hat. He had already donned a similar outfit, and had magically procured an umbrella from somewhere.

"It's the Balance of Payments," he said, as Moist struggled into the coat. "He never gets it right." There was a crash from somewhere, and water droplets rained down on them. "See?" Bent added.

"What's it doing?" said Moist.

Bent rolled his eyes. "Hell knows, Heaven suspects," he said. He raised his voice. "Hubert? We have a visitor!"

A distant splashing grew louder and a figure appeared around the edge of the glassware.

Rightly or wrongly, Hubert is one of those names you put a shape to. There may well be tall, slim Huberts, Moist would be the first to agree, but this Hubert was shaped like a proper Hubert, which is to say, stubby and plump. He had red hair—unusual, in Moist's experience, in the standard-model Hubert. It grew thickly, straight up from his head, like the bristles of a brush; about five inches up, someone had apparently cut it short with the aid of shears and a spirit level. You could have stood a cup and saucer on it.

"A visitor?" said Hubert nervously. "Wonderful! We don't get many down here!"

"Really?" said Moist. Hubert wore a long, white coat, with a breast pocket full of pencils.

"Hubert, this is Mr. Lipwig," said Bent. "He is here to . . . learn about us."

"I am Moist," said Moist, stepping forward with his best smile and an extended hand.

"Oh, I'm sorry. We should have hung the raincoats nearer the door," said Hubert. He looked at Moist's hand as if it was some interesting device, and then shook it carefully.

"You're not seeing us at our best, Mr. Lipwick," he said.

"Really?" said Moist, still smiling. How *does* the hair stay up like that, he wondered. Does he use glue, or what?

"Mr. Lipwig is the postmaster general, Hubert," said Bent.

"Is he? Oh. I don't get out of the cellar very much these days," said Hubert.

"Really," said Moist, his smile now a bit glassy.

"No, we're so close to perfection, you see," said Hubert. "I really think we're nearly there . . ."

"Mister Hubert believes that this . . . device is a sort of crystal ball for showing the future," said Bent, and rolled his eyes.

"*Possible* futures. Would Mr. Lipstick like to see it in operation?" said Hubert, vibrating with enthusiasm and eagerness. Only a man with a heart of stone would have said no, so Moist made a wonderful attempt at indicating that all his dreams were coming true.

"I'd love to," he said, "but what does it actually do?"

Too late, he saw the signs. Hubert grasped the lapels of his jacket, as if addressing a meeting, and swelled with the urge to communicate, or at least talk at length in the belief that it was the same thing.

"The Glooper, as it is affectionately known, is what I call a quote 'analogy machine' unquote. It solves problems not by considering them as a numerical exercise but by actually duplicating them in a form we can manipulate: in this case, the flow of money and its effects within our society becomes water flowing through a glass matrix, the Glooper. The geometrical shape of certain vessels, the operation of valves, and, although I say so myself, ingenious tipping buckets and flow-rate propellers enable the Glooper to simulate quite complex transactions. We can change the starting conditions, too, to learn the rules inherent in the system. For example, we can find out what happens if you halve the labor force in the city, by the adjustment of a few valves, rather than going out into the streets and killing people."

"A big improvement! Bravo!" said Moist desperately, and started to clap.

No one joined in. He shoved his hands in his pockets.

"Er . . . perhaps you would like a less, um, dramatic demonstration?" Hubert volunteered.

Moist nodded. "Yes," he said. "Show me . . . show me what happens when people get fed up with banks," he said.

"Ah, yes, a familiar one! Igor, set up program five!" Hubert shouted to some figure in the forest of glassware. There was the sound of squeaky screws being turned and the glug of reservoirs being topped up.

"Igor?" said Moist. "You have an Igor?"

"Oh, yes," said Hubert. "That's how I get this wonderful light. They know the secret of storing lightning in jars! But don't let that worry you, Mr. Lipspick. Just because I'm employing an Igor and working in a cellar doesn't mean I am some sort of madman, ha ha ha!"

"Ha ha," agreed Moist.

"Ha hah hah!" said Hubert. "Hahahahahaha!! Ahahahahaha**hhhhh!!!!!**—"

Bent slapped him on the back. Hubert coughed. "Sorry about that, it's the air down here," he mumbled.

"It certainly looks very . . . complex, this thing of yours," said Moist, striking out for normality.

"Er, yes," said Hubert, a little bit thrown. "And we are refining it all the time. For example, floats coupled to ingenious spring-loaded sluice gates elsewhere on the Glooper can allow changes in the level in one flask to automatically adjust flows in several other places in the system—"

"What's that for?" said Moist, pointing at random to a round bottle suspended in the tubing.

"Phase-of-the-moon valve," said Hubert promptly.

"The *moon* affects how money moves around?"

"We don't know. It might. The weather certainly does."

"Really?"

"Certainly!" Hubert beamed. "And we're adding fresh influences all the time. Indeed, I will not be satisfied until my wonderful machine can completely mimic every last detail of our great city's economic cycle!" A bell rang, and he went on: "Thank you, Igor! Let it go!"

Something clanked, and colored waters began to foam and slosh along the bigger pipes. Hubert raised not only his voice but also a long pointer.

"Now, if we reduce public confidence in the banking system—watch that tube there—you will see here a flow of cash out of the banks and into Flask 28, currently designated 'The Old Sock Under the Mattress.' Even quite rich people don't want their money outside their control. See the mattress getting fuller, or perhaps I should say . . . thicker?"

"That's a lot of mattresses," Moist agreed.

"I prefer to think of it as one mattress a third of a mile high."

"Really?" said Moist.

Slosh! Valves opened somewhere, and water rushed along a new path.

"Now see how bank lending is emptying as the money drains into the Sock?" *Gurgle!* "Watch Reservoir 11, over there. That means business expansion is slowing . . . there it goes, there it goes . . ." *Drip!* "Now watch Bucket 34. It's tipping, it's tipping . . . there! The scale on the left of Flask 17 shows collapsing businesses, by the way. See Flask 9 beginning to fill? That's foreclosures. Job losses is Flask 7 . . . and there goes the valve on Flask 28, as the socks are pulled out." *Flush!* "But what is there to buy? Over here we see that Flask 11 has also drained . . ." *drip*.

Except for the occasional gurgle, the aquatic activity subsided.

"And we end up in a position where we can't move because we're standing on our own hands, as it were," said Hubert. "Jobs vanishing, people without savings suffering, wages low, farms going back to wilderness, rampaging trolls coming down from the mountains—"

"They're here already," said Moist. "Some of them are even in the Watch."

"Are you *sure*?" said Hubert.

"Yes, they've got helmets and everything. I've seen them."

"Then I expect they'll be wanting to rampage back to the mountains," said Hubert. "I think I would, if I were them."

"You believe all that could really happen?" said Moist. "A bunch of tubes and buckets can tell you that?"

"They are correlated to events very carefully, Mr. Lipswick," said Hubert, looking hurt. "Correlation is everything. Did you know it is an established fact that hemlines tend to rise in times of national crisis?"

"You mean—?" Moist began, not at all certain how the sentence was going to end.

"Women's dresses get shorter," said Hubert.

"And that causes a national crisis? Really? How high do they go?"

Mr. Bent coughed a leaden cough. "I think perhaps *we* should go, Mr. Lipwig," he said. "If you have seen all you want, no doubt you are in a hurry to leave." There was a slight inflection on *leave*.

"What? Oh . . . yes," said Moist. "I probably should be getting along. Well, thank you, Hubert. It has been an education and no mistake."

"I just can't get rid of the leaks," said the little man, looking crestfallen. "I'll swear that every joint is watertight, but we never end up with the same amount of water that we started with."

"Of course not, Hubert," said Moist, patting him on the shoulder. "And that's because you're close to achieving perfection!"

"I am?" said Hubert, wide-eyed.

"Certainly. Everyone knows that at the end of the week you never have quite as much money as you think you should. It's a well-known fact!"

The sunrise of delight dawned on Hubert's face. *Topsy was right*, Moist told himself. *I am* good *with people.*

"Now demonstrated by the Glooper!" Hubert breathed. "I shall write a paper on it!"

"Or you could write it on paper!" said Moist, shaking him warmly by the hand. "Okay, Mr. Bent, let us tear ourselves away!"

When they were walking up the main stairs Moist said: "What relation is Hubert to the current chairman?"

"Nephew," said Bent. "How did you—?"

"I'm always interested in people," said Moist, smiling to himself. "And there's the red hair, of course. Why does Mrs. Lavish have two crossbows on her desk?"

"Family heirlooms, sir," lied Bent. It was a deliberate, flagrant lie, and he must have meant it to be seen as such. Family heirlooms. And she sleeps in her office. All right, she's an invalid, but people usually do that at home.

She doesn't intend to step out of the room. She's on guard. And she's very particular about who comes in.

"Do you have any interests, Mr. Bent?"

"I do my job with care and attention, sir."

"Yes, but what do you do in the evenings?"

"I double-check the day's totals in my office, sir. I find counting very . . . satisfying."

"You're very good at it, yes?"

"More than you can imagine, sir."

"So if I save ninety-three-point-forty-seven dollars a year for seven years at two and a quarter percent, compound, how—"

"Eight hundred and thirty-five-point-thirteen dollars calculated once annually, sir," said Bent calmly.

Yes, and twice you've known the exact time, thought Moist. And you didn't look at a watch. You *are* good with numbers. Inhumanly good, perhaps . . .

"No holidays?" he said aloud.

"I did a walking tour of the major banking houses of Überwald last summer, sir. It was most instructive."

"That must have taken weeks. I'm glad you felt able to tear yourself away!"

"Oh, it was easy, sir. Miss Drapes, who is the senior clerk, sent a coded clacks of the day's business to each of my lodging houses at the close of business every day. I was able to review it over my after-dinner strudel and respond instantly with advice and instructions."

"Is Miss Drapes a useful member of the staff?"

"Indeed. She performs her duties with care and alacrity." He paused. They were at the top of the stairs. Bent turned and looked directly at Moist.

"I have worked here all my life, Mr. Lipwig. Be careful of the Lavish family. Mrs. Lavish is the best of them, a wonderful woman. The others . . . are used to getting their own way."

Old family, old money. *That* kind of family. Moist felt a distant call, like the song of the skylark. It came back to taunt him every time, for example, he saw an out-of-towner in the street with a map and a perplexed expression, crying out to be relieved of his money in some helpful and hard-to-follow way.

"Dangerously so?" he said.

Bent looked a little affronted at this directness. "They are not at home to disappointment, sir. They have tried to declare Mrs. Lavish insane, sir."

"Really?" said Moist. "Compared to who?"

T HE WIND BLEW through the town of Big Cabbage, which liked to call itself The Green Heart of the Plains.

It was called Big Cabbage because it was home to The Biggest Cabbage in the World, and the town's inhabitants were not very creative when it came to names. People traveled miles to see this wonder; they'd go inside its concrete interior and peer out through the windows, buy cabbage-leaf bookmarks, cabbage ink, cabbage shirts, Captain Cabbage dolls, musical boxes carefully crafted from Kohl Rabi and cauliflower, which played "The Cabbage-Eater's Song," cabbage jam, kale ale, and green cigars made from a newly developed species of cabbage and rolled on the thighs of local maidens, presumably because they liked it.

Then there was the excitement of BrassicaWorld, where very small children could burst into terrified screams at the huge head of Captain Cabbage himself, along with his friends Cauliflower the Clown and Billy Broccoli. For older visitors there was, of course, the Cabbage Research Institute, over which a green pall always hung and downwind of which plants tended to be rather strange and sometimes turned to watch you as you passed.

And then . . . what better way to record the day of a lifetime than pose at the behest of the black-clad man with the iconograph, who took a picture of the happy family and promised a framed, colored result, sent right to their home, for a mere three dollars, S&H included, one dollar deposit to cover expenses, if you would be so good, sir, and may I say what wonderful children you have there, madam, they are a credit to you and no mistake, oh, and did I say that if you are not *delighted* with the framed picture then send no further money and we shall say no more about it?

The kale ale was generally pretty good, and there's no such thing as too much flattery where mothers are concerned, and, all right, the man had rather strange teeth, which seem determined to make a break from his mouth, but none of us is perfect and what was there to lose?

What there was to lose was a dollar, and they add up. Whoever said you can't fool an honest man wasn't one.

Around about the seventh family a watchman started taking a distant interest, so the man in dusty black made a show of taking the last name and address and strolled into an alley. He tossed the broken iconograph back on the pile of junk where he had found it—it was a cheap one and the imps had long since evaporated—and was about to set off across the fields when he saw the newspaper being bowled along by the wind.

To a man traveling on his wits, a newspaper was a useful treasure. Stuck down your shirt, it kept the wind off your chest. You could use it to light fires. For the fastidious, it saved a daily resort to dockweed, burdock, or other broad-leaved plants. And, as a last resort, you could read it.

This evening, the breeze was getting up. He gave the front page of the paper a cursory glance, and tucked it under his vest.

His teeth tried to tell him something, but he never listened to them. A man could go mad, listening to his teeth.

WHEN HE GOT back to the Post Office, Moist looked up the Lavish family in *Whom's*

Whom. They were indeed what was known as "old money," which meant that it had been made so long ago that the black deeds which had originally filled the coffers were now historically irrelevant. Funny, that: a brigand for a father was something you kept quiet about, but a slave-taking pirate for a great-great-great-grandfather was something to boast of over the port. Time turned the evil bastards into rogues, and *rogue* was a word with a twinkle in its eye and nothing to be ashamed of.

They'd been rich for centuries. The key players in the current crop of Lavishes, apart from Topsy, were her brother-in-law Marko Lavish and his wife, Capricia Lavish, daughter of a famous trust fund. They lived in Genua, as far away from other Lavishes as possible, which was a very Lavish thing to do. Then there were Topsy's stepchildren, the twins Cosmo and Pucci, who had, the story ran, been born with their little hands around each other's throats, like true Lavishes. There were also plenty more cousins, aunts, and genetic hangers-on, all watching one another like cats. From what he'd heard, the family business was traditionally banking, but the recent generations, buoyed by a complex network of long-term investments and ancient trust funds, had diversified into disinheriting and suing one another, apparently with great enthusiasm and a commendable lack of mercy. He recalled pictures of them in the *Times*' society pages, getting in or out of sleek black coaches and not smiling very much, in case the money escaped.

There was no mention of Topsy's side of the

family. They were Turvys, apparently not grand enough to be *Whom*s. Topsy Turvy . . . there was a music-hall sound to it, and Moist could believe that.

Moist's in box had been topped up in his absence. It was all unimportant stuff, and really didn't need anything from him, but it was this newfangled carbon paper that was the trouble. He got copies of everything, and they took up time.

It wasn't that he wasn't good at delegating. He was extremely good at delegating. But the talent requires people on the other end of the chain to be good at being delegated onto. They weren't. Something about the Post Office discouraged original thinking. The letters went in the slots, okay? There was no room for people who wanted to experiment with sticking them in their ear, up the chimney, or down the privy. It'd do them good to—

He spotted the flimsy pink clacks among the other stuff and tugged it out quickly.

It was from Spike!

He read:

SUCCESS. RETURNING DAY AFTER TOMORROW. ALL WILL BE REVEALED. S.

Moist put it down carefully.

Obviously she'd missed him terribly and was desperate to see him again, but she was stingy about spending Golem Trust money. Also, she'd probably run out of cigarettes.

Moist drummed his fingers on the desk. A year ago he'd asked Adora Belle Dearheart to be his wife, and she'd explained that, in fact, he was going to be her husband.

It was going to be . . . well, it was going to be sometime in the near future, when Mrs. Dearheart finally lost patience with her daughter's busy schedule and arranged the wedding herself.

But he was a nearly married man, however you looked at it. And nearly married men didn't get mixed up with the Lavish family. A nearly married man was steadfast and dependable and always ready to hand his nearly wife an ashtray. He had to be there for his oneday children, and make sure they slept in a well-ventilated nursery.

He smoothed out the message.

And he would stop the night-climbing, too. Was it grown-up? Was it sensible? Was he a tool of Vetinari? No!

But a memory stirred. Moist got up and went over to his filing cabinet, which he normally avoided at all costs.

Under "Stamps" he found the little report he'd had two months ago from Stanley Howler, the head of stamps. It noted in passing the continued high sales of one- and two-dollar stamps, which was higher than even Stanley had expected. Maybe "stamp money" was more prevalent than he'd thought. After all, the government backed it, right? It was even easy to carry. He'd have to check on exactly how much they—

There was a dainty knock at the door, and Gladys entered. She bore with extreme care a plate of ham sandwiches, made very, very thin, as only Gladys

could make them, which was to put one ham between two loaves and bring her shovel-sized hand
down on it very hard.

"I Anticipated That You Would Have Had No
Lunch, Postmaster," she rumbled.

"Thank you, Gladys," said Moist, mentally shaking himself.

"And Lord Vetinari Is Downstairs," Gladys went
on. "He Says There Is No Rush."

The sandwich stopped an inch from Moist's lips.

"He's in the *building*?"

"Yes, Mr. Lipwig."

"Wandering about by himself?" said Moist,
horror mounting.

"Currently He Is In The Blind Letter Office, Mr.
Lipwig."

"What is he doing there?"

"Reading The Letters, Mr. Lipwig."

No rush, thought Moist grimly. Oh, yes. Well,
I'm going to finish my sandwiches that the nice lady
golem has made for me.

"Thank you, Gladys," he said.

When she was gone, Moist took a pair of tweezers out of his desk drawer, opened the sandwich,
and began to disembowel it of the bone fragments
caused by Gladys's drop-hammer technique.

It was a little over three minutes later that the
golem reappeared, and stood patiently in front of
the desk.

"Yes, Gladys?" said Moist.

"His Lordship Desired Me To Inform You That
There Is Still No Rush."

Moist ran downstairs and Lord Vetinari was indeed sitting in the Blind Letter Office* with his boots on a desk, a sheaf of letters in his hand, and a smile on his face.

"Ah, Lipwig," he said, waving the grubby envelopes. "Wonderful stuff! Better than the crossword! I like this one: 'Duzbuns Hopsit pfarmerrsc.' I've put the correct address underneath." He passed the letter over to Moist.

He had written: "K. Whistler, Baker, 3 Pigsty Hill."

"There are three bakeries in the city that could be said to be opposite a pharmacy," said Vetinari, "but Whistler does those rather good curly buns that regrettably look as though a dog has just done his business on your plate and somehow managed to add a blob of icing."

"Well done, sir," said Moist weakly. At the other end of the room, Frank and Dave, who spent all their time deciphering the illegible, misspelled, misdirected, or simply insane mail that sleeted through the Blind Letter Office every day, were watching Vetinari in shock and awe. In the corner, Drumknott appeared to be brewing tea.

"I think it is just a matter of getting into the mind of the writer," Vetinari went on, looking at a letter

---

*The invention of which Moist was very proud. The people of Ankh-Morpork took a straightforward approach to letter-writing, which could be summarized as: If I know what I mean, so should you. As a result, the Post Office was used to envelopes addressed to "My brofer Jonn, tall, by the brij" or "Mrs. Smith wot Des, Dolly Sistres." The keen and somewhat worrying intellects employed in the Blind Letter Office enjoyed the challenge, and during their tea break they played chess in their heads.

covered with grubby fingerprints and what looked like the remains of someone's breakfast. He added: "In some cases, I imagine, there is a lot of room."

"Frank and Dave manage to sort out five out of every six," said Moist.

"They are veritable magicians," said Vetinari. He turned to the men, who smiled nervously and backed away, leaving the smiles hanging awkwardly in the air, as protection. He added: "But I think it is time for their tea break?"

The two looked at Drumknott, who was pouring tea into two cups.

"Somewhere else?" Vetinari suggested.

No express delivery had ever moved faster than Frank and Dave. When the door had shut behind them, Vetinari went on: "You have looked around the bank? Your conclusions?"

"I think I'd rather stick my thumb in a mincing machine than get involved with the Lavish family," said Moist. "Oh, I could probably do things with it, and the Mint needs a good shaking. But the bank needs to be run by someone who understands banks."

"People who understand banks got it into the position it is in now," said Vetinari. "And I did not become ruler of Ankh-Morpork by understanding the city. Like banking, the city is depressingly easy to understand. I have remained ruler by getting the city to understand *me*."

"I understood you, sir, when you said something about angels, remember? Well, it worked. I am a re-formed character and I will act like one."

"Even as far as the goldish chain?" said Vetinari, as Drumknott handed him a cup of tea.

"Damn right!"

"Mrs. Lavish was very impressed with you."

"She said I was an out-and-out crook!"

"High praise indeed, coming from Topsy," said Vetinari. He sighed. "Well, I can't force such a reformed person as you to"—he paused as Drumknott leaned down to whisper in his ear, and then continued—"well, clearly *I can* force you, but on this occasion I don't think I will. Drumknott, take this down, please. 'I, Moist von Lipwig, wish to make it clear that I have no desire or intention to run or be involved in the running of any bank in Ankh-Morpork, preferring instead to devote my energies to the further improvement of the Post Office and the clacks system.' Leave a space for Mr. Lipwig's signature and the date. And then—"

"Look, why is this necessary—" Moist began.

"—continue: 'I, Havelock Vetinari, etc. confirm that I have indeed discussed the future of the Ankh-Morpork banking system with Mr. Lipwig and fully accept his express wish to continue his fine work at the Post Office, freely and without hindrance or penalty.' Space for signature, etc. Thank you, Mr. Lipwig."

"What is all that about?" said Moist, bewildered.

"The *Times* seems to think I intend to nationalize the Royal Bank," said Vetinari.

"Nationalize?" said Moist.

"Steal," Vetinari translated. "I don't know how these rumors get about."

"I suppose even tyrants have enemies?" said Moist.

"Well put as usual, Mr. Lipwig," said Vetinari, giving him a sharp look. "Give him the memorandum to sign, Drumknott."

Drumknott did so, taking care to retrieve the pencil afterward with a rather smug look. Then Vetinari stood up and brushed off his robe.

"I well recall our interesting conversation about angels, Mr. Lipwig, and I recall telling you that you only get one," he said, a little stiffly. "Do bear that in mind."

IT WOULD APPEAR that the leopard *does* change his shorts, sir," mused Drumknott, as the evening mist drifted, waist-high, along the street.

"It would appear so, indeed. But Moist von Lipwig is a man *of* appearances. I'm sure he believes everything he said, but one must look beyond the surface to the Lipwig beneath, an honest soul with a fine criminal mind."

"You have said something similar before, sir," said the secretary, holding open the coach door, "but it seems that honesty has got the better of him."

Vetinari paused with his foot on the step.

"Indeed, but I take some heart, Drumknott, from the fact that, once again, he has stolen your pencil."

"In fact he has not, sir, because I was most careful to put it in my pocket!" said Drumknott, in some triumph.

"Yes," said Vetinari happily, sinking into the

creaking leather as Drumknott started to pat himself down with an increasing desperation, "I know."

T HERE WERE GUARDS in the bank at night. They patrolled the corridors in a leisurely way, whistling under their breath, safe in the knowledge the very best locks kept miscreants out and all the ground floor was paved with marble which, in the long, silent watches of the night, rang like a bell at every step. Some dozed, standing upright with their eyes half-open.

But someone ignored the locks of iron, passed through the bars of brass, trod soundlessly on the ringing tiles, moved under the very noses of the slumbering men. Nevertheless, when the figure walked through the big doors to the chairman's office, two crossbow bolts passed through it and splintered the fine woodwork.

"Well, you can't blame a body for trying," said Mrs. Lavish.

I AM NOT CONCERNED WITH YOUR BODY, MRS. TOPSY LAVISH, said Death.

"It's been quite a while since anyone was," sighed Topsy.

THIS IS THE RECKONING, MRS. LAVISH. THE FINAL ACCOUNTING.

"Do you always use banking allusions at a time like this?" said Topsy, standing up. Something remained slumped in the chair, but it wasn't Mrs. Lavish anymore.

I TRY TO ACKNOWLEDGE THE AMBIENCE, MRS. LAVISH.

"The 'Closing of the Ledger' would have the right ring, too."

THANK YOU. I SHALL MAKE A NOTE. AND NOW, YOU MUST COME WITH ME.

"I made my will just in time, it seems," said Topsy, letting her white hair down.

ONE SHOULD ALWAYS TAKE CARE OF ONE'S POSTER-ITY, MRS. LAVISH.

"My posterity? The Lavishes can kiss my bum, sir! I've fixed 'em for good. Oh yes! Now what, Mr. Death?"

Now? said Death. Now, YOU COULD SAY, COMES . . . THE AUDIT.

"Oh. There is one, is there? Well, I'm not ashamed."

THAT COUNTS.

"Good. It should," said Topsy.

She took Death's arm and walked with him through the doors and onto the black desert under the endless night.

After a while Mr. Fusspot sat up and started to whine.

THERE WAS A small article about the banking business in the *Times* next morning. It used the word *crisis* quite a lot.

Ah, here we are, thought Moist, when he got to paragraph four. Or, rather, here I am.

Lord Vetinari told the *Times*, "It is true that, with the permission of the bank's chairman, I discussed with the Postmaster General the possibility of him offering his services to the Royal Bank in these difficult times. He has declined, and the matter ends there. It is not the business of the government to run banks. The future of the Royal Bank of Ankh-Morpork is in the hands of its directors and shareholders."

And gods help it, thought Moist.

He tackled the in tray with vigor. He threw himself at the paperwork, checking figures, correcting spelling, and humming to himself to drown out the inner voice of temptation.

Lunchtime arrived, and with it a plate of one-foot-wide cheese sandwiches delivered by Gladys, along with the midday copy of the *Times*—

Mrs. Lavish had died in the night. Moist stared at the news. It said she had passed away quietly in her sleep, after a long illness.

He dropped the paper and stared at the wall. She'd seemed like someone hanging together by sheer grit and gin. Even so, that vitality, that spark . . . well, she couldn't hold on forever. So what would happen now? Ye gods, he was well out of it!

And it was probably not a good day to be Mr. Fusspot. He'd looked a waddly sort of dog, so he'd better learn to run *really quickly*.

The latest post that Gladys had brought up contained a long and thoroughly secondhand envelope addressed to him "personly" in thick black letters.

He slit it open with the letter opener and shook it out into the waste bin, just in case.

There was a folded newspaper inside. It was, it turned out, the *Times* from yesterday, and there was Moist von Lipwig on the front page. *Circled*.

Moist turned it over. On the other side, in tiny, neat handwriting, were the words:

> Dear Sir, I have took the small precawtion of loging certain affedavids with trusted associates. You will here from me again
>
> A friend

Take it slowly, take it slowly . . . It can't be from a friend. Everyone I think of as a friend can spell. This must be some kind of con, yes? But there were no skeletons in his closet . . .

Oh, all right, if you were going for the fine detail, there were, in fact, enough skeletons in his closet to fill a big crypt, with enough left over to equip a fun-fair house of horrors and maybe also make a macabre but mildly amusing ashtray. But they'd never been associated with the name Lipwig. He'd been careful about that. His crimes had died with Albert Spangler. A good hangman knows exactly how much rope to give a man, and had dropped him out of one life and into another.

Could anyone have recognized him? But he was the least recognizable person in the world when he wasn't wearing his golden suit! When he was young, his mother sometimes went home from school with the wrong child!

And when he wore the suit, people recognized the suit. He hid by being conspicuous . . .

It had to be a scam of some kind. Yes, that was it. The old "guilty secret" job. Probably no one got to a position like this without accumulating some things they'd rather not see made public. But it was a nice touch to include the bit about affidavits. It was there to set a nervous man to wondering. It suggested that the sender knew something so dangerous that you, the recipient, might try to silence him, and he was in a position to set the lawyers on you.

Hah! And he was being given some time in which, presumably, to stew. Him! Moist von Lipwig! Well, they might just find out how hot a stew could get. For now, he shoved the paper in a bottom drawer. Hah!

There was a knock at the door.

"Come in, Gladys," he said, rummaging in the in tray again.

The door opened and the worried, pale face of Stanley Howler appeared around it.

"It's me, sir. Stanley, sir," it said.

"Yes, Stanley?"

"Head of stamps at the Post Office, sir," Stanley added, in case pinpoint identification was required.

"Yes, Stanley, I know," said Moist patiently. "I see you every day. What is it that you want?"

"Nothing, sir," said Stanley. There was a pause, and Moist adjusted his mind to the world as seen through the brain of Stanley Howler. Stanley was very . . . precise, and as patient as the grave.

"What is the reason for you, coming here, to see me, today, Stanley?" Moist tried, enunciating carefully in order to deliver the sentence in bite-size chunks.

"There is a lawyer downstairs, sir," Stanley announced.

"But I've only just read the threatening—" Moist began, and then relaxed.

"A lawyer? Did he say why?" he said.

"A matter of great importance, he said. There's two watchmen with him, sir. And a dog."

"Really?" said Moist calmly. "Well, you'd better show them up, then."

He glanced at his watch.

Oh . . . kay . . . Not good.

The Lancre Flyer would be leaving in forty-five seconds. He knew he could be down that damn drainpipe in eleven seconds. Stanley was on his way below to bring them up here, call that thirty seconds, maybe. Get them off the ground floor, that was the thing. Scramble onto the back of the coach, jump off when it slowed down for the Hubwards Gate, pick open the tin chest he'd got stashed in the beams of the old stable in Lobbin Clout, get changed and adjust his face, stroll across the city to have a coffee in that shop near the main watch house, keep an eye on the clacks traffic for a while, stroll over to Hen and Chickens Court, where he had another trunk stored with "I Don't Know" Jack, get changed, leave with his little bag and his tweed cap (which he'd change for the old brown bowler in the bag in some alley, just in case Jack had a sudden attack of memory brought on by excessive money), and he'd mosey down to the slaughterhouse district and step into the persona of Jeff the Drover and hang out in the huge, fetid bar of the Butcher's Eagle, which was where the drovers traditionally damped down the road dust. There was a vampire in the Watch these days and they'd had a werewolf for years, too. Well, let those famously sharp noses snuff up the mixed cocktail stink of manure, fear, sweat, offal, and urine and see how they liked it! And that was just in the bar—if anything, it was worse in the slaughterhouses.

Then maybe he'd wait until evening to hitch a lift on one of the steaming dung carts heading out of the city, along with the other drunk drovers. The gate guards never bothered to check them. On the other hand, if his sixth sense was still squawking, then he'd run the thimble game with some drunk until he'd got enough for a little bottle of perfume and a cheap but decent thirdhand suit at some shonky shop and repair to Mrs. Eucrasia Arcanum's Lodging House for Respectable Working Men, where with a tip of a hat and some wire-rimmed spectacles he'd *be* Mr. Trespass Hatchcock, a wool salesman who stayed there every time his business brought him to the city and who brought her a little gift suitable for a widow of the age she'd like people to think she was. Yes, that'd be a better idea. At Mrs. Arcanum's the food was solid and plentiful. The beds were good and you seldom had to share.

Then he could make real plans.

The itinerary of evasion wound across his inner

eye at the speed of flight. The outer eye alighted on something less pleasing. There was a copper in the coach yard, chatting to a couple of the drivers. Moist recognized Sergeant Fred Colon, whose chief duty appeared to be ambling around the city, chattering to elderly men of the same age and demeanor as himself.

The watchman spotted Moist at the window and gave him a little wave.

No, it was going to get complicated and messy if he ran. He'd have to bluff it out up here. It wasn't as though he'd done anything wrong, technically. The letter had thrown him, that's all it was.

Moist was sitting at his desk looking busy when Stanley came back, ushering in Mr. Slant, the city's best-known and, at three hundred and fifty-one, probably also its oldest lawyer. He was accompanied by Sergeant Angua and Corporal Nobbs, widely rumored to be the Watch's secret werewolf. Corporal Nobbs was accompanied by a large wicker hamper and Sergeant Angua, carrying a large bag and a squeaky rubber bone, which she occasionally, in an absentminded way, squeaked. Things were looking up but strange.

The exchanged pleasantries were not that pleasant, this close to Nobby Nobbs and the lawyer, who smelled of embalming fluid, but when they were over, Mr. Slant said: "I believe you visited Mrs. Topsy Lavish yesterday, Mr. Lipwig."

"Oh, yes. Er . . . when she was alive," said Moist, and cursed himself and the unknown letter-writer. He was losing it, he really was.

"This is not a murder investigation, sir," said the sergeant calmly.

"Are you sure? In the circumstances—"

"We've made it our business to be sure, sir," said the sergeant, "*in the circumstances.*"

"Don't think it was the family, then?"

"No, sir. Or you."

"Me?" said Moist, suitably openmouthed at the suggestion.

"Mrs. Lavish was known to be very ill," said Mr. Slant. "And it seems that she took quite a shine to you, Mr. Lipwig. She has left you her little dog, Mr. Fusspot."

"And also a bag of toys, rugs, tartan coats, little booties, eight collars including one set with diamonds and, oh, a vast amount of other stuff," said Sergeant Angua. She squeaked the rubber bone again.

Moist's mouth shut.

"The dog," he said, in a hollow voice. "Just the dog? And the toys?"

"You were expecting something more?" said Angua.

"I wasn't expecting even that!" Moist looked at the hamper. It was suspiciously silent.

"I give him one of his little blue pills," said Nobby Nobbs helpfully. "They knocks him out for a little while. Don't work on people though. They tastes of aniseed."

"All this is a bit . . . odd, isn't it?" said Moist. "Why's the Watch here? The diamond collar?

Anyway, I thought the will wasn't read until after the funeral . . ."

Mr. Slant coughed. A moth flew out of his mouth.

"Yes indeed. But knowing the contents of her will, I thought it prudent to hasten to the Royal Bank and deal with the most . . ."

There was a very long pause. For a zombie, the whole of life is a pause, but it seemed that he was looking for the right word.

". . . *problematical* bequests immediately," he finished.

"Yes, well, I suppose the little doggie needs feeding," said Moist, "but I wouldn't have thought that—"

"The . . . . problem, if such it be, is in fact his paperwork," said Mr. Slant.

"Wrong pedigree?" said Moist.

"Not his pedigree," said Mr. Slant, opening his briefcase. "You may be aware that the late Sir Joshua left one percent share in the bank to Mr. Fusspot?"

A cold, black wind began to blow through Moist's mind.

"Yes," he said. "I am."

"The late Mrs. Lavish has left him another fifty percent. That, by the customs of the bank, means that he is the new chairman, Mr. Lipwig. And you own him."

"Hold on, an animal can't own—"

"Oh, but it can, Mr. Lipwig, it can!" said Slant, with lawyerly glee. "There is a huge body of case law. There was even, once, a donkey who was ordained and a tortoise who was appointed a judge. Obviously the more difficult trades are less well represented. No horse has yet held down a job as a carpenter, for example. But dog as chairman is relatively usual."

"This makes no sense! She hardly knows me!" And his mind chimed in with: *Oh yes she does! She had you bang to rights in a blink!*

"The will was dictated to me last night, Mr. Lipwig, in the presence of two witnesses and Mrs. Lavish's physician, who declared her very sound of mind if not of body." Mr. Slant stood up. "The will, in short, is legal. It does not have to make sense."

"But how can he, well, chair meetings? All he does with chairs is sniff the legs!"

"I assume he will act as chairman through you," said the lawyer. There was a squeak from Sergeant Angua.

"And what happens if he dies?" said Moist.

"Ah, thank you for reminding me," said Mr. Slant, taking another document from the thin and rather battered briefcase. "Yes, it says here: the shares will be distributed among any remaining members of the family."

"Any remaining members of the family? What, *his* family? I don't think he's had much of a chance to have one!"

"No, Mr. Lipwig," said Slant, "the Lavish family."

Moist felt the winds grow colder. "How long does a dog live?"

"An ordin'ry dog?" said Nobby Nobbs. "Or a dog

who stands between a bunch of Lavishes and another fortune?"

"Corporal Nobbs, that was a pertinent remark!" snapped Sergeant Angua.

"Sorry, Sarge."

"Ahem." A cough from Mr. Slant liberated another moth.

"Mr. Fusspot is used to sleeping in the Manager's Suite at the bank, Mr. Lipwig," he said. "You will sleep there too. It is a condition of the bequest."

Moist stood up. "I don't have to do any of this," he snapped. "It's not like I've committed a crime! You can't run people's lives from beyond the grav— well, *you* can, sir, no problem there, but she can't just—"

A further envelope was produced from the briefcase. Mr. Slant was smiling, which is never a good sign.

"Mrs. Lavish also wrote this personal heartfelt plea to you," he said. "And now, Sergeant, I think we should leave Mr. Lipwig alone."

They departed, although after a few seconds Sergeant Angua walked back in and, without saying a word or catching his eye, went over to the bag of toys and dropped the squeaky rubber bone.

Moist walked over to the basket and lifted the lid. Mr. Fusspot looked up, yawned, and then reared up on his cushion and begged. His tail wagged uncertainly once or twice and his huge eyes filled with hope.

"Don't look at me, kid," said Moist, and turned his back.

Mrs. Lavish's letter was drenched in lavender water, slightly spiced with gin. She wrote in a very neat, old-lady hand:

Dear Mr. Lipwig,

I feel that you are a dear, sweet man who will look after my little Mr. Fusspot. Please be kind to him. He has been my only friend in difficult times. Money is such a crude thing in these circumstances, but the sum of $20,000 annually will be paid to you (in arrears) for performing this duty, which I beg you to accept.

If you do not, or if he dies of unnatural causes, your arse will belong to the Guild of Assassins. $100,000 is lodged with Lord Downey, and his young gentlemen will hunt you down and gut you like the weasel you are, Smart Boy!

May the gods bless you for your kindness to a widow in distress.

Moist was impressed. Stick *and* carrot. Vetinari just used the stick, or hit you over the head with the carrot.

Vetinari! Now *there* was a man with some questions to answer!

The hairs on the back of his neck, trained by

decades of dodging in any case and suddenly made extra sensitive with Mrs. Lavish's words still bouncing in his skull, bristled in terror. Something came through the window and *thunked!* into the wall. But Moist was already diving for the carpet when the glass broke.

Shuddering in the door was a black arrow.

Moist crawled across the carpet, reached up, grabbed the arrow, and ducked down again.

In exquisite white writing, like the inscription on some ancient ring, on the arrow were the words:

"Guild of Assassins 'When Style Matters.'"

It had to be a warning shot, right? Just a little grace note, yes? A sort of emphasis? Just in case?

Mr. Fusspot took this opportunity to leap out of his basket and lick Moist's face. Mr. Fusspot didn't care who he was or what he'd done, he just wanted to be friends.

"I think," said Moist, giving in, "that you and me ought to go walkies."

The dog gave an excited little yip and went and tugged at the bag of accessories until it fell over. He disappeared inside, tail wagging madly, and came out dragging a little red velvet doggie coat on which the word *Tuesday* was embroidered.

"Lucky guess, boy," said Moist as he buckled it up. This was difficult, because he was being washed by dog goo all the while.

"Er, you wouldn't know where your lead is, would you?" Moist ventured, trying not to swallow.

Mr. Fusspot bounced off to the bag and returned again with a red leash.

"Oh . . . kay," said Moist. "This is going to be the fastest walky in the history of walkies. It is, in fact, going to be a runny . . ."

As he reached up for the door handle, the door opened anyway. Moist found himself staring up at two terra-cotta-colored legs that were as thick as tree trunks.

"I Hope You Are Not Looking Up My Dress, Mr. Lipwig?" rumbled far above.

At what, exactly? Moist thought.

"Ah, Gladys," he said. "Would you just go and stand at the window? Thank you!"

There was a little *tick!* sound and Gladys turned around, holding another black arrow between her thumb and forefinger. Its sudden deceleration in Gladys's grasp had caused it to catch fire.

"Someone Has Sent You An Arrow, Mr. Lipwig," she noted.

"Really? Just blow it out and put it in the in tray, will you?" said Moist, crawling out of the door. "I'm just going to see a man about a dog."

He picked up Mr. Fusspot and hurried down the stairs, through the thronged hall, down the stone steps—and there, pulling up to the curb, was a black coach. Ha! The man was always one jump ahead, right?

He wrenched open the door as the coach came to a stop, landed heavily in an unoccupied seat, with Mr. Fusspot barking happily in his arm, glared across the carpet, and said—

"Oh . . . sorry, I thought this was Lord Vetinari's coach . . ."

A hand slammed the door shut. It was wearing a large, black, and very expensive glove, with jet beads embroidered into it. Moist's gaze followed it up an arm to a face, which said:

"No, Mr. Lipwig. My name is Cosmo Lavish. I was just coming to see you. How do you do?"

CHAPTER 4

THE MAN . . . made things. He was an unsung craftsman, because the things he made never ended up with his name on them. No, they usually bore the names of dead men on them, men who were masters of their craft. He, in his turn, was the master of one craft. It was the craft of seeming.

"Do you have the money?"

"Yes." The man in the brown robe indicated the stolid troll next to him.

"Why did you bring that? Can't abide 'em."

"Five hundred dollars is a lot to carry, Mr. Morpeth. And a lot to pay for jewelry that isn't even silver, I may add," said the young man, whose name was Heretofore.

"Yes, well, that's the trick, ain't it?" said the old man, "I know this ain't exactly proper, what you're doing. An' I told you stygium's rarer than gold. It just don't sparkle . . . well, unless you do things wrong. Believe me, I could sell all I could get to the assassins. Those fine gentlemen do like their black, so they do. They love it to bits."

"It's not illegal. No one owns the letter V. Look, we've been through this. Let me see it."

The old man gave Heretofore a look, then opened a drawer and put a small box on top of his desk. He adjusted the reflectors on the lamps and said: "Okay, open it."

The young man lifted the lid, and there it was, black as night, the serifed V a deeper, sharper shadow.

He took a deep breath, reached out for the ring, and dropped it in horror.

"It's warm!"

There was a snort from the maker of things that seemed.

"That's stygium, that is. It drinks the light. If you was out in full daylight you'd be sucking your fingers and yellin'. Keep it in a box when it's bright outside, right? Or wear a glove over it if you're a swanker."

"It's perfect!"

"Yes. It is." The old man snatched the ring back, and Heretofore began to tumble into his own private Hell. "It's just like the real thing, ain' it," growled the seemer. "Oh, don't look surprised. You think I

don't know what I've made? I've seen the real one a
coupla' times, and this'd fool Vetinari hisself. That
takes a lot of forgetting."

"I don't know what you mean!" Heretofore protested.

"You *are* stupid, then."

"I told you, no one owns the letter $\mathbb{V}$!"

"You'll tell that to his lordship, will you? No, you
won't. But you'll pay me another five hundred. I'm
thinking of retiring anyway, and a little extra will
get me a long way away."

"We had an agreement!"

"An' now we're having another one," said Morpeth. "This time you're buying forgetfulness." The
maker of things that seemed beamed happily. The
young man looked unhappy and uncertain.

"This is priceless to someone, right?" Morpeth
prompted.

"All right, five hundred, damn you," said Heretofore.

"Except it's a thousand now," said the old man.
"See? You were too fast. You didn't haggle. Someone
really needs my little toy, right? Fifteen hundred all
in. You try to find anyone else in this city who can
work like me. An' if you open your mouth to say anything but 'yes' it'll be two thousand. Have it my way."

There was a longer pause, and Heretofore said:
"Yes. But I'll have to come back with the rest."

"You do that, mister. I'll be here waiting. There,
that wasn't too hard, was it? Nothing personal, it's
just business."

The ring went back in the box, the box went back

in the drawer. At a signal from the young man the troll dropped the bags on the floor and, job done, wandered off into the night.

Heretofore turned suddenly, and the seemer's right hand flew down behind the desk. It relaxed when the young man said: "You'll be here later, yes?"

"Me? I'm always here. See yourself out."

"You'll be here?"

"I just *said* yes, didn't I?"

In the darkness of the stinking hallway the young man opened the door, his heart thumping. A black-clad figure stepped inside. He couldn't see the face behind the mask, but he whispered: "Box is in the top left drawer. Some kind of weapon on the right side. Keep the money. Just don't . . . hurt him, okay?"

"Hurt? That's not why I'm here!" hissed the dark figure.

"I know, but . . . do it neatly, all right?"

And then Heretofore was shutting the door behind him.

It was raining. He went in the doorway opposite. It was hard to hear noises over the rain and the sound of overflowing gutters, but he fancied he heard, above all this, a faint thump. It may have been his imagination, because he did not hear the door open, or the approach of the killer, and he nearly swallowed his tongue when the man loomed in front of him, pressed the box into his hand, and vanished into the rain.

A smell of peppermint drifted out onto the street; the man was thorough, and had used a peppermint bomb to cover his scent.

You stupid, stupid old fool! Heretofore said, in the turmoil of his skull. *Why didn't you take the money and shut up! I had no choice! He wouldn't risk you telling anyone!*

Heretofore felt his stomach heave. He'd never meant it to be like this! He'd never meant for anyone to die! And then he threw up.

That was last week. Things hadn't got any better.

L ORD VETINARI HAS a black coach.
Other people also have black coaches.

Therefore, not everyone in a black coach is Lord Vetinari.

It was an important philosophical insight that Moist, to his regret, had forgotten in the heat of the moment.

There was no heat now. Cosmo Lavish was cool, or at least making a spirited effort to be so. He wore black, of course, as people do to show how rich they are, but the real giveaway was the beard.

It was, technically, a goatee similar to that of Lord Vetinari. A thin line of black hair came down each cheek, made a detour to loop equally thinly under the nose, and met in a black triangle just below the lip, thus giving what Cosmo must have thought was a look of menacing elegance. And indeed, on Vetinari it did. On Cosmo the elegant facial topiary floated unhappily on blue jowls glistening with little tiny beads of sweat, and gave the effect of a pubic chin.

Some master barber had to deal with it, hair by

hair, every day, and his job wouldn't have been made any easier by the fact that Cosmo had inflated somewhat since the day he adopted the style. There is a time in a thoughtless young man's life when his six-pack becomes a keg, but in Cosmo's case it had become a tub of lard.

And then you saw the eyes, and they made up for everything. They had the faraway look of a man who can already see you dead . . .

But probably not those of a killer himself, Moist hazarded. He probably bought death when he needed it. True, on fingers that were slightly too pudgy for them were ostensibly knobbly poison rings, but surely anyone *really* in the business wouldn't have so many, would they? Real killers didn't bother to advertise. And why was the elegant black glove on the other hand? That was an Assassins' Guild affectation. Yep, guild-school trained, then. Lots of upperclass kids went there for the education but didn't do the Black Syllabus. He probably had a note from his mother saying he was excused from stabbing.

Mr. Fusspot was trembling with fear or, perhaps, rage. In Moist's arms he was growling like a leopard.

"Ah, my stepmother's little dog," said Cosmo, as the coach began to move. "How sweet. I do not waste words. I will give you ten thousand dollars for him, Mr. Lipwig."

He held out a piece of paper in the ungloved hand.

"My note of hand for the money. Anyone in this city will accept it."

The voice of Cosmo was a kind of modulated sigh, as if talking was somehow painful.

Moist read:

Please pay the sum of Ten Thousand Dollars to Moist von Lipwig.

And it was signed across a one-penny stamp by Cosmo Lavish, with many a flourish.

Signed across a stamp . . . where had that come from? But you saw it more and more in the city, and if you asked anyone why, they said, " 'Cos it makes it legal, see?" And it was cheaper than lawyers, and so it worked.

And here it was, ten thousand dollars pointing directly at him.

How dare he try to bribe me, thought Moist. In fact, that was his second thought, that of the soon-to-be wearer of a goldish chain. His first thought, courtesy of the old Moist, was: *How dare he try to bribe me so* small.

"No," he said. "Anyway, I'll get more than that for looking after him for a few months!"

"Ah yes, but my offer is less . . . risky."

"You think?"

Cosmo smiled. "Come now, Mr. Lipwig. We're men of the world—"

"—you and I, yes?" Moist finished. "That's so *predictable*. Besides, you should have offered me more money first."

At this point something happened in the vicinity of Cosmo's forehead. Both eyebrows began to twist like Mr. Fusspot's when he was puzzled. They writhed for a moment, and then Cosmo saw Moist's expression, whereupon he slapped his brow and his momentary glare indicated that instant death would reward any comment.

He cleared his throat and said, "For what I can get free? We are making a very good case that my stepmother was insane when she made that will."

"She seemed sharp as a tack to me, sir," said Moist.

"With two loaded crossbows on her desk?"

"Ah, I see your point. Yes, if she was *really* sane, she'd have hired a couple of trolls with big, big clubs."

Cosmo gave Moist a long, appraising look, or what he clearly thought was one, but Moist knew that tactic. It was supposed to make the lookee think they were being weighed up for a serious kicking, but it could just as easily mean "I'll give him the ol' hard eyeball while I'm wondering what to do next." Cosmo might be a ruthless man, but he wasn't a stupid one. A man in a gold suit gets noticed, and *someone* would remember whose coach he got into.

"I fear that my stepmother has landed you into a lot of trouble," said Cosmo.

"I've been in trouble before," said Moist.

"Oh? When was that?" And this came sharp and sudden.

Ah. The past. Not a good place to go. Moist tried to avoid it.

"Very little is known about you, Mr. Lipwig," Cosmo went on. "You were born in Überwald, and you became our postmaster general. In between . . ."

"I've managed to survive," said Moist.

"An enviable achievement indeed," said Cosmo. He tapped on the side of the coach and it began to slow. "I trust it will continue. In the meantime, let me at least give you this . . ."

He tore the bill in half, and dropped the half that very emphatically did not carry his seal or signature onto Moist's lap.

"What is this for?" said Moist, picking it up while trying to restrain the frantic Mr. Fusspot with the other hand.

"Oh, just a declaration of good faith," said Cosmo, as the coach stopped. "One day you might feel inclined to ask me for the other half. But understand me, Mr. Lipwig, I don't usually take the trouble to do things the hard way."

"Don't bother to do so on my account, please," said Moist, wrenching the door open. Sator Square was outside, full of carts and people and embarrassingly potential witnesses.

For a moment, Cosmo's forehead did that . . . eyebrow thing again. He gave it a slap, and said, "Mr. Lipwig, you misunderstand. *This* was the hard way. Good-bye. My regards to your young lady."

Moist spun on the cobbles, but the door had slammed shut and the coach was speeding away.

"Why didn't you add 'We know where your children will go to school'?" he shouted after it.

What now? Hell's bells, he *had* been dropped right in it!

A little way up the street, the palace beckoned.

Vetinari had some questions to answer. How had the man arranged it? The Watch said she'd died of natural causes! But he'd been trained as an assassin, yes? A real one, specializing in poisons, maybe?

He strode in through the open gates, but the guards stopped him at the building itself. Moist knew them of old. There was probably an entrance exam for them. If they answered the question "What is your name?" and got it wrong, they were hired. There were *trolls* that could outthink them.

But you couldn't fool them, or talk them round. They had a list of people who could walk right in, and another of people who needed an appointment. If you weren't on either, you didn't get in.

However, one of their captains, bright enough to read large type, did recognize "Postmaster General" and "Chairman of the Royal Bank" and sent one of the lads knuckling off to see Drumknott, carrying a scribbled note. To Moist's surprise, ten minutes later, he was being ushered into the Oblong Office.

Seats around the big conference table at one end of the room were fully occupied. Moist recognized a few guild leaders, but quite a few were average-looking citizens, working men, men who looked ill at ease indoors. Maps of the city were strewn across the table. He'd interrupted something. Or, rather, Vetinari had interrupted something for him.

Lord Vetinari got up as soon as Moist entered, and beckoned him forward.

"Please excuse me, ladies, gentlemen, but I do need some time with the postmaster general. Drumknott, do take everyone through the figures again, will you? Mr. Lipwig, this way if you please."

Moist thought he heard muffled laughter behind them as he was ushered into what he at first thought was a high-ceilinged corridor, but which turned out to be a sort of an art gallery. Vetinari shut the door behind them. The click seemed, to Moist, to be very loud. His anger was draining fast, to be replaced by a very chilly feeling. Vetinari was a tyrant, after all. If Moist was never seen again, his lordship's reputation would only be enhanced.

"Do put down Mr. Fusspot," said Vetinari. "It will do the little chap good to run about."

Moist lowered the dog to the ground. It was like dropping a shield. And now he could take in what it was this gallery exhibited.

What he'd thought were carved stone busts were faces, made of wax. And Moist knew how and when they were made, too.

They were death masks.

"My predecessors," said Vetinari, strolling down the gallery. "Not a complete collection, of course. In some cases the head could not be found or was, as you might say, in a rather untidy state."

There was a silence. Foolishly, Moist filled it.

"It must be strange, having them look down on you every day," he managed.

"Oh, do you think so? I have to say I'd rather look down on *them*. Gross men, for the most part, greedy, venal, and clumsy. Cunning can do duty for thought up to a point, and then you die. Most of *them* died rich, fat, and terrified. They left the city the worse for their incumbency and the better for their death. But now the city works, Mr. Lipwig. We progress. We would not do so if the ruler was the kind of man who would kill elderly ladies, do you understand?"

"I never said—"

"I know exactly what you never said. You refrained from saying it very loudly." Vetinari raised an eyebrow. "I am extremely angry, Mr. Lipwig."

"But I've been dropped right in it!"

"Not by me," said Vetinari. "I can assure you that if I had, as your ill-assumed street patois has it, 'dropped you in it,' you would fully understand all meanings of 'drop' and have an unenviable knowledge of 'it.'"

"You know what I mean!"

"Dear me, is this the real Moist von Lipwig speaking, or is it just the man looking forward to his very nearly gold chain? Topsy Lavish knew she was going and simply changed her will. I salute her for it. The staff will accept you more easily, too. And she's done you a great favor."

"Favor? I was shot at!"

"That was just the Assassins' Guild dropping you a note to say they are watching you."

"There were two shots!"

"Possibly for emphasis?" said Vetinari, sitting down on a velvet-covered chair.

"Look, banking is supposed to be *dull*! Numbers, pensions, a job for life!"

"For life possibly, but apparently not for long," said Vetinari, clearly enjoying this.

"Can't you do something?"

"About Cosmo Lavish? Why should I? Offering to buy a dog is not illegal."

"But the whole family is—how did you know that? I didn't tell you!"

Vetinari waved a hand dismissively. "Know the

man, know the method. I know Cosmo. In this sort of situation he will not resort to force if money will work. He can be very personable when he wants to be."

"But I've heard about the rest of them. They sound a pretty poisonous bunch."

"I couldn't possibly comment. However, Topsy has helped you there. The Assassins' Guild won't take out a second contract on you. Conflict of interests, you see. I suppose technically they could accept a contract on the chairman, but I doubt if they will. Killing a lapdog? It would not look good on anyone's résumé."

"I didn't sign up to deal with something like this!"

"No, Mr. Lipwig, you signed up to die," snapped Vetinari, his voice suddenly as cold and deadly as a falling icicle. "You signed up to be justly hanged by the neck until dead for crimes against the city, against the public good, against the trust of man for man. And you were resurrected, because the city required you to be. This is about the city, Mr. Lipwig. It is always about the city. You know, of course, that I have plans?"

"It was in the *Times*. The Undertaking. You want to build roads and drains and streets under the city. There's some dwarf machine we've got hold of, called a Device. And the dwarfs can make waterproof tunnels. The Artificers' Guild is very excited about it all."

"I gather by your somber tones that you are not?"

Moist shrugged. Engines of any sort had never interested him. "I don't think much about it one way or another."

"Astonishing," said Vetinari, taken aback. "Well, Mr. Lipwig, you can at least guess at what we will need in very large amounts for this project."

"Shovels?"

"Finance, Mr. Lipwig. And I would have it, if we had a banking system suitable for the times. I have every confidence in your ability to . . . shake things up a little."

Moist tried one last throw. "The Post Office *needs* me—" he began.

"At the moment it does not, and you chafe at the thought," said Vetinari. "You are not a man for the humdrum. I hereby grant you leave of absence. Mr. Groat has been your deputy, and while he may not have your . . . flair, let us say, he will, I am sure, keep things moving along."

He stood up, indicating that the audience was at an end. "The city bleeds, Mr. Lipwig, and you are the clot I need. Go away and make money. Unlock the wealth of Ankh-Morpork. Mrs. Lavish gave you the bank in trust. Run it well."

"It's the dog that's got the bank, you know!"

"And what a trusting little face he has," said Vetinari, ushering Moist to the door. "Don't let me detain you, Mr. Lipwig. Remember—it's all about the city."

THERE WAS ANOTHER protest march going on when Moist walked to the bank. You got more and more of them lately. It was a funny thing, but everyone seemed to want to live under the despotic rule of the tyrannical Lord Vetinari. They poured into the city whose streets were apparently paved with gold.

It wasn't gold. But the influx was having an effect, no doubt about it. Wages were falling, to start with.

This march was against the employment of golems, who uncomplainingly did the dirtiest jobs, worked around the clock, and were so honest they paid their taxes. But they weren't human and they had glowing eyes, and people could get touchy about that sort of thing.

Mr. Bent must have been waiting behind a pillar. Moist was no sooner through the doors of the bank, Mr. Fusspot tucked happily under his arm, when the chief cashier was by his side.

"The staff are very concerned sir," he said, piloting Moist toward the stairs. "I took the liberty of telling them that you would speak to them later."

Moist was aware of the worried stares. And of other things, too, now that he was looking with an almost proprietorial eye. Yes, the bank had been built well, out of fine materials, but get past that and you could see the neglect and the marks of time. It was like the now-inconveniently-large house of a poor old widow who just couldn't see the dust anymore. The brass was rather tarnished, the red velvet curtains frayed and a little bald in places, the marble floor was only erratically shiny—

"What?" he said. "Oh, yes. Good idea. Can you get this place cleaned up?"

"Sir?"

"The carpets are mucky, the plush ropes are unraveled, the curtains have seen better centuries, and the brass needs a jolly good scrub. The bank should look smart, Mr. Bent. You might give money to a beggar but you wouldn't lend it to him, eh?"

Bent's eyebrows rose. "And that's the chairman's view, is it?" he said.

"The chairman? Oh, yes. Mr. Fusspot's very keen on clean. Isn't that right, Mr. Fusspot?"

Mr. Fusspot stopped growling at Mr. Bent long enough to bark a couple of times.

"See?" said Moist. "When you don't know what to do, comb your hair and clean your shoes. Words of wisdom, Mr. Bent. Jump to it."

"I shall elevate myself to the best of my ability, sir," said Bent. "Meanwhile, a young lady has called, sir. She seemed reluctant to give her name but said you would be pleased to see her. I have ushered her into the small boardroom."

"Did you have to open a window?" said Moist hopefully.

"No, sir."

That ruled out Adora Belle, then, to replace her with a horrifying thought. "She's not one of the Lavish family, is she?"

"No, sir. And it's time for Mr. . . . it's time for the chairman's lunch, sir. He has cold, boned chicken because of his stomach. I'll have it sent along to the small boardroom, shall I?"

"Yes, please. Could you rustle up something for me?"

"Rustle, sir?" Bent looked puzzled. "You mean steal?"

Ah, that *kind of man*, Moist thought.

"I meant find me something to eat," he translated.

"Certainly, sir. There is a small kitchen in the suite and we have a chef on call. Mrs. Lavish has lived here for some time. It will be interesting to have a master of the Royal Mint again."

"I like the sound of master of the Royal Mint," Moist said. "How about that, Mr. Fusspot?"

On cue, the chairman barked.

"Hmm," said Bent. "One final thing, sir. Could you please sign these?" He indicated a pile of paperwork.

"What are they? They're not minutes, are they? I don't do minutes."

"They are various formalities, sir. Basically, they add up to you signing a receipt for the bank on the chairman's behalf, but I am advised that Mr. Fusspot's paw mark should appear in the places ticked."

"Does *he* have to read all this?" said Moist.

"No, sir."

"Then I won't. It's a bank. You've given me the big tour. It's not as though it's got a wheel missing. Just show me where to sign."

"Just here, sir. And here. And here. And here. And here. And here. And here . . ."

T HE LADY IN the conference room was certainly an attractive woman, but since she worked for the *Times*, Moist felt unable to award her total ladylike status. Ladies didn't fiendishly quote exactly what you said but didn't exactly mean, or hit you around the ear with unexpectedly difficult questions. Well, come to think of it, they did, quite often, but *she* got paid for it.

But, he had to admit, Sacharissa Cripslock was fun.

"Sacharissa! This is a should-have-been-expected surprise!" he declared, as he stepped into the room.

"Mr. Lipwig! Always a pleasure!" said the woman. "So you are a dog's body now?"

That kind of fun. A bit like juggling knives. You were instantly on your toes. It was as good as a workout.

"Writing the headlines already, Sacharissa?" he said. "I am merely carrying out the terms of Mrs. Lavish's will." He put Mr. Fusspot on the polished tabletop and sat down.

"So you are now chairman of the bank?"

"No, Mr. Fusspot here is the chairman," said Moist. "Bark circumspectly at the nice lady with the busy pencil, Mr. Fusspot!"

"Woof," said Mr. Fusspot.

"Mr. Fusspot is the chairman," said Sacharissa, rolling her eyes. "Of course. And you take orders from him, do you?"

"Yes. I am master of the Royal Mint, by the way."

"A dog and his master," said Sacharissa. "How nice. And I expect you can read his thoughts because of some mystic bond between dog and man?"

"Sacharissa, I could not have put it better."

They smiled at each other. This was only round one. Both knew they were barely warming up.

"So, I take it that you would not agree with those who say that this is one last ruse by the late Mrs. Lavish to keep the bank out of the hands of the rest of her family, believed by some to be totally incapable of running it anywhere but further into the ground? Or would you confirm the opinion of many that the Patrician has every intention of bringing the city's uncooperative banking industry to heel, and finds in this situation the perfect opportunity?"

"Some who believe, those who say . . . who *are* these mysterious people?" said Moist, trying to raise an eyebrow as good as Vetinari's. "And how is it that you know so many of them?"

Sacharissa sighed. "And you wouldn't describe Mr. Fusspot as really little more than a convenient sock puppet?"

"Woof?" said the dog at the mention of his name.

"I find the very question offensive!" said Moist. "And so does he!"

"Moist, you are just no fun anymore." Sacharissa closed her notebook. "You're talking like . . . well, like a *banker*."

"I'm glad you think so." *Remember, just because she's shut the notebook doesn't mean you can relax!*

"No dashing around on mad stallions? Nothing to make us cheer? No wild dreams?" said Sacharissa.

"Well, I'm already tidying up the foyer."

Sacharissa's eyes narrowed. "Tidying the foyer? Who are you, and what have you done with the real Moist von Lipwig?"

"No, I'm serious. We have to clean up ourselves before we can clean up the economy," said Moist, and felt his brain shift seductively into a higher gear. "I intend to throw out what we don't need. For example, we have a room full of useless metal in the vault. That'll have to go."

Sacharissa frowned. "Are you talking about the *gold*?"

Where had that come from? Well, don't try to back away, or she'll go for the throat. Tough it out! Besides, it's good to see her looking astonished.

"Yes," he said.

"You can't be serious!"

The notebook was instantly flipped open, and Moist's tongue began to gallop. He couldn't stop it. It would have been nice if it had talked to him first. Taking over his brain, it said:

"Dead serious! I am recommending to Lord Vetinari that we sell it all to the dwarfs. We do not need it. It's a commodity and nothing more."

"But what's worth more than gold?"

"Practically everything. You, for example. Gold is heavy. Your weight in gold is not very much gold at all. Aren't you worth more than that?"

Sacharissa looked momentarily flustered, to Moist's glee. "Well, in a manner of speaking—"

"The only manner of speaking worth talking about," said Moist flatly. "The world is full of things worth more than gold. But we dig the damn stuff up and then bury it in a different hole. Where's the sense in that? What are we, magpies? Is it all about the gleam? Good heavens, *potatoes* are worth more than gold!"

"Surely not!"

"If you were shipwrecked on a desert island, what would you prefer, a bag of potatoes or a bag of gold?"

"Yes, but a desert island isn't Ankh-Morpork!"

"And that proves gold is only valuable because we agree it is, right? It's just a dream. But a potato is always worth a potato, anywhere. Add a knob of butter and a pinch of salt and you've got a meal, *anywhere*. Bury gold in the ground and you'll be worrying about thieves forever. Bury a potato and in due season you could be looking at a dividend of a thousand percent."

"Can I assume for a moment that you don't intend to put us on the potato standard?" said Sacharissa sharply.

Moist smiled. "No, it won't be that. But in a few days I shall be giving away money. It doesn't like to stand still, you know. It likes to get out and make new friends." The bit of Moist's brain that was trying to keep up with his mouth thought: *I wish I could make notes about this; I'm not sure I can remember it all.* But the conversations of the last day were banging together in his memory and making a kind of music. He wasn't sure he had all the notes yet, but there were bits he could hum. He just had to listen to himself for long enough to find out what he was talking about.

"By giving away you mean—" said Sacharissa.

"Hand over. Make a gift of. Seriously."

"How? Why?"

"All in good time!"

"You are smirking at me, Moist!"

No, I've frozen because I've just heard what my mouth said, Moist thought. *I don't have a clue, I've just got some random thoughts. It's . . .*

"It's about desert islands," he said. "And why this city isn't one."

"And that's it?"

Moist rubbed his forehead. "Miss Cripslock, Miss Cripslock . . . this morning I got up with nothing in mind but to seriously make headway with the paperwork and maybe lick the problem of that special 25p Cabbage Green stamp. You know, the one that'll grow into a cabbage if you plant it? How can you expect me to come up with a new fiscal initiative by teatime?"

"All right, but—"

"It'll take me at least until breakfast."

He saw her write that down. Then she tucked the notebook in her handbag.

"This is going to be fun, isn't it," she said, and Moist thought: *Never trust her when she's put her notebook away, either. She's got a good memory.*

"Seriously, I think this is an opportunity for me to do something big and important for my adopted city," said Moist, in his sincere voice.

"That's your sincere voice," she said.

"Well, I'm being sincere," said Moist.

"But since you raise the subject, Moist, what *were* you doing with your life before the citizens of Ankh-Morpork greeted you with open palms?"

"Surviving," said Moist. "In Überwald the old empire was breaking up. It was not unusual for a government to change twice over lunch. I worked at anything I could to make a living. By the way, I think you meant 'arms' back there," he added.

"And when you got here you impressed the gods so much that they led you to a treasure trove so that you could rebuild our post office."

"I'm very humble about that," said Moist, trying to look it.

"Ye-ess. And the gods-given gold was all in used coinage from the plains cities . . ."

"You know what, I've often lain awake wondering about that myself," said Moist, "and I reached the conclusion that the gods, in their wisdom, decided that the gift should be instantly negotiable." *I can go on like this for as long as you like*, he thought, *and you're trying to play poker with no cards. You can suspect all you like, but I gave that money back! Okay, I stole it in the first place, but giving it back counts for something, doesn't it? The slate is clean, isn't it? Well, acceptably grubby, yes?*

The door opened slowly, and a young and nervous woman crept in, holding a plate of cold, boned chicken. Mr. Fusspot brightened up as she placed it in front of him.

"Sorry, can we get you a coffee or something?" said Moist, as the girl headed back toward the door.

Sacharissa stood up. "Thank you, but no. I'm on a deadline, Mr. Lipwig. I'm sure we'll be talking again very soon."

"I'm certain of it, Miss Cripslock," said Moist.

She took a step toward him and lowered her voice.

"Do you know who that girl was?"

"No, I hardly know anyone yet."

"So you don't know if you can trust her?"

"Trust her?"

Sacharissa sighed. "This is not like you, Moist. She's just given a plate of food to the most valuable dog in the world. A dog that some people might like to see dead."

"Why shouldn't—" Moist began. They both turned to Mr. Fusspot, who was already licking the empty plate up the length of the table with an appreciative *gronf-gronf* noise.

"Er . . . can you see yourself out?" said Moist, hurrying toward the sliding plate.

"If you're in any doubt, stick your fingers down his throat!" said Sacharissa from the door with what Moist considered an inappropriate amount of amusement.

He grabbed the dog and hurried through the far door, after the girl. It led to a narrow and not particularly well-decorated corridor with a green door at the end, from which came the sound of voices.

Moist barged through it.

In the small, neat kitchen beyond, a tableau greeted him. The young woman was backed against a table, and a bearded man in a white suit was wielding a big knife. They looked shocked.

"What's going on!" Moist yelled.

"Er, er . . . you just ran through the door and shouted?" said the girl. "Was something wrong? I always give Mr. Fusspot his appetizer about now."

"And I'm doing his entrée," said the man, bringing the knife down on a tray of offal. "It's chicken necks stuffed with giblets, with his special toffee pudding for afters. And who's asking?"

"I'm the— I'm his owner," said Moist, as haughtily as he could manage.

The chef removed his white hat. "Sorry, sir, of course you are. The gold suit and everything. This is Peggy, my daughter. I'm Aimsbury, sir."

Moist had managed to calm down a little. "Sorry," he said. "I was just worried that someone might try to poison Mr. Fusspot . . ."

"We were just talking about that," said Aimsbury. "I thought that— Hold on, you don't mean me, do you?"

"No, no, certainly not!" said Moist to the man still holding a knife.

"Well, all right," said Aimsbury, mollified. "You're new, sir, you're not to know. That Cosmo kicked Mr. Fusspot once!"

"He'd poison anyone, he would," said Peggy.

"But I go down to the market every day, sir, and select the little dog's food myself. And it's stored downstairs in the cool room, and I have the only key."

Moist relaxed. "You couldn't knock out an omelet for me, could you?" he said.

The chef looked panicky.

"That's eggs, right?" he said nervously. "Never really got involved with cooking eggs, sir. He has a raw one in his steak tartare on Fridays and Mrs. Lavish used to have two raw ones in her gin and orange juice every morning, and that is about it between me n' eggs. I've got a pig's head sousing if you'd fancy some of that. Got tongue, hearts, mar- rowbone, sheep's head, nice bit o' dewlap, melts, slaps, lights, liver, kidneys, beccles—"

In his youth, Moist had been served a lot off that menu. It was exactly the sort of food that one should serve to kids if one wanted them to grow up skilled in the arts of bare-faced lying, sleight of hand, and camouflage. As a matter of course, Moist had hidden those strange, wobbly meats under his veg- etables, on one occasion achieving a potato twelve inches high.

Light dawned.

"Did you cook much for Mrs. Lavish?" said Moist.

"Nossir. She lived on gin, vegetable soup, her morning pick-me-up, and—"

"Gin," said Peggy firmly.

"So you're basically a dog chef?"

"Canine, sir, if it's all the same to you. You may have read my book? *Cooking with Brains*?" Aimsbury said this rather hopelessly, and rightly so.

"Unusual path to follow," said Moist.

"Well, sir, it enables me to . . . it's safer . . . well, the truth is, I have an allergy, sir." The chef sighed. "Show him, Peggy."

The girl nodded, and pulled a grubby card out of her pocket.

"Please don't say this word, sir," she said, and held it up.

Moist stared.

"You just can't avoid it in the catering business, sir," said Aimsbury miserably.

This wasn't the time, *really* wasn't the time. But if you weren't interested in people, then you didn't have the heart of a trickster.

"You're allergic to g— this stuff?" he said, correcting himself just in time.

"No, sir. The word, sir. I can handle the actual alium in question, I can even eat it, but the sound of it, well . . . "

Moist looked at the word again, and shook his head sadly.

"So I have to shun restaurants, sir."

"I can see that. How are you with the word . . . *leek*?"

"Yes, sir, I know where you're going, I've been there. Far leek, tar lick . . . no effect at all."

"Just *garlic*, then—oh, sorry . . ."

Aimsbury froze, with a distant expression on his face.

"Gods, I'm so sorry, I honestly didn't mean—" Moist began.

"I know," said Peggy wearily, "the word just forces its way out, doesn't it? He'll be like this for fifteen seconds, then he'll throw the knife straight ahead of him, and then he'll speak in fluent Quirmian for about four seconds, and then he'll be fine. Here"— she handed Moist a bowl containing a large brown lump—"you go back in there with the sticky-toffee pudding and I'll hide in the pantry. I'm used to it. And I can do you an omelet, too." She pushed Moist through the door and shut it behind him.

He put down the bowl, to the immediate and fully focused interest of Mr. Fusspot.

Watching a dog try to chew a large piece of toffee is a pastime fit for gods. Mr. Fusspot's mixed ancestry had given him a dexterity of jaw that was truly awesome. He somersaulted happily around the floor, making faces like a rubber gargoyle in a washing machine.

After a few seconds Moist distinctly heard the twang of a knife vibrating in woodwork, followed by a scream of: "*Nom d'une bouilloire! Pourquoi est-ce que je suis hardiment ri sous cape à par les dieux?*"

There was a knock at the double doors, followed instantly by the entry of Bent. He was carrying a large, round box.

"The suite is now ready for you, Master," he announced. "That is to say, for Mr. Fusspot."

"The suite?"

"Oh, yes. The chairman has a suite."

"Oh, that suite. He has to live above the shop, as it were?"

"Indeed. Mr. Slant has been kind enough to give me a copy of the conditions of the legacy. The chairman must sleep in the bank every night—"

"But I've got a perfectly good apartment in the—"

"Ahem. They are the Conditions, sir," said Bent. "You can have the bed, of course," he added generously. "Mr. Fusspot will sleep in his in tray. He was born in it, as a matter of interest."

"I have to stay locked up here *every night*?"

In fact, when Moist saw the suite the prospect looked much less like a penance. He had to open four doors even before he found a bed. It had a dining room, a dressing room, a bathroom, a separate flushing privy, a spare bedroom, a passage to the office, which was a kind of public room, and a little private study. The master bedroom contained a huge oak four-poster with damask hangings, and Moist fell in love with it at once. He tried it for size. It was so soft that it was like lying in a huge, warm puddle—

He sat bolt upright. "Did Mrs. Lavish—" he began, panic rising.

"She died sitting at her desk, Master," said Bent soothingly, as he untied the string on the big round box. "We have replaced the chair. By the way, she is to be buried tomorrow. Small Gods, at noon, family members only, by request."

"Small Gods? That's a bit down-market for a Lavish, isn't it?"

"I believe a number of Mrs. Lavish's ancestors are buried there. She did once tell me in a moment of confidence that she would be damned if she was going to be a Lavish for all eternity." There was a rustle of paper, and Bent added: "Your hat, sir."

"What hat?"

"For the master of the Royal Mint." Bent held it up.

It was a black silk hat. Once it had been shiny. Now it was mostly bald. Old tramps wore better hats.

It could have been designed to look like a big pile of dollars, it could have been a crown, it could have been set with small, jeweled scenes depicting embezzlement through the ages, the progression of negotiable currency from snot to little white shells and cows and all the way to gold. It could have said something about the magic of money. It could have been *good*.

A black top hat. No style. No style at all.

"Mr. Bent, can you arrange for someone to go over to the Post Office and get them to bring my stuff over here?" said Moist, looking glumly at the wreck.

"Of course, Master."

"I think 'Mr. Lipwig' will be fine, thank you."

"Yes, sir. Of course."

Moist sat down at the enormous desk and ran his hands lovingly across the worn green leather.

Vetinari, damn him, had been right. The Post Office had made him cautious and defensive. He'd run out of challenges, run out of *fun*.

Thunder grumbled, away in the distance, and the afternoon sun was being threatened by blue-black clouds. One of those heavy all-night storms was rolling in from the plains. There tended to be more crimes on rainy nights these days, according to the *Times*. Apparently it was because of the werewolf in the Watch: rain made smells hard to track.

After a while Peggy brought him an omelet containing absolutely no mention of the word *garlic*. And shortly after that, Gladys arrived with his wardrobe. All of it, including the door, carried under one arm. It bounced off the walls and ceiling as she lumbered across the carpet and dropped it in the middle of the big bedroom floor.

Moist went to follow her, but she held up her huge hands in horror.

"No, Sir! Let Me Come Out First!"

She clumped past him into the hallway. "That Was Nearly Very Bad," she said.

Moist waited to see if anything more was going to be forthcoming, and then prompted, "Why, exactly?"

"A Man And A Young Woman Should Not Be In The Same Bedroom," said the golem with solemn certitude.

"Er . . . how old are you, Gladys?" said Moist carefully.

"One Thousand And Fifty-Four Years, Mr. Lipwig."

"Er . . . right. And you are made of clay. I mean, everyone's made of clay, in a manner of speaking, but, as a golem, you are, as it were, er . . . *very* made of clay . . ."

"Yes, Mr. Lipwig, But I Am Not Married."

Moist groaned. "Gladys, what did the counter girls give you to read this time?" he said.

"It Is *Lady Deirdre Waggon's Prudent Advice For Young Women*," said Gladys. "It Is Most Interesting. It Is How Things Are Done."

She pulled a slim book out of the huge pocket in her dress. It had a chintzy look. Moist sighed. It was the kind of old-fashioned etiquette book that'd tell you Ten Things Not To Do With Your Parasol.

"I see," Moist said.

He didn't know how to explain. Even worse, he didn't know what he'd be explaining. Golems were . . . golems. Big lumps of clay with the spark of life in them. Clothes? What for? Even the male golems in the Post Office just had a lick of blue and gold paint to make them look smart—hold on, he was getting it now! There were *no* male golems! Golems were golems, and had been happy to be just golems for thousands of years. And now they were in modern Ankh-Morpork, where all kinds of races and people and ideas were shaken up and it was amazing what dripped out of the bottle.

Without a further word, Gladys clumped across the hallway, turned around, and stood still. The glow in her eyes settled down to a dull red. And that was it. She had decided to stay.

In his in tray, Mr. Fusspot snored.

Moist took out the half-note that Cosmo had given him.

Desert island. Desert island. I know I think best when I'm under pressure, but what exactly did I mean?

On a desert island gold is worthless. Food gets you through times of no gold much better than gold gets you through times of no food. If it comes to that, gold is worthless in a gold mine, too. The medium of exchange in a gold mine is the pickax.

Hmm. Moist stared at the bill. What does it need to make it worth ten thousand dollars? The seal and signature of Cosmo, that's what. Everyone knows he's good for it. Good for nothing *but* money, the bastard.

Banks use these all the time, he thought. Any bank in the Plains would give me the cash, withholding a commission, of course, because banks skim you top and bottom. Still, it's much easier than lugging bags of coins around. Of course I'd have to sign it too, otherwise it wouldn't be secure.

I mean, if it was blank after "pay," *anyone* could use it.

Desert island, desert island . . . on a desert island a bag of vegetables is worth more than gold, in the city gold is more valuable than the bag of vegetables.

This is a sort of equation, yes? Where's the value?

He stared.

It's in the city itself. The city says: In exchange for that gold, you will have all these things. The city is the magician, the alchemist in reverse. It turns worthless gold into . . . everything.

How much is Ankh-Morpork worth? Add it all up! The buildings, the streets, the people, the skills, the art in the galleries, the guilds, the laws, the libraries . . . billions? No. No money would be enough.

The city was one big gold bar. What did you need to back the currency? You just needed the city. The *city* says a dollar is worth a dollar.

It was a dream, but Moist was good at selling dreams. And if you could sell the dream to enough people, no one dared to wake up.

In a little rack on the desk was an ink pad and two rubber stamps, showing the city's coat of arms and the seal of the bank. But in Moist's eyes, there was a haze of gold around these simple things, too. They had value.

"Mr. Fusspot?" said Moist. The dog sat up in his tray, looking expectant.

Moist pushed his sleeves back and flexed his fingers.

"Shall we make some money, Mr. Chairman?" he said.

The chairman expressed unconditional agreement by means of going "Woof!"

"*Pay The Bearer The Sum Of One Dollar*" Moist wrote on a piece of crisp bank paper.

He stamped the paper with both stamps, and gave the result a long, critical look. It needed something more. You had to give people a show. The eye was everything.

It needed . . . a touch of gravitas, like the bank itself. Who'd bank in a wooden hut?

Hmm.

Ah, yes. It was all about the city, right? Underneath, he wrote, in large ornate letters:

Ad Urbem Pertinet

And, in smaller letters, after some thought:

Promitto fore ut possessori postulanti nummum unum solvem, an apte satisfaciam.

Signed Moist von Lipwig

pp The Chairman

Excuse me, Mr. Chairman," he said, and lifted the dog up. It was the work of a moment to press a front paw on the damp pad and leave a neat little footprint beside the signature.

Moist went through this a dozen or more times,

tucked five of the resulting bills under the blotter, and took the new money, and the chairman, for walkies.

COSMO LAVISH GLARED at his reflection in the mirror. Often he got it right in the glass three or four times in a row, and then—oh, the shame— he'd try it in public and people, if they were foolish enough to mention it, would say, "Have you got something in your eye?"

He'd even had a device constructed that pulled at one eyebrow repeatedly, by means of clockwork. He'd poisoned the man who made it, there and then, as he took delivery, chatting with him in his smelly little workshop while the stuff took hold. He'd been nearly eighty and Cosmo had been very careful, so it never came to the attention of the Watch. Anyway, at that age it shouldn't really count as murder, should it? It was more like a favor, really. And obviously he couldn't risk the old fool blabbing happily to someone after Cosmo had become Patrician.

On reflection, he thought, he should have waited until he was certain that the eyebrow-training machine was working properly. It had given him a black eye before he'd made a few hesitant adjustments.

How did Vetinari do it? It was what had got him the Patricianship, Cosmo was sure. Well, a couple mysterious murders had helped, admittedly, but it was the way the man could raise an eyebrow that kept him there.

Cosmo had studied Vetinari for a long time. It was easy enough, at social gatherings. He'd cut out every picture that appeared in the *Times*, too. What was the secret that kept the man so powerful and unscathed? How might he be understood?

And then one day he'd read in some book or other: "If you want to understand a man, walk a mile in his shoes."

And he'd had a great and glorious idea . . .

He sighed happily, and tugged at the black glove.

He'd been sent to the Assassins' school as a matter of course. It was the natural destination for young men of a certain class and accent. He'd survived, and had made study of poisons, because he believed that was Vetinari's specialty, but the place had bored him. It was so stylized now. They'd got so wrapped up in some ridiculous concepts of honor and elegance that they seemed to forget what it was an assassin was supposed to do . . .

The glove came free, and there it was.

Oh yes . . .

Heretofore had done *magnificently*.

Cosmo stared at the wondrous thing, moving his hand so that it caught the light. Light did strange things to stygium: sometimes it reflected silver, sometimes an oily yellow, sometimes it remained resolutely black. And it was warm, even here. In direct sunlight it would burst into flame. It was a metal that might have been intended for those who move in shadow . . .

The ring of Vetinari. Vetinari's signet ring. Such a small thing, and yet so powerful.

It was entirely without ornamentation, unless you counted the tiny border to the cartouche that surrounded the sharply incised and serifed single letter:

$$V$$

He could only guess at all the things his secretary had to do to get it. He'd had a replica made, "reverse-devised," whatever that was, from the wax seals it had so impressively stamped. And there had been bribes (expensive ones) and hints of hasty meetings and cautious exchanges and last-minute changes to get the replica exactly right—

And here the real one was, on his finger. Very much on his finger, in fact. From Cosmo's point of view, Vetinari also had very small fingers for a man, and getting the ring over the knuckle had been a real effort. Heretofore had fretted about getting it enlarged, foolishly not realizing that this would completely ruin it. The magic—and surely Vetinari had a magic all his own—would leak out. It wouldn't be totally the real thing anymore.

Yes, it had hurt like hell for a few days, but now he was floating above the pain, in a clear blue sky.

He prided himself on being no fool. He'd have known at once if his secretary had tried to palm off a mere copy on him. The shock that went up his arm when he slid the ring—all right, *forced* the ring over the knuckle—was enough to tell him that he had got the real thing. Already he could feel his thoughts getting sharper and faster.

He brushed a forefinger across the deeply cut V and looked up at Drumk—at Heretofore.

"You seem concerned, Heretofore," he said kindly.

"The finger has gone very white, sir. Almost pale blue. Are you sure it doesn't hurt?"

"Not a bit. I feel . . . utterly in control. You seem very . . . worried lately, Heretofore. Are you well?"

"Um . . . fine, sir," said Heretofore.

"You must understand I sent Mr. Cranberry with you for the best of reasons," said Cosmo. "Morpeth would have told someone, sooner or later, however much you paid him."

"But the boy in the hat shop—"

"Exactly the same situation. And it was a fair fight. Was that not so, Cranberry?"

Cranberry's shiny bald head looked up from his book. "Yes, sir. He was armed."

"Bu—" Heretofore began.

"Yes?" said Cosmo calmly.

"Er . . . nothing, sir. You are right, of course." In possession of a small knife and very drunk. Heretofore wondered how much that counted against a professional killer.

"I am, aren't I," said Cosmo in a kindly voice, "and you are excellent at what you do. As is Cranberry. I shall have another little quest for you soon, I feel it. Now do go and get your supper."

As Heretofore opened the door, Cranberry glanced up at Cosmo, who shook his head almost imperceptibly. Unfortunately for Heretofore, he had excellent peripheral vision.

He's going to find out, he's going to find out, he's going to find ooouuutttt!!! he moaned to himself, as he scurried along the corridors. It's the damn ring, that's what it is! It's not my fault Vetinari has thin fingers! He would have smelled a rat if the bloody thing had fitted! Why didn't he let me have it made bigger? Hah, and if I had he'd have sent Cranberry along later to murder the jeweler! I know he'll send him after me, I *know* it!

Cranberry frightened Heretofore. The man was soft-spoken and modestly dressed. And when Cosmo did not require his services he sat and read books all day. That upset Heretofore. If the man was an illiterate thug, things would, in some strange way, have been better, more . . . understandable. The man apparently had no body hair, either, and the gleam from his head could blind you in sunlight.

And it had all begun with a lie. Why had Cosmo believed him? Because he was mad, but regrettably not all the time; he was a sort of hobby madman. He had this . . . thing about Lord Vetinari.

Heretofore didn't spot that at first, he just wondered why Cosmo had fussed about his height at the job interview. And when Heretofore had told him he'd worked at the palace, he was hired on the spot.

And that was the lie, right there, although Heretofore preferred to think of it as an unfortunate conjunction of two truths.

Heretofore *had* indeed been employed for a while at the palace, and thus far Cosmo had not found out that this was as a gardener. He *had* been a minor secretary at the Armorers' Guild before that, which was why he'd felt confident in saying "I was a minor secretary and I was employed at the palace," a phrase that he felt Lord Vetinari would have examined with more care than the delighted Cosmo had done. And now here he was, advising a very important and clever man on the basis of as much rumor as he could remember or, in desperation, make up. And he was getting away with it. In his everyday business dealings, Cosmo was cunning, ruthless, and sharp as a tack, but when it came to anything to do with Vetinari, he was as credulous as a child.

Heretofore noticed that his boss occasionally called him by the name of the Patrician's secretary, but he was being paid fifty dollars a month, food and his own bed thrown in, and for that kind of money he'd answer to "Daisy." Well, perhaps not Daisy, but certainly Clive.

And then the nightmare had begun, and in the way of nightmares, everyday objects took on a sinister importance.

Cosmo had asked for an old pair of Vetinari's boots.

That had been a poser. Heretofore had never been inside the actual palace, but he'd got into the grounds that night by scaling the fence next to the old green garden gate, met one of his old mates, who had to stay up all night to keep the hothouse boilers going, had a little chat, and the following night returned for a pair of old but serviceable black boots, size eight, and information from the boot boy that his lordship wore down the left heel slightly more than the right.

Heretofore couldn't see any difference in the

boots presented, and no one was actually claiming as a fact that these were the fabled Boots Of Vetinari, but well-worn but still-useful boots floated down from the upper floors to the servants' quarters on a tide of noblesse oblige, and if these weren't the boots of the man himself then they had almost certainly, at the very least, sometimes been in the same room as his feet.

Heretofore handed over ten dollars for them and spent an evening wearing down the left heel enough to be noticeable. Cosmo paid him fifty dollars without flinching, although he did wince when he tried them on.

"If you want to understand a man, walk a mile in his shoes," he'd said, hobbling the length of his office. What insight he'd glean if they were the man's under-butler's shoes, Heretofore couldn't guess at, but after half an hour, Cosmo rang for a basin of cold water and some soothing herbs and the shoes had not made an appearance since.

And then there had been the black skullcap. That one had been the one stroke of luck in this whole business. It was even genuine. It was a safe bet that Vetinari bought them from Bolters in the Maul, and Heretofore had cased the place, entered when the senior partners were at lunch, spoken to the impecunious youth who worked the steamy cleaning and stretching machines in the back room—and found that one had been sent in for cleaning. Heretofore walked out with it, uncleaned, leaving the young man extremely pecunious and with instructions to wash a new cap for return to the palace.

Cosmo was beside himself, and wanted to know all the details.

Next evening, it turned out that the pecunious youth spent the evening in a bar and died outside in a drunken brawl around midnight, short of money and even shorter of breath. Heretofore's room was next to Cranberry's. On reflection, he'd heard the man come in late that night.

And now there was the signet ring. Heretofore had told Cosmo that he could get a replica made and use his contacts—his very expensive contacts—at the palace to get it swapped for the real thing. He'd been paid five thousand dollars!

Five thousand dollars!

And the boss was overjoyed. Overjoyed and mad. He'd got a fake ring but he swore it had the spirit of Vetinari flowing in it. Perhaps it did, because Cranberry became part of the arrangement. If you got drawn into Cosmo's little hobby, Heretofore realized too late, you died.

He reached his room, darted inside, and shut the door. Then he leaned on it.

He ought to run, right now. His savings by now could buy a lot of distance. But the fear subsided a little as he collected his thoughts.

They told him: Relax, relax. The Watch hadn't come knocking yet, had they? Cranberry was a professional, and the boss was full of gratitude.

So . . . why not one last trick? Make some real money! What could he "obtain" that the boss would pay him another five thousand for?

Something simple but impressive, that would be

the trick, and by the time he found out—if he ever did—Heretofore would be on the other side of the continent, with a new name and suntanned beyond recognition.

Yes . . . the very thing . . .

T HE SUN WAS HOT, and so were the dwarfs. They were mountain dwarfs and were not at home under open skies.

And what were they here for? The king wanted to know if anything valuable was taken out the hole that the golems were digging for the mad smoking woman, but they weren't allowed to set foot on it, because that would be trespassing. So they sat in the shade and sweated, while, about once a day, the mad smoking woman who smoked all the time came and laid . . . things on a crude trestle table in front of them. The things had this in common: they were dull.

There was nothing to mine here, everyone knew. It was barren silt and sand all the way down. There was no fresh water. Such plants as survived here stored winter rain in swollen, hollow roots, or lived off the moisture in the sea mist. The place contained nothing of interest. And what came out of the long sloping tunnel bore this out to the point of boredom.

There were bones of old ships, and occasionally the bones of old sailors. There were a couple of coins, one silver, one gold, which were not dull enough and were duly confiscated. There were broken pots and pieces of statue, which were puzzled over, part of an iron cauldron, an anchor with a few links of chain.

It was clear, the dwarfs considered as they sat in the shade, that nothing came here but by boat. But remember: in matters of commerce and gold, never trust anyone who could see over your helmet.

And then there were the golems. They hated golems, because they moved silently, for all their weight, and looked like trolls. They arrived and departed all the time, fetching timbers from who knew where, marching down into the dark . . .

And then one day golems came pouring out of the hole; there was a lengthy discussion, and the smoking woman marched over to the watchers. They watched her nervously, as fighters do when approached by a self-confident civilian they know they're not allowed to kill.

In broken dwarfish she told them that the tunnel had collapsed, and she was going to leave. Everything they'd dug out, she said, were gifts for the king. And she left, taking the wretched golems with her.*

That was last week. Since then the tunnel had completely fallen in and the blowing sand had covered everything.

THE MONEY LOOKED after itself. It sailed down the centuries, buried in paperwork, hidden

---

*The dwarfs didn't think to count them and see if any had been left behind. It wouldn't have made any difference, but later on the king might not have shouted at them so much.

behind lawyers, groomed, invested, diverted, converted, laundered, dried, ironed and polished, and kept safe from harm and taxes, and, above all, kept safe from the Lavishes themselves. They knew their descendents—they'd raised them, after all—and so, the money came with bodyguards of trustees, managers, and covenants, disgorging only a measured amount of itself to the next generation, enough to maintain the lifestyle with which their name had become synonymous and with a bit left over for them to indulge in the family tradition of fighting among themselves over, yes, the money.

Now they were arriving, each family branch and often each individual with their own lawyer and bodyguards, being careful about who they deigned to notice, just in case they inadvertently smiled at someone they were currently suing. As a family, people said, the Lavishes got along like a bagful of cats. Cosmo had watched them at the funeral, and they spent all their time watching one another, very much like cats, each one waiting for someone else to attack. But even so, it would have been a decently dignified occasion if only that moron nephew the old bitch had allowed to live in the cellar hadn't turned up in a grubby white coat and a yellow rain hat and kept on blubbing all through the ceremony. He had completely spoiled the occasion for everyone.

But now the funeral was over and the Lavishes were doing what they always did after funerals, which was talk about The Money.

You couldn't sit Lavishes around *a* table. Cosmo

had set out small tables in a pattern that represented
to the best of his knowledge the current state of the
alliances and minor fratricidal wars, but there was
a lot of shifting and scraping and threats of legal
action before people settled down. Behind, the alert
ranks of their lawyers paid careful attention, earning a total of a dollar every four seconds.

Apparently, the only relative that Vetinari had
was an aunt, Cosmo mused. That man had all the
luck. When *he* was Vetinari, there would have to be
a culling.

"Ladies and gentlemen," he said, when the hiss-
ing and name-calling had died away, "I am so glad
to see so many of you here today—"

"Liar!"

"Especially you, Pucci," said Cosmo, smiling at
his sister. Vetinari didn't have a sister like Pucci,
either. No one did, Cosmo was prepared to bet. She
was a fiend in vaguely human shape.

"You've still got something wrong with your
eyebrow, you know," said Pucci. She had a table by
herself, a voice like a saw encountering a nail, with
a slight additional touch of foghorn, and was always
referred to as "a society beauty," which showed just
how rich the Lavishes were. Cut in half, she might
make two society beauties, but not, at that point,
very beautiful ones. While it was said that men she
had spurned jumped off bridges in despair, the only
person known to have said this was Pucci herself.

"I'm sure you all know—" Cosmo began.

"Thanks to your-side-of-the-family's total in-
competence you have lost us the bank!"

That came from the far corner of the room, but it triggered a rising chorus of complaint.

"We are all Lavishes here, Josephine," he said sternly. "Some of us were even *born* a Lavish."

That didn't work. It ought to have done. It would have done for Vetinari, Cosmo was sure. But for Cosmo, it only upset people. The growls of objection got louder.

"Some of *us* make a better job of it!" snapped Josephine. She was wearing a necklace of emeralds, and they reflected a greenish light on her face. Cosmo was impressed.

Whenever possible, Lavishes married distant cousins, but it wasn't uncommon for a few, every generation, to marry outside, in order to avoid the whole "three thumbs" situation. The women found handsome husbands who did what they were told, while the men found wives who, amazingly, were remarkably good at picking up the petulance and shaved-monkey touchiness that was the mark of a true Lavish.

Josephine sat down with a poisonous look of satisfaction at the muttered chorus of agreement. She sprang up again, for an encore: "And what do you intend to do about this unforgivable situation? Your branch has put a mountebank in control of *our* bank! *Again!*"

Pucci spun in her seat. "How dare you say that about Father!"

"And how dare you say that about Mr. Fusspot!" said Cosmo.

It would have worked for Vetinari, he knew it. It would have made Josephine look silly and raised Cosmo's stock in the room. It would have worked for Vetinari, who could raise his eyebrow like a visual rim shot.

"What? What? What *are* you talking about?" said Josephine. "Don't be so silly, child! I'm talking about this Lipwig creature! He's a postman, for goodness' sake! Why haven't you offered him money?"

"I have," said Cosmo, and added for his inner ear: *I'll remember "child," you whey-faced old boot. When I am a master of the eyebrow we shall see what you say then!*

"And?"

"I believe he is not interested in money."

"Nonsense!"

"What about the little doggie?" said an elderly voice. "What happens if it passes away, gods forbid?"

"The bank comes back to us, Aunt Careful," said Cosmo to a very small old lady in black lace, who was engaged in some embroidery.

"No matter how the little doggie dies?" said Aunt Carefulness Lavish, paying fastidious attention to her needlework. "There is always the option of poison, I am sure."

With an audible *woosh*, Aunt Careful's lawyer rose to his feet and said: "My client wishes to make it clear that she is merely referring to the general availability of noxious substances in general and this is not intended to be and in no way should be taken as an espousal of any illegal course of action."

He sat down again, fee earned.*

"Regrettably, the Watch would be all over us like cheap chain mail," said Cosmo.

"Watchmen in our bank? Shut the door on them!"

"Times have moved on, Auntie. We can't do that anymore."

"When your great-grandfather pushed his brother over the balcony the Watch even took the body away for five shillings and a pint of ale all round!"

"Yes, Auntie. Lord Vetinari is the Patrician now."

"And he'd allow watchmen to clump around in our bank?"

"Without a doubt, Auntie."

"Then he is no gentleman," the aunt observed sadly.

"He lets vampires and werewolves into the Watch," said Miss Tarantella Lavish. "It's disgusting, the way they're allowed to walk the streets like real people."

—and something went *ping!* in Cosmo's memory. *He's just like real people*, said the voice of his father.

"This is your problem, Cosmo Lavish!" said Josephine, unwilling to see targets switched. "It was your wretched father who—"

"Shut up," said Cosmo calmly. "Shut up. And those emeralds do not suit you, by the way."

This was unusual. Lavishes might sue and conspire and belittle and slander, but there was such a thing as good manners, after all.

In Cosmo's head there was another ping, and his father saying, *And he's managed to hide what he is so*

---

*For considering implications and intervening with due clarification: $AM12.98p.

*well and at great pain. What he was is probably not even
there anymore. But you'd better know, in case he starts
acting funny . . .*

"My father rebuilt the business of the bank," said
Cosmo, the voice still ringing in his head as Josephine
drew breath for a tirade, "and you all let him. Yes,
you let him. You didn't care what he did so long as the
bank was available to you for all your little schemes,
the ones we so carefully conceal and don't talk about.
He bought out all the small shareholders, and you
didn't mind so long as *you* got your dividends. It was
just a shame that his choice in chums was flawed—"

"Not as bad as his choice of that upstart music-
hall girl!" said Josephine.

"—although his choice in his last wife was
not," Cosmo went on. "Topsy was cunning, devious, ruthless, and merciless. The problem I have is
simply that she was better at all this than you are.
And now I must ask you all to leave. I am going to
get our bank back. Do see yourselves out."

He got up, walked to the door, shut it carefully
behind, and then ran like hell for his study, where
he stood with his back to the door and gloated, an
exercise he had just the face for.

Good old Dad! Of course, that little talk had
been back when he was ten, and didn't have his own
lawyer yet, and hadn't fully embraced the Lavish
tradition of prickly and guarded involvement. But
Dad had been sensible. He hadn't just been giving
Cosmo advice, he'd been giving him ammunition
which could be used against the others. What else
was a father for?

Mr. Bent was . . . not just Mr. Bent. He was something out of nightmares. At the time the revelation had scared young Cosmo, and later on he'd been ready to sue his father over those sleepless nights, in the very best Lavish tradition, but he'd hesitated and that was just as well. It would all have come out in court and he'd have thrown away a wonderful gift.

So the Lipwig fellow thought he controlled the bank, did he? Well, you couldn't run the bank without Mavolio Bent, and by this time tomorrow he, Cosmo Lavish, would own Mr. Bent. Hmm, yes . . . leave it perhaps a little long-er. Another day of dealing with Lipwig's bizarre recklessness would wind up poor Mr. Bent to the point where Cranberry's special powers of persuasion would hardly be required. Oh, yes.

Cosmo pushed his eyebrow up. He was getting the hang of it, he was sure. He'd been just like Vetinari out there, hadn't he? Yes, he had. The look on the family's face when he'd told Josephine to shut up! Even the recollection made his spine tingle . . .

Was this the time? Yes, just for a minute, perhaps. He deserved it . . .

He unlocked a drawer in his desk, reached inside, and pressed the hidden button. On the other side of his desk a secret compartment slid out. From it, Cosmo took a small black skullcap that seemed as good as new. Heretofore was a genius.

Cosmo lowered the cap onto his head with great solemnity.

Someone knocked on the study door. This was pointless, since they then slammed it open.

"Locking yourself in your room again, bro?" said Pucci triumphantly.

At least Cosmo had strangled the impulse to snatch the cap from his head as if he'd been caught doing something dirty.

"It was not, in fact, locked, as you see," he said, "and you are forbidden to come within fifteen yards of me. I have an injunction."

"And you are not allowed to be within twenty yards of *me*, so you broke it first," said Pucci, pulling up a chair. She straddled it heavily and rested her arms on the back. The wood creaked.

"I wasn't the one who moved, I think?"

"Well, cosmically it's all the same," said Pucci. "You know, that's a dangerous obsession you have there."

Now Cosmo took off the cap.

"I'm simply trying to get inside the man," he said.

"A *very* dangerous obsession."

"You know what I mean. I want to know how his mind works."

"And this?" Pucci said, waving a hand at the large picture that hung on the wall opposite the desk.

"William Pouter's *Man with Dog*. It's a painting of Vetinari. Notice how the eyes follow you around the room."

"The dog's *nose* follows me around the room! Vetinari has a dog?"

"Had. Wuffles. Died some time ago. There's a little grave in the palace grounds. He goes there alone once a week and puts a dog biscuit on it."

"Vetinari does that?"

"Yes."

"Vetinari the cool, heartless, calculating tyrant?" said Pucci.

"Indeed!"

"You're lying to your sweet dear sister, yes?"

"You can choose to believe that if you wish." Cosmo exulted, deep inside. He loved to see that irate-chicken expression of furious curiosity on his sister's face.

"Information like that is worth money," she said.

"Indeed. And I'm only telling you because it's useless unless you know where he goes, at what time, and on which day. It just may be, dear sweet Pucci, that what you call my obsession is, in fact, of great practical use. I watch, study, and learn. And I believe that Moist von Lipwig and Vetinari must share some dangerous secret which could even—"

"But you just weighed in and offered Lipwig a bribe!" You could say this about Pucci: she was easy to confide in, because she never bothered to listen. She used the time to think about what to say next.

"A ridiculously small one. And a threat, too. And so now he thinks he knows all about me," said Cosmo, not even trying not to look smug. "And I know nothing about him, which is even more interesting. How did he turn up out of nowhere and immediately get one of the highest jobs in—"

"What the hell is that?" demanded Pucci, whose massive inquisitiveness was also hampered by the attention span of a kitten. She was pointing at the little diorama in front of the window.

"That? Oh—"

"Looks like an ornamental window-box. Is it Toy-town? What's that all about? Tell me right now!"

Cosmo sighed. He didn't actually dislike his sister—well, not more than the natural basic feeling of irksomeness all Lavishes felt for one another—but it was hard to like that loud, nasal, perpetually irritated voice, which treated anything Pucci didn't immediately understand, which was practically everything, as a personal affront.

"It is an attempt to achieve, by means of scale models, a view similar to that seen from the Oblong Office by Lord Vetinari," he explained. "It helps me think."

"That's crazy. What kind of dog biscuit?" said Pucci.

Information also traveled through Pucci's apprehension at different speeds. *It must be all that hair*, thought Cosmo.

"Tracklement's Yums," he said. "The bone-shaped ones that come in five different colors. But he never leaves a yellow one, because Wuffles didn't like them."

"You know they say Vetinari is a vampire?" said Pucci, going off on a tangent to a tangent.

"Do you believe it?" said Cosmo.

"Because he's tall and thin and wears black? I think it takes a bit more than that!"

"And is secretive and calculating?" said Cosmo.

"*You* don't believe it, do you?"

"No, and it wouldn't make any real difference if he was, would it? But there are other people with more . . . dangerous secrets. Dangerous to them, I mean."

"Mr. Lipwig?"

"He could be one, yes."

Pucci's eyes lit up. "You know something, don't you?"

"Not exactly, but I think I know where there is something to be known."

"Where?"

"Do you really want to know?"

"Of course I do!"

"Well, I have no intention of telling you," said Cosmo, smiling. "Don't let me detain you!" he added, as Pucci stormed out of the room.

Don't let me detain you. What a wonderful phrase Vetinari had devised. The jangling double meaning set up undercurrents of uneasiness in the most innocent of minds. The man had found ways of bloodless tyranny that put the rack to shame.

What a genius! And there, but for an eyebrow, went Cosmo Lavish.

He would have to make good the failings of cruel nature. The mysterious Lipwig was the key to Vetinari, and the key to Lipwig—

It was time to talk to Mr. Bent.

CHAPTER 5

Spending spree ❈ *Inadvisability of golem back-rubs*
❈ *Giving away money* ❈ *Some observations*
on the nature of trust ❈ *Mr. Bent has a visitor*
❈ *One of the family*

WHERE DO YOU test a bankable idea? Not in
a bank, that was certain. You needed to test
it where people paid far more attention to money,
and juggled their finances in a world of constant risk
where a split-second decision meant the difference
between triumphant profit or ignominious loss. Ge-
nerically it was known as the real world, but one of
its proprietary names was Tenth Egg
Street.

The Boffo Novelty and Joke
Shop, in Tenth Egg Street, J.
Proust prop., was a haven for
everyone who thought that
fart powder was the last word
in humor, which in many re-
spects it is. It had caught Moist's

eye, though, as a source of material for disguises and other useful things.

Moist had always been careful about disguises. A mustache that could come off at a tug had no place in his life. But since he had the world's most forgettable face, a face that was still a face in the crowd even when it was by itself, it helped, sometimes, to give people something to tell the Watch about. Spectacles were an obvious choice, but Moist achieved very good results with his own design of nose and ear wigs. Show a man a pair of ears that small songbirds had apparently nested in, watch the polite horror in his eyes, and you could be certain *that would be all he would remember.*

Now, of course, he was an honest man, but part of him felt it necessary that he should keep his hand in, just in case.

Today he bought a pot of glue and a large jar of fine gold sprinkles, because he could see a use for them.

"That will be 35p, Mr. Lipwig," said Mr. Proust. "Any new stamps coming along?"

"One or two, Jack," said Moist. "How's Ethel? And little Roger," he added, after only a moment's shuffle through the files in his head.

"Very well, thank you for asking. Can I get you anything else?" Proust added hopefully, in case Moist might have a sudden recollection that life would be considerably improved by the purchase of a dozen false noses.

Moist glanced at the array of masks, scary rubber hands, and joke noses, and considered his needs satisfied.

"Only my change, Jack," he said, and carefully laid one of his new creations on the counter. "Just give me half a dollar."

Proust stared at it as if it might explode or vent some mind-altering gas.

"What's this, sir?"

"A note for a dollar. A dollar bill. It's the latest thing."

"Do I have to sign it or anything?"

"No, that's the interesting bit. It's a dollar. It can be anyone's."

"I'd like it to be mine, thank you!"

"It is, now," said Moist. "But you can use it to buy things."

"There's no gold in it," said the shopkeeper, picking it up and holding it away from his body, just in case.

"Well, if I paid in pennies and shillings there would be no gold in them either, right? As it is, you're fifteen pence ahead, and that's a good place to be, agreed? And that note is worth a dollar. If you take it along to my bank, they'll give you a dollar for it."

"But I've already got a dollar! Er . . . haven't I?" Proust added.

"Good man! So why not go out in the street and spend it right now? Come on, I want to see how it works."

"Is this like the stamps, Mr. Lipwig?" said Proust, scrambling for something he could understand. "People sometimes pay me in stamps, me doing a lot of mail-order—"

"Yes! Yes! Exactly! Think of it as a big stamp.

Look, I'll tell you what, this is an introductory offer. Spend that dollar and I'll give you another bill for a dollar, so that you'll still have a dollar. So what are you risking?"

"Only if this *is*, like, one of the first dollar bills, right . . . well, my lad bought some of the first stamps you did, right, and now they're worth a mint, so if I hang on to it, it'll be worth money someday—"

"*It's worth money now!*" Moist wailed. That was the trouble with slow people. Give him a fool any day. Slow people took some time to catch up, but when they did they rolled right over you.

"Yes, but, see"—and here the shopkeeper grinned what he probably thought was an artful grin, which, in fact, made him look like Mr. Fusspot halfway through a toffee—"you're a sly one with them stamps, Mr. Lipwig, bringin' out different ones all the time. My granny says if it's true a man's got enough iron in his blood to make a nail then *you've* got enough brass in your neck to make a doorknob, no offense meant, she speaks her mind does my granny—"

"I've made the mail run on time, haven't I?"

"Oh, yes, Gran says you may be a Slippery Jim but you get things done, no doubt about it—"

"Right! Let's spend the damn dollar, then, shall we?" *Is it some kind of duplex magical power I have*, he wondered, *that lets old ladies see right through me but like what they see?*

And thus Mr. Proust decided to hazard his dollar in the shop next door, on an ounce of Jolly Sailor pipe tobacco, some mints, and a copy of *What Novelty?* And Mr. "Natty" Poleforth, once the exercise was explained to him, accepted the note and took it across the road to Mr. Drayman the butcher, who cautiously accepted it, after having things set out fair and square for him, in payment for some sausages and also gave Moist a bone "for your little doggie." It was more than likely that Mr. Fusspot had never seen a real bone before. He circled it carefully, waiting for it to squeak.

Tenth Egg Street was a street of small traders who sold small things in small quantities for small sums on small profits. In a street like that, you had to be small-minded. It wasn't the place for big ideas. You had to look at the detail. These were men who saw far more farthings than dollars.

Some of the other shopkeepers were already pulling down the shutters and closing up for the day. Drawn by the Ankh-Morporkian's instinct for something interesting, the traders drifted over to see what was going on. They all knew one another. They all dealt with one another. And everyone knew Moist von Lipwig, the man in the gold suit. The notes were examined with much care and solemn discussion.

"*It's just an IOU or marker, really.*"

"*All right, but supposing you needed the money?*"

"*But, correct me if I'm wrong, isn't the IOU the money?*"

"*All right then, who owes it to you?*"

"*Er . . . Jack here, because . . . no, hang on . . . it* is *the money, right?*"

Moist grinned as the discussion wobbled back and forth. Whole new theories of money were growing here like mushrooms, in the dark and based on bullshit. But these were men who counted every half-farthing and slept at night with the cash box under their bed. They'd weigh out flour and raisins and rainbow sprinkles with their eyes ferociously focused on the scale's pointer, because they were men who lived in the margins. If he could get the idea of paper money past them then he was home and, if not dry, then at least merely Moist.

"So you think these might catch on?" he said, during a lull.

The consensus was, yes, they could, but should look "fancier," in the words of Natty Poleforth—"You know, with more fancy lettering and similar."

Moist agreed, and handed a note to every man, as a souvenir. It was worth it.

"And if it all goes wahoonie-shaped," said Mr. Proust, "you've still got the gold, right? Locked up down there in the cellar?"

"Oh, yes, you've got to have the gold," said Mr. Drayman.

There was a general murmur of agreement, and Moist felt his spirits slump.

"But I thought we'd all agreed that you don't need the gold?" he said. In fact, they hadn't, but it was worth a try.

"Ah, yes, but it's got to be there *somewhere*," said Mr. Drayman.

"It keeps banks honest," said Mr. Poleforth, in the tone of plonking certainty that is the hallmark of that most knowledgeable of beings, The Man In The Pub.

"But I thought you understood," said Moist. "You don't *need* the gold!"

"Right, sir, right," said Mr. Poleforth soothingly. "Just so long as it's there."

"Er . . . do you happen to know *why* it has to be there?" said Moist.

"Keeps banks honest," said Mr. Poleforth, on the basis that truth is achieved by repetition. And with nods all round, this was the feeling of Tenth Egg Street. So long as the gold was somewhere, it kept banks honest and everything was okay. Moist felt humbled by such faith. If the gold was somewhere, herons would no longer eat frogs, either. But, in fact, there was no power in the world that could keep a bank honest if it didn't want to be.

Still, not a bad start to his first day, even so. He could build on it.

It began to rain, not hard, but the kind of fine rain where you can *almost* get away without an umbrella. No cabs bothered to trawl Tenth Egg Street for trade, but there was one at the curb in Losing Street, the horse sagging in the harness, the driver hunched into his greatcoat, the lamps flickering in the dusk. With the rain getting to the blobby, soaking stage, it was a sight for damp feet.

He hurried over, climbed in, and a voice in the gloom said, "Good evening, Mr. Lipwig. It's so nice to meet you at last. I'm Pucci. I'm sure we will be friends . . ."

"Now, you see, that was good," said Sergeant Colon of the Watch, as the figure of Moist von Lipwig disappeared around the corner, still accelerating. "He went right through the cab window without touching the sides and bounced off that bloke creepin' up. Very nice roll as he landed, I thought, and he still had hold of the little dog the whole time. Done it before, I shouldn't wonder. Nevertheless, I'm forced, on balance, to consider him a twit."

"The first cab," said Corporal Nobbs, shaking his head. "Oh dear, oh dear, oh *dear*. I would not have thought it of a man like him."

"My point exactly," said Colon. "When you know you've got enemies at large, never, ever get in the first cab. Fact of life. Even things what live under rocks know it."

They watched the former creeper gloomily picking up the remains of his iconograph, while Pucci screamed at him from the coach.

"I bet when the first cab was built, no one dared to get into it, eh, Sarge?" said Nobby happily. "I bet the first cabby used to go home every night starvin' on account of everyone knowin', right?"

"Oh, no, Nobby, people with no enemies at large would be okay, Nobby. Now let's go and report."

"What does it mean 'at large,' anyway," said Nobby as they ambled toward the Chitling Street watch house and the certain prospect of a cup of hot, sweet tea.

"It means large enemies, Nobby. It's as clear as the nose on your face. Especially yours."

"Well, she's a large girl, that Pucci Lavish."

"And nasty enemies to have, that family," Colon opined. "What's the odds?"

"Odds, Sarge?" said Nobby innocently.

"You're runnin' a book, Nobby. You always run a book."

"Can't get any takers, Sarge. For'gone conclusion," said Nobby.

"Ah, right. Sensible. Lipwig goin' to be found lyin' in chalk by Sunday?"

"No, Sarge. Everyone thinks he'll win."

MOIST WOKE UP in the big, soft bed and strangled a scream.

Pucci! Aaagh! And in a state of what the delicately inclined called "dishabille." He'd always wondered what dishabille looked like, but he'd never expected to see so much of it in one go. Even now, some of his memory cells were still trying to die.

But he wouldn't be Moist von Lipwig if a certain amount of insouciance didn't rise to heal the wounds. He'd got away, after all. Oh, yes. It wasn't as though it was the first window he'd jumped through. And the sound of Pucci's scream of rage was almost as loud as the crack the man's iconograph made as it hit the cobbles. The ol' honey-trap game. Hah. But it really was time he did something illegal, just to get his mind back to crooked. He wouldn't have got into the first cab a year ago, that was for sure. Mind you, it would be a strange jury that believed he could be attracted to Pucci Lavish; he couldn't see that standing up in court.

He got up, dressed, and listened hopefully for signs of life from the kitchen. In their absence, he made himself some black coffee.

Armed with this, he made his way into the office, where Mr. Fusspot dozed in his in tray and the official top hat sat, accusingly black.

Ah, yes, he was going to do something about that, wasn't he?

He reached into his pocket and pulled out the little pot of glue, which was one of the convenient ones with a brush in the lid, and after some careful spreading began to pour the glittering flakes as smoothly as he could.

He was still engrossed in this exercise when Gladys loomed in his vision like an eclipse of the sun, holding what turned out to be a bacon-and-egg sandwich two feet long and one-eighth-of-an-inch thick. She'd also picked up his copy of the *Times*.

He groaned.

He'd made the front page. He usually did. It was his athletic mouth. It ran away with him whenever he saw a notebook.

Er . . . he'd made page two, as well. Oh, and the lead editorial. Bugger, even the political cartoon, too, the one that was never much of a laugh.

First Urchin: "Why ain't Ankh-Morpork like a desert island?"

Second Urchin: "'Cos when yer on a desert island the sharks can't bite yer!"

It was side-splitting.

His bleary eyes strayed back to the editorial. *They*, on the other hand, could be quite funny, since they were based on the assumption that the world would be a much better place if it was run by journalists. They were—

What? What was this? "Time to consider the unthinkable . . . a wind of change blowing through the vaults at last . . . undoubted success of the new Post Office . . . stamps already a de facto currency . . . fresh ideas needed . . . youth at the helm . . ." Youth at the helm? This from William de Worde, who was almost certainly the same age as Moist but wrote editorials that suggested his bum was stuffed with tweed.

It was sometimes hard to tell in all the ponderousness what de Worde actually thought about anything, but it appeared through the rolling fog of polysyllables that the *Times* believed Moist von Lipwig to be, on the whole and all things considered, taking the long view and one thing with another, probably the right man in the right job.

He was aware of Gladys behind him when red light glinted off the brasswork on the desk.

"You Are Very Tense, Mr. Lipwig," she said.

"Yeah, right," said Moist, reading the editorial again. Ye gods, the man really did write as though he was chipping the letters in stone.

"There Was An Interesting Article About Back Rubs In The Ladies' Own Magazine," Gladys went on. Later on, Moist felt that perhaps he should have heeded the hopeful tone in her voice. But he was thinking: Not just carved, but with big serifs, too.

"They Are Very Good At Relieving Tension Caused By The Hurly-Burly Of Modern Life," Gladys intoned.

"Well, we certainly don't want any of that," said Moist, and everything went black.

The strange thing was, he thought, when Peggy and Aimsbury had brought him round and clicked his bones back into the appropriate sockets, that he actually felt a lot better. Perhaps that was the idea. Perhaps the hideous white-hot pain was there to make you realize that there were worse things in the world than the occasional twinge.

"I Am Very Sorry," said Gladys. "I Did Not Know That Was Going To Happen. It Said In The Magazine That The Recipient Would Experience A Delightful Frisson."

"I don't think that means you should be able to see your own eyeball," said Moist, rubbing his neck. Gladys's eyes dimmed so much that he was moved to add: "I feel much better now, though. It's so nice to look down and not see my heels."

"Don't you listen to him, it wasn't that bad," said Peggy, with sisterly fellow feeling. "Men always make a big fuss over a little pain."

"They Are Just Big Cuddly Babies, Really," said Gladys. That caused a thoughtful pause.

"Where did *that* come from?" said Moist.

"The Information Was Imparted To Me By Glenda At The Stamp Counter."

"Well, from now on I don't want you to—"

The big doors swung open. They let in a hubbub from the floors below, and riding the noise, like some kind of aural surfer, was Mr. Bent, saturnine and far too shiny for this time of the morning.

"Good morning, Master," he said icily. "The street outside is full of people. And might I take this opportunity to congratulate you on disproving a theory currently much in vogue at Unseen University?"

"Huh?" said Moist.

"There are, some risible people like to suggest, an infinite number of universes, in order to allow everything that may happen a place to happen in. This is, of course, nonsense, which they entertain only because they believe words are the same as reality. Now, however, I can disprove the theory, since in such an infinity of worlds there would have to be one where I would applaud your recent actions and, let me assure you, sir, infinity is not that big!" Mr. Bent drew himself up. "People are hammering on the doors! They want to close their accounts! I *told* you banking was about trust and confidence!"

"Oh dear," said Moist.

"They are asking for gold!"

"I thought that's what you prom—"

"It is only a *metaphorical* promise! I told you, it is based on the understanding that no one will actually demand it!"

"How many people want to withdraw their money?" said Moist.

"Nearly twenty!"

"Then they are making a lot of noise, aren't they?"

Mr. Bent looked uncomfortable.

"Well, there are some others," he said. "A few misguided people are seeking to open accounts, but—"

"How many?"

"About two or three hundred, but—"

"*Opening* accounts, you say?" said Moist. Mr. Bent was squirming.

"Only for trifling sums, a few dollars here and there," he said dismissively. "It would appear that they think you have 'something up your sleeve.'" The inverted commas shuddered, like a well-bred girl picking up a dead vole.

Some of Moist recoiled. But part of him began to feel the wind on his face.

"Well, let's not disappoint them, shall we?" he said, picking up the gold top hat, which was still a bit sticky. Bent glared at it.

"The other banks are furious, you know," he said, high-stepping hurriedly after Moist as the master of the Royal Mint headed for the stairs.

"Is that good or bad?" said Moist over his shoulder. "Listen, what's the rule about bank-lending? I heard it once. It's about interest."

"Do you mean 'borrow at one-half, lend at two, go home at three'?" said Bent.

"Right! I've been thinking about that. We could shave those numbers, couldn't we?"

"This is Ankh-Morpork! A bank has to be a fortress! That is *expensive*!"

"But we could alter them a bit, couldn't we? And we don't pay interest on balances of less than a hundred dollars, correct?"

"Yes, that is so."

"Well, from now on anyone can open an account with five dollars and we'll start paying interest a lot earlier. That'll smooth out the lumps in the mattresses, won't it?"

"Master, I protest! Banking is not a game!"

"Dear Mr. Bent, it *is* a game. And it's an old game, called 'What can we get away with?'"

A cheer went up. They had reached an open landing that overlooked the hall of the bank like a pulpit overlooks the sinners, and a field of faces stared up at Moist in silence for a moment. Then someone called out: "Are you going to make us all rich, Mr. Lipwig?"

Oh damn, thought Moist, *why* are *they all here?*

"Well, I'm going to do my best to get my hands on your money!" he promised.

This got a cheer. Moist wasn't surprised. Tell someone you were going to rob them and all that happened was that you got a reputation as a truthful man.

The waiting ears sucked at his tongue, and his common sense went and hid. It heard his mouth add: "And so I can get more of it, I think—that is to say, the chairman thinks—that we should be looking at one percent interest on all accounts that have five dollars in them for a whole year."

There was a choking sound from the chief cashier, but no great stir from the crowd, most of whom were of the Sock Under The Mattress persuasion. In fact, the news did not appear to please. Then someone raised his hand and said: "That's a lot to pay just to have you stick our money in your cellar, isn't it?"

"No, it's what I'll pay *you* to let me stick your money in my cellar for a year," said Moist.

"You will?"

"Certainly. Trust me."

The inquirer's face twisted into the familiar mask of a slow thinker trying to speed up.

"So where's the catch?" he managed.

Everywhere, thought Moist. *For one thing, I won't be storing it in my cellar, I'll be storing it in someone else's pocket. But you really don't need to know that right now.*

"No catch," he said. "If you put a hundred dollars on deposit, then after a year it'll be worth one hundred and one dollars."

"That's all very well for you to say, but where would the likes of me get a hundred dollars?"

"Right here, if you invest just one dollar and wait for—how long, Mr. Bent?"

The chief cashier snorted. "Four hundred and sixty-one years!"

"Okay, it's a bit of a wait, but your great-great-great-etc.-grandchildren will be proud of you," said Moist, above the laughter. "But I'll tell you what I'll do; if you open an account here today for, oh, five dollars, we'll give you a free dollar on Monday. A free dollar to take away, ladies and gentlemen, and where are you going to get a better deal than—"

"A real dollar, pray, or one of these *fakes*?"

There was a commotion near the door, and Pucci Lavish swept in. Or, at least, tried to sweep. But a good sweep needs planning, and probably a rehearsal. You shouldn't just go for it and hope. All you get is a lot of shoving.

The two heavies, there to clear a path through the press of people, got defeated by sheer numbers, which meant that the rather slimmer young men leading her exquisitely bred blond hounds got stuck behind them. Pucci had to shoulder her way through.

It could have been *so good*, Moist felt. It had all the right ingredients, the black-clad bruisers so menacing, the dogs so sleek and blond. But Pucci herself had been blessed with beady, suspicious little eyes and a generous upper lip which combined to the long neck to put the honest observer in mind of a duck who'd just been offended by a passing trout.

Someone should have told her that black was not her color, that the expensive fur could have looked better on its original owners, that if you were going to wear high heels then this week's fashion tip was "Don't Wear Sunglasses At The Same Time," because when you walked out of the bright sunlight into the relative gloom of, say, a bank, you would lose all sense of direction and impale the foot of one of your own bodyguards. Someone should have told her, in fact, that true style comes from innate cunning and mendacity. You can't buy it.

"Miss Pucci Lavish, ladies and gentlemen!" said Moist, starting to clap as Pucci whipped her sunglasses off and advanced on the counter with murder in her eye. "One of the directors who will join us *all* in making money."

There was some clapping from the crowd, most

of whom had never seen Pucci before but wanted the free show.

"I say! Listen to me! Everyone listen to me," she commanded. She waved what seemed to Moist to look very much like his experimental dollar bills. "This is just worthless paper! This is what he will be giving you!"

"No, it's the same as an open check or a banker's draft," said Moist.

"Really? We shall see! I say! Good people of Ankh-Morpork! Do any of you think this piece of paper could be worth a dollar? Would anyone give me a dollar for it?" Pucci waved the paper dismissively.

"Dunno. What is it?" said someone, and there was a buzz from the crowd.

"An experimental bank note," said Moist, over the growing hubbub. "Just to try out the idea."

"How many of them are there, then?" said the inquiring man.

"About twelve," said Moist.

The man turned to Pucci. "I'll give you five dollars for it, how about that?"

"Five? It says it's worth one!" said Pucci, aghast.

"Yeah, right. Five dollars, miss."

"Why? Are you insane?"

"I'm as sane as the next man, thank you, young lady!"

"Seven dollars here!" said the next man, raising a hand.

"This is madness!" wailed Pucci.

"Mad?" said the next man. He pointed a finger at

Moist. "If I'd bought a pocketful of the black penny stamps when that feller brought them out last year, I'd be a rich man!"

"Anyone remember the Triangular Blue?" said another bidder. "Fifty pence it cost. I put one on a letter to my aunt; by the time it got there it was worth fifty dollars! And the ol' baggage wouldn't give it back!"

"It's worth a hundred and sixty now," said someone behind him. "Auctioned at Dave's Stamp and Pin Emporium last week. Ten dollars is my bid, miss!"

"Fifteen here!"

Moist had a good view from the stairs. A small consortium had formed at the back of the hall, working on the basis that it was better to have small shares than none at all.

Stamp collecting! It had started on day one, and then ballooned like some huge . . . thing, running on strange, mad rules. Was there any other field where flaws made things worth more? Would you buy a suit just because one arm was shorter than the other? Or because a bit of spare cloth was still attached? Of course, when Moist had spotted this, he'd put in flaws on purpose, as a matter of public entertainment, but he certainly hadn't planned for Lord Vetinari's head to appear upside down just once on every sheet of Blues. One of the printers had been about to destroy them when Moist brought him down with a flying tackle.

The whole business was unreal, and unreal was Moist's world. Back when he'd been a naughty boy he'd sold dreams, and the big seller in that world was the one where you got very rich by a stroke of luck. He'd sold glass as diamonds because greed clouded men's eyes. Sensible, upright people, who worked hard every day, nevertheless believed, against all experience, in money for nothing. But the stamp collectors . . . they believed in small perfections. It was possible to get one small part of the world *right*. And even if you couldn't get it right, you at least knew what was missing. It might be, f'rinstance, the flawed 50p Triangular Blue, but there were still six of them out there, and who knew what piece of luck might attend the dedicated searcher?

Rather a lot of luck would be needed, Moist had to admit, because four of them were safely tucked away for a rainy day in a little lead box under the floorboards in Moist's office. Even so, two were out there somewhere, perhaps destroyed, lost, eaten by snails, or—and here hope lay thick as winter snow—were in some unregarded bundle of letters at the back of a drawer somewhere.

—and Miss Pucci simply didn't know how to work a crowd. She stomped and demanded attention and bullied and insulted and it didn't help that she'd called them "good people," because no one likes an outright liar. And now she was losing her temper, because the bidding had reached thirty-four dollars. And now—

—she'd torn it up!

"That's what *I* think of this silly money!" she announced, throwing the pieces in the air. Then she stood there, panting and looking triumphant, as if she'd done something clever.

A kick in the teeth to everyone there. It made you want to cry, it really did. Oh, well.

He pulled one of the new notes out of his pocket and held it up.

"Ladies and gentlemen!" he announced, "I have here one of the *increasingly rare* first-generation One Dollar notes"—he had to pause for the laughter—"signed by myself and the chairman. Bids over forty dollars, please! All proceeds to the little kiddies!"

He ran it up to fifty, bouncing a couple of bids off the wall. Pucci stood ignored and steaming with rage for a while and then flounced out. It was a good flounce, too. She had no idea how to handle people and she tried to make self-esteem do the work of self-respect, but the girl could flounce better than a fat turkey on a trampoline.

The lucky winner was already surrounded by his unlucky fellow bidders by the time he reached the bank's doors. The rest of the crowd surged toward the counters, not sure what was going on but determined to have a piece of it.

Moist cupped his hand and shouted, "And this afternoon, ladies and gentlemen, Mr. Bent and myself will be available to discuss bank loans!" This caused a further stir.

"Smoke and mirrors, Mr. Lipwig," said Bent, turning away from the balustrade. "Nothing but smoke and mirrors . . ."

"But done without smoke and in a total absence of a mirror, Mr. Bent!" said Moist cheerfully.

"And the 'kiddies'?" said Bent.

"Find some. There's bound to be an orphanage

that needs fifty dollars. It'll have to be an anonymous donation, of course."

Bent looked surprised. "Really, Mr. Lipwig? I'll make no bones about saying that you seem to me to be the sort of man who makes a great Razz Arm Ma Tazz about giving money to charity." He made razzmatazz sound like some esoteric perversion.

"Well, I'm not. Do good by stealth, that is my watchword." *It'll get found out soon enough,* he added to himself, *and then I'm not only a jolly good chap but a decently modest one, too.*

I wonder . . . am I really a bastard or am I just really good at thinking like one?

Nothing nudged at his mind. Tiny hairs on the back of his neck were twitching. Something was wrong, out of place . . . dangerous.

He turned and looked down again at the hall. People were milling around, forming into lines, talking in groups—

In a world of movement, the eye is drawn to stillness. In the middle of the banking hall, unheeded by the throng, a man was standing as if frozen in time. He was all in black, with one of those flat, wide hats often worn by the more somber Omnian sects. He just . . . stood. And watched.

Just another gawker along to see the show, Moist told himself, and knew at once that he was lying. The man was causing a weight in his world.

I have lodged affidavits . . .

Him? About what? Moist had no past. Oh, a dozen aliases had managed a pretty busy and eventful past between them, but they had evaporated along with Albert Spangler, hanged by the neck until not-quite-dead and awoken by Lord Vetinari, who'd offered Moist von Lipwig a life all shiny and new—

Ye gods, he was getting jumpy, just because some old guy was looking at him with a funny little smile! *No one* knew him! He was Mr. Forgettable! If he walked around the town without the gold suit on, he was just another face. "Are you all right, Mr. Lipwig?"

Moist turned and looked into the face of the chief cashier.

"What? Oh . . . no. I mean yes. Er . . . have *you* ever seen that man before?"

"What man would that be?"

Moist turned back to point out the man in black, but he was gone.

"Looked like a preacher," he mumbled. "He was . . . well, he was looking at me."

"Well, sir, you do rather invite it. Perhaps you'd agree that the golden hat was a mistake?"

"I like the hat! There's no other hat like it!"

Bent nodded. "Fortunately, this is true, sir. Oh, dear. Paper money. A practice used only by the heathen Agateans . . ."

"Heathen? They've got far more gods than us! And over there gold is worth less than iron!"

Moist relented. Bent's face, usually so controlled and aloof, had crumpled like a piece of paper. "Look, I've been reading. The banks issue coins to four times the amount of the gold they hold. That's a nonsense we could do without. It's a dream world. This city is rich enough to be its own gold bar!"

"They're trusting you for no good reason," said Bent. "They trust you because you make them laugh. I do not make people laugh, and this is not my world. I don't know how to smile like you do and talk like you do. Don't you understand? There must be something which has a worth that goes beyond fashion and politics, a worth that endures. Are you putting Vetinari in charge of my bank? What guarantees the savings that those people are thrusting over our counter?"

"Not what, who. It's me. I am personally going to see that this bank does not fail."

"You?"

"Yes."

"Oh yes, the man in the gold suit," said Bent sourly. "And if all else fails, will you pray?"

"It worked last time," said Moist calmly.

Bent's eye twitched. For the first time since Moist had met him, he seemed . . . lost.

"I don't know what you want me to *do*!"

It was almost a wail. Moist patted him on the shoulder.

"Run the bank, like you always have. I think we should set up some loans, with all this cash coming in. Are you a good judge of character?"

"I thought I was," said Bent. "Now? I have no idea. Sir Joshua, I am sorry to say, was not. Mrs. Lavish was very, very good, in my opinion . . ."

"Better than you could possibly know," said Moist.

"Good. I shall take the chairman for his walkies, and then . . . we'll spread some money around. How about that?"

Mr. Bent shuddered.

T HE *TIMES* DID an early afternoon edition with a big picture on the front page, of the queue of customers winding out of the bank. Most of them wanted to get in on the act, whatever the act turned out to be, and the rest were queuing on the basis that there might be something interesting at the other end. There was a boy selling the paper, and people were buying it to read the story entitled "Huge Queue Swamps Bank," which seemed a bit odd to Moist. They were *in* the queue, weren't they? Was it only real if they read about it?

"There are already some . . . people wishing to inquire about loans, sir," said Bent, behind him. "I suggest you let me deal with them."

"No, we both will, Mr. Bent," said Moist, turning away from the window. "Show them into the down-stairs office, please."

"I really think you should leave this to me, sir. Some of them are rather new to the idea of bank-ing," Bent persisted. "In fact, I don't think some of them have ever been in a bank before, except per-haps during the hours of darkness."

"I would like you to be present, of course, but I will make the final decision," said Moist, as loftily as he could manage. "Aided by the chairman, naturally."

"*Mr. Fusspot?*"

"Oh yes."

"He is an expert judge, is he?"

"Oh yes!"

Moist picked up the dog and headed for the office. He could feel the chief cashier glaring at his back.

But Bent had been right. Some of the people waiting hopefully to see him about a loan were thinking in terms of a couple of dollars until Friday. They were easy enough to deal with. And then there were others . . .

"Mr. Dibbler, isn't it?" said Moist. He knew it was, but you had to speak like that when you sat behind a desk.

"That's right, sir, man and boy," said Mr. Dibbler, who had a permanently eager, rodent-like cast to his countenance. "I could be someone else if you like."

"And you sell pork pies, sausages, rat-on-a-stick . . ."

"Er, I *pervay* them, sir," Dibbler corrected him, "on account of being a perveyor."

Moist looked at him over the paperwork. Claude Maximillian Overton Transpire Dibbler, a name bigger than the man himself. Everyone knew C.M.O.T. Dibbler. He sold pies and sausages off a tray, usually to people who were the worse for drink, who then became the worse for pies.

Moist had eaten the odd pork pie and occasional sausage in a bun, however, and that very fact interested him. There was something about the stuff that drove you back for more. There had to be some secret ingredient, or maybe the brain just didn't believe what the taste buds told it, and wanted to feel once again that flood of hot, greasy, not entirely organic, slightly crunchy substances surfing across the tongue. So, you bought another one.

And, it had to be said, there were times when a Dibbler sausage in a bun was just what you wanted. Sad, yet true. Everyone had moments like that. Life brought you so low that for a vital few seconds that charivari of strange greases and worrying textures was your only friend in all the world.

"Do you have an account with us, Mr. Dibbler?"

"Yessir, thankyousir," said Dibbler, who had refused an invitation to put down his tray and sat with it held defensively in front of him. The bank seemed to make the streetwise trader nervous. Of course, it was meant to. That was the reason for all the pillars and marble. It was there to make you feel out of place.

"Mr. Dibbler has opened an account with five dollars," said Bent.

"And I have brought along a sausage for your little doggie," said Dibbler.

"Why do you need a loan, Mr. Dibbler?" said Moist, watching Mr. Fusspot sniff the sausage carefully.

"I want to expand the business, sir," said Dibbler.

"You've been trading for more than thirty years," said Moist.

"Yessir, thankyousir."

"And your products are, I think I can say, unique . . ."

"Yessir, thankyousir."

"So I imagine that now you need our help to open a chain of franchised cafés trading on the Dibbler name, offering a variety of meals and drinks bearing your distinctive likeness?" said Moist.

Mr. Fusspot jumped down from the desk with the sausage held gently in his mouth, dropped it in the corner of the office, and tried industriously to kick the carpet over it.

Dibbler stared at Moist, and then said, "Yessir, if you insist, but actually I was thinking about a barrow."

"A barrow?" said Bent.

"Yessir. I know where I can get a nice little secondhand one with an oven and everything. Painted up nice, too. Wally the Gimp is quitting the jacket-potato business 'cos of stress and he'll let me have it for fifteen dollars, cash down. A not-to-be-missed opportunity, sir." He looked nervously at Mr. Bent and added, "I could pay you back at a dollar a week."

"For twenty weeks," said Bent.

"Seventeen," said Moist.

"But the dog just tried to—" Bent began.

Moist waved away the objection. "So we have a deal, Mr. Dibbler?"

"Yessir, thankyousir," said Dibbler. "That's a good idea you've got there, about the chain and everything, though, and I thank you. But I find that in this business it pays to be mobile."

Mr. Bent counted out fifteen dollars with bad grace and began to speak as soon as the door closed behind the trader.

"Even the dog wouldn't—"

"But humans will, Mr. Bent," said Moist. "And therein lies genius. I think he makes most of his money on the mustard, but there's a man who can sell sizzle, Mr. Bent. And that is a seller's market."

The last prospective borrower was heralded first by a couple of muscular men who took up positions on either side of the door, and then by a smell that overruled even the persistent odor of a Dibbler sausage. It wasn't a particularly bad smell; it put you in mind of old potatoes or abandoned tunnels—it was what you got when you started out with severely foul stink and then scrubbed hard but ineffectually, and it surrounded King like an emperor's cloak.

Moist was astonished. King of the Golden River, they called him, because the foundation of his fortune was the daily collection of the urine his men made from every inn and pub in the city. The customers paid him to take it away, and the alchemists, tanners, and dyers paid him to bring it to them.

But that was only the start.

Harry King's men took away *everything*. You saw their carts everywhere, especially around dawn. Every rag-and-bone man and rubbish picker, every dunnikin diver, every gongfermor, every scrap-metal merchant . . . you worked for Harry King, they said, because a broken leg was bad for business, and Harry King was all about business. They said that if a dog in the street looked even a bit strained, a King's man would be there in a flash to hold a shovel under its arse, because prime dog muck fetched 9p a bucket from the high-class tanners. They paid Harry. The city paid Harry. Everyone paid Harry. And what he couldn't sell back to them in more fragrant form went to feed his giant compost heaps downriver, which on frosty days sent up such great plumes of steam that kids called them the cloud factories.

Apart from his hired help, Harry was accompanied by a skinny young man clutching a briefcase.

"Nice place you got here," said Harry, sitting down in the chair opposite Moist. "Very sound. The wife's been on at me to get curtains like that. I'm Harry King, Mr. Lipwig. I've just put fifty thousand dollars in your bank."

"Thank you very much, Mr. King. We shall do our best to look after it."

"You do that. And now I'd like to borrow one hundred thousand, thank you," said Harry, pulling out a fat cigar.

"Have you got any security, Mr. King?" said Bent.

Harry King didn't even look at him. He lit the cigar, puffed it into life, and waved it in the general direction of Bent.

"Who's this, Mr. Lipwig?"

"Mr. Bent is our chief cashier," said Moist, not daring to look at Bent's face.

"A clerk, then," said Harry King dismissively, "an' that was a clerk's question."

He leaned forward. "My name is Harry King. That's your security, right there, an' it should be good for a hundred grand in these parts. *Harry King*. Everyone knows me. I pay what's owing an' I take what's owed, my word, don't I just. My handshake is my fortune. Harry King."

He slammed his huge hands down on the table. Except for the pinkie of his left hand, which was missing, there was a heavy gold ring on each of them, and each ring was incised with a letter. If you saw them coming at you, as for instance in an alley, because you'd been skimming something off the take, the last name you would see would be H°A°R°R°Y°K°I°N°G. It was a fact worth keeping in the forefront of your brain, in the interests of *keeping* the forefront of your brain.

Moist looked up into the man's eyes.

"We shall need a lot more than that," growled Bent, from somewhere above Moist.

Harry King didn't bother to look up. He said, "I only talks to the organ grinder."

"Mr. Bent, could you step outside for a few minutes," said Moist brightly, "and perhaps Mr. King's . . associates will do the same?"

Harry King nodded almost imperceptibly.

"Mr. Lipwig, I really—"

"Please, Mr. Bent."

The chief cashier snorted, but followed the thugs out of the office. The young man with the briefcase made as if to leave as well, but Harry waved him back into his seat.

"You want to watch that Bent," he said to Moist. "There's something funny about him."

"Odd, maybe, but he wouldn't like to be called funny. So, why does Harry King need money, Mr. King? Everyone knows you're rich. Has the bottom dropped out of the dog-muck business? Or vice versa?"

"I'm cons-sol-id-ating," said King, grinning. "This Undertaking business . . . there's going to be a few opportunities for a man in the right place. There's land to buy, palms to grease . . . you know how it is. But them other banks, they won't lend to King of the Golden River, for all it's my lads what keeps their cesspits fragrant as a violet. Them stuck-up ponces'd be up to their ankles in their own piss if it weren't for me, but they holds their noses when I walks by, oh yeah." He stopped, as if a thought had occurred to him, and went on. "Well most people do, o'course, it's not like a man can take a bath every five bloody minutes, but that bunch of bankers still gives me the cold shoulder even when the wife has scrubbed me raw. How dare they! I'm a better risk than most of their smarmy customers, you can bet on that. I employs a thousand people in this city, mister, one way or another. That's a thousand families lookin' to me for their dinner. I might be about muck, but I don't muck about."

He's not a crook, Moist reminded himself. He pulled himself out of the gutter and beat his way to the top in a world where a length of lead pipe was the standard negotiating tool. That world wouldn't trust paper. In that world, reputation was all.

"A hundred thousand is a lot of money," he said aloud.

"You'll give it to me, though," said King, grinning. "I knows you will, 'cos you're a chancer, same as me. I can smell it on you. I smell a lad who's done a thing or two in his time, eh?"

"We all have to eat, Mr. King."

"Course we do. Course we do. An' now we can sit back like a coupla judges an' be pillows of the community, eh? So we'll shake hands on it like the gentlemen we ain't. This here," he went on, laying a huge hand on the shoulder of the young man, "is Wallace, my clerk what does the sums for me. He's new, on account of the last one I had I caught fiddlin' me. That was a laugh, as you can imagine!"

Wallace didn't smile.

"I probably can," said Moist. Harry King guarded his various premises with creatures that could only be called dogs because wolves aren't that insane. And they were kept hungry. There were rumors, and Harry King was probably happy about that. It paid to advertise. You didn't double-cross Harry King. But it worked both ways.

"Wallace can talk numbers with your monkey," said Harry, standing up. "You'll want to squeeze me, right enough. Business is business, and don't I know it. What do you say?"

"Well I'd say we have an agreement, Mr. King," Moist said. Then he spat on his hand, and held it out.

It was worth it to see the look on the man's face.

"I didn't know bankers did that," said Harry.

"They don't often shake hands with Harry King, then," said Moist. That was probably overdoing it, but King winked, spat on his own hand, and grasped Moist's. Moist had been prepared, but even so, the man's grip ground his finger bones together.

"You're more full of bullshit than a frightened herd on fresh pasture, Mr. Lipwig."

"Thank you, sir. I take that as a compliment."

"And just to keep your monkey happy, I'll deposit the deeds of the paper mill, the big yard, and a few other properties," said Harry. "Give 'em to the man, Wallace."

"You should have said that in the first place, Mr. King," said Moist, as some impressive scrolls were handed over.

"Yeah, but I didn't. Wanted to make sure of you. When can I have my money?"

"Soon. When I've printed it."

Harry King wrinkled his nose. "Oh, yeah, the paper stuff. Me, I like money that clinks, but Wallace here says paper's the coming thing." He winked. "And it's not like I can complain, since ol' Spools buys his paper off'f me these days. Can't turn me nose up at me own manufacture now, can I? Good day to you, sir!"

Mr. Bent strode back into the office twenty minutes later, his face like a tax demand, to find Moist staring vaguely at a sheet of paper on the worn green leather of the desk.

"Sir, I must protest—"

"Did you nail him down to a good rate?" said Moist.

"I pride myself that I did, but the way you—"

"We will do well out of Harry King, Mr. Bent, and he will do well out of us."

"But you're turning my bank into some sort of—"

"Not counting our friend Harry, we took in more than four thousand dollars today," said Moist briskly. "Most of them were from what you'd call poor people, but there's far more of them than rich people. We can set that money to work. And we won't lend to scoundrels this time, don't you worry about that. I'm a scoundrel, and I can spot them a mile off. Please pass on our compliments to the counter staff. And now, Mr. Bent, Mr. Fusspot and I are going to see a man about making money."

TEEMER AND SPOOLS had gone up in the world because of the big stamp contract. They'd always done the best printing work in any case, but now they had the men and muscle to bid for all the big contracts. And you could trust them. Moist always felt rather guilty when he went into the place; Teemer and Spools seemed to represent everything that he only pretended to be.

There were plenty of lights on when he went in. And Mr. Spools was in his office, writing in a ledger. He looked up and, when he saw Moist, smiled the smile you save for your very best customer.

"Mr. Lipwig! What can I do for you? Do take a seat! We don't see so much of you these days!"

Moist sat and chatted, because Mr. Spools liked to chat.

Things were difficult. Things were always difficult. There were a lot more presses around these days. T&S were staying ahead of the game by staying on top of it. Regrettably, said Mr. Spools, with a straight face, their "friendly" rivals, the wizards at Unseen University Press, had come a cropper with their talking books—

"Talking books? That sounds a good idea," said Moist.

"Quite possibly," said Spools, with a sniff. "But these weren't meant to talk, and certainly not to complain about the quality of their glue and the hamfistedness of the typesetter. And of course now the university can't pulp them."

"Why not?"

"Think of the screaming! No, I pride myself that we are still riding the wave. Er . . . was there something special you wanted?"

"What can you do with this?" said Moist, putting one of the new dollars on the table.

Spools picked it up and read it carefully. Then, in a faraway voice, he said: "I did hear something. Does Vetinari know you're planning this?"

"Mr. Spools, I'll bet he knows my shoe size and what I had for breakfast."

The printer put down the bill as if it were ticking.

"I can see what you are doing. Such a small thing, and yet so dangerous."

"Can you print them?" said Moist. "Oh, not that one. I made up a batch just to test the idea. I meant high-quality bank notes, if I can find an artist to draw them."

"Oh, yes. We are a byword for quality. We're building a new press to keep pace with demand. But what about security?"

"What, in here? No one has ever bothered you so far, have they?"

"No, they haven't. But up until now we haven't

had lots of money lying around, if you see what I mean."

Spools held the note up and let it go. It wafted gently from side to side until it landed on the desk.

"So light, too," he went on. "A few thousand dollars would be no problem to carry."

"But kind of hard to melt down. Look, build the new press in the Mint. There's a lot of space. End of problem."

"Well, yes, that would make sense. But a press is a big thing to move, you know. It'll take days to shift it. Are you in a hurry? Of course you are."

"Hire some golems. Four golems will lift anything. Print me dollars by the day after tomorrow and the first thousand you print are a bonus."

"Why are you always in such a *hurry*, Mr. Lipwig?"

"Because people don't like change. But make the change happen fast enough and you go from one type of normal to another."

"Well, we could hire some golems, I suppose," said the printer. "But I fear there are other difficulties less easy to overcome. Do you realize that if you start printing money then you *will* get forgeries? It's not worth the trouble, maybe, for a 20p stamp, but if you want, say, a ten-dollar note . . . ?" He raised his eyebrows.

"Probably, yes. Problems?"

"Big ones, my friend. Oh, we can help. Decent linen paper with a pattern of raised threads, watermarks, a good spirit ink, change the plates often to keep it sharp, little tricks with the design . . . and make it complex, too. That's important. Yes, we could do it for you. They will be expensive. I strongly suggest you find an engraver as good as this . . ."

Mr. Spools unlocked one of the lower drawers of his desk and tossed a sheet of 50p green "Tower of Art" stamps onto the blotter. Then he handed Moist a large magnifying glass.

"That's top-quality paper, of course," the printer said as Moist stared.

"You're getting very good. I can see every detail," Moist breathed, poring over the sheet.

"No," said Spools, with some satisfaction. "In fact, you cannot. You *might*, though, with this." He unlocked a cupboard and handed Moist a heavy brass microscope.

"He's put in more detail than we did," he said, as Moist focused. "It's at the very limit of what metal and paper can be persuaded to do. It is, I declare, a work of genius. He would be your salvation."

"Amazing," said Moist. "Well, we've got to have him! Who does he work for now?"

"No one, Mr. Lipwig. He is in prison, awaiting the noose."

"Owlswick Jenkins?"

"You testified against him, Mr. Lipwig," said Spools mildly.

"Well . . . yes, but only to confirm that they were our stamps he was copying, and how much we might be losing! I didn't expect he'd be hanged!"

"His lordship is always touchy when it's a case of

treason against the city, as he describes it. I think Jenkins was badly served by his lawyer. After all, his work made our stamps look like the real forgeries. You know, I got the impression the poor chap didn't really realize what he was doing was wrong."

Moist recalled the watery, frightened eyes and the expression of helpless puzzlement.

"Yes," he said. "You may be right."

"Could you perhaps use your influence with Vetinari to—"

"No. It wouldn't work."

"Ah? Are you sure?"

"Yes," said Moist flatly.

"Well, you see, there's only so much we can do. We can even number the bills automatically now. But the artwork must be of the finest kind. Oh dear. I'm sorry. I wish I could help. We owe you a great debt, Mr. Lipwig. So much official work is coming in now that we'd *need* the space in the Mint. My word, we're practically the government's printer!"

"Really?" said Moist. "That's very . . . interesting."

IT RAINED UNGRACEFULLY. The gutters gargled and tried to spit. Occasionally the wind caught the cascading overflow from the rooftops and slapped a sheet of water across the face of anyone who looked up. But this was not a night to look up. This was a night to scurry, bent double, for home.

Raindrops hit the windows of Mrs. Cake's boardinghouse, specifically the one in the rear room occupied by Mavolio Bent, at the rate of twenty-seven a second, plus or minus fifteen percent.

Mr. Bent liked counting. You could trust numbers, except perhaps for pi, but he was working on that in his spare time and it was bound to give in sooner or later.

He sat on his bed, watching the numbers dance in his head. They'd always danced for him, even in the bad times. And the bad times had been so very bad. Now, perhaps, there were more ahead.

Someone knocked at his door. He said, "Come in, Mrs. Cake."

The landlady pushed open the door.

"You always know it's me, don't you, Mr. Bent," said Mrs. Cake, who was more than a trifle nervous about her best lodger. He paid his rent on time—exactly on time—and he kept his room scrupulously clean and, of course, he was a professional gentleman. All right, he had a haunted look about him and there was that odd business with him carefully adjusting the clock before he went to work every day, but she was prepared to put up with that. There was no shortage of lodgers in this crowded city, but clean ones who paid regularly and never complained about the food were thin enough on the ground to be worth cherishing, and if they put a strange padlock on their wardrobe, well, least said soonest mended.

"Yes, Mrs. Cake," said Bent. "I always know it's you because there is a distinctive one-point-four seconds between the knocks."

"Really? Fancy!" said Mrs. Cake, who rather

liked the sound of *distinctive*. "I always say you're the man for the adding up. Er . . . there is going to be three gentlemen downstairs asking after you . . ."

"When?"

"In about two minutes," said Mrs. Cake.

Bent stood up in one unfoling moment, like a jack-in-the-box.

"Men? What will they be wearing?"

"Well, er, just, you know, clothes?" said Mrs. Cake uncertainly. "Black clothes. One of them will give me his card, but I won't be able to read it because I'll have my wrong spectacles on. Of course, I could go and put the right ones on, obviously, but I get such a headache if I don't let a premonition go right. Er . . . and now you're going to say, 'Please let me know when they arrive, Mrs. Cake.'" She looked at him expectantly. "Sorry, but I had a premonition that I'd come up to tell you I had a premonition, so I thought I'd better. It's a bit silly, but none of us can change how we're made, I always say."

"Please let me know when they arrive, Mrs. Cake," said Bent. Mrs. Cake gave him a grateful look before hurrying away.

Mr. Bent sat down again. Life with Mrs. Cake's premonitions could get a little intricate at times, especially now they were getting recursive, but it was part of the Elm Street ethos that you were charitable toward the foibles of others in the hope of a similar attitude to your own. He liked Mrs. Cake, but she was wrong. You *could* change how you were made. If you couldn't, there was no hope.

After a couple of minutes he heard the ring of the

bell, the muted conversation, and went through the motions of surprise when she knocked on his door.

Bent inspected the visiting card.

"Mr. Cosmo? Oh. How strange. You had better send them up." He paused, and looked around. Subdivision was rife in the city now. The room was exactly twice the size of the bed, and it was a narrow bed. Three people in here would have to know one another well. Four would know one another well whether they wanted to or not. There was a small chair, but Bent kept it on top of the wardrobe, out of the way.

"Perhaps just Mr. Cosmo," he suggested.

The man was proudly escorted in a minute later.

"Well, this is a wonderful little hideaway, Mr. Bent," Cosmo began. "So handy for, um—"

"Nearby places," said Bent, lifting the chair off the wardrobe. "There you are, sir. I don't often have visitors."

"I'll come straight to the point, Mr. Bent," said Cosmo, sitting down. "The directors do not like the, ha, direction things are going. I'm sure you don't, either."

"I could wish for them to be otherwise, sir, yes."

"He should have held a director's meeting!"

"Yes, sir, but bank rules say he needn't do so for a week, I'm afraid."

"He will ruin the bank!"

"We are, in fact, getting many new customers, sir."

"You can't possibly like the man? Not *you*, Mr. Bent?"

"He is easy to like, sir. But you know me, sir. I do

not trust those who laugh too easily. The heart of a fool is in the house of mirth. He should not be in charge of your bank."

"I like to think about it as our bank, Mr. Bent," said Cosmo generously, "because, in a very real way, it *is* ours."

"You are too kind, sir," said Bent, staring down at the floorboards visible through the hole in the cheap oilcloth which was itself laid bare, in a very real way, by the bald patch in the carpet which, in a very real way, was his.

"You joined us quite young, I believe," Cosmo went on. "My father himself gave you a job as trainee clerk, didn't he?"

"That is correct, sir."

"He was very . . . understanding, my father," said Cosmo. "And rightly so. No sense in dredging up the past." He paused for a little while to let this sink in. Bent was intelligent, after all. No need to use a hammer when a feather would float down with as much effect.

"Perhaps you could find some way that will allow him to be removed from office without fuss or bloodshed? There must be something," he prompted. "No one just steps out of nowhere. But people know even less about his past than they do about, for the sake of argument, yours."

Another little reminder. Bent's eye twitched.

"But Mr. Fusspot will still be chairman," he mumbled, while the rain rattled on the glass.

"Oh yes. But I'm sure he will then be looked after by someone who is, shall we say, better capable of translating his little barks along more traditional lines?"

"I see."

"And now I must be going," said Cosmo, standing up. "I'm sure you have a lot of things to"—he looked around the barren room which showed no sign of real human occupation, no pictures, no books, no debris of living, and concluded—"do?"

"I will go to sleep shortly," said Mr. Bent.

"Tell me, Mr. Bent, how much do we pay you?" said Cosmo, glancing at the wardrobe.

"Forty-one dollars per month, sir," said Bent.

"Ah, but of course you get wonderful job security."

"So I had hitherto believed, sir."

"I just wonder why you choose to live here?"

"I like the dullness, sir. It expects nothing of me."

"Well, time to go," said Cosmo, slightly faster than he really should. "I'm sure you can be of help, Mr. Bent. You have always been a great help. It would be such a shame if you could not be of help at this time."

Bent stared at the floor. He was trembling.

"I speak for all of us when I say that we think of you as one of the family," Cosmo went on. He rethought this sentence with reference to the peculiar charms of the Lavishes and added: "But in a good way."

CHAPTER 6

Jailbreak ❁ *The prospect of a kidney sandwich*
❁ *The barber-surgeon's knock* ❁ *Suicide by paint,
inadvisability of* ❁ *Angels at one remove*
❁ *Igor goes shopping* ❁ *The use of understudies at a
hanging, reflections on* ❁ *Places suitable for putting a head*
❁ *Moist awaits the sunshine* ❁ *Tricks with your brain*
❁ *"We're going to need some bigger notes"*
❁ *Fun with root vegetables* ❁ *The lure of clipboards*
❁ *The impossible cabinet*

On the roof of the Tanty, the city's oldest jail, Moist was more than moist. He'd reached the point where he was so wet that he should be approaching dryness from the other end.

With care, he lifted the last of the oil lamps from the little semaphore tower on the flat roof, and tossed its contents into the howling night. They had been only

half-full, in any case. It was amazing that anyone had even bothered to light them on a night like this.

He felt his way back to the edge of the roof and located his grapnel, moving it gently around the stern crenellation and then letting out more rope to lower it down to the invisible ground. Now he had the rope around the big stone bulk he slid down holding on to both lengths and pulled the rope down after him. He stashed both grapnel and rope among the debris in an alley; it would be stolen within an hour or so.

Right, then. Now for it . . .

The Watch armor he'd lifted from the bank's locker room fitted like a glove. He'd have preferred it to fit like a helmet and breastplate. But, in truth, it probably didn't look any better on its owner, currently swanking along the corridors in the bank's own shiny but impractical armor. It was common knowledge that the Watch's approach to uniforms was one-size-doesn't-exactly-fit-anybody, and that Commander Vimes disapproved of armor that didn't have that kicked-by-trolls look. He liked armor to state clearly that it had been doing its job.

He took some time to get his breath back, and then walked around to the big black door and rang the bell. The mechanism rattled and clanked.

They wouldn't rush, not on a night like this.

He was as naked and exposed as a baby lobster. He hoped he'd covered all the angles, but angles were, what did they call it, he'd gone to a lecture at the university . . . ah, yes. Angles were fractal. Each one was full of smaller angles. You couldn't cover them all. The watchman at the bank might be called back to work and find his locker empty, someone might have seen Moist take it, Jenkins might have been moved . . . The hell with it. When time was pressing you just had to spin the wheel and be ready to run.

Or, in this case, lift the huge door knocker in both hands and bring it down sharply, twice, on the nail.

He waited until, with difficulty, a small hatch in the big door was pulled aside.

"What?" said a petulant voice in a shadowy face.

"Prisoner pickup. Name of Jenkins."

"What? It's the middle of the bleedin' night!"

"Got a signed Form 37," said Moist stolidly.

The little hatch slammed shut.

He waited in the rain again. This time it was three minutes before it opened.

"What?" said a new voice, marinated in suspicion.

Ah, good. It was Bellyster. Moist was glad of that. What he was going to do tonight was going to make one of the wardens a very uncomfortable screw, and some of them were decent enough, especially on death row. But Bellyster was a real old-school screw, a craftsman of small evils, the kind of bully that would take every opportunity to make a prisoner's life misery. It wasn't just that he'd gob in your bowl of greasy skilly, but he wouldn't even have the common decency to do it where you couldn't see him. He picked on the weak and frightened, too. And there was one good thing. He hated the Watch, and the feeling was mutual. A man could use that.

"Come for a pris'ner," Moist complained. "An' I been standing in the rain for five minutes!"

"And you shall continue to do so, my son, oh, yes indeed, until I'm ready. Show me the docket!"

"Says here Jenkins, Owlswick," said Moist.

"Let me see it, then!"

"They said I has to hand it over when you give me the pris'ner," said Moist, a model of stolid insistence.

"Oh, we have a lawyer here, do we? All right, Abe, let my learned friend in."

The little hatch slid back and, after some more clanking, a wicket door opened. Moist stepped through.

"Have I seen you before?" said Bellyster, his head on one side.

"Only started last week," said Moist. Behind him, the gate was locked again. The slamming of the bolts echoed in his head.

"Why's there only one of you?" Bellyster demanded.

"Don't know, sir. You'd have to ask my mum and dad."

"Don't you be funny with me! There should be two on escort duty!"

Moist gave a wet and weary shrug of pure disinterest.

"Should there? Don't ask me. They just told me he's a little piece of piss who'll be no trouble. You can check if you like. I heard the palace wants to see him right away."

The palace. That changed the gleam in the warden's nasty little eyes. A sensible man didn't get in the way of the palace. And sending out some dim newbie to do a thankless task on a wild night like this made sense; it was exactly what Bellyster would have done.

He held out his hand and demanded: "Docket!"

Moist handed over the flimsy paper. The man read it, lips perceptibly moving, clearly willing it to be wrong in some way. There'd be no problem there, however much the man glared; Moist had pocketed a handful of the forms while Mr. Spools was making him a cup of coffee.

"He's goin' to hang in the morning," Bellyster said, holding the sheet up to the lantern. "What d'they want him for now?"

"Dunno," said Moist. "Get a move on, will you? I'm on my break in ten minutes."

The warden leaned forward. "Just for that, friend, I *will* go and check. Just one escort? Can't be too careful, can I? Enjoy the rain."

Oh . . . kay, thought Moist. All going according to plan. He'll be ten minutes having a nice cup of tea, just to teach me a lesson, five minutes to find out the clacks isn't working, about one second to decide that he'd be blowed if he was going to sort out the fault on a night like this, another second to think: the paperwork was okay, he'd checked for the watermark, and that was the main thing . . . call it twenty minutes, give or take.

Of course, he could be wrong. Anything could happen. Bellyster could be rounding up a couple of his mates right now, or maybe he'd get someone to run out the back way and find a real copper. The future was uncertain. Exposure could be a few seconds away.

It didn't get any better than this.

Bellyster left it for twenty-two minutes. Footsteps approached, slowly, and Jenkins appeared, tottering under the weight of the irons, with Bellyster prodding him occasionally with his stick. There was no way the little man could have gone any faster, but he was going to get prodded anyway.

"I don't think I'm going to need the shackles," said Moist quickly.

"You ain't getting 'em," said the warden. "The reason bein', you buggers never bring 'em back!"

"Okay," said Moist. "C'mon, it's freezing out here."

Bellyster grunted. He was not a happy man. He bent down, unlocked the shackles, and stood up with his hand once again on the man's shoulder. His other hand thrust out, holding a clipboard.

"Sign!" he commanded. Moist did.

And then came the magic bit. It was why the paperwork was so important in the greasy world of turnkeys, thief-takers, and bang-beggars, because what really mattered at any one moment was habeas corpus: whose hand is on the collar? Who is responsible for this corpus?

Moist had been through this before as the body in question, and knew the drill. The prisoner moved on a trail of paper. If he was found without a head, then the last person to have signed for a prisoner whose hat was *not* resting on his neck might well have to answer some stern questions.

Bellyster pushed the prisoner forward and spake the time-honored words.

"To you, sir!" he barked. "Habby arse corparse!"

Moist thrust the clipboard back at him and laid his other hand on Owlswick's other shoulder.

"*From* you, sir!" he replied. "I habby his arse all right!"

Bellyster grunted, and removed his hand. The deed was done, the law was observed, honor was satisfied, and Owlswick Jenkins—

—looked up sadly at Moist, kicked him hard in the groin, and went off down the street like a hare.

As Moist bent double, all he was aware of outside his little world of pain was the sound of Bellyster laughing himself silly and shouting, "Your bird, milord! You habbyed him all right! Ho yus!"

Moist HAD MANAGED to walk normally by the time he got back to the little room he rented from "I Don't Know" Jack. He struggled into the golden suit, dried off the armor, bundled it into the bag, stepped out into the alley, and hurried back to the bank.

It was harder to get it back in than it had been to get it out. The guards changed over at the same time as the staff left, and in the general milling about, Moist, wearing the tatty gray suit he wore when he wanted to stop being Moist von Lipwig and turn into the world's most unmemorable man, had strolled out unquestioned. It was all in the mind: the night guards started guarding when everyone had gone home, right? So people *going* home were no problem, or, if they were, they were not mine.

The guard who finally turned up to see who was struggling to unlock the front door gave him a bit of trouble until a second guard, who was capable of modest intelligence, pointed out that if the chairman wanted to get into the bank at midnight then that was fine. He was the damn boss, wasn't he? Don't you read the papers? See gold suit? And he had a key! So what if he had a big fat bag? He was coming *in* with it, right? If he was *leaving* with it, might be a different matter, ho ho, just my little joke, sir, sorry about that sir . . .

It was amazing what you could do if you had the nerve to try, thought Moist, as he bid the men goodnight. F'rinstance, he'd been so theatrically working the key in the lock because it was a Post Office key. He didn't have one for the bank yet.

Even putting the armor back in the locker was not a problem. The guards still walked set routes and the buildings were big and not very well lit. The locker room was empty and unregarded for hours at a time.

A lamp was still alight in his new suite. Mr. Fusspot was snoring on his back in the middle of the in tray. A night-light was burning by the bedroom door. In fact there were two, and they were the red, smoldering eyes of Gladys. "Would You Like Me To Make You A Sandwich, Mr. Lipwig?"

"No thank you, Gladys."

"It Would Be No Trouble. There Are Kidneys In The Ice Room."

"Thank you, but no, Gladys. I'm really not hungry," said Moist, carefully shutting the door.

Moist lay on the bed. Up here, the building was absolutely silent. He'd grown used to his bed in the Post Office, where there was always noise drifting up from the yard.

But it was not the silence that kept him awake. He stared up at the ceiling and thought: Stupid, stupid, stupid! In a few hours there would be a shift change at the Tanty. People wouldn't get too worried about the missing Owlswick until the hangman turned up, looking busy, and then there would be a nervous time when they decided who was going to go to the palace to see if there was any chance of being allowed to hang their prisoner this morning.

The man would be miles away by now, and not even a vampire or a werewolf could smell him on a wet and windy night like this. They couldn't pin anything on Moist, but in the cold, wet light of two a.m., he could imagine bloody Commander Vimes worrying at this, picking away at it in that thick-headed way of his.

He blinked. *Where* would the little man run to? He wasn't part of a gang, according to the Watch. He'd just made his own stamps. What kind of a man goes to the trouble of forging a ha'penny stamp?

What kind of a man . . .

Moist sat up.

Could it be that easy?

Well, it might be. Owlswick was crazy enough in a mild, bewildered sort of way. He had the look of one who'd long ago given up trying to understand the world beyond his easel, a man for whom cause and effect had no obvious linkage. Where would a man like that hide?

Moist lit the lamp and walked over to the battered wreckage of his wardrobe. Once again he selected the tatty gray suit. It had sentimental value; he had been hanged in it. And it was an unmemorable suit for an unmemorable man, with the additional advantage, unlike black, of not showing up in the dark.* Thinking ahead, he went into the kitchen, too, and stole a couple of dust rags from a cupboard.

The corridor was reasonably well lit by the lamps every few yards. But lamps create shadows, and in one of them, beside a huge Ping Dynasty vase from Hunghung, Moist was just a patch of gray on gray.

A guard walked past, treacherously silent on the thick carpet. When he'd gone, Moist hurried down the flight of marble steps and tucked himself behind a potted palm that someone had thought necessary to put there.

The floors of the bank all opened onto the main hall which, like the one in the Post Office, went from ground floor to roof. Sometimes, depending on the layout, a guard on a floor above could see the floor below. Sometimes, the guards walked over uncarpeted marble. Sometimes, on the upper floors, they crossed patches of fine tiling, which rang like a bell.

---

*Every Assassin knew that real black often stood out in the dark, because the night in the city is usually never full black, and that gray or dark green merge much better. But they wore black anyway, because style trumps utility every time.

Moist stood and listened, trying to pick up the rhythm of the patrols. There were more than he'd expected. Come on lads, you're working security, what about the traditional all-night poker game! Don't you know how to behave?

It was like a wonderful puzzle. It was better than night-climbing, better even than Extreme Sneezing! And the really good thing about it was this: if he was caught, why, he was just testing the security! Well done, lads, you found me . . .

But he mustn't be caught.

A guard came upstairs, walking slowly and deliberately. He leaned against the balustrade and, to Moist's annoyance, lit the stub of a cigarette. Moist watched from between the fronds while the man leaned comfortably on the marble, looking down at the floor below. He was sure that guards weren't supposed to do this. And smoking, too!

After a few reflective drags, the guard dropped the butt, trod on it, and continued up the stairs.

Two thoughts struggled for dominance in Moist's mind. Screaming slightly louder was: He had a crossbow! Do they shoot first to avoid having to ask questions later? But also there, vibrating with indignation, was a voice saying: He stubbed out that damn cigarette right there on the marble! Those tall brass wossnames with the little bowls of white sand are there for a *reason*, you know!

When the man had disappeared above him, Moist ran down the rest of the flight, slid across the polished marble on his dust-rag-covered boots, found the door that led down to the basement, opened it quickly, and remembered just in time to close it quietly behind him.

He shut his eyes and waited for cries or sounds of pursuit.

He opened his eyes.

There was the usual brilliant light at the far end of the undercroft, but there was no rushing of water. Only the occasional drip demonstrated the depth of the otherwise all-pervading silence.

Moist walked carefully past the Glooper, which tinkled faintly, and into the unexplored shadows beneath the wonderful fornication.

If we build it, wilt thou comest? he thought. But the hoped-for god never came. It was sad but, in some celestial way, a bit stupid. Well, wasn't it? Moist had heard that there were maybe millions of little gods floating around in the world, living under rocks, blown about like tumbleweeds, clinging to the topmost branches of trees . . . They awaited the big moment, the lucky break that might end up with a temple and a priesthood and worshipers to call your own. But they hadn't come here, and it was easy to see why.

Gods wanted belief, not rational thinking. Building the temple first was like giving a pair of wonderful shoes to a man with no legs. Building a temple didn't mean you believed in gods, it just meant you believed in architecture.

Something akin to a workshop had been built on the end wall of the undercroft, around a huge and ancient fireplace. An Igor was working over an intense, blue-white flame, carefully bending a piece of glass pipe. Behind him, green liquid surged and fizzed in giant bottles: Igors seemed to have a natural affinity with lightning.

You could always recognize an Igor. They went out of their way to be recognized. It wasn't just the musty dusty old suits, or even the occasional extra digit or mismatched eyes. It was that you could probably stand a ball on the top of their head without it falling off.

The Igor looked up.

"Good morning, thur. And you are . . . ?"

"Moist von Lipwig," said Moist. "And you would be Igor."

"Got it in one, thur. I have heard many good thingth about you."

"Down here?"

"I alwayth keep an ear to the ground, thur."

Moist resisted the impulse to look down. Igors and metaphors didn't go well together.

"Well, Igor . . . the thing is . . . I want to bring someone into the building without troubling the guards, and I wonder if there was another door down here?"

What he did not say, but what passed between them on the ether, was: You're an Igor, right? And when the mob are sharpening their sickles and trying to break down the door, *the Igor is never there*. Igors were masters of the unobtrusive exit.

"There ith a thmall door we ueth, thur. It can't be opened from the outthide tho itth never guarded."

Moist looked longingly at the rainwear on its stand.

"Fine. Fine. I'm just popping out, then."

"You're the bothth, thur."

"And I shall be popping back shortly with a man. Er . . . a gentleman who is not anxious to meet civic authority."

"Quite, thur. Give them a pitchfork and they think they own the bloody plathe, thur."

"But he's not a murderer or anything."

"I'm an Igor, thur. We don't athk quethtionth."

"Really? Why not?"

"I don't know, thur. I didn't athk."

Igor took Moist to a small door that opened into a grimy, trash-filled stairwell, half-flooded by the unremitting rain. Moist paused on the threshold, the water already soaking into the cheap suit.

"Just one thing, Igor . . ."

"Yeth, thur?"

"When I walked past the Glooper just now, there was water in it."

"Oh, yeth, thur. Ith that a problem?"

"It was moving, Igor. Should that be happening at this time of night?"

"That? Oh, jutht thyphonic variableth, thur. It happenth all the time."

"Oh, the old syphonics, eh? Ah, well, that's a relief—"

"Jutht give the barber-thurgeon'th knock when you return, thur."

"What is the—"

The door closed.

Igor went back to his workbench and fired up the gas again.

Some of the little glass tubes lying beside him on a piece of green felt looked . . . odd, and reflected the light in disconcerting ways.

The point about Igors . . . the thing about Igors . . .

Well, most people looked no further than the musty suit, lank hair, cosmetic clan scars, and stitching, and the lisp. And this was probably because, apart from the lisp, this was all there was to see.

And people forgot, therefore, that most of the people who employed Igors were not conventionally sane. Ask them to build a storm attractor and a set of lightning-storage jars and they would laugh at you.* They needed, oh, how they needed, someone in possession of a fully working brain, and every Igor was guaranteed to have at least one of those. Igors were, in fact, smart, which was why they were always elsewhere when the fiery torches hit the windmill.

And they were perfectionists. Ask them to build you a device and you wouldn't get what you asked for.

You'd get what you *wanted*.

In its web of reflections, the Glooper glooped. Water rose in a thin glass tube and dripped into a little glass bucket, which tipped into a tiny seesaw and caused a tiny valve to open.

OWLSWICK JENKINS'S RECENT abode, according to the *Times*, was Short Alley. There wasn't a house number, because Short Alley was only

---

*In fact they would probably laugh at you if you said "sausages." They laugh at lots of things.

big enough for one front door. The door in question was shut, but hanging by one hinge. A scrap of black-and-yellow rope indicated, for those who hadn't spotted the clue of the door, that the place had come to the recent attention of the Watch.

The door fell off the hinge when Moist pushed at it, and landed in the stream of water that was gushing down the alley.

It wasn't much of a search, because Owlswick hadn't bothered to hide. He was in a room on the first floor, surrounded by mirrors and candles, a dreamy look on his face, peacefully painting.

He dropped the brush when he saw Moist, grabbed a tube that lay on a bench, and held it in front of his mouth, ready to swallow.

"Don't make me use this! Don't make me use this!" he warbled, his whole body trembling.

"Is it some kind of toothpaste?" said Moist. He sniffed the very lived-in air of the studio and added: "That could help, you know."

"This is Uba Yellow, the most poisonous paint in the world! Stand back or I will die horribly!" said the forger. "Er . . . in fact, the *most* poisonous paint is probably Agatean White, but I've run out of that, it is most vexing." It occurred to Owlswick that he had lost the tone slightly, and he quickly raised his voice again. "But this is pretty poisonous, all the same!"

A gifted amateur picks up a lot, and Moist had always found poisons interesting.

"An arsenical compound, eh?" said Moist. Everyone knew about Agatean White. He hadn't heard of Uba Yellow, but arsenic came in many inviting shades. Just don't lick your brush.

"It's a horrible way to die," he said. "You more or less melt over several days."

"I'm not going back! I'm not going back!" squeaked Owlswick.

"They used to use it to make skin whiter," said Moist, moving a little closer.

"Get back! I'll use it! I swear I'll use it!"

"That's where we get the phrase 'drop-dead gorgeous,'" said Moist, closing in.

He snatched at Owlswick, who rammed the tube in his mouth. Moist tugged it out, pushing the forger's clammy little hands out of the way, and examined it.

"Just as I thought," he said, pocketing the tube. "You forgot to take the cap off. It's the kind of mistake amateurs always make!"

Owlswick hesitated, and then said: "You mean there's people who commit suicide professionally?"

"Look, Mr. Jenkins, I'm here to—" Moist began.

"I'm not going back to that jail! I'm not going back!" said the little man, backing away.

"That's fine by me. I want to offer you a—"

"They watch me, you know," Owlswick volunteered. "All the time."

Ah. This was slightly better than suicide by paint, but only just.

"Er . . . you mean in jail?" said Moist, just to make sure.

"They watch me everywhere! There's one of Them right behind you!"

Moist stopped himself from turning, because that way madness lay. Mind you, quite a lot of it was standing right here in front of him.

"I'm sorry to hear that, Owlswick," said Moist. "That's why—"

Moist hesitated, and thought: —not? It had worked on him.

"That's why I'm going to tell you about angels," he said.

P‌EOPLE SAID THERE were more thunderstorms now that Igors were living in the city. There was no more thunder now, but the rain fell as if it had got all night.

Some of it swirled over the top of Moist's boots as he stood in front of the bank's unobtrusive side door and tried to remember the barber-surgeon's knock.

Oh, yes. It was the old one that went *rat tat a tat-tat TAT TAT!*

Or, to put it another way: Shave and a haircut—no legs!

The door opened instantly.

"I would like to apologithe about the lack of creak, thur, but the hingeth jutht don't theem to—"

"Just give me a hand with this lot, will you?" said Moist, bent under the weight of two heavy boxes. "This is Mr. Jenkins. Can you make up a bed for him down here? And is there any chance you could change what he looks like?"

"More than you could poththibly imagine, thur," said Igor happily.

"I was thinking of, well, a shave and a haircut. You can do that, can't you?"

Igor gave Moist a pained look.

"It is true that *technically* thurgeonth can perform tonthorial operations—"

"No no, don't touch his throat, please."

"That meanth yeth, I can give him a haircut, thur," Igor sighed.

"I have had my tonsils out when I was ten," said Owlswick.

"Would you like thome more?" said Igor, looking for some bright edge to the situation.

"This is wonderful light!" Owlswick exclaimed, ignoring the offer. "It's like day!"

"Jolly good," said Moist. "Now get some sleep, Owlswick. Remember what I told you. In the morning, *you* are going to design the first proper one-dollar bank note, understand?"

Owlswick nodded, but his mind was already elsewhere.

"You're with me on this, are you?" said Moist loudly. "A note so good that no one else could do it? I showed you my attempt, yes? I know you can do better, of course."

He looked nervously at the little man. He wasn't insane, Moist was sure, but it was clear that mostly, for him, the world happened elsewhere.

Owlswick paused in the act of unpacking his box.

"Um . . . I can't make things up," he said.

"What do you mean?" said Moist.

"I don't know how to make things up," said Owls-wick, staring at a paintbrush as if expecting it to whistle.

"But you're a forger! Your stamps look better than ours!"

"Er . . . yes. But I don't have your . . . I don't know how to get started . . . I mean, I need something to work from . . . I mean, once it's there, I can . . ."

It must be about four o'clock, thought Moist. Four o'clock! I *hate* it when there are two four o'clocks in the same day . . .

He snatched a piece of paper from Owlswick's box, and pulled out a pencil.

"Look," he said, "you start with . . ."

What?

"Richness," he told himself, aloud, "richness and solidarity, like the front of the bank. Lots of ornate scrolling, which is hard to copy. A . . . panorama, a cityscape . . . yes! Ankh-Morpork, it's all about the city! Vetinari's head, because they'll expect that, and a Great Big One, so they get the message. Oh, the coat of arms, we must have that. And down here"—the pencil scribbled fast—"a space for the chairman's signature, pardon me, I mean paw print. On the back . . . well, we are talking fine detail, Owlswick. Some god would give us a bit of gravi-tas. One of the jollier ones. What's the name of that god with the three-pronged fork? One like him, anyway. Fine lines, Owlswick, that's what we want. Oh, and a boat. I like boats. Tell 'em it's worth a dollar again, too. Um . . . oh yes, mystic stuff doesn't hurt, people'll believe in any damn thing if it sounds old and mysterious. Doth not a penny to the widow outshine the unconquered sun?"

"What does that mean?"

"I haven't the foggiest idea," said Moist, "I just made it up." He sketched away for a while and then pushed the paper across to the awestruck Owlswick.

"Something like that," he said. "Have a go. Think you can make something of it?"

"I'll try," Owlswick promised.

"Good. I'll see you tomo—later on. Igor here will look after you."

Owlswick was already staring at nothing. Moist pulled Igor aside.

"Just a shave and a haircut, okay?"

"As you with, thur. Am I right in thinking that the gentleman doeth not want any entanglementth with the Watch?"

"Correct."

"No problem there, thur. Could I thuggetht a change of name?"

"Good idea. Any suggestions?"

"I like the name Clamp, thur. And for a firtht name, Exorbit thpringth to mind," Igor sprayed.

"Really. Where did it spring from? No, don't answer that. Exorbit Clamp . . ." Moist hesitated, but at this time of the night, why argue? Especially when it was this time of the morning. "Exorbit Clamp it is, then. Make certain he forgets even the name of Jenkins," Moist added, with what, he later realized, was in the circumstances a definite lack of foresight.

Moist slipped back up to bed without ever having to duck out of sight. No guard is at his best in the small hours. The place was locked up tight, wasn't it? Who would break in?

Down in the well-fornicated vault, the artist formerly known as Owlswick stared at Moist's sketches and felt his brain begin to fizz. It was true that he was not, in any proper sense, a madman. He *was*, by certain standards, very sane. Faced with a world too busy, complex, and incomprehensible to deal with, he'd reduced it to a small bubble just big enough to hold him and his palette. It was nice and quiet in there. All the noises were far away, and They couldn't spy on him.

"Mr. Igor?" he said.

Igor looked up from a crate in which he had been rummaging. He held what looked like a metal colander in his hands.

"How may I be of thurvith, thur?"

"Can you get me some old books with pictures of gods and boats and maybe some views of the city too?"

"Indeed, thur. There ith an antiquarian booktheller in Lobbin Clout." Igor put the metal device aside, pulled a battered leather bag from under the table, and, after a moment's thought, put a hammer in it.

Even in the world of the newly fledged Mr. Clamp, it was still so late at night that it was too early in the morning.

"Er . . . I'm sure it can wait until daylight," he volunteered.

"Oh, I alwayth thhop at night, thur," said Igor, "when I'm after . . . bargainth."

Moist woke fully dressed and far too early, with Mr. Fusspot standing on his chest and squeaking his rubber bone very loudly. As a result, Moist was being dribbled on in no small way.

Behind Mr. Fusspot was Gladys. Behind her were two men in black suits.

"His lordship has agreed to see you, Mr. Lipwig," said one of them quite cheerfully.

Moist tried to wipe the slobber off his lapel, and only succeeded in shining the suit.

"Do I *want to see him*?"

One of the men smiled.

"*Ooooh yes!*"

"A hanging always makes me hungry," said Lord Vetinari, working carefully on a hard-boiled egg. "Don't you find this so?"

"Um . . . I've only been hanged once," said Moist. "I didn't feel like eating much."

"I think it is the chilly early-morning air," said Vetinari, apparently not hearing this. "It puts an edge on the appetite."

He looked directly at Moist for the first time, and appeared concerned.

"Oh dear, you're not eating, Mr. Lipwig? You

must *eat*. You look a little peaky. I trust your job is not getting on top of you?"

Somewhere en route to the palace, Moist thought, he must have stepped into another world. It had to be something like that. It was the only explanation.

"Er . . . who was hanged?" he said.

"Owlswick Jenkins, the forger," said Vetinari, devoting himself again to the surgical removal of the white from the yolk. "Drumknott, perhaps Mr. Lipwig would like some fruit? Or some of that bowel-lacerating grain-and-nut concoction you favor so much?"

"Indeed, sir," said the secretary.

Vetinari leaned forward as if inviting Moist to join a conspiracy and added, "I believe the cook does kippers for the guards. Very fortifying. You really do look quite pale. Don't you think he looks pale, Drumknott?"

"Verging on the wan, sir."

It was like having acid dropped slowly into your ear. Moist thought frantically, but the best he could come up with was: "Was it a well-attended hanging?"

"Not very. I don't think it was properly advertised," said Vetinari, "and, of course, his crime was not associated with buckets of gore. That always makes the crowd cheer as you know. But Owlswick Jenkins was there, oh yes. He never cut a throat but he bled the city, drop by drop."

Vetinari had removed and eaten the whole of the white of the egg, leaving the yolk glowing and unsullied.

What would I have done if I was Vetinari and

found my prison was about to become a laughing-stock? There's nothing like laughter for undermining authority, Moist thought. More important, what would *he* have done if he was him, which of course he is . . .

You'd hang someone else, that's what you'd do. You'd find some wretch of the right general shape who was waiting in the slammer for the hemp fandango and cut him a deal. Oh, he'd hang right enough, but under the name of Owlswick Jenkins. News would get out that the stand-in had been pardoned but died accidentally or something, and his dear ol' mum or his wife and kids would get an anonymous bag of wonga and escape a little bit of shame.

And then the crowd would get their hanging. Now, with any luck, Bellyster had a job washing spittoons, justice or something vaguely similar would be seen to be done, and the message would be sent out that crimes against the city should be contemplated exclusively by those with cast-iron necks, and even then, only maybe.

Moist realized he was touching his own neck. Sometimes he woke up in the night, even now, just a moment after the void opened under his feet—

Vetinari was looking at him. It wasn't exactly a smile on his face, but Moist got the nape-twitching feeling that, when he tried to think like Vetinari, his lordship slid in on those thoughts like some big black spider on a bunch of bananas and scuttled around where he shouldn't.

And the certainty hit him. Owlswick wouldn't

have died *anyway*. Not with a talent like that. He would have dropped through the trapdoor to a new life, just as Moist had. He'd have woken up to be given the angel offer, which for Owlswick would have been a nice light room somewhere, three meals a day, his potty emptied on demand, and all the ink he wanted. From an Owlswick point of view, he'd be getting heaven. And Vetinari . . . would get the world's best forger, working *for* the city.

Oh, damn. I'm right in his way. I'm in Vetinari's *way*.

The orange-gold ball of the rejected yolk glowed on Vetinari's plate.

"Your wonderful plans for paper money are progressing?" said his lordship. "I'm hearing such a lot about them."

"What? Oh . . . yes. Er . . . I'd like to put your head on a dollar bill, please."

"But of course. A good place to put a head, considering all the places a head might be put."

Like a spike, yeah. He needs me, Moist thought, as the totally-not-a-threat sank in. But how much?

"Look, I—"

"Possibly your fertile mind can assist me with a little puzzle, Mr. Lipwig." Vetinari dabbed at his lips and pushed back his chair. "Do follow me. Drumknott, please bring the ring. And the tongs, of course, just in case."

He led the way out onto the balcony, trailed by Moist, and leaned on the balustrade with his back to the foggy city.

"Still a lot of cloud about, but I think the sun

should break through at any time, don't you think?" he said.

Moist glanced up at the sky. There was a patch of pale gold among the billows, like the yolk of an egg. What was the man doing?

"Pretty soon, yes," he ventured.

The secretary handed Vetinari a small box.

"That's the box for your signet ring," said Moist.

"Well done, Mr. Lipwig, observant as ever! Do take it."

Guardedly, Moist picked up the ring. It was black and had an odd, organic feel to it. The V seemed to stare at him.

"Do you notice anything unusual about it?" said Vetinari, watching him carefully.

"Feels warm," said Moist.

"Yes it does, doesn't it," said Vetinari. "That is because it is made of stygium. It's called a metal, but I strongly believe that it is an alloy, and a magically constructed one at that. The dwarfs sometimes find it in the Loko Region, and it is extremely expensive. One day I shall write a monograph on its fascinating history, but for now, all I will say is that it is usually only of interest to those who, by inclination or lifestyle, move in darkness—and also, of course, to those who find a life without danger hardly worth living. It can kill, you see. In direct sunshine it heats within a few seconds to a temperature that will melt iron. No one knows why."

Moist glanced up at the hazy sky. The boiled-egg glow of the sun drifted into another bank of fog. The ring cooled.

"Occasionally there is a fad among young assassins for stygium rings. Classically, they wear an ornate black glove over the ring during the day. It's all about risk, Mr. Lipwig. It's about living with Death in your pocket. I swear, there are people who will pull a tiger's tail for mischief. Of course, people who are interested in coolth rather than danger just wear the glove. Be that as it may, less than two weeks ago the only man in the city who carries a stock of stygium and knows how to work it was murdered, late at night. The murderer dropped a peppermint bomb afterward. Who do you think did it?"

I'm not going to look up, thought Moist. *This is just a game. He wants me to sweat.*

"What was taken?" he said.

"The Watch does not know, because, you see, what was taken was, de facto, not there."

"All right, what was left behind?" said Moist, and thought: *He's not looking at the sky, either . . .*

"Some gems and a few ounces of stygium in the safe," said Vetinari. "You didn't ask how the man was killed."

"How was—"

"Crossbow shot to the head, while he was seated. Is this exciting, Mr. Lipwig?"

"Hit man, then," said Moist desperately. "It was planned, because he'd brought the bomb. Maybe the dead man didn't pay a debt. Perhaps he was a fence and tried to pull a scam. There's not enough information!"

"There never is," said Vetinari. "My cap comes

back from the cleaners subtly changed, and a young man who works there dies in a brawl. A former gardener here comes in at the dead of night to buy a rather worn pair of Drumknott's old boots. Why? Perhaps we shall never know. Why was a picture of myself stolen from the Royal Art Gallery last month? Who benefits?"

"Uh, why was this stygium left in the safe?"

"Good question. The key was in the man's pocket. So what is our motive?"

"Not enough information! Revenge? Silence? Maybe he's made something he shouldn't? Can you make a dagger out of this stuff?"

"Ah, I think you are getting warm, Mr. Lipwig. Not about a weapon, because accretions of stygium much bigger than a ring tend to explode without warning. But he was a rather greedy man, that is true."

"An argument over something?" said Moist. Yes, I *am* getting warm, thank you! And what are the tongs for? To pick it up after it's dropped through my hand?

The light was growing; he could see faint shadows on the wall, he felt the sweat trickle down his spine—

"An interesting thought. Do give me that ring back," said Vetinari, proffering the box.

Hah! So it was just a show to scare him, after all, Moist thought, flicking the wretched ring into the box. I've never even *heard* of stygium before today! He must have made it up—

He sensed the heat before it, and saw the ring blaze white-hot as it fell into the box. The lid snapped shut, leaving a purple hole in Moist's vision.

"Remarkable, isn't it," said Vetinari. "Incidentally, I think you were needlessly silly to hold it all that time. I'm not a monster, you know."

No, monsters don't play tricks with your brain, thought Moist. *At least, while it's still inside your head . . .*

"Look, about Owlswick, I didn't mean—" he began, but Vetinari held up a hand.

"I don't know what you are talking about, Mr. Lipwig. In fact, I invited you here in your capacity as de facto deputy chairman of the Royal Bank. I want you to loan me—that is to say, the city—half a million dollars at two percent. You are, of course, at liberty to refuse."

So many thoughts scrambled for the emergency exit in Moist's brain that only one remained:

We're going to need some bigger notes . . .

Moist RAN BACK to the bank, and straight to the little door under the stairs. He liked it down in the undercroft. It was cool and peaceful, apart from the gurgling of the Glooper and the screams.

That last bit was wrong, wasn't it?

The pink poisons of involuntary insomnia slopped around in his head as he broke into a run.

The former Owlswick was sitting in a chair, apparently clean-shaven except for a pointy little beard. Some kind of metal helmet had been attached to his head, and from it wires ran down into some glowing, clicking device that only an Igor would want to understand. The air smelled of thunderstorms.

"What are you doing to this poor man?" Moist yelled.

"Changing hith mind, thur," said Igor, pulling a huge knife switch.

The helmet buzzed. Clamp blinked.

"It tickles," he said. "And, for some reason, it tastes of strawberries."

"You're putting lightning right into his head!" said Moist. "That's barbaric!"

"No, thur. Barbarianth don't have the capabilitieth," said Igor smoothly. "All I'm doing, thur, ith taking out all the bad memorieth and thtoring them"—here he pulled a cloth aside to reveal a big jar full of green liquid, containing something rounded and studded with still more wires—"into thith!"

"You're putting his brain into a . . . parsnip?"

"It ith a turnip," said Igor.

"It's amazing what they can do, isn't it," said a voice by Moist's elbow. He looked down.

Mr. Clamp, now helmetless, beamed up at him. He looked shiny and alert, like a better class of shoe salesman. Igor had even managed a suit transplant.

"Are you all right?" said Moist.

"Fine!"

"What did . . . it feel like?"

"Hard to explain," said Clamp. "But it sounded like the smell of raspberries tastes."

"Really? Oh. I suppose that's all right, then. And you really feel okay, in yourself?" said Moist, probing for the dreadful drawback. It had to be there. But Owls— Exorbit looked happy and full of confidence and vim, a man ready to take what life threw at him and knock it out of the court.

Igor was winding up his wiring with what, under all those scars, was a very smug look on what was probably his face.

Moist felt a pang of guilt. He was an Überwald boy, he'd come down the Vilinus Pass like everyone else, trying to seek his fortune—correction, everybody else's fortune—and he had no right to pick up the fashionable lowland prejudice against the clan of Igors. After all, didn't they simply put into practice what so many priests professed to believe: that the body was just a rather heavy cheap suit clothing the invisible, everlasting soul, and *therefore*, swapping around bits and pieces like spare parts was surely no worse than running a shonky shop for used clothing? It was a constant source of hurt amazement to Igors that people couldn't see that this was both sensible and provident, at least up until the time when the axe slipped and you needed someone to lend a hand in a hurry. At a time like that, even an Igor looked good.

Mostly they looked . . . serviceable. Igors, with their obliviousness to pain, wonderful healing powers, and marvelous ability to carry out surgery on themselves with the aid of a hand mirror, could presumably *not* look like a stumpy butler who'd been left in the rain for a month. Igorinas always looked stunning, but there was always something—a beautifully curved scar under one eye, a ring of decorative stitching around a wrist—that was for the Look. That was always disconcerting, but an Igor always had his heart in the right place. Or *a* heart, at least.

"Well, er . . . well done, Igor," Moist managed. "Ready to make a start on the ol' dollar bill, then, Mr., er, Clamp?"

Mr. Clamp's smile was full of sunbeams. "Done it!" he announced. "Did it this morning!"

"Surely not!"

"Indeed I have! Come and see!" The little man walked over to a table and lifted a sheet of paper.

The bank note gleamed, in purple and gold. It gave off money in rays. It seemed to float above the paper like a small magic carpet. It said wealth and mystery and tradition—

"We're going to make so much money!" said Moist. *We'd better*, he added to himself. *We'll need to print at least six hundred thousand of these, unless I can come up with some bigger denominations.*

But there it was, so beautiful you wanted to cry, and make lots more like it, and put them in your wallet.

"How did you do it so quickly?"

"Well, a lot of it is just geometry," said Mr. Clamp. "Mr. Igor here was kind enough to make me a little device which was a great help there. It's not finished, of course, and I haven't even started on the other side yet. I think I'll make a start on that now, in fact, while I'm still fresh."

"You think you can do *better*?" said Moist, awed in the presence of genius.

"I feel so . . . full of energy!" said Clamp.

"That would be the elecktrical fluid, I expect," said Moist.

"No, I mean I can see so clearly what needs to be done! Before, it was all like some horrible weight I had to lift, but now everything is clear and light!"

"Well, I'm glad to hear it," said Moist, not entirely certain that he was. "Do excuse me, I have a bank to run."

He hurried through the arches and entered the main hall via the unassuming door in time to very nearly collide with Bent.

"Ah, Mr. Lipwig, I wondered where you were—"

"Is this going to be important, Mr. Bent?"

The chief cashier looked offended, as if he'd ever trouble Moist about anything that was not important.

"There are lots of men outside the Mint," he said. "With trolls and carts. They *say* you want them to install a"—Bent shuddered—"a printing engine!"

"That's right," said Moist. "They're from Teemer and Spools. We must print the money here. It'll look more official and we can control what goes out of the doors."

"Mr. Lipwig. You are turning the bank into a . . . a circus!"

"Well, I'm the man with the top hat, Mr. Bent, so I suppose I'm the ringmaster!"

He said it with a laugh, to lighten the mood a little, but Bent's face was a sudden thundercloud.

"Really, Mr. Lipwig? And whoever told you the ring-master runs the circus? You are very much mistaken, sir! Why are you cutting off the other shareholders?"

"Because they don't know what a bank is about. Come with me to the Mint, will you?"

He strode through the main hall, having to dodge and weave between the queues.

"And you know what a bank is about, do you, sir?" said Bent, following behind in his jerky flamingo step.

"I'm learning. Why do we have one queue in front of each clerk?" Moist demanded. "It means that if one customer takes up a lot of time, the whole queue has to wait. Then they'll start hopping sideways from one queue to another and the next thing you know someone has a nasty head wound. Have one big queue and tell people to go to the next clerk free. People don't mind a long queue if they can see that it's moving— Sorry, sir!"

This was to a customer he'd collided with, who steadied himself, grinned at Moist, and spoke in a voice from a past that should have stayed buried. "Why, if it isn't my old friend Albert. You're doin' well for yourself, ain't you?" the stranger went on, spluttering the words through ill-fitting teeth. "You in your shuit o' lightsh!"

Moist's past life flashed before his eyes. He didn't even need to go to the bother of dying, although he felt as though he was going to.

It was Cribbins! It could only be Cribbins!

Moist's memory sandbagged him, one bag after another. The teeth! Those damn false teeth! They were that man's pride and joy. He'd prized them out of the mouth of an old man he'd robbed, while the poor devil lay dying of fear! He'd joked that they had a mind of their own! And they spluttered and popped and slurped and fitted so badly that they once turned around in his mouth and bit him in the throat! He used to take them out and talk to them! And, aargh, they were so old, and the stained teeth had been carved from walrus ivory and the spring was so strong that sometimes it'd force the top of his head back so that you could see right up his nose!!

It all came back like a bad oyster.

He was just Cribbins. No one knew his first name. They'd teamed up oh, ten years ago, and they'd run the old legacy con in Überwald one winter. He was much older than Moist and still had the serious personal problem that made him smell of bananas.

And he was a nasty piece of work. Professionals had their pride. There had to be some people you wouldn't rob, some things you didn't steal. And you had to have style. If you didn't have style, you'd never fly.

Cribbins didn't have style. He wasn't violent, unless there was absolutely no chance of retaliation, but there was some generalized, wretched, wheedling malice about the man that had got on Moist's soul.

"Is there a problem, Mr. Lipwig?" said Bent, glaring at Cribbins.

"What? Oh . . . no . . ." said Moist.

It's a shakedown, he thought. *That bloody picture in the paper. But he can't prove a thing, not a thing.*

"You are mistaken, sir," said Moist. He looked around. The queues were moving, and no one was paying them any attention.

Cribbins put his head on one side and gave Moist an amused look. "Mishtaken, shir? Could be. I could be mishtaken. Life on the road, making new chums every day, you know—well, you wouldn't, would you, on account of not being Albert Shpangler. Funny, though, 'cos you have his smile, sir, hard to change a man's smile, and your smile ish, like, in front of your face, like you is shlooking out from behind it *slurp*. Just like young Albert's smile. Bright lad he wash, very quick, very quick, I taught him everything he knew."

—And that took about ten minutes, Moist thought, *and a year to forget some of it. You're the sort that gives criminals a bad name—*

"Course, sir, you're wonderin', can the leopard change his shorts? Can that ol' rascal I knew all them years ago have forsook the wide and wobbly for the straight an' narrow?" He glanced at Moist, and amended: "Whoopsh! No, course you ain't, on account of you never seein' me before. But I was scrobbled in Pseudopolis, you see, thrown into the clink for malicious lingering, and that's where I found Om."

"Why? What had he done?" It was stupid, but Moist couldn't resist it.

"Do not jest, sir, do not jest," said Cribbins solemnly. "I am a changed man, a changed man. It is my task to pass on the good news, shir." Here, with the speed of a snake's tongue, Cribbins produced a battered tin from inside his greasy jacket. "My crimes weigh me down like chains of hot iron, shir, like chains, but I am a man anxious to unburden himshelf by means of good works and confession, the last bein' mosht important. I have to get a lot off my chest before I can sleep easy, shir." He rattled the box. "For the kiddies, shir?"

This would probably work better if I hadn't seen you do this before, Moist thought. The penitent thief must be one of the oldest cons in the book.

He said: "Well, I'm glad to hear it, Mr. Cribbins. I'm sorry I'm not the old friend you are looking for. Let me give you a couple of dollars . . . for the kiddies."

The coin clanked on the bottom of the tin. "Thank you kindly, Mishter Shpangler," said Cribbins.

Moist flashed a little smile. "In fact I'm not Mr. Spangler, Mr.—"

I called him Cribbins! Just then! I called him Cribbins! Did he tell me his name? Did he notice? He must have noticed!

"—I beg your pardon, l mean Reverend," he managed, and the average person would not have noticed the tiny pause and quite-adroit save. But Cribbins wasn't average.

"Thank you, Mr. Lipwig," he said, and Moist heard the drawn out *mister* and the explosively sardonic "Lipwig." They meant "Gotcha!"

Cribbins winked at Moist and strolled off

through the banking hall, shaking his tin, his teeth accompanying him with a medley of horrible dental noises.

"Woe and thrice woe *szss!* is the man who stealssh by words, for his tongue shall cleave to the roof of his mouth *pock!* spare a few coppersh for the poor orphans *sweessh!* Brothers and shisters! to those *svhip!* that hath shall be giventh, generally spheaking . . ."

"I shall call the guards," said Mr. Bent firmly. "We don't allow beggars in the bank."

Moist grabbed his arm. "No," he said urgently, "not with all these people in here. Manhandling a man of the cloth and all that. It won't look good. I think he'll be going soon."

Now he'll let me stew, thought Moist, as Cribbins headed nonchalantly toward the door. *That's his way. He'll spin it out. Then he'll hit me for money, again and again.*

Okay, but what could Cribbins *prove*? But did there need to be proof? If he started talking about Albert Spangler, it could get bad. Would Vetinari throw him to the wolves? He might. He probably would. You could bet your hat that he wouldn't play the resurrection game without lots of contingency plans.

Well, he had some time, at least. Cribbins wouldn't go for a quick kill. He liked to watch people wriggle.

"Are you all right?" said Bent. Moist came back to reality.

"What? Oh, fine," he said.

"You should not encourage that sort of person in here, you know."

Moist shook himself.

"You are right about that, Mr. Bent. Let's get to the Mint, shall we?"

"Yes, sir. But I warn you, Mr. Lipwig, these men will not be won over by fancy words!"

"INSPECTORS . . ." SAID Mr. Shady, ten minutes later, turning the word over in his mouth like a candy.

"I need people who value the high traditions of the Mint," said Moist, and did not add: *Like making coins very, very slowly and taking your work home with you.*

"Inspectors," said Mr. Shady again. Behind him, the Men of the Sheds held their caps in their hands and watched Moist owlishly, except when Mr. Shady was speaking; then they stared at the back of the man's neck.

They were all in Mr. Shady's official shed, which was built high up on the wall, like a swallow's nest. It creaked whenever anyone moved.

"And of course, some of you will still be needed to deal with the outworkers," Moist went on, "but in the main it will be your job to see that Mr. Spools's men arrive on time, comport themselves as they should, and observe proper security."

"Security," said Mr. Shady, as if tasting the word. Moist saw a flicker of evil light in the eyes of the Men. It said: These buggers will be taking over our Mint but they'll have to go past *us* to get out of the door. Hoho!

"And of course you can keep the sheds," said Moist. "I also have plans for commemorative coins and other items, so your skills will not be wasted. Fair enough?"

Mr. Shady looked at his fellows and then back to Moist.

"We'd like to talk about this," he said.

Moist nodded at him, and at Bent, and led the way down the creaking, swaying staircase to the floor of the Mint, where the parts of the new press were already being stacked up. Bent gave a little shudder when he saw it.

"They won't accept, you know," he said with unconcealed hope in his voice. "They've been doing things the same way here for hundreds of years! And they are craftsmen!"

"So were the people who used to make knives out of flint," said Moist. In truth, he'd been amazed at himself. It must have been the encounter with Cribbins. It had made his brain race. "Look, I don't like to see skills unused," he said, "but I'll give them better wages and a decent job and use of the Sheds. They wouldn't get an offer like that in a hundred years—"

Someone was coming down the swaying stairs. Moist recognized him as Young Alf, who, amazingly, had managed to be employed in the Mint while still too young to shave though definitely old enough to have spots.

"Er, the men say, will there be badges?" said the boy.

"Actually, I was thinking of uniforms," said Moist.

"Silver breastplate with the city's coat of arms on it and lightweight silver chain mail, to look impressive when we have visitors."

The boy pulled a piece of paper out of his pocket and consulted it.

"What about clipboards?" he said.

"Certainly," said Moist. "And whistles, too."

"And, er, it's def'nite about the Sheds, right?"

"I'm a man of my word," said Moist.

"You are a man *of* words, Mr. Lipwig," said Bent as the boy scuttled back up the rocking steps, "but I fear they will lead us into ruin. The bank needs solidarity, reliability . . . everything that gold represents!"

Moist spun around. It had not been a good day. It had not been a good night, either.

"Mr. Bent, if you do not like what I am doing, feel free to leave. You'll have a good reference and all the wages due to you!"

Bent looked as though he'd been slapped.

"Leave the bank? *Leave* the bank? How could I do that? How dare you!"

A door slammed above them. They looked up. The Men of the Sheds were coming down the stairs in solemn procession.

"Now we shall see," hissed Bent. "These are men of solid worth. They'll have nothing to do with your gaudy offer, Mr. . . . . Ringmaster!"

The Men reached the bottom of the steps. Without a word they all looked at Mr. Shady, except for Mr. Shady, who looked at Moist.

"The sheds stay, right?" he said.

"You're giving in?" said Mr. Bent, aghast. "After hundreds of years?"

"We-ll," said Mr. Shady, "me and the boys had a bit of a talk and, well, at a time like this, a man's got to think of his shed. And the outworkers will be all right, right?"

"Mr. Shady, I'd go to the barricades for the elim," said Moist.

"And we talked to some of the lads from the Post Office last night and they said we could trust Mr. Lipwig's word 'cos he's as straight as a corkscrew."

"A corkscrew?" said Bent, shocked.

"Yeah, we asked about that, too," said Shady. "And they said he acts curly but that's okay 'cos he damn well gets the corks out!"

Mr. Bent's expression went blank. "Oh," he said. "This is clearly some kind of judgment-clouding joke, which I do not understand. If you will excuse me, I have a great deal of work to attend to."

His feet rising and falling, as though he was walking on an invisible staircase, Mr. Bent departed in jerky haste.

"Very well, gentlemen, thank you for your helpful attitude," said Moist, watching the retreating figure, "and for my part I will get those uniforms ordered this afternoon."

"You're a fast mover, Master," said Mr. Shady.

"Stand still and your mistakes catch up with you!" said Moist. They laughed, because he'd said it, but the face of Cribbins rose up in his mind and, quite unconsciously, he put his hand in his pocket and touched the blackjack. He'd have to learn how to use it now, because a weapon you held and didn't know how to use belonged to your enemy.

He'd bought it—why? Because it was like the lock picks, a token to prove, if only to himself, that he hadn't given in, not all the way, that a part of him was still free. It was like the other ready-made identities, the escape plans, the caches of money and clothes. They told him that any day he could leave all this, melt into the crowd, say good-bye to the paperwork and the timetable and the endless, endless *wanting*.

They told him that he could give it up anytime he liked. Any hour, any minute, any second. And because he could, he didn't . . . every hour, every minute, every second. There had to be a reason why.

"Mr. Lipwig! Mr. Lipwig!"

A young clerk dodged and weaved through the busyness of the Mint, and stopped in front of Moist, panting.

"Mr. Lipwig, there's a lady in the hall to see you and we've thanked her for not smoking three times and she's still doing it!"

The image of the wretched Cribbins vanished, and was replaced with a much better one.

Ah, yes. *That* reason.

MISS ADORA BELLE Dearheart, known to Moist as Spike, was standing in the middle of the banking hall. Moist just headed for the smoke.

"Hello, you," she said, and that was that. "Can

you take me away from all this?" She gestured with her nonsmoking hand. Staff had meaningfully surrounded her with tall brass ashtrays, full of white sand.

Moist shifted a couple of them, and let her out.

"How was—" he began, but she interrupted.

"We can talk on the way."

"Where are we going?" Moist asked hopefully.

"Unseen University," said Adora Belle, heading for the door. She had a large woven bag on her shoulder. It was apparently stuffed with straw.

"Not lunch then?" said Moist.

"Lunch can wait. This is important."

"Oh."

I̶T WAS LUNCHTIME at Unseen University, where *every* meal is important. It was hard to find a time when some meal or other was not in progress there. The library was unusually empty, and Adora Belle walked up to the nearest wizard who did not seem gainfully employed and demanded: "I want to see the Cabinet of Curiosity right away!"

"I don't think we have anything like that," said the wizard. "Who's it by?"

"Please don't lie. My name is Adora Belle Dearheart, so as you can imagine I've got a pretty short temper. My father brought me with him when you people asked him to come and look at the Cabinet, about twenty years ago. You wanted to find out how the doors worked. Someone must remember. It was in a big room. A very big room. And it had lots and lots of drawers. And the funny thing about them was—"

The wizard raised his hands quickly, as if to ward off further words. "Can you wait just one minute?" he suggested.

They waited for five. Occasionally, a pointy-hatted head peered around a bookshelf to look at them, and ducked away if it thought it'd been spotted.

Adora Belle lit a fresh cigarette. Moist pointed to a sign which said IF YOU ARE SMOKING, THANK YOU FOR BEING BEATEN ABOUT THE HEAD.

"That's just for show," said Adora Belle, expelling a stream of blue smoke. "All wizards smoke like chimneys."

"Not in here, I notice," said Moist, "and possibly this is because of all the highly inflammable books? It might be a good idea to—"

He felt the swish of the air and got a whiff of rain forest as something heavy swung overhead and disappeared upward into the gloom, now trailing a stream of blue smoke.

"Hey, someone took my—" Adora Belle began, but Moist pushed her out of the way as the thing swung back again and a banana knocked his hat off.

"They are a bit more definite about things here," he said, picking up his hat. "If it's any comfort, the Librarian probably *intended* to hit me. He can be quite gallant."

"Ah, you're Mr. Lipwig, I recognize the suit!" said an elderly wizard, who clearly hoped he was appearing as if by magic but, in fact, had appeared as if by stepping out from behind a bookcase. "I know I am the Chair of Indefinite Studies here, for my sins. And you, ahaha, by a process of elimination, will be Miss Dearheart, who remembers the Cabinet of Curiosity?" The Chair of Indefinite Studies stepped closer and looked conspiratorial. He lowered his voice. "I wonder if I can persuade you to forget about it?"

"Not a chance," said Adora Belle.

"We like to think of it as one of our better-kept secrets, you see . . ."

"Good. I'll help you keep it," said Adora Belle.

"Nothing I could say could change your mind?"

"I don't know," said Adora Belle. "*Abracadabra*, maybe? Got your spell book?" Moist was impressed at that. She could be s . . . spiky.

"Oh . . . *that* type of lady," said the Chair of Indefinite Studies wearily. "*Modern*. Oh well, I suppose you'd better come with me, then."

"What's this all about please?" hissed Moist, as they followed the wizard.

"I need something translated," said Adora Belle, "in a hurry."

"Aren't you glad to see me?"

"Oh yes. Lots. But I need something translated in a hurry."

"And this cabinet thing can help?"

"Perhaps."

"Perhaps? 'Perhaps' could wait until after lunch, couldn't it? If it was 'definitely,' now, I could have seen the point—"

"Oh dear, I'm afraid I'm lost again, and through

no fault of my own, I might add," grumbled the Chair of Indefinite Studies. "I'm afraid, they keep changing the parameters and they do leak so, I don't know, what with one thing and another you can't call your door your own these days . . ."

"What were your sins?" said Moist, giving up on Adora Belle.

"Pardon? Oh dear, what is that stain on the ceiling? Probably best not to know . . ."

"What were the sins you committed in order to become the Chair of Indefinite Studies?" Moist persisted.

"Oh, I just tend to say that for something to say," said the wizard, opening a door and slamming it again quickly. "But right now I'm inclined to think I must have committed a few, and they must have been *whoppers*. It's just unbearable at the moment, of course. They're saying that everything in the whole wretched universe is technically indefinable, but what am I supposed to do about it? And of course this damn Cabinet is playing havoc with the place again; I thought we'd seen the last of it fifteen years ago . . . Oh, yes, mind the squid, we're a bit puzzled about that, actually . . . ah, here's the right door," the Chair sniffed, "and it's twenty-five feet away from where it ought to be. What did I tell you . . ."

The door opened and then it was just a matter of knowing where to start. Moist opted for letting his jaw drop, which was clean and simple.

The room was bigger than it ought to be. No room ought to be more than a mile across, especially when outside in the corridor, which looked quite ordinary if you ignored the giant squid; it appeared to have perfectly normal rooms on either side of it. It shouldn't have a ceiling so high that you couldn't see it, either. It simply should not fit.

"It's quite easy to do this, actually," said the Chair of Indefinite Studies, as they stared. "At least, so they tell me," he added wistfully. "Apparently, if you shrink time you can expand space."

"How do they do that?" Moist asked, staring at the . . . structure that was the Cabinet of Curiosity.

"I'm proud to say I haven't got the faintest idea," said the Chair. "Frankly, I'm afraid I got rather lost round about the time we stopped using dribbly candles. I know it's technically my department but I find it best just to let them get on with it. They do insist on trying to explain things, which of course does not help . . ."

Moist, if he'd had any mental picture at all, was expecting a cabinet. After all, that's what it was called, yes?

But what filled most of the impossible room was a tree, in the general shape of a venerable spreading oak. It was a tree in winter; there were no leaves. And then, when the mind had found a familiar, friendly simile, it had to come to terms with the fact that the tree was made of filing cabinets. They appeared to be wooden ones, but this didn't help much.

High up in what had to be called the branches, wizards on broomsticks were engaged in who-knew-what. They looked like insects.

"It *is* a bit of a shock when you see it for the first time, isn't it," said a friendly voice.

Moist looked around at a young wizard, at least by the standards of wizards, who had round spectacles, a clipboard, and the shiny sort of expression that says: I probably know more than you can possibly imagine, but I am still reasonably happy to talk even to people like you.

"You're Ponder Stibbons, right?" said Moist. "The only one who does any work in the university?"

Other wizards turned their heads at this, and Ponder went red.

"That's quite untrue! I just pull my weight, like any other member of the faculty," he said, but a slight tone to his voice suggested that perhaps the other faculty members had far too much weight and not enough pull. "I am in charge of the Cabinet Project, for my sins."

"Why? What did *you* do?" said Moist, at sea in a world of sin. "Something worse?"

"Er . . . volunteered to take it over," said Ponder. "And I have to say we have learned more in the last six months than in the past twenty-five years. The Cabinet is a truly amazing artifact."

"Where did you find it?"

"In the attic, tucked behind a collection of stuffed frogs. We think people gave up trying to make it work years ago. Of course, that was back in the dribbly-candle era," said Ponder, earning a snort from the Chair of Indefinite Studies. "Modern technomancy is somewhat more useful."

"All right, then," said Moist, "*what does it do?*"

"We don't know."

"How does it work?"

"We don't know."

"Where did it come from?"

"We don't know."

"Well, that seems to be all," said Moist sarcastically. "Oh no, one last one: what is it? And let me tell you, I'm agog."

"That may be the wrong sort of question to ask," said Ponder, shaking his head. "Technically it appears to be a classic Bag of Holding but with n mouths, where n is the number of items in an eleven-dimensional universe, which are not currently alive, not pink, and can fit in a cubical drawer 14.14 inches on a side, divided by P."

"What's P?"

"That may be the wrong sort of question."

"When I was a little girl, it was just a magic box," Adora Belle broke in, in a dreamy voice. "It was in a much smaller room and when it unfolded a few times there was a box with a golem's foot in it."

"Ah, yes, in the third iteration," said Ponder. "They couldn't get much further than that in those days. Now, of course, we've got controlled recursion and aim-driven folding that effectively reduces collateral boxing to 0.13 percent, a twelvefold improvement in the last year alone!"

"That's great!" said Moist, feeling that it was the least he could do.

"Does Miss Dearheart want to see the item again?" said Ponder, lowering his voice.

Adora Belle still had a faraway look in her eyes.

"I think so," said Moist. "She's very big on golems."

"We were about to fold up for today in any case," said Ponder. "It won't hurt to pick up the Foot on the way."

He took a large megaphone from a bench and held it to his lips.

"THE CABINET CLOSES IN THREE MINUTES, GENTLEMEN. ALL RESEARCHERS INSIDE THE SAFETY AREA NOW, PLEASE. BE THERE OR BE SQUARE!"

"Be there or be square?" said Moist, as Ponder lowered the megaphone.

"Oh, a couple of years ago someone ignored the warning and, um, when the Cabinet folded up, he temporarily became a curiosity."

"You mean he ended up inside a fourteen-inch cube?" said Moist, horrified.

"Mostly. Look, we really *would* be very happy if you didn't tell anyone about the Cabinet, thank you. We know how to use it, we think, but it might not be the way it was intended to be used. We don't know what it's for, as you put it, or who built it or even if they are completely the wrong questions to ask. Nothing in it is bigger than about fourteen inches square, but we don't know why this is, or who it is who decides they are curious, or why, and we certainly don't know why it contains nothing pink. It's all very embarrassing. I'm sure you *can* keep a secret, Mr. Lipwig?"

"You'd be amazed."

"Oh? Why?"

"That's the wrong kind of question."

"You do know *something* quite important about

the Cabinet," said Adora Belle, apparently waking up. "You know it wasn't built for or by a girl between the ages of four and, oh, eleven years old."

"How do we know that?"

"No pink. Trust me. No girl in that age group would leave out pink."

"Are you sure? That's wonderful!" said Ponder, making a note on his clipboard. "That's certainly worth knowing. Let's get the Foot, then, shall we?"

The broomstick-riding wizards had touched down now. Ponder cleared his throat and picked up the megaphone. "ALL DOWN? WONDERFUL. HEX—BE SO GOOD AS TO FOLD, PLEASE!"

There was silence for a while, and then a distant clattering noise began to grow, up near the ceiling. It sounded like gods shuffling wooden playing cards that happened to be a mile high.

"Hex is our thinking engine," said Ponder. "We'd hardly be able to explore the box at all without him."

The clattering was becoming louder and faster.

"You might find your ears aching," said Ponder, raising his voice. "Hex tries to control the speed, but it takes finite time for the ventilators to get air back into the room. THE VOLUME OF THE CABINET CHANGES VERY FAST, YOU SEE!"

This was shouted against the thunder of collapsing drawers. They slammed in on themselves far too fast for the human eye to follow as the edifice shrank and folded and slid and rattled down into house size, shed size, and, finally, in the middle of the huge space, unless it was some kind of time, stood a small polished cabinet, about a foot and a half on a side, standing on four beautifully carved legs.

The Cabinet's doors clicked shut.

"Slowly unfold to specimen 1,109," said Ponder, in the ringing silence.

The doors opened. A deep drawer slid out.

It went on sliding.

"Just follow me," said Ponder, strolling toward the Cabinet. "It's fairly safe."

"Er, a drawer about a hundred yards long has just slid out of a box about fourteen inches square," said Moist, in case he was the only one to notice.

"Yes. That's what happens," said Ponder, as the drawer slid back about halfway. Its side, Moist saw, was a line of drawers. So drawers opened . . . out of drawers. Of course, Moist thought, in eleven-dimensional space that was the wrong thing to think.

"It's a sliding puzzle," said Adora Belle, "but with lots more directions to slide."

"That is a very graphic analogy which aids under-standing wonderfully while being, strictly speaking, wrong in every possible way," said Ponder.

Adora Belle's eyes narrowed. She had not had a cigarette in ten minutes.

The long drawer extruded another drawer at right angles. All along the sides of it were, yes, yet more drawers. One of these extended slowly.

Moist took a risk and tapped on what appeared to be perfectly ordinary wood. It made a perfectly ordinary noise.

"Should I worry that I just saw a drawer slide through another drawer?" he said.

"No," said Ponder. "The Cabinet is trying to make four-dimensional sense of something that is happening in eleven or, possibly, ten."

"Trying? Do you mean it's alive?"

"Aha! The right type of question!"

"I bet you don't know the answer, though."

"You are correct. But you must admit it's an interesting question not to know the answer to. And, yes, here we have the Foot. Hold and collapse please, Hex."

The drawers collapsed back into themselves in a series of crashes, much shorter and less dramatic than before, leaving the Cabinet looking demure and antique and slightly bow-legged. It had little claws as feet, a cabinet-maker's affectation that always annoyed Moist in a low-grade way. Did they think the things moved around in the night? Or maybe the Cabinet really did.

And the Cabinet's doors were open. Nestling inside, and only just fitting, was a golem's foot, or at least most of one.

Once, golems were delicate and beautiful. Once, the very best sculptors probably made them to rival the most beautiful of statues, but long since then the fumble-fingered many who could barely make a snake out of clay found that bashing the stuff into the shape of a big, hulking gingerbread man worked just as well.

This foot was one of the early kind. It was made

of a clay like white china, with patterns of tiny raised markings in yellow, black, and red. A little brass plate in front of it was engraved, in Überwaldean: FOOT OF UMNIAN GOLEM, MIDDLE PERIOD.

"Well, whoever made the Cabinet comes from—"

"Anyone looking at the labels sees it in their native tongue," said Ponder wearily. "The markings apparently indicate that it did indeed come from the city of Um, according to the late Professor Flead."

"Um?" said Moist. "Um what? They weren't sure what to call the place?"

"Just Um," said Ponder. "Very ancient. About sixty thousand years, I believe. Back in the Clay Age."

"The first golem-makers," said Adora Belle. She unslung the bag and started to rummage in the straw.

Moist tapped the foot. It seemed eggshell-thin.

"It's some sort of ceramic," said Ponder. "No one knows how they made it. The Umnians even baked *boats* out of the stuff."

"Did they work?"

"Up to a point," said Ponder. "Anyway, the city was totally destroyed in the first war with the ice giants. There's nothing there now. We think that the foot was put in the Cabinet a long time ago."

"Or will be dug up some time in the future, perhaps?" said Moist.

"That could very well be the case," said Ponder gravely.

"In which case, won't that be a bit of a problem? I mean, can it be in the ground and in the cabinet at the same time?"

"That, Mr. Lipwig, is—"

"The wrong type of question?"

"Yes. The box exists in ten or possibly eleven dimensions. Practically anything may be possible."

"Why only eleven dimensions?"

"We don't know," said Ponder. "It might be simply that more would be silly."

"Can you take the foot out, please?" said Adora Belle, who was now brushing wisps of straw off a long package.

Ponder nodded, lifted out the relic with great care, and placed it gently on the bench behind them.

"What would have happened if you had drop—" Moist began.

"Wrong type of question, Mr. Lipwig!"

Adora Belle put the bundle down beside the Foot and unwrapped it with care.

It contained a part of a golem's arm, two feet long.

"I knew it! The markings are the same!" she said. "And there's a lot more on my piece. Can you translate it?"

"Me? No," said Ponder. "The arts are not my field," he added, in a way that suggested his was a pretty superior field with much better flowers in it. "You need Professor Flead."

"You mean the one who's dead?" said Moist.

"He's dead at the moment, but I'm sure that in the interests of discretion my colleague Dr. Hicks can arrange for the professor to talk to you after lunch."

"When he'll be less dead?" said Moist.

"When Dr. Hicks has had lunch," said Ponder patiently. "Professor Flead will be pleased to receive visitors, er, especially Miss Dearheart. He is the world expert on Umnian. Every word has hundreds of meanings, I understand."

"Can I take the Foot?" said Adora Belle.

"No," said Ponder. "It's ours."

"That was the wrong type of answer," said Adora Belle, picking up the Foot. "On behalf of the Golem Trust, I am acquiring this golem. If you can prove ownership, we will pay you a fair price for it."

"Would that it were that simple," said Ponder, politely taking it from her, "but, you see, if a Curiosity is taken away from the Cabinet Room for more than fourteen hours and fourteen seconds, the Cabinet stops working. Last time it took us three months to restart it. But you can drop in at any time to, er, check that we're not mistreating it."

Moist laid a hand on Adora Belle's arm to forestall an Incident.

"She's very passionate about golems," he said. "The Trust digs them up all the time."

"That's very commendable," said Stibbons. "I'll talk to Dr. Hicks. He's the head of the Department of Postmortem Communications."

"Postmortem Com . . ." Moist began. "Isn't that the same as necroman—"

"I said *the Department of Postmortem Communications*," said Ponder very firmly. "I suggest you come back at three o'clock."

❋ ❋ ❋

"**D**ID ANYTHING ABOUT that conversation strike you as normal?" said Moist, as they stepped out into the sunlight.

"Actually, I thought it went very well," said Adora Belle.

"This wasn't how I imagined your homecoming," said Moist. "Why the rush? Is there some problem?"

"Look, we found four golems at the dig," said Adora Belle.

"That's . . . good, yes?" said Moist.

"Yes! And you know how deep they were?"

"I couldn't guess."

"Guess!"

"I don't know!" said Moist, bewildered at suddenly having to play "What's My Depth?" "Two hundred feet down? That's more than—"

"Half a mile underground."

"Impossible! That's deeper than coal!"

"Keep it down, will you? Look, is there somewhere we can go and talk?"

"How about—the Royal Bank of Ankh-Morpork? There's a private dining room."

"And they'll let us eat there, will they?"

"Oh yes. The chairman is a great friend of mine," said Moist.

"He is, is he?"

"He certainly is," said Moist. "Why, only this morning he licked my face!"

Adora Belle stopped and turned to stare at him. "Really?" she said. "Then it's just as well I got back when I did."

CHAPTER 7

The joy of collops
❋ *Mr. Bent goes out to lunch* ❋ *The Dark Fine Arts*
❋ *Amateur thespians, avoidance of embarrassment by*
❋ *The Pen of Doom!* ❋ *Professor Flead gets cozy*
❋ *Lust comes in many varieties* ❋ *A hero of banking!*
❋ *Cribbins's cup runneth over*

THE SUN SHONE through the window of the bank's dining room onto a scene of perfect pleasure.

"You should sell tickets," said Adora Belle dreamily, with her chin in her hands. "People who are depressed would come here and go away cured."

"It's certainly hard to watch it happening and be sad," said Moist.

"It's the enthusiastic way he tries to turn his mouth inside out," said Adora Belle.

 There was a gulp from Mr. Fusspot as the last of the sticky toffee pudding went down. He then turned the bowl over hopefully, in case there was any more. There never had been, but Mr. Fusspot was not a dog to bow down to the laws of causality.

"So . . ." said Adora Belle, "a mad old lady—all right, a very *astute* mad old lady—died and gave you her dog, which sort of wears this bank on its collar, and you've told everyone that gold is worth less than potatoes, and you broke a dastardly criminal out of your actual death row, he's in the cellar designing 'bank notes' for you, you've upset the nastiest family in the city, people are queuing to join the bank because you make them laugh . . . what have I missed?"

"I think my secretary is, uh, getting sweet on me. Well, I *say* secretary, she's sort of assumed that she is."

Some fiancées would have burst into tears or shouted. Adora Belle burst out laughing.

"And she's a golem," said Moist.

The laughter stopped. "That's not possible. They don't work that way. Anyway, why should a golem think he's female? It's never happened before."

"I bet there haven't been many emancipated golems before. Besides, why should he think he's male? And she bats her eyelashes at me . . . well, that's what she thinks she's doing, I think. The counter girls are behind this. Look I'm serious. Trouble is, so is she."

"I'll have a word with him . . . or, as you say, her."

"Good. The other thing is, there's this man—"

Aimsbury poked his head around the door. He was in love.

"Would you like some *more* minced collops, miss?" he said, waggling his eyebrows as if to indicate that the joys of minced collops were a secret known only to a few.*

"You've still got more?" said Adora Belle, looking down at her plate. Not even Mr. Fusspot could have cleaned it better, and she'd already cleaned it twice.

"Do you know what they are?" said Moist, who'd settled again for an omelet made by Peggy.

"Do you?"

"No!"

"Nor do I. But my granny used to make them and they are one of my happiest childhood memories, thank you very much. Don't spoil it." Adora Belle beamed at the delighted chef. "Yes please, Aimsbury, just a little more then. And could I just say that the flavor could really be brought out by just a touch of gar—"

66 Y OU ARE NOT eating, Mr. Bent," said Cosmo. "Perhaps a little of this pheasant?"

The chief cashier looked around nervously, uneasy in this grand house full of art and servants. "I . . . I want to make it clear that my loyalty to the bank is—"

"—beyond question, Mr. Bent. Of course." Cosmo pushed a silver tray toward him. "Do eat something. Now you have come all this way."

"But you are hardly eating at all, Mr. Cosmo. Just bread and water!"

---

*Fortunately, this is the case.

"I find it helps me think. Now, what was it you wanted to—"

"They all *like* him, Mr. Cosmo! He just talks to people and they like him! And he is really set on dismissing gold. Think of it, sir! Where would we find true worth? He says it's all about the city but that puts us at the mercy of *politicians*! It's trickery again!"

"A little brandy would do you good, I think," said Cosmo. "And what you say is solid-gold truth, but where is our way forward?"

Bent hesitated. He did not like the Lavish family. They crawled over the bank like ivy, but at least they didn't try to change things and at least they believed in gold. And they weren't *silly*.

Mavolio Bent had a definition of "silly" that most people would have considered a touch on the broad side. Laughter was silly. Theatricals, poetry, and music were silly. Clothes that weren't gray, black, or at least of undyed cloth were silly. Pictures of things that weren't real were silly (pictures of things that were real were unnecessary). The ground state of being was silliness, which had to be overcome with every mortal fiber.

Missionaries from the stricter religions would have found in Mavolio Bent an ideal convert, except that religion was extremely silly.

Numbers were not silly. Numbers held everything together. And gold was not silly. The Lavishes believed in counting and in gold. Mr. Lipwig treated numbers as if they were something to play with, and he said gold was just lead on holiday! That was more than silly, it was inappropriate behavior, a scourge that he had torn from his breast after years of struggle.

The man had to go. Bent had worked his way up the echelons of the bank over many years, fighting every natural disadvantage, and it hadn't been to see this . . . person make a mockery of it all! No!

"A man came to the bank again today," he said. "He was very odd. And he seemed to know Mr. Lipwig, but he called him Albert Spangler. Talked as if he knew him from long ago and I think Mr. Lipwig was upset at that. Name of Cribbins, or so Mr. Lipwig called him. Very old clothes, very dusty. He made out he was a holy man, but I don't think so."

"And that was what was odd, was it?"

"No, Mr. Cosmo—"

"Just call me Cosmo, Malcolm. We surely needn't stand on ceremony."

"Er . . . yes," said Mavolio Bent. "Well, no, it wasn't that. It was his teeth. They were those dine-chewers, and they moved and rattled when he spoke, causing him to slurp."

"Ah, the old type with the springs," said Cosmo. "Very good. And Lipwig was annoyed?"

"Oh, yes. And the strange thing was, he said he didn't know the man but he called him by name."

Cosmo smiled. "Yes, that is strange. And the man left?"

"Well, yes, si— Mr.— Cosmo," said Bent. "And then I came here."

"You have done very well, Matthew! Should the man come in again, could you please follow him and try to find out where he is staying?"

"If I can, si— Mr.— Cosmo."

"Good man!" Cosmo helped Bent out of his chair, shook his hand, waltzed him to the door, opened the door, and ushered him out all in one smooth, balletic movement.

"Hurry back, Mr. Bent, the bank needs you!" he said, closing the door. "He's a strange creature, don't you think, Drumknott?"

I wish he'd stop doing that, Heretofore thought. *Does he think he's Vetinari? What do they call those fishes that swim alongside sharks, making themselves useful so they don't get eaten? That's me, that's what I'm doing, just hanging on, because it's much safer than letting go.*

"How would Vetinari find a badly dressed man, new to the city, with ill-fitting teeth, Drumknott?" said Cosmo.

Fifty dollars a month and all found, thought Heretofore, snapping out of a brief marine nightmare. *Never forget it. And in another few days you're free.*

"He makes much use of the Beggars' Guild, sir," he said.

"Ah, of course. See to it."

"There will be expenses, sir."

"Yes, Drumknott, I'm conscious of the fact. There are always expenses. And the other matter?"

"Soon, sir, soon. This is not a job for Cranberry, sir. I'm having to bribe at the highest level." Heretofore coughed. "Silence is expensive, sir . . ."

❈ ❈ ❈

MOIST ESCORTED ADORA Belle back to the university in silence. But the important thing was that nothing had been broken and no one was killed.

Then, as if reaching a conclusion after much careful thought, Adora Belle said: "I worked in a bank for a while, you know, and hardly anyone got stabbed."

"I'm sorry, I forgot to warn you. And I did push you out of the way in time."

"I must admit that the way you threw me to the floor quite turned my head."

"Look, I'm sorry, okay? And so is Aimsbury! And now will you tell me what all this is about? You found four golems, right? Have you brought them back?"

"No, the tunnel collapsed before we got down that far. I told you, they were half a mile down, under millions of tons of sand and mud. For what it's worth, we think there was a natural ice dam up in the mountains, which burst and flooded half the continent. The stories about Um say it was destroyed in a flood, so that fits. The golems were washed away with the rubble, which ended up against some chalk cliffs by the sea."

"How did you find out they were down there? It's . . . well, it's nowhere!"

"The usual way. One of our golems heard one singing. Imagine that. It's been underground for sixty thousand years . . ."

In the night under the world, in the pressure of the depth, in the crushing of the dark . . . a golem sang. There were no words. The song was older than words; it was older than tongues. It was the call of the common clay, and it carried for miles. It traveled along fault lines, made crystals sing in harmony in dark, unmeasured caverns, followed rivers that never saw the sun . . .

. . . and out of the ground and up the legs of a golem from the Golem Trust, who was pulling a wagon loaded with coal along the region's one road. When he arrived in Ankh-Morpork, he told the Trust. That was what the Trust did: it found golems.

Cities, kingdoms, countries came and went, but the golems that priests had baked from clay and filled with holy fire tended to go on forever. When they had no more orders, no more water to fetch or wood to hew, perhaps because the land was now on the ocean floor or the city was inconveniently under fifty feet of volcanic ash, they did nothing but wait for the next order. They were, after all, property. They obeyed whatever instructions were written on the little scroll in their head. Sooner or later, rock erodes. Sooner or later a new city would arise. One day there would be orders.

Golems had no concept of freedom. They knew they were artifacts; some even still bore, on their clay, the finger marks of the long-dead priests. Golems were made to be owned.

There had always been a few in Ankh-Morpork, running errands, doing chores, pumping water deep underground, unseen and silent and not getting in anyone's way. Then, one day, someone freed a golem by inserting in its head the receipt for the money he'd paid for it. And then he told it that it owned itself.

A golem could not be freed by orders, or a war, or a whim. But it could be freed by freehold. When you have been a possession, then you really understand what freedom means, in all its magnificent terror.

Dorfl, the first freed golem, had a plan. He worked hard, around the clock he had no time for, and bought another golem. The two golems worked hard and bought a third golem . . . and now there was the Golem Trust, which bought golems, found golems entombed underground or in the depths of the sea, and helped golems buy themselves.

In the booming city golems *were* worth their weight in gold. They would accept small wages but they earned them for twenty-four hours a day. It was still a bargain—stronger than trolls, more reliable than oxen, and more indefatigable and intelligent than a dozen of each, a golem could power every machine in a workshop.

This didn't make them popular. There was always a reason to dislike a golem. They didn't drink, eat, gamble, swear, or smile. They worked. If a fire broke out, they hurried to it en masse and put it out and then walked back to what they had been doing. No one knew why a creature that had been baked into life had the urge to do this, but all it won them was a kind of awkward resentment. You couldn't be grateful to an unmoving face with glowing eyes.

"How many are down there?" said Moist.

"I told you. Four."

Moist felt relieved. "Well, that's good. Well done. Can we have a proper celebratory meal tonight? Of something the animal wasn't so attached to? And then, who knows—"

"There may be a snag," said Adora Belle slowly.

"No, really?"

"Oh, please." Adora Belle sighed. "Look, the Umnians were the first golem-builders, do you understand? Golem legend says that the Umnians invented golems. It's easy to believe, too. Some priest baking a votive offering says the right words, and the clay sits up. It was their only invention. They didn't need any more. Golems built their city, golems tilled their fields. They invented the wheel, but as a children's toy. They didn't need wheels, you see. You don't need weapons, either, when you've got golems instead of city walls. You don't even need shovels—"

"You're not going to tell me they built fifty-foot-high killer golems, are you?"

"Only a man would think of that."

"It's our job," said Moist. "If you don't think of fifty-foot-high killer golems first, someone else will."

"Well, there's no evidence of them," said Adora Belle briskly. "The Umnians never even worked iron. They did work bronze, though . . . and gold."

There was something about the way *gold* was left hanging there that Moist didn't like.

"Gold," he said.

"Umnian is a very complex language," said Adora

Belle quickly. "None of the Trust golems know much about it, so we can't be certain—"

"Gold," said Moist, his voice leaden.

"So, when the digging team found caves down there, we came up with a plan. The tunnel was getting unstable anyway, so they closed it off, we said it had collapsed, and by now the team will have brought the golems out under the sea and be bringing them underwater all the way into the city," said Adora Belle.

Moist pointed at the golem's arm in its bag. "That one isn't gold," he said hopefully.

"We found a lot of golem remains about halfway down," said Adora Belle with a sigh. "The others are deeper . . . er, perhaps because they are heavier."

"Gold's twice the weight of lead," said Moist gloomily.

"The buried golem is singing in Umnian, which is the most complex language ever," said Adora Belle. "I can't be certain of our translation, so I thought, let's start by getting them into Ankh-Morpork, where they will be safe."

Moist took a deep breath. "Do you know how much trouble you can get into by breaking a contract with a dwarf?"

"Oh, come on! I'm not starting a war!"

"No, you're starting a legal action! And with the dwarfs that's even worse! You told me the contract said you couldn't take precious metals out of the land!"

"Yes, but these are golems. They're alive."

"Look, you've taken—"

"—*may have taken*—"

"—all right, *may have taken*, good grief, *tons* of gold out of dwarf land—"

"Golem Trust land—"

"—All right, but there was a covenant! Which you broke when you took—"

"—didn't take. It walked off by itself," said Adora Belle calmly.

"For heavens' sake, only a woman could think like this! You think because you believe there's a perfectly good justification for your actions the legal issues don't matter! And here am I, *this* close to persuading people here that a dollar doesn't have to be round and shiny and I'm finding that at any minute four big shiny beaming golems are going to stroll into town, waving and glittering at everybody!"

"There's no need to get hysterical," said Adora Belle.

"Yes, there is! What there isn't a need for is staying calm!"

"Yes, but that's when you come alive, right? That's when your brain works best. You always find a way, right?"

And there was nothing you could do about a woman like that. She just turned herself into a hammer and you ran right into her.

Fortunately.

They'd reached the entrance to the university. Above them loomed the forbidding statue of Alberto Malich, the founder. It had a chamber pot on its head. This had inconvenienced the pigeon which, by family tradition, spent most of its time perched on Alberto's head and now wore on its own head a miniature version of the same pottery receptacle.

Must be Rag Week again, thought Moist. *Students, eh? Love 'em or hate 'em, you're not allowed to hit 'em with a shovel.*

"Look, golems or not, let's have dinner tonight, just you and me, up in the suite. Aimsbury would love it. He doesn't often get a chance to cook for humans and it'd make him feel better. He'll do anything you want, I'm sure."

Adora Belle gave him a lopsided look. "I thought you'd suggest that, so I ordered sheep's head. He was overjoyed."

"Sheep's head," said Moist gloomily, "you know I hate food that stares back. I won't even look a sardine in the face."

"He promised to blindfold it."

"Oh, *good.*"

"My granny made a wonderful sheep's head mold," said Adora Belle. "That's where you use pig's trotters to thicken the broth so that when it gets cold you—"

"You know, sometimes there's such a thing as too much information?" said Moist. "This evening, then. Now let's go and see your dead wizard. You should enjoy it. There's bound to be skulls."

THERE WERE SKULLS. There were black drapes. There were complex symbols drawn on the floor. There were spirals of incense from black thuribles. And in the middle of all this the

Head of Postmortem Communications, in a fearsome mask, was fiddling with a candle.

He stopped when he heard them come in, and straightened up hurriedly.

"Oh, you're early," he said, his voice somewhat muffled by the fangs. "Sorry. It's the candles. They should be cheap tallow for the proper black smoke, but wouldn't you know it, they've given me beeswax. I *told* them just dribbling is no good to me, acrid smoke is what we want. Or what *they* want, anyway. Sorry, John Hicks, head of department. Ponder has told me all about you."

He took off the mask and extended a hand. The man looked as though he'd tried, like any self-respecting necromancer, to grow a proper goatee beard, but owing to some basic lack of malevolence it had turned out a bit sheepish. After a few seconds Hicks realized why they were staring, and pulled off the fake rubber hand with the black fingernails.

"I thought necromancy was banned," said Moist.

"Oh, we don't do necromancy here," said Hicks. "What made you think that?"

Moist looked around at the furnishings, shrugged, and said, "Well, I suppose it first crossed my mind when I saw the way the paint was flaking off the door and you can still just see a crude skull and the letters NECR . . ."

"Ancient history, ancient history," said Hicks, quickly. "*We* are the Department of Postmortem Communications, a force for good, you understand? Necromancy, on the other hand, is a very bad form of magic done by evil wizards."

"And since you are not evil wizards, what you are doing can't be called necromancy?"

"Exactly!"

"And, er, what defines an evil wizard?" said Adora Belle.

"Well, doing necromancy would definitely be there right on top of the list."

"Could you just remind us what you *are* going to do?"

"We're going to talk to the late Professor Flead," said Hicks.

"Who is dead, yes?"

"Very much so. Extremely dead."

"Isn't that just a *tiny* bit like necromancy?"

"Ah, but, you see, for necromancy you require skulls and bones and a general necropolitan feel," said Dr. Hicks. He looked at their expressions. "Ah, I see where you're going here," he said, with a little laugh that cracked a bit around the edges. "Don't be deceived by appearances. *I* don't need all this. Professor Flead does. He's a bit of a traditionalist, and wouldn't get out of his urn for anything less than the full Rite of Souls complete with the Dread Mask of Summoning." He twanged a fang.

"And that's the Dread Mask of Summoning, is it?" said Moist. The wizard hesitated for a moment before saying: "Of course."

"Only it looks just like the Dread Sorcerer mask they sell in Boffo's shop in Tenth Egg Street," said Moist. "Excellent value at five dollars, I thought."

"I, er, think you must be mistaken," said Hicks.

"I don't think so," said Moist, "you left the label on."

"Where? Where?" The I'm-not-a-necromancer-at-all snatched up the mask and turned it over in his hands, looking for—

He saw Moist's grin and rolled his eyes.

"All right, yes," he muttered. "We lost the real one. Everything gets lost around here, you just wouldn't believe it. They're not clearing up the spells properly. Was there a huge squid in the corridor?"

"Not this afternoon," said Adora Belle.

"Yes, what's the reason for the squid?"

"Oooh, let me tell you about the squid!" said Hicks.

"Yes?"

"You *don't* want to know about the squid!"

"We don't?"

"Believe me! Are you sure it wasn't there?"

"It's the sort of thing you notice," said Adora Belle.

"With any luck that one's worn off, then," said Hicks, relaxing. "It really is getting impossible. Last week everything in my filing cabinet filed itself under W. No one seems to know why."

"And you were going to tell us about the skulls," said Adora Belle.

"All fake," said Hicks.

"Excuse *me*?" The voice was dry and crackly and came from the shadows in the far corner.

"Apart from Charlie, of course," Hicks added hurriedly. "He's been here for *ever*."

"I'm the backbone of the department," said the voice, a shade proudly.

"Look, shall we get started?" said Hicks, rummaging in a black velvet sack. "There are some hooded black robes on the hook behind the door. They're just for show, of course, but nec— Postmortem Communications is all about theater, really. Most of the people we . . . communicate with are wizards, and frankly, they don't like change."

"We're not going to do anything—ghoulish, are we?" said Adora Belle, looking at a robe doubtfully.

"Apart from talk to someone who's been dead for three hundred years," said Moist. He was not naturally at ease in the presence of skulls. Humans have been genetically programmed not to be, ever since monkey times, because (a) whatever turned that skull into a skull might still be around and you should head for a tree *now*, and (b) skulls look like they're having a laugh at one's expense.

"Don't worry about that," said Hicks, taking a small ornamental jar out of the black bag and polishing it on his sleeve. "Professor Flead willed his soul to the university. He's a bit crabby, I have to say, but he can be cooperative if we put on a decent show." He stood back. "Let's see . . . grisly candles, Circle of Namareth, Glass of Silent Time, the Mask, of course, the Curtains of, er, Curtains, and," here he put a small box down beside the bottle, "the vital ingredients."

"Sorry? You mean all those expensive-sounding other things *aren't* vital?" said Moist.

"They're more like . . . scenery," said Hicks, adjusting the hood. "I mean, we could all sit around reading the script out loud, but without the costumes and scenery who'd want to turn up? Are you interested in the theater at all?" he added, in a hopeful voice.

"I go when I can," said Moist guardedly, because he recognized the hope in the man's voice.

"You didn't by any chance see *'Tis Pity She's an Instructor in Unarmed Combat* at the Little Theater recently? It was put on by the Dolly Sisters Players?"

"Uh, no, I'm afraid not."

"I played Sir Andrew Fartswell," said Dr. Hicks, in case Moist was due a sudden attack of recollection.

"Oh, that was *you* was it?" said Moist, who'd met actors before. "Everyone at work was talking about t!"

I'm okay so long as he doesn't ask which night they talked about, he thought. There's always one night in every play when something hilariously dreadful happens. But he was lucky; an experienced actor knows when not to push his luck.

Instead, Hicks said, "Do you know ancient languages?"

"I can do Basic Droning," said Moist.

"ꓦ ꓐꓱꓱ ꓶꓵꓶꓶꓐ ꓷꓡꓱꓱꓶꓚ ꓐꓡꓚꓶꓱ. Is this ancient enough for you?" said Adora Belle, and made Moist's spine tingle. The private language of the golems was usually hell on the human tongue, but it sounded unbearably sexy when Adora Belle uttered it. It was like silver in the air.

"What was that?" said Hicks.

"The common language of golems for the last twenty thousand years," said Adora Belle.

"Really? Most, er, moving . . . er . . . We'll begin . . ."

I N THE COUNTING house no one dared to look up as the desk of the chief cashier rumbled around on its turntable like some ancient tumbrel. Papers flew under Mavolio Bent's hands while his brain drowned in poisons and his feet treadled continually to release the dark energies choking his soul.

He didn't calculate, not as other men saw it. Calculation was for people who couldn't see the answer turning gently in their head. To see was to know. It always had been.

The mound of accumulated paperwork dwindled as the fury of his thinking wracked him.

There were new accounts being opened all the time. And why? Was it because of trust? Probity? An urge toward thrift? Was it because of anything that could be called worth?

No! It was because of Lipwig! People whom Mr. Bent had never seen before and hoped never to see again were pouring into the bank, their money in boxes, their money in piggy banks, and quite often their money in socks. Sometimes they were actually wearing the socks!

And they were doing this because of words! The bank's coffers were filling up because the wretched Mr. Lipwig made people laugh and made people hope. People *liked* him. No one had ever liked Mr. Bent, as far as he was aware. Oh, there had been a mother's love and a father's arms, the one chilly, the other too late, but where had they got him? In the end he'd been left alone. So he'd run away and found the gray caravan and entered a new life based on numbers and on worth and solid respect, and he had worked his way up and yes, he was a man of worth and yes, he had respect. Yes, respect. Even Mr. Cosmo respected him.

And now here was Lipwig, and who was he? No one seemed to know, except for the suspicious man with the unstable teeth. One day there was no Lipwig, next day he was the postmaster general! And now he was in the bank, a man whose worth was in his mouth and who showed no respect for anyone! And he made people laugh—and the bank filled up with money!

And did the Lavishes lavish anything on you? said a familiar little voice in his head. It was a hated little part of himself that he had beaten and starved and punched back into its wardrobe for years. It wasn't the voice of his conscience. *He* was the voice of his conscience. It was the voice of the . . . the mask.

"No!" snapped Bent. Some of the nearest clerks looked up at the unaccustomed noise and then hurriedly lowered their heads for fear of catching his eye. Bent stared fixedly at the sheet in front of him, watching the numbers roll past. Rely on the numbers! They didn't let you down . . .

Cosmo doesn't respect you, you fool, you fool. You have run their bank for them and cleaned up after them! You made, they spent . . . and they laugh at you. You know they do. Silly Mr. Bent with his funny walk, silly, silly, silly . . .

"Get away from me, *get away*," he whispered.

The people like him because he likes them. No one likes Mr. Bent.

"But I have worth. I have value!" Mr. Bent pulled another worksheet toward himself and sought solace in its columns. But he was pursued . . .

Where was your worth and value when you made the numbers dance, Mr. Bent? The innocent numbers? You made them dance and somersault and cartwheel when you cracked your whip, and they danced into the wrong places, didn't they, because Sir Joshua demanded his price! Where did the gold dance off to, Mr. Bent? Smoke and mirrors!

"No!"

In the counting house all the pens ceased moving for a few seconds, before scribbling again with frantic activity.

Eyes watering with shame and rage, Mr. Bent tried to unscrew the top from his patent fountain pen. In the muted silence of the banking hall, the sound of the green pen being deployed had the same effect as the sound of the axman sharpening his blade. Every clerk bent low to his desk. Mr. Bent Had Found A Mistake. All anyone could do was keep their eyes on the paper in front of them and hope against hope that it was not theirs.

Someone, and please gods it would not be them, would have to go and stand in front of the high desk. They knew that Mr. Bent did not like mistakes: Mr.

Bent believed that mistakes were the result of a deformity of the soul.

At the sound of the Pen of Doom, one of the senior clerks hurried to Mr. Bent's side. Those workers who risked being turned to water by the ferocity of Mr. Bent's stare essayed a quick glance and saw her being shown the offending document. There was a distant *tut-tut* sound. Her tread as she came down the steps and crossed the floor echoed in deadly, praying silence. She did not know, as she scurried, button-boots flashing, to the desk of one of the youngest and newest clerks, that she was about to meet a young man who was destined to go down in history as one of the great heroes of banking.

T HE DARK ORGAN music filled the Department of Postmortem Communications. Moist assumed it was all part of the ambience, although the mood would have been more precisely obtained if the tune it was playing did not appear to be "Cantata and Fugue for Someone Who Has Trouble with the Pedals."

As the last note died, after a long illness, Dr. Hicks spun around on the stool and raised the mask.

"Sorry about that, I have two left feet sometimes. Could you both just chant a bit while I do the mystic waving, please? Don't worry about words. Anything seems to work if it sounds sepulchral enough."

As he walked around the circle, chanting variants on *oo!* and *raah!*, Moist wondered how many bankers raised the dead during the course of an afternoon. Probably not a high number. He shouldn't be doing this, surely. He should be out there making money. Owls— Clamp must have finished the design by now. He could be holding his first note in his hands by tomorrow! And then there was damn Cribbins, who could be talking to anyone. True, the man had a rap sheet as long as a roller towel, but the city worked by alliances and if he met up with the Lavishes then Moist's life would unravel all the way back to the gallows—

"In my day we at least hired a decent mask," growled an elderly voice. "I say, is that a *woman* over there?"

A figure had appeared in the circle, without any bother or fuss, apart from the grumbling. It was in every respect the picture of a wizard—robed, pointy-hatted, bearded, and elderly, with the addition of a silvery monochrome effect overall and some slight transparency.

"Ah, Professor Flead," said Hicks, "it's kind of you to join us . . ."

"You know you brought me here and it's not as if I had anything else to do," said Flead. He turned back to Adora Belle and his voice became pure syrup. "What is your name, my dear?"

"Adora Belle Dearheart."

The warning tone of voice was lost on Flead.

"How delightful," he said, giving her a gummy smile. Regrettably, this made little strings of saliva vibrate in his mouth like the web of a very old spider.

"And would you believe me if I told you that you bear a striking resemblance to my beloved concubine Fenti, who died more than three hundred years ago? The likeness is astounding!"

"I'd say that was a pickup line," said Adora Belle.

"Oh dear, such cynicism," sighed the late Flead, turning to the Head of Postmortem Communications.

"Apart from this young lady's wonderful chanting, it was frankly a mess, Hicks," he said sharply. He tried to pat Adora Belle's hand, but his fingers passed right through.

"I'm sorry, professor, we just don't get the funding these days," said Hicks.

"I know, I know. It was ever thus, Doctor. Even in my day, if you needed a corpse you had to go out and find your own! And if you couldn't find one, you jolly well had to make one! It's all so *nice* now, so damn *correct*. So a fresh egg *technically* does the trick, but whatever happened to style? They tell me they've made an engine that can think now, but of course the Fine Arts are always last in the queue! And so I'm brought to this: one barely competent Postmortem Communicator and two people from Central Groaning!"

"Necromancy is a fine art?" said Moist.

"None finer, young man. Get things just a tiny bit wrong and the spirits of the vengeful dead may enter your head via your ears and blow your brains out down your nose."

The eyes of Moist and Adora Belle focused on

Dr. Hicks like those of an archer on his target. He waved his hands frantically and mouthed "Not very often!"

"What is a pretty young woman like you doing here, hmm?" said Flead, trying to grab Adora Belle's hand again.

"I'm trying to translate a phrase from Umnian," she said, giving him a wooden smile and absent-mindedly wiping her hand on her dress.

"Are women allowed to do that sort of thing these days? What fun! One of my greatest regrets, you know, is that when I was in possession of a body I didn't let it spend enough time in the company of young ladies . . ."

Moist looked around to see if there was any kind of emergency lever. There had to be *something*, if only in the event of nasal brain explosion.

He sidled up to Hicks.

"It's going to go really bad in a moment!" he hissed.

"It's all right, I can banish him to the Undead Zone in a moment," Hicks whispered.

"That won't be far enough if she loses her temper! I once saw her put a stiletto heel right through a man's foot while she was smoking a cigarette. She hasn't had a cigarette for more than fifteen minutes, so there's no telling what she'll do!"

But Adora Belle had pulled the golem's arm out of her bag, and the late Professor Flead's eyes twinkled with something more compelling than romance. Lust comes in many varieties.

He picked up the arm. That was the second surprising thing. And then Moist realized that the arm was still there, by Flead's feet, and what he was lifting was a pearly, tenuous ghost.

"Ah, part of an Umnian golem," he said. "Bad condition. Immensely rare. Probably dug up on the site of Um, yes?"

"Possibly," said Adora Belle.

"Hmm. Possibly, eh?" said Flead, turning the spectral arm around. "Look at the wafer-thinness! Light as a feather but strong as steel while the fires burned within! There has been nothing like them since!"

"I might know where such fires still burn," said Adora Belle.

"After sixty thousand years? I think not, madam!"

"I think otherwise."

She could say things in that tone of voice and turn heads. She projected absolute certainty. Moist had worked hard for years to get a voice like that.

"Are you saying *an Umnian golem has survived*?"

"Yes. Four of them, I think," said Adora Belle.

"Can they sing?"

"At least one can."

"I'd give anything to see one before I die," said Flead.

"Er . . ." Moist began.

"Figure of speech, figure of speech," said Flead, waving a hand irritably.

"I think that could be arranged," said Adora Belle. "In the meantime, we've transcribed their song into Boddely's Phonetic Runes." She dipped into her bag and produced a small scroll. Flead reached out, and once again an iridescent ghost of the scroll was now in his hands.

"It appears to be gibberish," he said, glancing at it, "although I have to say that Umnian always does at first glance. I shall need some time to work it out. Umnian is entirely a contextual language. Have you seen these golems?"

"No, our tunnel collapsed. We can't even talk to the golems who were digging anymore. Song doesn't travel well under salt water. But we think they are . . . unusual golems."

"Golden, probably," said Flead, the words leaving a thoughtful silence in their wake.

Then Adora Belle said: "Oh." Moist shut his eyes; on the inside of the lids, the gold reserves of Ankh-Morpork walked up and down, gleaming.

"Anyone who researches Um finds the golden golem legend," said Flead. "Sixty thousand years ago some witch doctor sitting by a fire made a clay figure and worked out how to make it live and that was the only invention they ever needed, do you understand? Even had horse golems, did you know that? No one has ever been able to create one since. Yet the Umnians never worked iron! They never invented the spade or the wheel! Golems herded their animals and spun their cloth! The Umnians did make their own jewelry, though, which largely consisted of scenes of human sacrifice, badly executed in every sense of the word. They were incredibly inventive in that area. A theocracy, of course," he added, with a shrug. "I don't know what it is about stepped pyramids that brings out the worst in a god . . . Anyway, yes, they did work gold. They dressed their priests in it. Quite possibly they made a few golems out of it. Or, equally, the 'golden golems' was a metaphor referring to the *value* of golems to the Umnians. When people wish to express the concept of worth, *gold* is always the word of choice—"

"Isn't it just," murmured Moist.

"—or it is simply a legend without foundation. Exploration of the site has never found anything except a few fragments of broken golems," said Flead, sitting back and making himself comfortable on empty air.

He winked at Adora Belle. "Perhaps you looked elsewhere? One story tells us that upon the death of all the humans, the golems walked into the sea . . . ?" The question mark hung in the air like the hook it was.

"What an interesting story," said Adora Belle, poker-faced.

Flead smiled. "I will find the sense of this message. Of course you will come and see me again tomorrow? ⅄ᒪᕋ Ɛⴼⴼⴼ ⅂⧸ⴼƐⴼ⅂⧸⅂ Ⴟ⅂ⴼƐⴼⴸⴸⴸ⅂!"

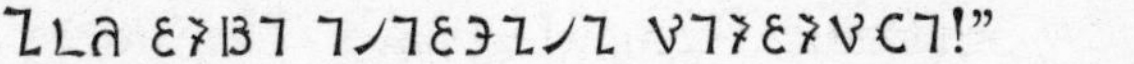

Moist didn't like the sound of that, whatever it was. It didn't help that Adora Belle was smiling.

Flead added: "ᕋⴹ⅂ Ɜᒪ ⅄ᒪᕋ �601Ɛ1 ⴼⴸᒪᕋ⧸ ᖼᒪⴺ1Ɛ1? ⧸ⴹ11 ⴹⴼᕋ1 Ɜᒪ Ⴖⴼ11⅄ᒪⴼⴼ⧸1 ႶⴼƐ⧸1!"

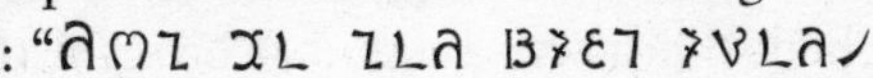

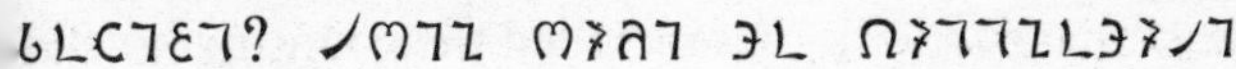

"Have you, *sir*?" said Adora Belle, laughing.

"No, but I have an excellent memory!"

Moist frowned. He liked it better when she was giving the old devil the cold shoulder.

"Can we go now?" he said.

❄ ❄ ❄

PROBATIONARY TRAINEE JUNIOR Clerk Hammersmith Coot watched Miss Drapes looming ever closer, with slightly less apprehension than his older colleagues did, and they knew this was because the poor kid had not been there long enough to know the meaning of what was about to happen.

The senior clerk put the paper on his desk with some force. The total had been ringed around in green ink which was still wet. "Mr. Bent," she said, with a tincture of satisfaction, "says you must do this again. *Properly.*"

And because Hammersmith was a well-brought-up young man and because this was only his first week in the bank, he said, "Yes, Miss Drapes," took the paper neatly, and set to work.

There were many different stories told about what happened next. In years to come, clerks measured their banking experience in how close they were when the Thing Happened. There were disagreements on what was actually said. Certainly there was no violence, no matter what some of the stories implied. But it was a day that brought the world, or at least that part of it that included the counting house, to its knees.

Everyone agreed that Hammersmith spent some time working on the percentages. They say he produced a notebook—a personal notebook, which was an offense in itself—and did some work in it. Then,

after, some say fifteen minutes, some say nearly half
an hour, he walked back to the desk of Miss Drapes,
and declared, "I'm sorry, Miss Drapes, but I can't
find where the mistake is. I have checked my work-
ings and believe my total is correct."

His voice was not loud, but the room went silent.
In fact, it was more than silent. The sheer straining
of hundreds of ears meant spiders spinning cobwebs
near the ceiling wobbled in the aural suction. He
was sent back to his desk to "do it again and don't
waste people's time," and after a further ten minutes, some say fifteen, Miss Drapes went to his desk
and looked over his shoulder.

Most people agree that after half a minute or so
she picked up the paper, pulled a pencil from the
tight bun on the back of her head, ordered the
young man out of his seat, sat down, and spent
some time staring at the numbers. She got up. She
went to the desk of another senior clerk. Together
they pored over the piece of paper. A third clerk
was summoned. He copied out the offending columns, worked on them for a while, and looked up,
his face gray. No one needed to say it aloud. By now
all work had stopped but Mr. Bent, up on the high
stool, was still engrossed in the numbers before
him and, significantly, he was muttering under his
breath.

People sensed it in the air.

Mr. Bent had Made a Mistake.

The most senior clerks conferred hastily in a
corner. There was no higher authority that they

could appeal to. Mr. Bent *was* the higher authority, second only to the inexorable Lord of Mathematics. In the end it was left to the luckless Miss Drapes, who so recently had been the agent of Mr. Bent's displeasure, to write on the document: "I am sorry, Mr. Bent, I believe the young man is right." She slipped this at the bottom of a number of working sheets that she was delivering to the in tray, dropped it in as the tray rumbled past, and then the sound of her little boots echoed as she rushed, weeping, the length of the hall to the ladies' restroom, where she had hysterics.

The remaining members of the staff looked around warily, like ancient monsters who can see a second sun getting bigger in the sky but have absolutely no idea what they should do about it. Mr. Bent was a fast man with an in tray and by the look of it there were about two minutes or less before he was confronted with the message. Suddenly and all at once, they fled for the exits.

"AND HOW WAS that for you?" said Moist, stepping out into the sunlight.

"Do I detect a note of peevishness?" said Adora Belle.

"Well, my plans for today did not include dropping in to chat with a three-hundred-year-old letch."

"I think you mean lych, and anyway he was a ghost, not a corpse."

"He was letching!"

"All in his mind," said Adora Belle. "Your mind, too."

"Normally you go crazy if people try to patronize you!"

"True. But most people aren't able to translate a language so old that even golems can hardly understand a tenth of it. Get a talent like that and it could be *you* getting the girls when you are three centuries dead."

"You were just flirting to get what you wanted?"

Adora Belle stopped dead in the middle of the square to confront him. "And? *You* flirt with people all the time. You flirt with the whole world! That's what makes you *interesting*, because you're more like a musician than a thief. You want to play the world, especially the fiddly bits. And now I'm going home for a bath. I got off the coach this morning, remember?"

"This morning," said Moist, "I found that one of my staff had swapped the mind of another of my staff with that of a turnip."

"Was that good?" said Adora Belle.

"I'm not sure. In fact I'd better go and check. Look, we've both had a busy day. I'll send a cab at half past seven, all right?"

CRIBBINS WAS ENJOYING himself. He'd never been much for reading, up until now. Oh, he *could* read, and write too, in a nice cursive script that people thought was quite distinguished. And he'd always liked the *Times* for its clear, readable font, and had, with the aid of some scissors and a pot of paste, often accepted its assistance in producing those missives that attract attention not by fine writing but by having the messages created in cut-out words and letters and even whole phrases, if you were lucky. Reading for pleasure had passed him by, however. But he was reading now, oh yes, and it was extremely pleasurable, goodness yes! It was amazing what you could find if you knew what you were looking for! And now, all his Hogswatches were about to come at once—

"A cup of tea, Reverend?" said a voice by his side. It was the plump lady in charge of the *Times*' back issues department, who had taken to him as soon as he doffed his hat to her. She had the slightly wistful, slightly hungry look that so many women of a certain age wore when they'd decided to trust in gods because of the absolute impossibility of continuing to trust in men.

"Why, thank you, shister," he said, beaming. "And is it not written: 'The eleemosynary cup is more worthy than the thrown hen'?"

Then he noticed the discreet little silver ladle pinned to her bosom, and that her earrings were two tiny spatulas. The holy symbols of Anoia, yes. He'd just been reading about Anoia in the religious pages. All the rage these days, thanks to the help of young Spangler. Started out way down the ladder as the Goddess Of Things That Get Stuck In Drawers, but the talk in the religious pages was that she was being tipped for Goddess Of Lost Causes, a very profitable area, very profitable *indeed* for a man with a flexible approach but, and he sighed inwardly, it was not such a good idea to do business when the god in question was active, in case Anoia got angry and found a new use for a spatula. Besides, he'd soon be able to put all that behind him. What a clever lad young Spangler had turned out to be! Smarmy little devil! This wasn't going to be over quick, oh no. This was going to be a pension for life. And it'd be a long, long life, or else—

"Is there anything more I can get you, Reverend?" said the woman anxiously.

"My cup runneth over, shister," said Cribbins.

The woman's anxious expression intensified. "Oh, I'm sorry, I hope it hasn't gone on the—"

Cribbins carefully put his hand over the cup. "I meant that I am more than shatisfied," he said, and he was. It was a bloody miracle, that's what it was. If Om was going to hand them out like this, he might even start believing in Him.

And it got better the more you thought about it, Cribbins told himself, as the woman hurried away. How'd the kid done it? There must have been cronies. The hangman, for one, a couple of jailers . . .

Reflectively, he removed his false teeth with a twang, swilled them gently in the tea, patted them dry with his handkerchief and wrestled them back into his mouth a few seconds before footsteps told him the woman was returning. She was positively vibrating with genteel courage.

"Excuse me, Reverend, but can I ask a favor?" she said, going pink.

"Og orsk . . . ugger! usht arg ogent—" Cribbins turned his back, and against a chorus of snaps and twoings dragged the wretched dentures around the right way. Damned things! Why he had ever bothered to lever them out of the old man's mouth, he'd never know.

"I do beg your pardon, shister, a little dental mishap there . . ." he murmured, turning back and dabbing at his mouth. "Pray continue."

"It's funny you should say that, Reverend," said the woman, her eyes bright with nervousness, "because I belong to a small group of ladies who run, well, a god-of-the-month club. Er . . . that is, we pick a god and believe in him . . . or her, obviously, or it, although we draw the line at the ones with teeth and too many legs, er, and foreign ones, of course, and then we pray to them for a month and then we sit down and discuss it. Well, there's so many, aren't there. Thousands! We've never really considered Om, though, but if you would care to give us a little talk next Tuesday I'm sure we'll be happy to give him a jolly good try!"

Springs pinged as Cribbins gave her a huge smile.

"What is your name, shister?" he asked.

"Berenice," she said. "Berenice, er, Houser."

Ah, no longer using the bastard's name, very wise, thought Cribbins. "What a wonderful idea, Berenish," he said. "I would consider it a pleshure!"

She beamed.

"There wouldn't be any biscuits, would there, Berenish?" Cribbins added.

Ms. Houser blushed. "I believe I have some chocolate ones somewhere," she volunteered, as if letting him in on a big secret.

"May Anoia rattle your drawers, shister," said Cribbins to her retreating back.

Wonderful, he thought, as she bustled off, blushing and happy. He tucked his notebook into his jacket and sat back and listened to the ticking of the clock on the wall and the gentle snores of the beggars, who were the normal habitués of this office on a hot afternoon. All was peaceful, settled, organized, just like life ought to be.

It was going to be the gravy boat for him from this day forward.

If he was very, very careful.

M OIST RAN DOWN the lengths of the vaults toward the brilliant light at the far end. There was a tableau of peacefulness. Hubert was standing in front of the Glooper, occasionally tapping a pipe. Igor was blowing some curious glass creation over his little forge, and Mr. Clamp, formerly known as Owlswick Jenkins, was sitting at his desk with a faraway look on his face.

Moist sensed the doom ahead. Something was wrong. It might not be even a particular thing, it was just a sheer platonic wrongness—and he did not like Mr. Clamp's expression at all.

Nevertheless, the human brain, which survives by hoping from one second to another, will always endeavor to put off the moment of truth. Moist approached the desk, rubbing his hands together. "How's it going then, Owl— I mean Mr. Clamp," he said. "Finished it yet, have we?"

"Oh, yes," said Clamp, a strange, mirthless little smile on his face. "Here it is."

On the desk in front of him was the other side of the first proper dollar bill ever to be designed. Moist had seen pictures quite like it, but they had been when he was four years old, in nursery school. The face of what was presumably meant to be Lord Vetinari had two dots for eyes and a broad grin. The panorama of the vibrant city of Ankh-Morpork appeared to consist of a lot of square houses, with a window, all square, in each corner and a door in the middle.

"I think it's one of the best things I have ever done," said Clamp.

Moist patted him convivially on the shoulder and then marched toward Igor, who was already looking defensive.

"What have you done to that man?" said Moist.

"I have made him a well-balanthed perthonality, no longer bethet with anxthietieth, fearth, and the demonth of paranoia," said Igor.

Moist glanced at Igor's workbench, a brave thing to do by any standards. On it was a jar with something indistinct floating in it. Moist looked closer, another minor act of heroism when you were in an Igor-rich environment.

It was not a happy turnip. It was blotchy. It was bouncing gently from one side of the jar to another, occasionally turning over. "I see," said Moist. "But it would appear, regrettably, that by giving our friend the relaxed and hopeful attitude toward life of, not to put too fine a point on it, a turnip, you have also given him the artistic abilities of, and I have no hesitation in using the term again, a turnip."

"But he ith much happier in himthelf," said Igor.

"Granted, but how much of himself is, and I really don't wish to keep repeating myself here, of a root-vegetable-like nature?"

Igor considered this for some time. "Ath a medical man, thir," he said, "I mutht conthider what ith betht for the pathient. At the moment he ith happy and content and hath no careth in the world. Why would he give up all thith for a mere fathility with a penthil?"

Moist was aware of an insistent *bonk-bonk*. It was the turnip banging itself against the side of the jar. "That is an interesting and philosophical point," he said, once again looking at Clamp's happy yet somewhat unfocused expression. "But it seems to me that all those nasty little details were what made him, well, him." The frantic banging of the vegetable grew louder. Igor and Moist stared from the jar to the eerily smiling man.

"Igor, I'm not sure you know what makes people tick."

Igor gave an avuncular little chuckle. "Oh, believe *me*, thur—"

"Igor?" said Moist.

"Yeth, marthter," said Igor gloomily.

"Go and fetch the damn wires again, will you."

"Yeth, marthter."

❊   ❊   ❊

Moist got back upstairs again to find himself in the middle of a panic. A tearful Miss Drapes spotted him and click-clicked over, at speed.

"It's Mr. Bent, sir. He just rushed out, yelling! We can't find him anywhere!"

"Why are you looking?" said Moist, and then realized he'd said it aloud. "I meant, what is the reason for you looking?"

The story unfolded. As Miss Drapes talked, Moist got the impression that all the other listeners were getting the point and he wasn't.

"So, okay, he made a mistake," he said. "No harm done, is there? It's all been sorted out, right? A bit embarrassing, I dare say . . ." But, he reminded himself, an error is worse than a sin, isn't it.

But that's plain daft, his sensible self pointed out. He could have said something like, "You see? Even I can make a mistake through a moment's inattention! We must be forever vigilant!" Or he could have said, "I did this on purpose to test you!" Even schoolteachers know *that* one. I can think of half a dozen ways to wriggle out of something like that. But then I'm a wriggler. I don't think he's ever wriggled in his life.

"I hope he hasn't done something . . . silly," said Miss Drapes, fishing a crumpled handkerchief out of a sleeve.

Something . . . silly, thought Moist. That's the phrase people used when they were thinking about someone jumping into the river or taking the entire contents of the medicine box in one go. Silly things like that.

"I've never met a less silly man," he said.

"Well, er . . . we've always wondered about him, to be honest," said a clerk. "I mean, he's in at dawn and one of the cleaners told me he's often in here late at night— What? What? That hurt!"

Miss Drapes, who had nudged him hard, now whispered urgently in his ear. The man deflated and looked awkwardly at Moist.

"Sorry, sir, I spoke out of turn," he mumbled.

"Mr. Bent is a good man, Mr. Lipwig," said Miss Drapes. "He drives himself hard."

"Drives all of you hard, it seems to me," said Moist.

This attempt at solidarity with the laboring masses didn't seem to hit the mark.

"If you can't stand the heat, get off the pot, that's what I say," said a senior clerk, and there was a general murmur of agreement.

"Er, I think you get out of the kitchen," said Moist. "'Get off the pot' is the alternative when—"

"Half the chief cashiers in the Plains have worked in this room," said Miss Drapes. "And quite a few managers, now. And Miss Lee, who's deputy manager of Apsly's Commercial Bank in Sto Lat, she got the job because of the letter Mr. Bent wrote. *Bent-trained*, you see. That counts for a lot. If you've got a reference from Mr. Bent, you can walk into any bank and get a job with a snap of your fingers."

"And if you stay, the pay here is better than anywhere," a clerk put in. "He told the Board, if they want the best, they'd have to pay for it!"

"Oh, he's demanding," said another clerk, "but I hear they're all working for a human resources manager at Pipeworth's Bank now, and if it comes to that I'll take Mr. Bent any day of the week. At least he thinks I'm a person. I was hearing where she was timing how long people spent in the privy!"

"They call it time-and-motion study," said Moist. "Look, I expect Mr. Bent just wants to be alone for a while. Who was he yelling at, the lad who'd made a mistake? . . . Or didn't make it, I mean."

"That was young Hammersmith," said Miss Drapes. "We sent him home because he was in a bit of a state. And no, he wasn't really shouting at him. He wasn't really shouting *at* anybody. He was—" she paused, searching for a word.

"Gibbering," said the clerk who had spoken out of turn, giving the turn another twist, "and you don't all have to look at me like that. You all *heard* him. And he looked as though he'd seen a ghost."

Clerks were wandering back into the counting house in ones and twos. They'd searched everywhere, was the general agreement, and there was strong support for the theory that he'd gone out through the Mint, it being rather busy in there with all the work still going on. Moist doubted it. The bank was old, and old buildings have all sorts of crannies, and Mr. Bent had been here for—

"How long has he been here?" he wondered aloud.

The general consensus was "since the mind of man can remember" but Miss Drapes, who seemed for some reason to have made herself well informed on the subject of Mavolio Bent, volunteered that it was thirty-nine years and he got a job when he was thirteen by sitting on the steps all night until the chairman came to work and impressing him with his command of numbers. He went from messenger boy to chief cashier in twenty years.

"Speedy!" said Moist.

"Never had a day off for illness, either," Miss Drapes concluded.

"Well. Perhaps he's entitled to some now," said Moist. "Do you know where he lives, Miss Drapes?"

"Mrs. Cake's boardinghouse."

"Really? That's a bit"—Moist stopped and chose from a number of options—"low rent, isn't it?"

"He says that as a bachelor it meets his needs," said Miss Drapes, and avoided Moist's gaze.

Moist could feel the day slipping away from him. But they were all staring at him. There was only one thing he could say if he was to maintain his image.

"Then I think I ought to see if he's gone there," said Moist. Their faces broke into smiles of relief. He added: "But I think that one of you should come with me. After all, you know him." *It looks as though I don't,* he thought.

"I'll fetch my coat," said Miss Drapes. The only reason that her words came out at the speed of sound was that she couldn't make them go any faster.

CHAPTER 8

As below, so above ❊ *No pain without gain*
❊ *A mind for puzzles* ❊ *Mr. Bent's sad past*
❊ *Something in the wardrobe* ❊ *Wonderful money*
❊ *Thoughts on madness, by Igor* ❊ *A pot thickens*

HUBERT TAPPED THOUGHTFULLY on one of the Glooper's tubes.

"Igor?" he said.

"Yeth, marthter?" said Igor, behind him.

Hubert jumped.

"I thought you were over by your lightning cells!" he managed.

"I wath, thur, but I am here now. What wath it you wanted?"

"You've wired up all the valves, Igor. I can't make any changes!"

"Yeth, thur," said Igor calmly. "There would be amathingly dire conthequentheth, thur."

"But I want to change some parameters, Igor," said Hubert, absentmindedly taking a rain hat off the peg.

"I am afraid there ith a problem, thur. You athked me to make the Glooper ath accurate ath poththible."

"Well, of course. Accuracy is vital."

"It ith . . . extremely accurate, thur," said Igor, looking uncomfortable. "Poththibly *too* accurate, thur."

This "poththibly" caused Hubert to grope for an umbrella.

"How can anything be too accurate?"

Igor looked around. Suddenly, he was on edge. "Would you mind if I wind down on the lisp a little, sir?"

"Can you *do* that?"

"Oh yeth . . . or, indeed, yes, sir. But it's a clan thing, you see. It's expected, like the stitcheth. But I think you will find the explanation hard enough to understand as it is."

"Well, er, thank you. Go ahead, please."

It was quite a long explanation. Hubert listened with care, his mouth open. The term "cargo cult" whirled past, and was followed by a short dissertation on the hypothesis that all water, everywhere, knows where all the other water is, some interesting facts about hyphenated silicon and what happens to it in the presence of cheese, the benefits and hazards of morphic resonation in areas of high background magic, the truth about identical twins, and the fact that if the fundamental occult maxim "as above, so below" was true, then so was "as below, so above" . . .

The silence that followed was broken only by the tinkle of water in the Glooper, and the sound of the former Owlswick's pencil as he worked away with demon-haunted skill.

"Do you mind going back to lisping, please?" said Hubert. "I don't know why, it just sounds better that way."

"Very good, thur."

"All right. Now, are you really saying that I can now *change the economic life of the city* by adjusting the Glooper? It's like a witch's wax doll and I've got all the pins?"

"That ith correct, thur. A very nice analogy."

Hubert stared at the crystal masterpiece. The light in the undercroft was changing all the time as the economic life of the city pumped itself around the tubes, some of them no thicker than a hair.

"It's an economic model, in fact, which is the real thing?"

"They are identical, thur."

"So with one hammer blow I could throw the city into an irrevocable economic crash?"

"Yeth, thur. Do you want me to fetch a hammer?"

Hubert stared up at the rushing, trickling, foaming thing that was the Glooper and his eyes bulged. He started to giggle but it grew very quickly into a laugh.

"Hahah! Ahahahah!!! AHAHAHAHA!!! . . . can you get me a glass of water, please? . . .

HAHAHAHA!!! Hahahahahah!! . . . HAHA
HAHA!!!—"

The laughter stopped abruptly.

"That can't be right, Igor."

"Really, thur?"

"Yes indeed! Look at our old friend Flask 244a!
Can you see it? It's empty!"

"Indeed, thur?"

"Indeed *indeed*," said Hubert. "Flask 244a represents the gold in our very own vaults, Igor. And
ten tons of gold just don't get up and walk away!
Eh? HAHAHAHA!!! Could you get me that glass
of water I asked for? Hahahah ahah!! . . . HAHA
HAHA!!!—"

A SMILE PLAYED around Cosmo's lips, which
was a dangerous playground for anything as
innocent as a smile.

"All of them?" he said.

"Well, all the counting-house clerks," said Heretofore. "They just ran out into the street. Some of
them were in tears."

"A panic, in fact," murmured Cosmo. He looked
at the picture of Vetinari opposite his desk and was
sure it winked at him.

"Apparently it was some problem with the chief
cashier, sir."

"Mr. Bent?"

"Apparently he made a mistake, sir. They said he

was muttering to himself and then just ran out of the room. They said that some of the staff had gone back in to search for him."

"Mavolio Bent made a mistake? I think not," said Cosmo.

"They say he ran off, sir."

Cosmo very nearly raised an eyebrow without mechanical aid. It was that close.

"Ran off? Was he carrying any large and heavy bags? They usually do."

"I believe he wasn't, sir," said Heretofore.

"That would have been . . . helpful."

Cosmo leaned back in his chair, pulled off the black glove for the third time today, and held out his hand at arm's length. The ring did look impressive, especially against the pale blue of his finger.

"Have you ever seen a run on a bank, Drumknott?" he said. "Have you ever seen the crowds fighting for their money?"

"No, sir," said Heretofore, who was beginning to worry again. The tight boots had been, well, funny, but surely a finger shouldn't look that color?

"It's a dreadful sight. It's like watching a beached whale being eaten alive by crabs," said Cosmo, turning his hand so that the light showed up the shadowy V. "It may squirm in its agony, but there can be only one outcome. It is a terrible thing, if done properly."

This *is* how Vetinari thinks, his soul exulted. Plans can break down. You cannot plan the future. Only presumptuous fools plan. The wise man *steers*.

"As a director of the bank and, of course, a concerned citizen," he said dreamily, "I shall now write a letter to the *Times*."

"Yes, sir, of course," said Heretofore, "and shall I send for a jeweler, sir? I understand they have some fine little snips that—"

"No pain without gain, Drumknott. It sharpens my thinking." The glove went back on.

"Er . . ." and then Heretofore gave up. He'd tried his best, but Cosmo was bent on his own destruction, and all a sensible man could do was to make as much money as possible and then stay alive to spend it.

"I've had another stroke of luck, sir," he ventured. He'd have liked more time, but it was clear that time was getting short.

"Indeed? What is this?"

"That project I have been working on . . ."

"Very expensively? Yes?"

"I believe I can get you Vetinari's stick, sir."

"You mean his *sword stick*?"

"Yes, sir. As far as I know, the blade has never been drawn in anger."

"I understood it was always close to him."

"I didn't say it would be easy, sir. Or cheap. But after much, much work I now see a clear way," said Heretofore.

"They say the steel of the blade was taken from the iron in the blood of a thousand men . . ."

"So I have heard, sir."

"Have *you* seen it?"

"Very briefly, sir."

For the first time in his career, Heretofore found himself feeling sorry for Cosmo. There was a kind of yearning in the man's voice. He didn't want to usurp Vetinari. There were plenty of people in the city who wanted to usurp Vetinari. But Cosmo wanted to *be* Vetinari.

"What was it like?" The voice was pleading. Poison from the sickening finger must have got to his brain, thought Heretofore. But his mind is pretty poisonous to begin with. Perhaps they will be friends.

"Er . . . well, the handle and scabbard are just like yours, sir, but a little worn. The blade, though, is gray and looks—"

"Gray?"

"Yes, sir. It looks aged and slightly pitted. But here and there, when the light catches it, there are little red and gold flecks. I have to say that it looks ominous."

"The flecks of light would be the blood, of course," said Cosmo thoughtfully, "or, possibly, yes, very possibly the trapped souls of those who died to make the dreadful blade."

"I had not thought of that, sir," said Heretofore, who had spent two nights with a new blade, some hematite, a brass brush, and some chemicals to produce a weapon that looked as though it'd spring for your throat of its own accord.

"You could get it tonight?"

"I think so, sir. It will be dangerous, of course."

"And require yet more expense, I imagine," said

Cosmo, with rather more insight than Heretofore
would have expected in his current state.

"There are so many bribes, sir. He will not be
happy when he finds out, and I daren't risk the time
it would take to make an exact replacement."

"Yes. I see."

Cosmo pulled off the black glove again and
looked at his hand. There seemed to be some greenish tint to his finger now, and he wondered if there
was some copper in the ring's alloy. But the pink,
almost red streaks moving up his arm looked very
healthy.

"Yes. Get the stick," he murmured, turning
his hand to catch the light from the lamps. Odd,
though, he couldn't feel any heat on the finger, but
that didn't matter.

He could see the future so clearly. The shoes,
the cap, the ring, the stick . . . Surely, as he filled
the occult space occupied by Vetinari, the wretched
man would feel himself getting weaker and more
confused, and he'd get things wrong and make mistakes . . . "See to it, Drumknott," he said.

Lord Havelock Vetinari pinched the
bridge of his nose. It had been a long day and
was clearly going to be a long evening.

"I think I need a moment to relax. Let's get it
over with," he said.

Drumknott walked over to the long table, which
at this time of day held copies of several editions of

the *Times*, his lordship being keen on keeping track of what people thought was going on.

Vetinari sighed. People told him things all the time. Lots of people had been telling him things in the last hour. They told him things for all sorts of reasons: to gain some credit; to gain some money; for a favor quid pro quo; out of malice, mischief, or, suspiciously, out of a professed regard for the public good. What it amounted to was no information but a huge, Argus-eyed ball of little, wiggling factoids, out of which some information could, with care, be teased.

His secretary laid before him the paper, carefully folded to the correct page and place, which was occupied by a square filled with a lot of smaller squares, some of them containing numbers.

"Today's 'Jikan no Muda,' sir," he said. Vetinari glanced at it for a few seconds, and then handed it back to him.

The Patrician shut his eyes, drummed his fingers on the desktop for a moment. "Hmm . . . nine six three one seven four"—Drumknott scribbled hastily as the numbers streamed, and Vetinari eventually concluded—"eight four seven three. And I'm sure they used that one last month. On a Monday, I believe."

"Seventeen seconds, sir," said Drumknott, his pencil still catching up.

"Well, it has been a tiring day," said Vetinari. "And what is the point? Numbers are easy to outwit. They can't think back. The people who devise the crosswords, now they are indeed devious. Who would know that 'pysdxes' are ancient Ephebian carved-bone needle holders?"

"Well, you, sir, of course," said Drumknott, carefully stacking the files, "and the curator of Ephebian antiquities at the Royal Art Museum, 'Puzzler' of the *Times*, and Miss Grace Speaker, who runs the pet shop in Pellicool Steps."

"We should keep an eye on that pet shop, Drumknott. A woman with a mind like that content to dispense dog food? I think not."

"Indeed, sir. I shall make a note."

"I'm pleased to hear that your new boots have ceased squeaking, by the way."

"Thank you, sir. They have broken in nicely."

Vetinari stared pensively at the day's files.

"Mr. Bent, Mr. Bent, Mr. Bent," he said. "The mysterious Mr. Bent. Without him, the Royal Bank would be in far more trouble than it has been. And now that it *is* without him, it will fall over. It revolves around him. It beats to his pulse. Old Lavish was frightened of him, I'm sure. He said he thought that Bent was a . . ." he paused.

"Sir?" said Drumknott.

"Let us just accept the fact that he has, in every way, proved to be a model citizen," said Vetinari. "The past is a dangerous country, is it not?"

"There is no file on him, sir."

"He has never drawn attention to himself. All I know for sure is that he arrived here as a child, on a cart owned by some traveling accountants . . ."

❊ ❊ ❊

"What, like tinkers and fortune-tellers?" said Moist, as the cab rocked its way through streets that grew narrower and darker.

"I suppose you could say so," said Miss Drapes with a hint of disapproval. "They do big, you know, circuits all the way up to the mountains, doing the books for little businesses, helping people with their taxes, that sort of thing." She cleared her throat. "Whole families of them. It must be a wonderful life."

"Every day a new ledger," said Moist, nodding gravely, "and by night they drink beer, and happy, laughing accountants dance the Double-Entry Polka to the sound of accordions . . ."

"Do they?" said Miss Drapes nervously.

"I don't know. It would be nice to think so," said Moist. "Well, that explains something, at least. He was obviously ambitious. All he could hope for on the road was being allowed to steer the horse, I suppose."

"He was thirteen," said Miss Drapes, and she blew her nose loudly. "It's so sad." She turned a tearful face toward Moist.

"There's something *dreadful* in his past, Mr. Lipstick. They say one day some men came to the bank and asked—"

"This is it, Mrs. Cake's," said the cabman, pulling up sharply, "an' that'll be eleven pence and don't ask me to hang about 'cos they'll have the 'orse up on bricks and its shoes off in a wink."

The door of the boardinghouse was opened by

the hairiest woman Moist had ever seen, but in the area of Elm Street you learned to discount this sort of thing. Mrs. Cake was famously accommodating to the city's newly arrived undead, giving them a safe and understanding haven until they could get on their feet, however many they had.

"Mrs. Cake?" he said.

"Mother's at church," said the woman. "She said to expect you, Mr. Lipwig."

"You have a Mr. Bent staying here, I believe?"

"The banker? Room seven on the second floor. But I don't think he's in. He's not in trouble, is he?"

Moist explained the situation, aware all the while of doors opening a fraction in the shadows beyond the woman. The air was sharp with the smell of disinfectant; Mrs. Cake believed that cleanliness was more to be trusted than godliness and, besides, without that sharp note of pine half the clientele would be driven mad by the smell of the other half.

And in the middle of all this was the silent, featureless room of Mr. Bent, chief cashier. The woman, who volunteered that her name was Ludmilla, let them in, very reluctantly, with a master key.

"He's always been a good guest," she said. "Never a moment's trouble."

One glance took in everything: the narrow room, the narrow bed, the clothes hanging neatly around the walls, the tiny jug-and-basin set, the incongruously large wardrobe. Lives collect clutter, but Mr. Bent's did not. Unless, of course, it was all in the wardrobe.

"Most of your long-term guests are unde—"

"—differently alive," said Ludmilla sharply.

"Yes, of course, so I'm wondering why . . . Mr. Bent would stay here."

"Mr. Lipwick, what *are* you suggesting?" said Miss Drapes.

"You must admit it's rather unexpected," said Moist. And, because she was already distraught enough, he didn't add: *I don't have to suggest anything. It suggests itself. Tall. Dark. Gets in before dawn, leaves after dark. Mr. Fusspot growls at him. Compulsive counter. Obsessive over detail. Gives you a gentle attack of the creeps which makes you feel mildly ashamed. Sleeps on a long, thin bed. Stays at Mrs. Cake's, where the vampires hang up. It's not very hard to connect the dots.*

"This isn't about the man who was here the other night, is it?" said Ludmilla.

"What man would that be?"

"Didn't give a name. Just said he was a friend. All in black, had a black cane with a silver skull on it. Nasty piece of work, Mum said. Mind you," Ludmilla added, "she says that about nearly everyone. He had a black coach."

"Not Lord Vetinari, surely."

"Oh, no, Mum's all for him, except she thinks he ought to hang more people. No, this one was pretty stout, Mum said."

"Oh, really?" said Moist. "Well, thank you, ma'am. Well perhaps we should be going. By the way, do you by any chance have a key to that wardrobe?"

"No key. He put a new lock on it years ago, but Mum didn't complain because he's never any trouble. It's one of those magic ones they sell at the university," Ludmilla went on, as Moist examined the lock. The trouble with the wretched magical ones was that just about *anything* could be a key, from a word to a touch.

"It's rather strange that he hangs all his clothes on the walls, isn't it?" he said, straightening up.

Ludmilla looked disapproving. "We don't use the word *strange* in this household."

"Differently normal?" Moist suggested.

"That'll do." There was a warning glint in Ludmilla's eye. "Who can say who is truly normal in this world?"

Well, being someone whose fingernails don't visibly extend when they're annoyed would be a definite candidate, thought Moist. "Well, we should get back to the bank," he said. "If Mr. Bent turns up, do tell him that people are looking for him."

"And care about him," said Miss Drapes quickly, and then put a hand over her mouth and blushed.

I just want to make money, thought Moist, as he led the trembling Miss Drapes back to the area where cabs dared to go. *I thought life in banking was profitable boredom punctuated by big cigars. Instead, it has turned out differently normal. The only really sane person in there is Igor, and possibly the turnip. And I'm not sure about the turnip.*

He dropped the snuffling Miss Drapes off at her lodgings in Welcome Soap, with a promise to let her know when the errant Mr. Bent broke cover, and took the cab onward to the bank. The night guards had already arrived, but quite a few clerks were still hanging around, apparently unable to come to terms with the new reality. Mr. Bent had been a fixture, like the pillars.

Cosmo had been round to see him. It wouldn't have been a social call.

What *had* it been? A threat? Well, no one liked being beaten up. But perhaps it was more sophisticated. Perhaps it was *we'll tell people you are a vampire*. To which a sensible person would reply: Stick it where the sun shineth not. That would have been a threat twenty years ago, but today? There were plenty of vampires in the city, neurotic as hell, wearing the black ribbon to show they'd signed the pledge, and in general getting on with, for want of a better word, their lives. Mostly, people just accepted it. Day after day went past with no trouble, and so the situation became regarded as normal. Differently normal, but still normal.

Okay, Mr. Bent had kept quiet about his past, but that was hardly a pitchforking matter. He'd been sitting in a bank for forty years doing sums, for heavens' sake.

But perhaps he didn't see it that way. You measured common sense with a ruler, other people measured it with a potato.

He didn't hear Gladys approach. He just became aware that she was standing behind him.

"I Have Been Very Worried About You, Mr. Lipwig," she rumbled.

"Thank you, Gladys," he said cautiously.

"I Will Make You A Sandwich. You Like My Sandwiches."

"That would be kind of you, Gladys, but Miss Dearheart will be joining me shortly for dinner upstairs."

The glow in the golem's eyes faded for a moment and then grew brighter.

"Miss Dearheart."

"Yes, she was here this morning."

"A Lady."

"She's my fiancée, Gladys. She will be here quite a lot, I expect."

"Fiancée," said Gladys. "Ah, Yes. I Am Reading *Twenty Tips To Make Your Wedding Go With A Swing.*"

Gladys's eyes dimmed. She turned around and plodded toward the stairs.

Moist felt like a heel. Of course, he *was* a heel. But that didn't make feeling like one feel any better. On the other hand, she—damn, he . . . it . . . Gladys was the fault of misplaced female solidarity. What could he hope to achieve against that? Adora Belle would have to do something about it.

He was aware that one of the senior clerks was hovering politely.

"Yes?" he said. "Can I help you?"

"What do you want us to do, sir?"

"What's your name?"

"Spittle, sir. Robert Spittle."

"Why are you asking me, Bob?"

"Because the chairman goes *woof*, sir. Safes need locking up. So does the ledger room. Mr. Bent had all the keys. It's Robert, sir, if you don't mind."

"Are there any spare keys?"

"There might be in the chairman's office, sir," said Spittle.

"Look . . . Robert, I want you to go home and get a good night's sleep, okay? And I'll find the keys and turn every lock I can find. I'm sure Mr. Bent will be with us tomorrow, but if he's not, I'll call a meeting of the senior clerks. I mean, hah, you must know how it all works!"

"Well, yes. Of course. Only . . . well . . . but . . ." The clerk's voice faded into silence.

But there's no Mr. Bent, thought Moist. *And he delegated with the same ease that oysters tango. What the hell are we going to do?*

"There's people here? So much for banker's hours," said a voice from the doorway. "In trouble again I hear."

It was Adora Belle, and of course she meant "Hello! It's good to see you."

"You look stunning," said Moist.

"Yes, I know," said Adora Belle. "What's happening? The cabbie told me all the staff had walked out of your bank."

Later Moist thought: That was when it all went wrong. You have to leap on the stallion of rumor before he's out of the yard, so that you might be able to pull on the reins. You should have thought: What did it look like, with staff running out of the bank? You should have run to the *Times* office. You should have got in the saddle and turned it right around, there and then.

But Adora Belle did look stunning. Besides, all that had happened was that a member of staff had a funny turn and left the building. What could anyone make of that?

And the answer, of course, was: Anything they wanted to.

He was aware of someone else behind him.

"Mr. Lipwig, thur?"

Moist turned. It was even less fun looking at Igor when you'd just been looking at Adora Belle.

"Igor, this is really not the time—" Moist began.

"I know I'm not thupothed to come upthairth, thur, but Mr. Clamp thayth he hath finithed hith drawing. It ith very good."

"What was all that about?" said Adora Belle. "I think I nearly got two of the words."

"Oh, there's a man down in the forni—the cellar, who is designing a dollar note for me. Paper money, in fact."

"Really? I'd love to see that."

"You *would*?"

I T WAS TRULY wonderful. Moist looked at the back and the front of the dollar-note designs. Under Igor's brilliant white lights they looked rich as plum pudding and more complicated than a dwarf contract.

"We're going to make so much money," he said aloud. "Wonderful job, Owls— Mr. Clamp!"

"I'm going to hold on to the Owlswick," said the artist nervously. "It's the Jenkins that matters, after all."

"Well, yes," said Moist, "there must be dozens of Owlswicks around." He looked at Hubert, who was on a stepladder and peering hopelessly at the tubing.

"How's it going, Hubert?" he said. "The money's still rushing around okay, is it?"

"What? Oh, fine. Fine. Fine," said Hubert, almost knocking over the ladder in his haste to get down. He looked at Adora Belle with an expression of uncertain dread.

"This is Adora Belle Dearheart, Hubert," said Moist, in case the man was about to flee. "She is my fiancée. She's a woman," he added, in view of the worried look.

Adora Belle held out her hand and said: "Hello, Hubert."

Hubert stared.

"It's okay to shake hands, Hubert," said Moist carefully. "Hubert's an economist. That's like an alchemist, but less messy."

"So you know how the money moves around, do you, Hubert?" said Adora Belle, shaking an unresisting hand.

At last the notion of speech dawned on Hubert.

"I welded one thousand and ninety-seven joints," he said, "and blew the law of diminishing returns."

"I shouldn't think anyone's ever done that before," said Adora Belle.

Hubert brightened up. This was easy!

"We are not doing anything wrong, you know!" he said.

"I'm sure you aren't," said Adora Belle, trying to pull her hand away.

"It can keep track of every dollar in the city, you know. The possibilities are endless! But, but, but, um, of course we're not upsetting things in any way!"

"I'm very glad to hear it, Hubert," said Adora Belle, tugging harder.

"Of course we are having teething troubles! But everything is being done with immense care! Nothing has been lost because we've left a valve open or anything like that!"

"How intriguing!" said Adora Belle, bracing her left hand on Hubert's shoulder and wrenching the other one free.

"We have to go, Hubert," said Moist. "Keep up the good work, though. I'm very proud of you."

"You *are*?" said Hubert. "Cosmo said I was insane, and wanted Auntie to sell the Glooper for scrap!"

"Typical hidebound, old-fashioned thinking," said Moist. "This is the Century of the Anchovy. The future belongs to men like you, who can tell us how everything works."

"It does?" said Hubert.

"You mark my words," said Moist, ushering Adora Belle firmly toward the distant exit.

When they were gone, Hubert sniffed the palm of his hand and shivered.

"They were nice people, weren't they," he said.

"Yeth, marthter."

Hubert looked up at the glittering, trickling pipes of the Glooper, faithfully mirroring in its ebbing and flowing the tides of money around the city.

Just one blow could rattle the world. It was a terrible responsibility.

Igor joined him. They stood in a silence broken only by the sloshing of commerce.

"What shall I *do*, Igor?" said Hubert.

"In the Old Country we have a thaying," Igor volunteered.

"A what?"

"A thaying. We thay, 'If you don't want the monthter you don't pull the lever.'"

"You don't think I've gone mad, do you, Igor?"

"Many great men have been conthidered mad, Mr. Hubert. Even Dr. Hanth Forvord wath called mad. But I put it to you: could a madman have created a revolutionary living-brain extractor?"

66 I S HUBERT QUITE . . . normal?" said Adora Belle, as they climbed the marble staircase toward dinner.

"By the standards of obsessive men who don't get out into the sunlight?" said Moist. "Pretty normal, I'd say."

"But he acted as if he'd never seen a woman before!"

"He's just not used to things that don't come with a manual," said Moist.

"Hah," said Adora Belle, "why is it only men that get like that?"

Earns a tiny wage working for golems, thought Moist. *Puts up with graffiti and smashed windows because of golems. Camps out in wilderness, argues with powerful men. All for golems.* But he didn't say anything, because he'd read the manual.

They had reached the managerial floor. Adora Belle sniffed.

"Smell that? Isn't that just wonderful?" she said. "Wouldn't it turn a rabbit into a carnivore?"

"Sheep's head," said Moist gloomily.

"Only to make the broth," said Adora Belle. "All the soft wobbly bits get taken out first. Don't worry. You've just been put off by the old joke, that's all."

"What old joke?"

"Oh, come *on*! A boy goes into a butcher's shop and says, 'Mum says can we please have a sheep's head and you're to leave the eyes in 'cos it's got to see us through the week.' You don't get it? It's using *see* in the sense of to last and also in the sense of, well, to see . . ."

"I just think it's a bit unfair to the sheep, that's all."

"Interesting," said Adora Belle. "You eat nice, anonymous lumps of animals but think it's unfair to eat the other bits? You think the head goes off thinking, 'At least he didn't eat *me*?' Strictly speaking, the more we eat of an animal the happier its species should be, since we wouldn't need to kill so many of them."

Moist pushed open the double doors, and the air was full of wrongness again.

There was no Mr. Fusspot. Normally he'd be waiting in his in tray, ready to greet Moist with a big, slobbery welcome. But the tray was empty.

The room seemed larger, too, and this was because it also contained no Gladys.

There was a little blue collar on the floor. The smell of cooking filled the air.

Moist ran down the passage to the kitchen, where the golem was standing solemnly by the stove, watching the rattling lid of a very large pot. Grubby foam slid down and dripped onto the stove.

Gladys turned when she saw Moist.

"I Am Cooking Your Dinner, Mr. Lipwig."

The dark moppets of dread played their paranoid hopscotch across Moist's inner eyeballs.

"Could you just put the ladle down and step away from the pot, please?" said Adora Belle, suddenly beside him.

"I Am Cooking Mr. Lipwig's Dinner," said Gladys, with a touch of defiance. The scummy bubbles, it seemed to Moist, were getting bigger.

"Yes, and it looks as if it's nearly done," said Adora Belle. "So I Would Like To See It, Gladys."

There was silence.

"Gladys?"

In one movement the golem handed her the ladle and stood back, half a ton of living clay moving as lightly and silently as smoke.

Cautiously, Adora Belle lifted the pot's lid and plunged the ladle into the seething mass.

Something scratched at Moist's boot. He looked down into the worried goldfish eyes of Mr. Fusspot.

Then he looked back at what was rising out of the pot, and realized that it was at least thirty seconds since he'd last drawn a breath.

Peggy came bustling in. "Oh, there you are, you naughty boy!" she said, picking up the little dog. "Would you believe it, he got all the way down to the cold room!" She looked around, brushing hair out of her eyes. "Oh, Gladys, I did tell you to move it onto the cool plate when it started to thicken!"

Moist looked at the rising ladle, and in the flood of relief various awkward observations scrambled to be heard.

I've been in this job less than a week. The man I really depend on has run away screaming. I'm going to be exposed as a criminal. That's a sheep's head . . .

And—thank you for the thought, Aimsbury—it's wearing sunglasses.

CHAPTER 9

"I'M AFRAID I have to close the office now, Reverend," the voice of Ms. Houser broke into Cribbins's dreams. "We open up again at nine o'clock tomorrow," it added hopefully.

Cribbins opened his eyes. The warmth and the steady ticking of the clock had lulled him into a wonderful doze.

Ms. Houser was standing there, not gloriously naked and pink as so recently featured in the reverie, but in a plain brown coat and an unsuitable hat with feathers in it.

Suddenly awake, he fumbled urgently in his pocket for his dentures, not trusting them with the custody of his mouth while he slept. He turned his head away in a flurry of unaccustomed embarrassment, as he fought to get them in, and then fought again to get them in and the right way up. They always fought back. In desperation he wrenched them out and banged them sharply on the arm of the chair once or twice to break their spirit before ramming them into his mouth once more.

"Wshg!" said Cribbins, and slapped the side of his face. "Why, thank you, ma'am," he said, dabbing at his mouth with his handkerchief. "I am sorry about that, but I'm a martyr to them, I shwear."

"I didn't like to disturb you," Ms. Houser went on, her horrified expression fading. "I'm sure you needed your sleep."

"Not sleeping, ma'am but contemplating," said Cribbins, standing up. "Contemplating the fall of the unrighteous and the elevation of the godly. Is it not said that the last shall be first and the first shall be last?"

"You know, I've always been a bit worried about that," said Ms. Houser. "I mean, what happens to the people who aren't first but aren't really last, either? You know . . . jogging along, doing their best?" She strolled toward the door in a manner which, quite as subtly as she thought, invited him to accompany her.

"A conundrum indeed, Berenice," said Cribbins, following her. "The holy texts don't mention it, but I have no doubt that . . ." His forehead creased. Cribbins was seldom troubled by religious questions, and this one was pretty difficult. He rose to it like a born theologian. "I have no doubt that they will be found shtill jogging along, but *possibly in the opposite direction*."

"Back toward the last?" she said, looking worried.

"Ah, dear lady, remember that they will by then be the first."

"Oh yes, I hadn't thought of it like that. That's the only way it could work, unless of course the original first would wait for the last to catch up."

"That would be a miracle indeed," said Cribbins, watching her lock the door behind them. The evening air was sharp and unwelcoming after the warmth of the newspaper room, and made the prospect of another night in the flophouse in Monkey Street seem doubly unwelcome. He needed his own miracle right now, and he had a feeling that one was shaping up right here.

"I expect it's very hard for you, Reverend, finding a place to stay," Ms. Houser said. He couldn't make out her expression in the gloom.

"Oh, I have faith, shister," he said. "If Om does not come, He shendsh— Arrg!"

And at a time like this! A spring had slipped! It was a judgment!

But agonizing as it was, it might yet have its blessing. Ms. Houser was bearing down on him with the look of a woman determined to do good at any price.

Oh, it hurt, though; it had snapped right across his tongue.

A voice behind him said, "Excuse me, I couldn't

help noticing . . . are you Mr. Cribbins, by any chance?"

Enraged by the pain in his mouth, Cribbins turned with murder in his heart, but "That's Reverend Cribbins, thank you," said Ms. Houser, and his fists unclenched.

"'Shme," he muttered.

A pale young man in an old-fashioned clerk's robe was staring at him.

"My name is Heretofore," he said, "and if you *are* Cribbins, I know a rich man who wants to meet you. It could be your lucky day."

"Ish zat sho?" muttered Cribbins. "And if zat man ish called Coshmo, I want to meet *him*. It could be hish lucky day, too. Ain't we the lucky ones!"

66 **Y**OU MUST HAVE had a moment of dread," said Moist, as they relaxed in the marble-floored sitting room. At least, Adora Belle relaxed. Moist was searching.

"I don't know what you're talking about," she said, as he opened a cupboard.

"Golems weren't built to be free. They don't know how to handle . . . stuff."

"They'll learn. And she wouldn't have hurt the dog," said Adora Belle, watching him pace the room.

"You weren't sure. I heard the way you were talking to her. 'Put down the ladle and turn around slowly' sort of thing." Moist pulled open a drawer.

"Are you looking for something?"

"Some bank keys. There should be a set of them somewhere around."

Adora Belle joined in. It was that or argue about Gladys. Besides, the suite had a great many drawers and cupboards, and it was something to do while dinner was prepared.

"What is *this* key for?" she asked after a mere few seconds. Moist turned. Adora Belle held up a silvery key on a ring.

"No, there'll be a lot more than that," said Moist. "Where did you find that, anyway?"

She pointed to the big desk. "I just touched the side *here* and— Oh, it didn't do it this time . . ."

It took Moist more than a minute to find the trigger that slid the little drawer out. Shut, it disappeared seamlessly into the grain of the wood.

"It must be for something important," he said, heading for another desk. "Maybe he kept the rest of the keys somewhere else. Just try it on anything. I've just been camping here, really. I don't know what's in half of these drawers."

He returned to a bureau and was sifting through its contents when he heard a click and a creak behind him and Adora Belle said, in a rather flat voice: "You did say he entertained young ladies up here, right?"

"Apparently, yes. Why?"

"Well, that's what I *call* entertainment."

Moist turned. The door of a heavy cupboard stood wide-open.

"Oh, no," he said. "What's all *that* for?"

"You *are* joking?"

"Well, yes, all right. But it's all so . . . so black."

"And leathery," said Adora Belle. "Possibly rubbery, too."

They advanced on the museum of inventive erotica just revealed. Some of it, freed at last from confinement, unfolded, slid, or, in a few cases, bounced onto the floor.

"This"— Moist prodded something, which went *spoing!*—"is, yes, rubbery. Definitely rubbery."

"But all this here is pretty much frilly," said Adora Belle. "He must have run out of ideas."

"Either that or there were no more ideas to be had. I think he was eighty when he died," said Moist, as a seismic shift caused some more piles to slide and slither downward.

"Well done him," said Adora Belle. "Oh, and there's a couple of shelves of books, too," Adora Belle went on, investigating the gloom at the back of the cupboard. "Just here, behind the rather curious saddle and the whips. Bedtime reading, I assume."

"I don't think so," said Moist, pulling out a leather-bound volume and flicking it open at a random page. "Look, it's the old boy's journal. Years and years of it. Good grief, there's *decades*."

"Let's publish it and make a fortune," said Adora Belle, kicking the heap. "Plain covers, of course."

"No, you don't understand. There may be something in here about Mr. Bent! There's some secret . . ."

Moist ran a finger along the spines. "Let's see, he's fifty-two, he came here when he was about thirteen, and a few months later some people came looking for him. Old Lavish didn't like the look of them— Ah!"

He pulled out a couple of volumes. "These should tell us something, they're around the right time . . ."

"What are these, and why do they jingle?" Adora Belle said, holding up a couple of strange devices.

"How should I know?"

"You're a man."

"Well, yes. And? I mean, I don't go in for this stuff."

"You know, I think it's like horseradish," said Adora Belle thoughtfully.

"Pardon?"

"Like . . . well, horseradish is good in a beef sandwich, so you have some. But one day a spoonful just doesn't cut the mustard—"

"As it were," said Moist, fascinated.

"—and so you have two, and soon it's three, and eventually there's more horseradish than beef, and then one day you realize the beef fell out and you didn't notice."

"I don't think that is the metaphor you're looking for," said Moist, "because I have known you to make yourself a horseradish sandwich."

"All right, but it's still a good one," said Adora Belle. She reached down and picked up something from the floor.

"Your keys, I think. What they were doing in there we shall never know, with any luck."

Moist took them. The ring was heavy with keys of all sizes.

"And what shall we do with all this stuff?" Adora Belle kicked the heap again. It quivered, and somewhere inside something squeaked.

"Put it back in the cupboard?" Moist suggested uncertainly. The pile of passionless frippery had a brooding, alien look, like some sea monster of the abyss that had been dragged unceremoniously from its native darkness into the light of the sun.

"I don't think I could face it," said Adora Belle. "Let's just leave the door open and let it crawl back by itself. Hey!" This was to Mr. Fusspot, who'd trotted smartly out of the room with something in his mouth.

"Tell me that was just an old rubber bone," she said. "Please?"

"No-oh," said Moist, shaking his head. "I think that would definitely be the wrong description. I think it was . . . was . . . it was not an old rubber bone, is what it was."

66 **N**OW LOOK," SAID Hubert, "don't you think we'd know if the gold had been stolen? People talk about that sort of thing! I'm pretty certain it's a fault in the crossover multivalve, right here." He tapped a thin glass tube.

"I don't think the Glooper ith wrong, thur," said Igor gloomily.

"Igor, you realize that if the Glooper is right then I'll have to believe there is practically no gold in our vaults?"

"I believe the Glooper ith not in error, thur." Igor took a dollar out of his pocket and walked over to the well.

"If you would be tho good ath to watch the 'lotht money' column, thur?" he said, and dropped the coin into the dark waters. It gleamed for a moment as it sank beyond the pockets of mankind.

In one corner of the Glooper's convoluted glass tubing a small blue bubble drifted up, dawdling from side to side as it rose, and burst on the surface with a faint *gloop*.

"Oh dear," said Hubert.

T HE COMIC CONVENTION, when two people are dining at a table designed to accommo-date twenty, is that they sit at either end. Moist and Adora Belle didn't try it, but instead huddled to-gether. Gladys stood at the other end, a napkin over one arm, her eyes two sullen glows.

The sheep skull didn't help Moist's frame of mind at all. Peggy had arranged it as a centerpiece, with flowers around it, but the cool sunglasses were get-ting on his nerves.

"How good is a golem's hearing?" he said.

"Extremely," said Adora Belle. "Look, don't worry, I have a plan."

"Oh, good."

"No, seriously. I'll take her out tomorrow."

"Can't you just—" Moist hesitated, and then mouthed: *"change the words in her head?"*

"She's a free golem!" said Adora Belle sharply. "How would *you* like it?"

Moist remembered Owlswick and the turnip. "Not much," he admitted.

"With free golems you should change minds by persuasion. I think I can do that."

"Aren't your golden golems due to arrive tomorrow?"

"I hope so."

"It's going to be a busy day. I'm going to launch paper money and you're going to march gold through the streets."

"We couldn't leave them underground. Anyway, they might not be golden. I'll go and see Flead in the morning."

"*We* will go and see him. Together!"

She patted Moist's arm. "Never mind. There could be worse things than golden golems."

"I can't think what they are," said Moist, a phrase that he later regretted. "I'd like to take people's minds off gold—"

He stopped and stared at the sheep, which stared back in a calm enigmatic way. For some reason Moist felt it should have a saxophone and a little black beret.

"Surely they looked in the vault," he said aloud.

"Who looked?" said Adora Belle.

"That's where he'd go. The one thing you can depend on, right? The foundation of all that's worthy?"

"Who'd go?"

"Mr. Bent is in the gold vault!" said Moist, standing up so quickly that his chair fell over. "He's got all the keys!"

"Sorry? Is this the man who went haywire after making a simple mistake?"

"That's him. He's got a Past."

"One of those with a capital P?"

"Exactly. Come on, let's get down there!"

"I thought we were going to have a romantic evening?"

"We will! Right after we get him out!"

T HE ONLY SOUND in the vaults was the tap-tap-tapping of Adora Belle's foot.

It was really annoying Moist as he paced up and down in front of the gold room, by the light of silver candlesticks that had been gracing the dining-room table.

"I just hope Aimsbury is keeping the broth warm," said Adora Belle. *Tap-tap tap-tap.*

"Look," said Moist. "Firstly, to open a safe like this you need to have a name like Fingers McGee, and secondly, these little lock picks aren't up to the job."

"Well, let's go and find Mr. McGee. He's probably got the right sort." *Tap-tap. Tap-tap.*

"That won't be any good because, thirdly, there's probably no such person, and, fourthly, the vault is locked from the inside and I think he's left the key in the lock, which is why none of these work." He waved the key ring. "Fifthly, I'm trying to turn the key from this side with tweezers, an old trick which, it turns out, does not work!"

"Good. So we can go back to the suite?" *Tap-tap tap-tap*.

Moist peered again through the little spyhole in the door. A heavy plate had been slid across it on the inside, and he could just make out a glimmer of light around the edges. There was a lamp in there. What there was not, as far as he knew, was any kind of ventilation. It looked as though the vault had been built before the idea of breathing caught on. It was a man-made cave, built to contain something you never intended to take out. Gold didn't choke.

"I don't think we have the option," he said, "because sixthly, he's running out of air. He may even be dead!"

"If he's dead, can we leave him until tomorrow? It's freezing down here."

Tap-tap tap-tap.

Moist looked up at the ceiling. It was made of ancient oak beams, strapped together with iron bands. He knew what old oak could be like. It could be like steel, only nastier. It blunted axes and bounced hammers back in their owners' faces.

"Can't the guards help?" Adora Belle ventured.

"I doubt it," said Moist. "Anyway, I don't particularly want to encourage the idea that they can spend the night breaking into the vault."

"But they're mostly City Watch, aren't they?"

"So? When a man is legging it for the horizon with as much gold as he can carry he doesn't worry much about what his old job was. I'm a criminal. Trust me."

He walked toward the stairs, counting under his breath.

"And *now* what are you doing?"

"Working out which part of the bank is directly over the gold," said Moist. "But you know what? I think I already know. The gold room is right under his desk."

T HE LAMP HAD burned low, and oily smoke swirled and settled on the sacks where Mr. Bent lay curled up in a tight ball.

There was sound above, and voices muffled by the ancient ceiling. One of them said: "I can't budge it. All right, Gladys, over to you."

"Is This Ladylike Behavior?" a second voice rumbled.

"Oh yes, it counts as moving furniture," said a voice that was clearly female.

"Very Well. I Shall Lift It Up And Dust Underneath It."

There was the thunder of wood being scraped on wood, and a little dust fell onto the piled bullion.

"Very Dusty Indeed. I Shall Fetch A Broom."

"Actually, Gladys, I'd like you to lift up the floor now," said the first voice.

"There May Be Dust Underneath That Too?"

"I'm certain of it."

"Very Well."

There were several thumps that made the beams creak, and then a rumble of: "It Does Not Say Anything About Dusting Under The Floor In Lady Waggon's Book Of Household Management."

"Gladys, a man may be dying under there!"

"I See. That Would Be Untidy." The beams rattled under a blow. "Lady Waggon Says That Any Bodies Found During A Weekend Party Should Be Disposed Of Discreetly, In Case Of Scandal."

Three more blows, and a beam shattered.

"Lady Waggon Says Watchmen Are Disrespectful And Do Not Wipe Their Dirty Boots."

Another beam cracked. Light lanced down. A hand the size of a shovel appeared, grabbed one of the iron straps, and snapped it—

Moist peered into the gloom, while smoke poured up past him.

"He's down there! Ye gods, this reeks!"

Adora Belle looked over his shoulder.

"Is he alive?"

"I certainly hope so." Moist eased himself between the beams and dropped onto the bullion boxes.

After a moment he called up: "There's a pulse. And there's a key in the lock, too. Can you come down the stairs and give me a hand?"

"Er . . . we have visitors," Adora Belle called down.

A couple of helmeted heads were now outlined against the light. Damn it! Using off-duty watchmen was all very well, but they tended to take their badges everywhere with them, and were just the sort of people who'd jump to conclusions merely because they'd found a man standing in the wreckage of a bank vault after hours. The words "Look, I can explain" presented themselves for utterance, but Moist strangled them just in time. It was his bank, after all.

"Well, what do *you* want?" he demanded.

This was sufficiently unexpected to throw the men, but one of them rallied.

"Is this your bank vault, sir?" he said.

"I'm the deputy chairman, you idiot! And there's a sick man down here!"

"Did he fall when you were breaking into the vault, sir?"

Oh gods, you just couldn't budge a born copper. They just kept going, in that patient, grinding tone. When you were a policeman, everything was a crime.

"Officer—you *are* a copper, right?"

"Constable Haddock, sir."

"Well, constable, can we get my colleague into the fresh air? He's wheezing. I'll unlock the door down here."

Haddock nodded to the other guard, who hurried away toward the stairs.

"If you had a key, sir, why did you break in?"

"To get him out, of course!"

"So how—"

"It's all perfectly sensible," said Moist. "Once I've got out of here we will all have a laugh."

"I shall look forward to that, sir," said Haddock, "because I like a laugh."

TALKING TO THE Watch was like tap-dancing on a landslide. If you were nimble, you could stay upright, but you couldn't steer and there were no brakes and you just knew that it was going to end in a certain amount of fuss.

It wasn't Constable Haddock anymore. It had stopped being Constable Haddock just as soon as Constable Haddock had found that the pockets of the master of the Royal Mint contained a velvet roll of lock picks and a blackjack, and it then became Sergeant Detritus.

Lock picks, as Moist knew, were technically not illegal. Owning them was fine. Owning them while standing in someone else's house was not fine. Owning them while being found in a stricken bank vault was so far from fine it could see the curvature of the universe.

So far, to Sergeant Detritus, so good. However, the sergeant's grasp began to slip when confronted with the evidence that Moist quite legitimately had the keys for the vault he had broken into. This seemed to the troll to be a criminal act in itself, and he'd toyed for a while with the charge "Wasting Watch time by breaking in when you didn't have to."* He didn't understand about the visceral need for the lock picks; trolls didn't have a word for machismo in the same way that puddles don't have a word for water. He also had a problem with the mind-set and actions of the nearly late Mr. Bent. Trolls don't go mad, they get mad. So he gave up, and it became Captain Carrot.

Moist knew him of old. He was big and smelled

---

*"Wasting Watch time" is an offense committed by citizens who have found ways of wasting said time that haven't already been invented by the Watch themselves.

of soap, and his normal expression was one of blue-eyed innocence. Moist couldn't see behind that amiable face, just couldn't see a thing. He could read most people but the captain was a closed book in a locked bookcase. And the man was always courteous, in that really annoying way police have.

He said, "Good evening," politely, as he sat down opposite Moist in the little office that had suddenly become an interview room. "Can I start, sir, by asking you about the three men down in the cellar? And the big glass . . . thing?"

"Mr. Hubert Turvy and his assistants," said Moist. "They are studying the economic system of the city. They're not involved in *this*. Come to think of it, I'm not involved in this either! There is, in fact, no *this*. I have explained all this to the sergeant."

"Sergeant Detritus thinks you are too smart, Mr. Lipwig," said Captain Carrot, opening his notebook.

"Well, yes, I expect he thinks that about most people, doesn't he?"

Carrot's expression changed not one iota.

"Can you tell me why there is a golem downstairs who is wearing a dress and keeps ordering my men to wipe their dirty boots?" he said.

"Not without sounding mad, no. What has this got to do with anything?"

"I don't know, sir. I hope to find out. Who is Lady Deirdre Waggon?"

"She writes rather out-of-date books on etiquette and household management, for young ladies who would like to be the type of women who have time to arrange flowers. Look, is this relevant?"

"I don't know that, sir. I am endeavoring to assess the situation. Can you tell me why a small dog is running around the building, in possession of what I shall call a wind-up clockwork item of an intimate nature?"

"I think it is because my sanity is slipping away," said Moist. "Look, the only thing that is important here is that Mr. Bent had . . . a nasty turn and locked himself in the gold vault. I had to get him out quickly."

"Ah, yes, the gold vault," said the captain. "Can we talk about the gold for a moment?"

"What's wrong with the gold?"

"I was hoping you could tell us, sir. I believe you wanted to sell it to the dwarfs?"

"What? Well, yes, I said that, but it was only to make a point—"

"A point," said Captain Carrot solemnly, writing this down.

"Look, I know how this sort of thing goes," said Moist. "You just keep me talking in the hope that I'll suddenly forget where I am and say something stupid and incriminating, right?"

"Thank you for that, sir," said Captain Carrot, turning over another page in his notebook.

"Thank me for what?"

"For telling me you know how this sort of thing goes, sir."

See? Moist told himself, this is what happens when you get too comfortable. You lose the edge. Even a copper can outsmart you.

The captain looked up. "I will tell you, Mr.

Lipwig, that some of what you say has been corroborated by an unbiased witness who could not possibly be an accomplice."

"You talked to Gladys?" said Moist.

"Gladys being?"

"She's the one going on about dirty boots."

"How can a golem be a 'she,' sir?"

"Ah, I know this one. The correct answer is: How can a golem be a 'he'?"

"An interesting point, sir. That explains the dress, then. Out of interest, how much weight would you say a golem can carry?"

"I don't know. A couple of tons, maybe. What are you getting at?"

"I don't know, sir," said Carrot cheerfully. "Commander Vimes says that when life hands you a mess of spaghetti, just keep pulling until you find the meatball. In fact, your story agrees, insofar as he understood events, with what we have been told by a Mr. Fusspot."

"You talked to the *dog*?"

"Well, he is the chairman of the bank, sir," said the captain.

"How did you understand what— Ah, you have a werewolf, right?" said Moist, grinning.

"We don't confirm that, sir."

"Everyone knows it's Nobby Nobbs, you know."

"Do they, sir? Gosh. Anyway, your movements this evening are accounted for."

"Good. Thank you." Moist started to rise.

"However, your movements earlier this week, sir, are not." Moist sat down again.

"Well? I don't have to account for them, do I?"

"It might help us, sir."

"How would it help you?"

"It might help us understand why there is no gold in the vault, sir. It's a small detail in the great scheme of things, but it is something of a puzzler."

At which point, somewhere close at hand, Mr. Fusspot began to bark . . .

COSMO LAVISH SAT at his desk with his fingers steepled in front of his mouth, watching Cribbins eat. Not many people in a state to make a choice had ever done this for more than thirty seconds.

"The soup is good?" he said.

Cribbins lowered the bowl after one lengthy final gurgle.

"Champion, Your Lordship." Cribbins removed a gray rag from his pocket and—

He's going to take his teeth out, right now, here at the table, thought Cosmo. *Amazing. Ah, yes, and there's still bits of carrot in them . . .*

"Don't hesitate to repair your teeth," he said, as Cribbins removed a bent fork from a pocket.

"I'm a martyr to them, shir," said Cribbins. "I'll shwear they're out to get me." Springs twanged as he fought them with the fork and then, apparently satisfied, he wrestled them back onto his gray gums and champed them into place.

"That's better," he announced.

"Good," said Cosmo. "And now, in view of the nature of your allegations, which Drumknott here has carefully transcribed and you have signed, let me ask you: why have you not gone to Lord Vetinari?"

"I've knowed men escape the noose, sir," said Cribbins. "It ain't too hard if you've got the readies. But I never heard of one get a big plum job the very next day. Gov'ment job, too. Then suddenly he's a banker, no leshsh. Shomeone's watching over him, and I don't think it's a bleeding fairy. If I wash to go to Vetinari, then I'd be a bit silly, right. But he's got your bank, and you ain't, which is a shame. Sho I'm your man, shir."

"At a price, I have no doubt."

"Well, yes, something in the way of expenses would help, yesh."

"And you are *sure* that Lipwig and Spangler are one and the same?"

"It's the smile, shir. You never forget it. And he has this gift of chatting to people, he makes people want to do things his way. It's like magic, the little ingrate."

Cosmo stared at him and then said, "Give the reverend fifty dollars, Drum— Heretofore, and direct him to a good hotel. One where they might have a hot tub available."

"*Fifty dollarsh?*" growled Cribbins.

"And then please go ahead with that little acquisition, will you?"

"Yes, sir. Of course."

Cosmo pulled a piece of paper toward him, dipped a pen in the inkwell, and began to write furiously.

"Fifty dollarsh?" said Cribbins again, appalled at the minimum wage of sin.

Cosmo looked up and stared at the man as if seeing him for the first time and not enjoying the novelty.

"Hh, yes. Fifty dollars indeed for now, Reverend," said Cosmo soothingly. "And in the morning, if your memory is still as good, we will all look forward to a richer and righteous future. Do not let me detain you."

He returned to his paperwork.

Heretofore grabbed Cribbins's arm and towed him forcibly out of the room. He'd seen what Cosmo was writing.

VetinariVetinariVetinari VetinariVetinariVetinari
VetinariVetinariVetinari VetinariVetinariVetinari
VetinariVetinariVetinari VetinariVetinariVetinari
VetinariVetinariVetinari VetinariVetinariVetinari
VetinariVetinariVetinari VetinariVetinariVetinari
VetinariVetinariVetinari VetinariVetinariVetinar . . .

It was time for the sword stick, he thought. Get it, hand it over, take the money, and run.

T HINGS WERE QUIET in the Department of Postmortem Communications. They were never very loud at the best of times, although you always got, when the sounds of the university slid into silence, the reedy little gnat-sized voices leaking through from The Other Side.

The trouble was, thought Hicks, that too many of his predecessors had never had any kind of a life outside the department, where social skills were not a priority, and even when dead had completely failed to get a life, either. So they hung around the department, reluctant to leave the place. Sometimes, when they were feeling strong and the Dolly Sisters Players were doing a new production, he let them out to paint the scenery.

Hicks sighed. That was the trouble with working in the DPC, you could never exactly be the boss. In an ordinary job people retired, wandered back to the ol' workplace a few times while there were those who remembered them, and then faded into the ever-swelling past. But the former staff here never seemed to go . . .

There was a saying: "Old necromancers never die." When he told them this, people would say ". . . and?" and Hicks would have to reply, "That's all of it, I'm afraid. Just 'Old necromancers never die.'"

He was just tidying up for the night when, from his shadowy corner, Charlie said: "Somebody coming through, well, I *say* some body . . ."

Hicks spun around. The magic circle was glowing and a pearly pointy hat was already rising through the solid floor.

"Professor Flead?" he said.

"Yes, and we must hurry, young man," said the shade of Flead, still rising.

"But I banished you! I used the Ninefold Erasure! It banishes everything!"

"I wrote it," said Flead, looking smug. "Oh, don't

worry, I'm the only one it doesn't work on. Ha, I'd be a damn fool to design a spell to work on myself, eh?"

Hicks pointed a shaking finger. "You put in a hidden portal, didn't you!"

"Of course. A bloody good one. Don't worry, I'm the only one who knows where it is, too." The whole of Flead was floating above the circle now. "And don't try to look for it, a man of your limited talent will never find the hidden runes."

Flead looked around the room. "Isn't that wonderful young lady here?" he said hopefully. "Well, never mind. You must get me out of this place, Hicks. I want to see the fun!"

"Fun? What fun?" said Hicks, a man planning to look through the Ninefold Erasure spell very, very carefully.

"I know what kind of golems are coming!"

W HEN HE WAS a child, Moist had prayed every night before going to bed. His family were very active in the Plain Potato Church, which shunned the excesses of the Ancient and Orthodox Potato Church. Its followers were retiring, industrious, and inventive, and their strict adherence to oil lamps and homemade furniture made them stand out in the region where most people used candles and sat on sheep.

He'd hated praying. It felt as though he was opening a big black hole into space, and at any moment *something* might reach through and grab him. This may have been because the standard bedtime prayer included the line "If I die before I wake," which on bad nights caused him to try and sit up until morning.

He'd also been instructed to use the hours before sleep to count his blessings.

Lying here now, in the darkness of the bank, rather cold and significantly alone, he sought for some.

His teeth were good and he wasn't suffering from premature hair loss. There! That wasn't so hard, was it?

And the Watch hadn't actually arrested him, as such. But there was a troll guarding the vault, which had ominous black and yellow ropes strung around it.

No gold in the vault. Well, even that wasn't entirely true. There was five pounds of it, at least, coating the lead ingots. Someone had done a pretty good job there. That was a silver lining, right? At least it was *some* gold. It wasn't as if there was no gold at *all*, right?

He was alone because Adora Belle was spending a night in the cells for assaulting an officer of the Watch. Moist considered that this was unfair. Of course, depending on what kind of day a copper has had there is no action, short of being physically somewhere else, that may not be construed as assault, but Adora Belle hadn't actually *assaulted* Sergeant Detritus; she'd merely attempted to stab his huge foot with her shoe, which resulted in a broken heel and a twisted ankle. Captain Carrot said this had been taken into consideration.

The clocks of the city chimed four, and Moist considered his future, specifically in terms of length.

Look on the bright side. He might just be hanged.

He should have gone down to the vaults on day one, with an alchemist and a lawyer in tow. Didn't they ever audit the vaults? Was it done by a bunch of jolly decent chaps who'd poke their head into some other chap's vault and sign off on it quickly, so's not to miss lunch? Can't go doubting a chap's word, eh? Especially when you didn't want him to doubt yours.

Maybe the late Sir Joshua had blown it all on exotic leather goods and young ladies. How many nights in the arms of beautiful women were worth a sack of gold? The price of a good woman was proverbially above rubies, so a skillfully bad one was worth presumably a lot more.

He sat up and lit the candle, and his eye fell on Mr. Lavish's journal on the bedside table.

Thirty-nine years ago . . . well, it was the right year, and since at the moment he had nothing else to do . . .

The luck that had been draining from his boots all day came back to him. Even though he wasn't certain what he was looking for, he found it on the sixth random page:

"A pair of funny-looking people came to the bank today, asking for the boy Bent. I bade the staff send them away. He is doing exceedingly well. One wonders what he must have suffered."

Quite a lot of the journal seemed to be in some sort of code, but the nature of the secret symbols suggested that Mr. Lavish painstakingly recorded

every amorous affair. You had to admire his directness, at least. He'd worked out what he wanted to get
from life, and had set out to get as much of it as he
could. Moist had to take his hat off to the man.

And what had *he* wanted? He'd never sat down to
think about it. But mostly, he wanted tomorrow to
be different from today.

He looked at his watch. Four fifteen, and no one
about but the guards. There were watchmen on the
main doors. He was indeed not under arrest, but
this was one of those civilized little arrangements:
he was not under arrest, provided that he didn't try
to act like a man who was not under arrest.

Ah, he thought, as he pulled on his trousers, there
was another small blessing: he had been there when
Mr. Fusspot proposed to the werewolf—

—which was, by then, balancing on one of the
huge ornamental urns that grew like toadstools in
the bank's corridors. It was rocking. So was Corporal Nobbs, who was laughing himself sick at—

—Mr. Fusspot, who was bouncing up and down
with wonderfully optimistic enthusiasm. But he was
holding in his mouth his new toy, which appeared
to have been mysteriously wound up, and beneficent
fate had decreed that at the top of each jump, its
unbalancing action would cause the little dog to do
one slow cartwheel in the air.

And Moist thought: So, the werewolf is female
and has a Watch badge on her collar, and I've seen
that hair color before. Hah!

But his gaze had gone straight back to Mr.

Fusspot, who was jumping and spinning with a look of total bliss on his little face—

—and then Captain Carrot had plucked him out of the air, the werewolf fled, and the show was over. But Moist would always have the memory. Next time he walked past Sergeant Angua he'd growl under his breath, although that would probably constitute assault.

Now, fully dressed, he went for a walk along endless corridors.

The Watch had put a lot of new guards in the bank for the night. Captain Carrot was clever, you had to give him that. They were trolls. Trolls were very hard to talk around to your point of view.

He could sense them watching him everywhere he went. There wasn't one at the door into the undercroft, but Moist's heart sank when he neared the pool of brilliant light around the Glooper and saw one standing by the door to freedom.

Owlswick was lying on a mattress and snoring, his paintbrush in his hand. Moist envied him.

Hubert and Igor were working on the tangle of glassware which, Moist could swear, looked bigger every time he came down here.

"What's wrong?"

"Wrong? Nothing. Nothing's wrong!" said Hubert. "It's all fine! Is something wrong? Why do you think something is wrong? What would make you think there's something wrong?"

Moist yawned.

"Any coffee? Tea?" he suggested.

"For you, Mr. Lipwig," said Igor, "I will make thplot."

"Splot? *Real* Splot?"

"Indeed, thur," said Igor smugly.

"You can't buy it here, you know."

"I am aware of that, thur. It hath now been outlawed in motht of the old country, too," said Igor, rummaging in a sack.

"Outlawed? It's been outlawed? But it's just an herbal drink! My granny used to make it!"

"Indeed, it wath very traditional," Igor agreed. "It put hairth on your chetht."

"Yes, she used to complain about that."

"This an alcoholic beverage?" said Hubert nervously.

"Absolutely not," said Moist. "My granny never touched alcohol." He thought for a moment and then added: "Except maybe aftershave. Splot's made from tree bark."

"Oh? Well, that sounds nice," said Hubert.

Igor retired to his jungle of equipment, and there was the clinking of glassware. Moist sat down at the cluttered bench.

"How's it going in your world, Hubert?" he said. "The water gurgling around okay, is it?"

"It's fine! Fine! It's all fine! Nothing is wrong at all!" Hubert went blank, fished out his notebook, glanced at a page, and put it back. "How are you?"

"Me? Oh, great. Except that there should be ten tons of gold in the gold vaults and there isn't."

It sounded as though a glass had broken in the

direction of Igor, and Hubert stared in horror at Moist.

"Ha? Hahahaha?" he said. "Ha ha ha ha a HAHAHA !! **HA HA HA!!! HA HA—**"

There was a blur as Igor leaped the table and grabbed Hubert. "Thorry, Mr. Lipwig," he said over his shoulder, "thith can go on for hourth—"

He slapped Hubert twice across the face and pulled a jar out of his pocket.

"Mr. Hubert? How many fingerth am I holding up?"

Hubert slowly focused.

"Thirteen?" he quavered.

Igor relaxed, and dropped the jar back into his pocket. "Jutht in time. Well done, thur!"

"I am so sorry—" Hubert began.

"Don't worry about it. I'm feeling a bit that way myself," said Moist.

"So . . . this gold . . . have you any idea who took it?"

"No, but it must have been an inside job," said Moist. "And now the Watch are going to pin it on me, I suspect."

"Will that mean you won't be in charge?" said Hubert.

"I doubt I'll be allowed to run the bank from inside the Tanty."

"Oh dear," said Hubert, looking at Igor. "Um . . . what would happen if it was put back?"

Igor coughed loudly.

"I think that's unlikely, don't you?" said Moist.

"Yes, but Igor told me that when the Post Office burned down last year the gods themselves gave you the money to rebuild it!"

"Harrumph," said Igor.

"I doubt if that's likely twice," said Moist. "And I don't think there's a god of banking."

"One might take it on for the publicity," said Hubert desperately. "It could be worth a prayer."

"Harrumph!" said Igor, louder this time.

Moist looked from one to the other. *Okay*, he thought, *something's going on, and I'm not going to be told what it is.*

Pray to the gods to get a big heap of gold? When had that ever worked?

Well, last year it worked, true, but that was because I already knew where a big heap of gold was buried. The gods help those who help themselves, and my word, didn't I help myself.

"You think it's really worth it?" said Moist.

A small, steaming mug was placed in front of him.

"Your Thplot," said Igor. The words "Now please drink it up and go" accompanied it in every respect but the vocal.

"Do *you* think I should pray, Igor?" said Moist, watching his face.

"I couldn't thay. The Igor position on prayer is that it is nothing more than hope with a beat to it."

Moist leaned closer and whispered, "Igor, as one Überwald lad to another, your lisp just departed."

Igor's frown grew. "Thorry, thur, I have a lot on my mind," he said, rolling his eyes to indicate the nervous Hubert.

"My fault, I'm disturbing you good people," said Moist, emptying the cup in one go. "Any minute now the dhdldlkp;kvyv vbdf[;jvjvf;llljvmmk;vvbvl mbnxgcgbnme—"

Ah yes, Splot, thought Moist. It contained herbs and all natural ingredients. But belladonna was an herb, and arsenic was natural. There was no alcohol in it, people said, because alcohol couldn't survive. But a cup of hot Splot got men out of bed and off to work when there was six feet of snow outside and the well was frozen. It left you clear-headed and quick-thinking. It was only a shame that the human tongue couldn't keep up.

Moist blinked once or twice and said, "Ughx . . ."

He said his good-byes, even if they were his "gnyrxs," and headed back up the length of the undercroft, the light from the Glooper pushing his shadow in front of him. Trolls watched him suspiciously as he climbed the steps, trying to keep his feet from flying away from him. His brain buzzed, but it had nothing to do. There was nothing to grab hold of, to worry a solution from. And in an hour or so, the country edition of the *Times* would be out and, very shortly after, so would he. There would be a run on the bank, which is a horrifying thing at best, and the other banks wouldn't help him out, would they, because he wasn't a chap. Disgrace and ignominy and Mr. Fusspot were staring him in the face, but only one of them was licking it.

He'd made it to his office, then. Splot certainly took your mind off all your little problems by rolling them into the big one of keeping all of yourself on one planet. He accepted the little dog's ritual slobbering kiss, got off his knees, and made it as far as the chair.

Okay . . . sitting down, he could do that. But his mind raced.

People would be here soon. There were too many unanswered questions. What to do, what to do? Pray? Moist wasn't too keen on prayer, not because he thought the gods didn't exist but because he was afraid they might. All right, Anoia had got a good deal out of him and he'd noticed her shiny new temple the other day, its frontage already hung with votive egg-slicers, fondant whisks, ladles, parsnip butterers, and many other useless appliances donated by grateful worshipers who had faced the prospect of a life with their drawers stuck. Anoia delivered, because she specialized. She didn't even pretend to offer a paradise, eternal verities, or any kind of salvation. She just left you with a smooth pulling action and access to the forks. And practically no one had believed in her before he'd picked her, at random, as one of the gods to thank for the miraculous windfall. Would she remember?

If he had some gold stuck in a drawer, then maybe. Turning dross into gold, probably not. Still, you turned to the gods when all you had left was a prayer.

He wandered into the little kitchen and took a ladle off the hook. Then he went back to the office and rammed it into a desk drawer, where it stuck, this being the chief function of ladles in the world.

Rattle your drawers, that was it. She was attracted to the noise, apparently.

"Oh Anoia," he said, tugging at the drawer handle. "This is me, Moist von Lipwig, penitent sinner. I don't know if you remember? We are, all of us, mere utensils, stuck in drawers of our own making, and none more than I. If you could find time in your busy schedule to unstick me in my hour of need you will not find me wanting in gratitude, yea indeed, when we put statues of the gods on the roof of the new Post Office. I never liked the urns on the old one. Covered in gold leaf, too, by the way. Thanking you in anticipation, amen."

He gave the drawer one last tug. The ladle sprang out, twanging through the air like a leaping salmon, and smashed a vase in the corner.

Moist decided to take that as a hopeful sign. You were supposed to smell cigarette smoke if Anoia was present, but since Adora Belle had spent more than ten minutes in this room, there was no point in sniffing.

What next? Well, the gods helped those who helped themselves, and there was always one last Lipwig-friendly option. It floated up in his mind: wing it.

CHAPTER 10

WING IT! There's nothing left. Remember the nearly gold chain? This is the other end of the rainbow. Talk yourself out of a situation you can't talk your way out of. Make your own luck. Put on a show. If you fall, let them remember how you turned it into a dive. Sometimes the finest hour is the last one.

He went to the wardrobe and took out the *best*

golden suit, the one he wore on special occasions. Then he went and found Gladys, who was staring out of the window.

He had to speak her name quite loudly before she turned to face him, very slowly.

"They Are Coming," she said.

"Yes, they are," said Moist, "and I'd better look my best. Could you press these trousers, please?"

Wordlessly, Gladys took the pants from him, held them against the wall, and ran a huge palm down them before handing them back. Moist could have shaved with the crease. Then she turned back to the window.

Moist joined her. There was already a crowd in front of the bank, and coaches were pulling up as he watched. There were a fair number of guards around, too. A brief flash indicated that Otto Chriek of the *Times* was already taking pictures. Ah, yes, a deputation was now forming. People wanted to be in at the death. Sooner or later, someone would hammer at the door. Blow that for a game of soldiers. He couldn't let that happen.

Wash, shave, trim errant nose hairs, brush teeth. Comb hair, shine boots. Don hat, walk down stairs, unlock door very slowly so that the click was unlikely to be heard outside, wait until he heard a tread getting louder.

Moist opened the door, sharply.

"Well, gentlemen?"

Cosmo Lavish wobbled as the knock failed to connect, but recovered and thrust a sheet of paper at him.

"Emergency audit," he said. "These gentlemen"—and here he indicated a number of worthy-looking men behind him—"are representatives of the major guilds and some of the other banks. This is standard procedure and you can't stand in their way. You will

note that we have brought Commander Vimes of
the Watch. When we have established that there is
indeed no gold in the vault, I shall instruct him to
arrest you on suspicion of theft."

Moist glanced at the commander. He did not like
the man much, and was certain that Vimes did not
like him at all. He was even more certain, though,
that Vimes did not readily take orders from the likes
of Cosmo Lavish.

"I'm sure that the commander will do as he sees
fit," said Moist meekly. "You know the way to the
vault. I am sorry it's a bit of a mess at the moment."

Cosmo half-turned, to make certain the crowd
heard everything he said. "You are a thief, Mr.
Lipwig. A cheat and a liar, an embezzler and have
no dress sense whatsoever."

"I say, that's a bit on the harsh side," said Moist as
the men swept through. "I happen to think I dress
rather snappily!"

Now he was alone on the steps, facing the crowd.
They weren't a mob yet, but it could only be a matter
of time.

"Can I help anyone else?" he said.

"What about our money?" said someone.

"What about it?" said Moist.

"Says in the paper you've got no gold," said the
inquirer.

He pushed a damp copy of the *Times* toward
Moist. The newspaper had, on the whole, been quite
restrained. He had expected bad headlines, but the
story was a single column on the front page and it
was full of "we understand that"s and "we believe

that"s and "the *Times* had been informed that"s and all the phrases that journalists use when they are dealing with facts about large sums of money they don't fully understand and are not quite certain that what they have been told is true.

He looked up into the face of Sacharissa Cripslock.

"Sorry," she said, "but there were watchmen and guards all around the place last night and we didn't have much time. And frankly, Mr. Bent's . . . attack was enough of a story in its own right. Everyone knows he runs the bank."

"The chairman runs the bank," said Moist stiffly.

"No, Moist, the chairman goes *woof*," said Sacharissa. "Look, didn't you sign anything when you took over the job? A receipt or something?"

"Well, maybe. There was a mass of paperwork. I just signed where I was told. So did Mr. Fusspot."

"Ye gods, the lawyers would have fun with that," said Sacharissa, her notebook magically appearing in her hand. "And it's no joke, either.* He could end up in debtors' prison!"

"Kennel," said Moist. "He goes *woof*, remember? And that's not going to happen."

Sacharissa bent down to pat Mr. Fusspot on his little head, and froze in mid-bend.

"*What* has he got in his—?" she began.

"Sacharissa, can we go into this later? I really have not got time for it right now. I swear by any three gods you believe in, even though you are a journalist, that when this is over I will give you a

---

*The strange thing about what lawyers have fun with is that *no one* else ever sees the joke.

story that will tax even the *Times'* ability to avoid inelegant and suggestive subjects. Trust me."

"Yes, but it looks like a—" she began.

"Ah, so you *do* know what it is and I don't need to explain," said Moist briskly.

He handed the paper back to its worried owner. "You are Mr. Cusper, aren't you?" he said. "You have a balance of seven Ankh-Morpork dollars with us, I believe?" For a moment the man looked impressed. Moist was really good at faces. "I told you we aren't bothered about gold here," said Moist.

"Yeah, but . . ." the man began. "Well, it's not much of a bank if people can take the gold out of it, is it?" he said.

"But it doesn't make any difference," said Moist. "I did tell you all."

They looked uncertain. In theory, they should be stampeding up the steps. Moist knew what was holding them back. It was hope. It was the little voice inside that said: This isn't really happening. It was the voice that drove people to turn out the same pocket three times in a fruitless search for lost keys. It was mad belief that the world is bound to start working properly again if I truly believe, and there *will* be keys. It was the voice that said "This can't be happening" very loudly, in order to drown out the creeping dread that it was.

He had about thirty seconds, while hope lasted.

And then the crowd parted. Pucci Lavish did not know how to make an entrance. Harry King, on the other hand, did. The milling, uncertain throng opened up like the sea in front of a hydrophobic prophet, leaving a channel that was suddenly lined on either side by large, weathered-looking men with broken noses and a useful cross-section of scars. Along this recent avenue strode Harry King, trailing cigar smoke. Moist managed to stand his ground until Mr. King was a foot away, and made sure to look him in the eye.

"How much money did I put in your bank, Mr. Lipwig?" asked Harry.

"Er, I believe it was fifty thousand dollars, Mr. King," said Moist.

"Yes, I believe it was something like that," said Mr. King. "Can yer guess what I am going to do now, Mr. Lipwig?"

Moist did not guess. The Splot was still circulating in his system, and, in his brain, the answer clanged like a funeral bell. "You're going to put some more in, aren't you, Mr. King?"

Harry King beamed, as if Moist was a dog that had just done a new trick. "That's right, Mr. Lipwig! I thought to myself, Harry, I thought, fifty thousand dollars seems a bit on the lonely side, so I've come along to round it up to sixty thousand dollars."

On signal, some more of Harry King's men came up behind him, carrying large chests between them. "Most of it's gold and silver, Mr. Lipwig," said Harry. "But I know you got lots of bright young men who can count it all up for you."

"This is very kind of you, Mr. King," said Moist, "but at any minute the auditors are going to come back and the bank is going to be in big, big trouble. Please! I can't accept your money."

Harry leaned closer to Moist, enveloping him in cigar smoke and a hint of decayed cabbage. "I know you're up to something," he whispered, tapping the side of his nose. "The bastards are out to get you, I can see that! I know a winner when I sees one, and I know you've got something up your sleeves, eh?"

"Just my arms, Mr. King, just my arms," said Moist.

"And long may you keep them," said Harry, slapping him on the back.

The men filed past Moist and deposited their cases on the floor.

"I don't need a receipt," said Harry. "You know me, Mr. Lipwig. You know you can trust me, just like I *know* I can trust you."

Moist shut his eyes, just for a moment. To think that he had worried about ending the day hanging.

"Your money is safe with me, Mr. King," he said.

"I know," said Harry King. "And when you've won the day, I'll send young Wallace along and he'll have a little chat with your monkey about how much interest I'm gonna get paid on this little lot, all right? Fair's fair?"

"It certainly is, Mr. King."

"Right," said Harry. "Now I'm off to buy some land."

There was some uncertain murmuring from the crowd, as he departed. The new deposit had thrown them. It had thrown Moist, too. People were wondering what Harry King knew. So was Moist. It was a terrible thing, to have someone like Harry believing in you.

Now the crowd had evolved a spokesman, who said, "Look, what's going on? Has the gold gone or not?"

"I don't know," said Moist. "I haven't had a look today."

"You say that as if it doesn't matter," said Sacharissa.

"Well, as I have explained," Moist said, "the city is still here. The bank is still here. I am still here." He cast a glance toward Harry King's broad, retreating back. "For the moment. So we don't need the gold cluttering up the place, do we?"

Cosmo Lavish appeared in the door behind Moist. "So, Mr. Lipwig, it would appear that you are a trickster to the end."

"I beg your pardon?" said Moist.

Other members of the ad hoc audit committee were pushing their way out, looking satisfied. They had, after all, been woken up very early in the morning, and those who are awakened very early in the morning expect to kill before breakfast.

"Have you finished already?" said Moist.

"Surely you must know why we were brought here," said one of the bankers. "You know very well that last night the City Watch found no gold in your vaults. We can confirm this unhappy state of affairs."

"Oh well, you know how it is with money," said Moist. "You think you are flat-broke and there it was all the time in your other trousers."

"No, Mr. Lipwig, the joke is on you," said Cosmo. "The bank is a sham."

He raised his voice. "I would advise all the investors you have misled to take their money back while they can!"

"*No!* Squad, to me!"

Commander Vimes pushed his way through the bewildered bankers at the same time as half a dozen troll officers pounded up the steps and ended up shoulder to shoulder in front of the double doors.

"Are you a bloody fool, sir?" said Vimes, nose to nose with Cosmo. "That sounded to me like incitement to riot! This bank is closed until further notice!"

"I am a director of the bank, Commander," said Cosmo. "You cannot keep me out."

"Watch me," said Vimes. "I suggest you direct your complaint to his lordship. Sergeant Detritus!"

"Yessir!"

"Nobody goes in there without a chitty signed by me. And Mr. Lipwig, you will *not* leave the city, understood?"

"Yes, Commander." Moist turned to Cosmo. "You know, you're not looking well," he said. "That's not a good complexion you have there."

"No more words, Lipwig." Cosmo leaned down. Up close, his face looked even worse, like the face of a wax doll, if a wax doll could sweat. "We'll meet in court. It's the end of the road, Mr. Lipwig. Or should I say . . . Mr. Spangler?"

Oh, gods, I should have done something about Cribbins, thought Moist. *I was too busy trying to make money . . .*

And there was Adora Belle, being ushered

through the crowd by a couple of watchmen who were also acting as crutches. Vimes hurried down the steps as if he'd been expecting her.

Moist became aware that the background noise of the city was getting louder. The crowd had noticed it too. Somewhere, something big was happening, and this little confrontation was just a sideshow.

"You think you are clever, Mr. Lipwig?" said Cosmo.

"No, I *know* I am clever. I think I'm unlucky," said Moist. But he thought: *I didn't have that many customers, surely? I can hear screams!*

With triumphant shouting behind him, he pushed his way down to Adora Belle and the cluster of coppers.

"Your golems, right?" he said.

"Every golem in the city just stopped moving," said Adora Belle. Their gazes met.

"They're coming?" said Moist.

"Yes, I think they are."

"Who are?" said Vimes suspiciously.

"Er, them?" said Moist, pointing.

A few people came running around the corner from the Maul and sprinted, gray-faced, past the crowd outside the bank. But they were only the flecks of foam driven before the tidal wave of people fleeing from the river area, and the wave of people broke on the bank as if it was a rock in the way of the flood.

Floating on the sea of heads, as it were, was a circular canvas about ten feet across, of the sort that gets used to catch people who very wisely jump from

burning buildings. The four people carrying it were
Dr. Hicks and four other wizards, and it was at this
point you would notice the chalked circle and the
magic symbols. In the middle of the portable magic
circle sat Professor Flead, belaboring the wizards
unsuccessfully with his ethereal staff. They fetched
up alongside the steps as the crowd ran onward.

"I am sorry about this," panted Hicks, "it's the
only way we could get him here and he insisted, oh
how he insisted . . ."

"Where's the young lady?" Flead shouted. His
voice was barely audible in the living daylight.
Adora Belle pushed her way through the policemen.

"Yes, Professor Flead?" she said.

"I have found your answer! I have spoken with
several Umnians!"

"I thought they all died thousands of years ago!"

"Well, it *is* a department of necromancy," Flead
said. "But I must admit they were a wee bit indistinct, even for me. Can I have a kiss? One kiss, one
answer?"

Adora Belle looked at Moist. He shrugged. The
day was totally beyond him. He wasn't flying anymore; he was simply being blown along by the gale.

"All right," she said. "But no tongues."

"Tongues?" said Flead sadly. "I wish."

There was the briefest of pecks, but the ghostly
necromancer beamed. "Wonderful," he said. "I feel
at least a hundred years younger."

"You have done the translations?" said Adora
Belle. And at that moment Moist felt a vibration
under foot.

"What? Oh that," said Flead. "It was those gold golems you were talking about—"

—and another vibration, enough to cause a sense of unease in the bowels—

"—although it turns out that the word in context doesn't mean 'gold' at all. There are more than one hundred and twenty things it can mean, but in this case, taken in conjunction with the rest of the paragraph, it means 'a thousand.'"

The street shook again.

"Four *thousand* golems, I think you'll find," said Flead cheerfully. "Oh, and here they are now!"

T HEY CAME ALONG the streets six abreast, wall to wall and ten feet high, water and mud cascading off of them. The city echoed to their tread.

They did not trample people, but mere market stalls and coaches splintered under their massive feet. They spread out as they moved, fanning out across the city, thundering down side streets, heading for the gates of Ankh-Morpork, which were always open, because there was no point in discouraging customers.

And there were the horses, perhaps no more than a score in all the hurrying throng, saddles built into the clay of their backs, overtaking the two-legged golems, and not a man watched but thought: Where can I get one of those? The rest of the golems marched on with the sound of thunder, heading out of the city.

One man-shaped golem stopped in the middle of Sator Square, dropped on one knee, raised a fist as if in salute, and went still. The horses halted beside it, as if awaiting riders.

And when the many-walled city of Ankh-Morpork had one more wall, out beyond the gates, they stopped. As one, they raised their right hands in a fist. Shoulder to shoulder, ringing the city, the golems . . . guarded. Silence fell.

In Sator Square, Commander Vimes looked up at the poised fist and then at Moist.

"Am I under arrest?" said Moist meekly.

Vimes sighed. "Mr. Lipwig," he said, "there's no word for what you are."

THE PALACE'S BIG ground-floor council room was packed. Most people had to stand. Every guild, every interest group, and everyone who just wanted to say they had been there . . . was there. The crowd overflowed into the palace grounds and out onto the streets. Children were climbing on the golem in the square, despite the efforts of the watchmen who were guarding it.*

There was a large ax buried in the big table, Moist noticed; the force of it had split the wood. It had clearly been there for some time. Perhaps it was some kind of warning, or some kind of symbol. This was a council of war, after all, but without the war.

---

*Who was being guarded from whom was not, at this point, either certain or germane. *Guarding was in the process of happening.*

"—However, we are already getting some very threatening notes from the other cities," said Lord Vetinari, "so it is only a matter of time."

"Why?" said Archchancellor Ridcully of Unseen University, who had managed to get a seat by dint of elevating its protesting occupant out of it. "All the things are doin' is standin' around outside the walls, yes?"

"Quite so," said Vetinari, "and it's called aggresive defense. That is practically a declaration of war." He gave a sad little sigh, the sign of a brain shifting down a gear. "May I remind you of the famous dictum of General Tacticus: 'Those who desire war, prepare for war'? Our city is surrounded by a wall of creatures each one of which, I gather, could only be stopped by a siege weapon. Miss Dearheart," he paused to give Adora Belle a sharp little smile, "has been kind enough to bring Ankh-Morpork an army capable of conquering the world, although I'm happy to accept her assurance that she didn't actually mean to."

"Then why don't we?" said Lord Downey, head of the Assassins' Guild.

"Ah, Lord Downey. Yes, I thought someone would say that," said Vetinari. "Miss Dearheart? You have studied these golems."

"I've had half an hour!" Adora Belle protested. "Hopping on one foot, I might add!"

"Nevertheless, you are our expert. And you have had the assistance of the famously deceased Professor Flead."

"He kept trying to see up my dress!"

"Please, madam?"

"They have no chem that I can get at," said Adora Belle. "There's no way of opening their heads! As far as we can tell they have one overriding imperative, which is to defend the city. And that's all. It's actually carved into their clay."

"Nevertheless, there is such a thing as preemptive defense. That might be construed as 'guarding.' In your opinion, would they attack another city?"

"I don't think so. Which city would you like me to test them on, my lord?" Moist shuddered. Sometimes Adora Belle just didn't care.

"None," said Vetinari. "We are not going to have another wretched empire while I am Patrician. We've only just got over the last one. Professor Flead, have you been able to give them any instructions at all?"

All heads turned to Flead and his portable circle, which had remained near the door out of the sheer impossibility of struggling further into the room.

"What? No! I am certain I have the gist of Umnian, but I cannot make it move a step! I have tried every likely command, to no avail. It is most vexing!" He waved his staff at Dr. Hicks. "Come on, make yourself useful, you fellows. One more try!"

"I think I might be able to communicate with them," said Moist, staring at the ax, but his voice was lost in the disturbance as the grumbling students tried to manhandle the portable magic circle back through the crowded doorway.

Let me just work out why, he thought. *Yep . . . yep. It's actually . . . simple. Far too simple for a committee.*

"As' chairman of the, Merchant's' Guild gentle-men may, I point out that these thing's represent a valuable labor force in this' city—" said Mr. Robert Parker.*

"No slaves in Ankh-Morpork!" said Adora Belle, pointing a finger at Vetinari. "You've always said that!"

Vetinari lifted an eyebrow at her. Then he held the eyebrow and raised her a further eyebrow. But Adora Belle was unabashable.

"Miss Dearheart, *you* have yourself explained that they have no chem. You *cannot* free them. I am ruling that they are tools, and since they regard themselves as servants of the city, I will treat them as such." He raised both hands at the general uproar, and went on: "They will not be sold and will be treated with care, as tools should be. They will work for the good of the city and—"

"No, that would be a terribly bad idea!" A white coat was struggling to get to the front of the crowd. It was topped by a yellow rain hat.

"And you are . . . ?" said Vetinari.

The figure removed its yellow hat, looked around, and went rigid. A groan managed to escape from its mouth.

"Aren't you Hubert Turvy?" said Vetinari. Hubert's face remained locked in a mask of terror, so Vetinari, in a kinder tone, added, "Do you want some time to think about that last question?"

---

* As a member of the Ancient and Venerable Order of Greengrocers, Mr. Parker was honor-bound never to put his punctuation in the right place.

"I . . . only . . . just heard . . . about . . ." Hubert began.

Hubert looked around at the hundreds of faces, and blinked.

"Mr. Turvy, the alchemist of money?" Vetinari prompted. "It may be written down on your clothes somewhere?"

"I think I can assist here," said Moist, and elbowed his way to the tongue-tied economist.

"Hubert," he said, putting a hand on the man's shoulder, "all the people are here because they want to hear your amazing theory that demonstrates the inadvisability of putting these new golems to work. You don't want to disappoint them, do you? I know you don't meet many people, but everyone's heard of your wonderful work. Can you help them understand what you just shouted?"

"We are agog," said Lord Vetinari.

In Hubert's head, the rising terror of crowds was overturned by the urge to impart knowledge to the ignorant, which meant everyone except him. His hands grasped the lapels of his jacket. He cleared his throat.

"Well, the problem is that, considered as a labor force, the golems are capable of doing the work per day of one hundred and twenty thousand men."

"Think of what they could do for the city!" said Mr. Cowslick of the Artificers' Guild.

"Well, yes. To begin with, they would put one hundred and twenty thousand men out of work," said Hubert, "but that would only be the start. They do not require food, clothing or shelter. Most people spend their money on food, shelter, clothing, entertainment, and, not least, taxes. What would these golems spend it on? The demand for many things would drop and further unemployment would result. You see, circulation is everything. The money goes around, creating wealth as it goes."

"You seem to be saying that these things could beggar us!" said Vetinari.

"There would be . . . difficult times," said Hubert.

"Then what course of action do you propose, Mr. Turvy?"

Hubert looked puzzled. "I don't know, sir. I didn't know I had to find solutions as well."

"Any of the other cities would attack us if they had these golems," said Lord Downey, "and surely we don't have to think of their jobs, do we? Surely a little bit of conquest would be in order?"

"An empirette, perhaps?" said Vetinari sourly. "We use our slaves to create more slaves? But do we want to face the whole world in arms? For that is what we would do, at the finish. The best that we could hope for is that some of us would survive. The worst is that we would triumph. Triumph and rot. That is the lesson of history, Lord Downey. Are we not rich enough?"

That started another clamor.

Moist, unnoticed, pushed his way through the heaving crowd until he reached Dr. Hicks and his crew, who were fighting their way back to the big golem.

"Can I come with you, please?" he said. "I want to try something."

Hicks nodded, but while the portable circle was being dragged out in the street, he said, "I think Miss Dearheart tried everything. The professor was very impressed."

"There's something she didn't try. Trust me. Talking of trust, who are these lads holding the blanket?"

"My students," said Hicks, trying to keep the circle steady.

"They *want* to study necro— er, postmortem communications? Why?"

"Apparently it's good for getting girls," sighed Hicks. There were sniggers.

"In a necromancy department? What kind of girls do they get?"

"No, it's because when they graduate they get to wear the hooded black robe and the skull ring. I think the term one of them used was 'babe magnet.'"

"But I thought wizards aren't allowed to marry?"

"Marriage?" said Hicks. "Oh, I don't think they are concerned about *that*."

"We never were in my day!" shouted Flead, who was being shaken back and forth as the circle was dragged through the crowds. "Can't you blast some of these people with Black Fire, Hicks? You're a necromancer, for the sake of the seven hells! You are not supposed to be *nice*! Now that I can see what's going on I think I shall have to spend a lot more time in the department!"

"Could I have a quiet word?" whispered Moist to Hicks. "The lads can manage by themselves.

can't they? Tell them to catch up with us at the big golem."

He hurried on, and was not at all surprised to find Hicks hurrying to catch up with him. He pulled the not-really-a-necromancer into the shelter of a doorway and said: "Do you trust your students?"

"Are you mad?"

"It's just that I have a little plan to save the day, the downside of which is that Professor Flead will no longer, alas, be available to you in your department."

"By 'unavailable' you mean . . . ?"

"Alas, you would never see him again," said Moist. "I can tell that would be a blow."

Hicks coughed. "Oh dear. He wouldn't be able to come back at all?"

"I think not."

"Are you sure?" said Hicks carefully. "No possibility?"

"I'm pretty sure."

"Hm. Well, of course, it would indeed be a blow."

"A big blow. A big blow," Moist agreed.

"I wouldn't want him . . . hurt, of course."

"Anything but. Anything but," said Moist, trying not to laugh. We humans are good at this curly thinking, aren't we, he thought.

"And he has had a good innings, when all's said and done."

"Two of them," said Moist, "when you come to think about it."

"What do you want us to do?" said Hicks, against

the distant shouts of the ghostly professor berating the students.

"There's such a thing, I believe, as . . . an insorcism?"

"Those? We're not allowed to do those! They're totally against university rules!"

"Well, wearing the black robe and the skull ring has got to count for something, hasn't it? I mean, your predecessors would turn in their dark coffins if they thought you wouldn't agree to the minor naughtiness I have in mind . . ." And Moist explained, in one simple sentence.

Louder shouts and curses indicated that the portable circle was almost upon them.

"Well, Doctor?" said Moist.

A complex spectra of expressions chased one another across Dr. Hicks's face.

"Well, I suppose . . ."

"Yes, Doctor?"

"Well, it'd be like sending him to Heaven, right?"

"*Exactly!* I couldn't have put it better myself!"

"Anyone could put it better than this bunch!" snapped Flead, right behind him. "The department has really been allowed to go uphill since my day! Well, we shall see what we can do about that!"

"Before you do, Professor, I *must* speak to the golem," said Moist. "Can you translate for me?"

"Can but won't," snapped Flead.

"You tried to help Miss Dearheart just earlier on."

"*She* is *attractive*. Why should I bequeath to you knowledge it took me a century to acquire?"

"Because there's fools back there who want to use these golems to start a war?"

"Then that will reduce the number of fools."

In front of them now was the lone golem. Even kneeling, this one's face was level with Moist's eyes. The head turned to look blankly at him. The guards around the golem, on the other hand, looked at Moist with deep suspicion.

"We are going to perform a little magic, officers," Moist told them.

The corporal in charge looked as if this did not meet with his approval.

"We've got to guard it," he pointed out, eyeing the black robes and the shimmering Professor Flead.

"That's fine, we can work around you," said Moist. "Do please stay. I'm sure there's not much risk."

"Risk?" said the corporal.

"Although perhaps it might be better if you fanned out to keep the public away," Moist went on. "We would not want anything to happen to members of the public. If, perhaps, you could push them back a hundred yards or so?"

"Told to stay here," said the corporal, looking Moist up and down. He lowered his voice. "Er, aren't you the postmaster general?"

Moist recognized the look and the tone. Here we go . . .

"Yes, indeed," he said.

The watchman lowered his voice still further. "So, er, do you by any chance have any of the blue—"

"Can't help you there," said Moist quickly, reach-

ing into his pocket, "but I do just happen to have
here a couple of very rare 50p green stamps with
the highly amusing 'misprint' that caused a bit of a
stir last year, you may remember. These are the only
two left. *Very* collectible."

A small envelope appeared in his hand. Just as
quickly, it vanished into the corporal's pocket.

"We can't let anything happen to members of the
public," he said, "so I suggest we'd better keep them
back a hundred yards or so."

"Good thinking," said Moist.

A few minutes later, Moist had the square to himself, the watchmen having worked out quite quickly
that the further back from danger they pushed
the public the further from said danger they, too,
would be.

And now, Moist thought, for the Moment of
Truth. If possible, though, it would become the
Moment of Plausible Lies, since most people were
happier with them.

The Umnian golems were bigger and heavier
than the ones commonly seen around the town, but
they were beautiful. Of course they were—they had
probably been *made* by golems. And their builders
had given them what looked like muscles, and calm,
sad faces. In the last hour or so, in defiance of the
watchmen, the lovable kids of the city had managed
to scrawl a black mustache on this one.

O . . . kay. Now for the professor . . .

"Tell me, Professor, do you *enjoy* being dead?" he
said.

"Enjoy? How can anyone enjoy it, you fool?" said Flead.

"Not much fun?"

"Young man, the word *fun* is not applicable to existence beyond the grave," said Flead.

"And is that why you hang around the department?"

"Yes! It may be run by amateurs these days, but there's always something going on."

"Certainly," said Moist. "However, I'm wondering if someone of your . . . interests would not find them better served somewhere where there is always something coming off."

"I do not understand your meaning."

"Tell me, Professor, have you heard of the Pink PussyCat Club?"

"No, I have not. Cats are not normally pink in these times, are they?"

"Really? Well, let me tell you about the Pink PussyCat Club," said Moist. "Excuse us, Dr. Hicks." He waved away Hicks, who winked and led his students back to the crowd. Moist put his arm around the ghostly shoulders. It was uncomfortable to hold it there with no actual shoulder to take the weight, but style was everything in these matters.

The watchers heard some urgent whispering pass to and fro, and then Flead said, "You mean it's . . . smutty?"

Smut, thought Moist. *He really* is *old*.

"Oh, yes. Even, I might go so far as to say, suggestive."

"Do they show their . . . ankles?" said Flead, his eyes gleaming.

"Ankles," said Moist. "Ye— yes, I rather think they do." *Ye gods*, he wondered, *is he that old?*

"All the time?"

"Twenty-four hours a day. They never clothe," said Moist. "And sometimes they spin around a pole upside down. Take it from me, Professor, for you, eternity might not be long enough."

"And you just want a few words translated?"

"A small glossary of instructions."

"And then I can go?"

"Yes!"

"I have your word?"

"Trust me. I'll just explain this to Dr. Hicks. He may take some persuading."

Moist strolled over to the huddles of people who weren't necromancers at all. The postmortem communicator's response was other than he expected. Second thoughts were arising.

"I wonder if we'd be doing the right thing, setting *him* loose in a pole-dancing establishment?" said Hicks doubtfully.

"No one will see him. And he can't touch. They are very big on not touching in that place. I'm told."

"Yes, I suppose all he can do is ogle the young ladies." There was some sniggering from the students.

"So? They're paid to be ogled at," said Moist. "They are professional oglees. It's an ogling establishment. For oglers. And you heard what's going on in the palace. We could be at war in a day. Do you trust that lot? Trust me."

"You use that phrase an awful lot, Mr. Lipwig," said Hicks.

"Well, I'm very trustworthy. Ready, then? Hold back until I summon you, and then you can take him to his last resting place."

T HERE WERE PEOPLE in the crowd, with sledgehammers. You'd have a job to crack a golem if it didn't want you to, but he ought to get them out of here as soon as possible.

This probably wouldn't work. It was too simple. But Adora Belle had missed it, and so had Flead. The corporal now so bravely holding back the crowds wouldn't have, because it was all about orders, but nobody had asked him. You just had to think a little.

"Come on, young man," said Flead, still where his bearers had left him and backed away. "Let's get on with it, shall we?"

Moist took a deep breath.

"Tell me how to say: 'Trust me, and only me. Form ranks of four and march ten miles hubward of the city. Walk slowly,'" he said.

"Hee, hee. You are a sharp one, Mr. Lipstick!" said Flead, his mind full of ankles. "But it won't work, you know. We tried things like that."

"I can be very persuasive."

"It won't work, I tell you. I have found not one single word that they will react to."

"Well, Professor, it's not what you say, it's the way

that you say it, isn't it? Sooner or later it's all about style."

"Hah! You are a fool, man."

"I thought we had a deal, Professor? And I shall want a number of other phrases." He looked around at the golem horses, as still as statues. "And the one phrase I shall need is the equivalent of 'giddyup' and while I think of it I shall need 'whoa,' too. Or do you want to go back to the place where they've never heard of pole-dancing?"

CHAPTER 11

THINGS WERE GETTING heated in the conference room. This, to Lord Vetinari, was not a problem. He was a great believer in letting a thousand voices be heard, because this meant that all he actually needed to do was *listen* only to the ones that had anything useful to say, "useful" in this case being defined in the classic civil-service way as "inclining to my point of view." In his experience, it was a number generally smaller than ten.

The people who wanted a thousand, etc., really meant that they wanted their own voice to be heard while the other nine hundred ninety-nine were ignored, and for this purpose the gods had invented the committee. Vetinari was very good at committees, especially when Drumknott took the minutes. What the iron maiden was to stupid tyrants, the committee was to Lord Vetinari; it was only slightly more expensive,* far less messy, considerably more efficient, and, best of all, you had to *force* people to climb inside the iron maiden.

He was just about to appoint the ten noisiest people onto a Golem Committee that could be locked in a distant office, when a dark clerk appeared, apparently out of a shadow, and whispered something in Drumknott's ear. The secretary leaned down toward his master.

"Ah, it would seem that the golems are gone," said Vetinari cheerfully, as the dutiful Drumknott stepped back.

"Gone?" said Adora Belle, trying to see across to the window. "What do you mean, gone?"

"Not here anymore," said Vetinari. "Mr. Lipwig, it seems, has taken them away. They are leaving the vicinity of the city in an orderly fashion."

"But he can't do that!" Lord Downey was enraged. "We haven't decided what to do with them yet!"

"He, however, has," said Lord Vetinari, beaming.

"He shouldn't be allowed to leave the city! He is a bank robber! Commander Vimes, do your duty and arrest him!" This was from Cosmo.

Vimes's look would have frozen a saner man.

"I doubt if he's going far, *sir*," he said. "What do you wish me to do, Your Lordship?"

---

*The only real expense was tea and biscuits halfway through, which seldom happened with the iron maiden.

"Well, the ingenious Mr. Lipwig appears to have a purpose," said Vetinari, "so perhaps we should go and find out what it is?"

The crowd made for the door, where it got stuck and fought itself.

As it piled out into the street, Vetinari put his hands behind his head and leaned back with his eyes shut. "I love democracy. I could listen to it all day. Get the coach out, will you, Drumknott?"

"That is being done at this moment, sir."

"Did you put him up to this?"

Vetinari opened his eyes. "Miss Dearheart, always a pleasure," he murmured, waving away the smoke. "I thought you were gone. Imagine my delight at finding you are not."

"Well, did you?" said Adora Belle, her cigarette noticeably shortening as she took another drag. She smoked as if it were a kind of warfare.

"Miss Dearheart, I believe it would be impossible for me to put Moist von Lipwig up to anything that could be more dangerous than the things he finds to do of his own free will. While you were away, he took to climbing high buildings for fun, picked every lock in the Post Office, and took up with the Extreme Sneezing fraternity, who are frankly insane. He needs the heady whiff of danger to make his life worth living."

"He never does that sort of thing when *I'm* here!"

"Indeed. Can I invite you to ride with me?"

"What did you mean by saying 'indeed' like hat?" said Adora Belle suspiciously.

Vetinari raised an eyebrow. "By now, if I have

been adept at judging the way your fiancé thinks, we should be going to see an enormous hole . . ."

WE'RE GOING TO *need stone*, thought Moist as the golems dug. *Lots of stone. Can they make mortar? Of course they can. They're the Lancre Army Knife of tools.*

It was fearful, the way they could dig, even in this worn-out, hopeless soil. Dirt was fountaining into the air. Half a mile away, the Old Wizarding Tower, a landmark on the road to Sto Lat, brooded over an area of scrub and desolation that was unusual on the heavily farmed plains. A lot of magic had been used here once. Plants grew twisty or not at all. The owls that haunted the ruins made sure their meals came from a distance away. It was the perfect site. No one wanted it. It was a wasteland, and a wasteland shouldn't be allowed to go to waste.

What a weapon, he thought, as his golem horse circled the diggers. They could collapse a city in a day. What a terrible force they would be in the wrong hands.

Thank goodness they are in mine . . .

The crowd was keeping its distance, but was also getting bigger and bigger. The city had turned out to watch. To be a true citizen of Ankh-Morpork was to never miss a show. As for Mr. Fusspot, he was apparently having the time of his life standing on the horse's head. There's nothing a small dog likes more than a high place from which to yap madly at people . . . no, actually, there was, and the chairman had managed to wedge his toy between a clay ear and his paw, and stopped barking to growl every time Moist made a tentative grab at it.

"Mr. Lipwig!"

He looked around to see Sacharissa hurrying toward him, waving her notebook. *How does she do it?* he wondered, watching her as, dirt raining around her, she scurried past lines of digging golems. *She's even here before the Watch.*

"You have a golem horse, I see," she shouted as she reached him. "It looks beautiful."

"It's rather like riding a flowerpot that you can't steer," Moist yelled to make himself heard over the noise. "The saddle could use some padding, too. Good, though, aren't they? Notice how they keep shifting all the time, just like the real thing?"

"And why are the golems burying themselves?"

"I ordered them to!"

"But they are immensely valuable!"

"Yes. So we should keep them safe, right?"

"But they belong to the city!"

"They were taking up a lot of room, don't you think? I'm not claiming them, in any case!"

"They could do wonderful things for the city, couldn't they?" More people were arriving now and gravitating toward the man in the golden suit, because he was always good value for money.

"Like embroil it in a war or create an army of beggars? My way's better!"

"I'm sure you are going to tell us what it is!" shouted Sacharissa.

"I want to base the currency on them! I want to make them into money! Gold that guards itself! You can't fake it!"

"You want to put us on the golem standard?"

"Certainly! Look at them! How much are they worth?" shouted Moist, as his horse reared very convincingly. "They could build canals and dam floods, level mountains and make roads! If we need them to, they will! And if we don't, then they'll help to make us rich by doing nothing! The dollar will be so sound you could bounce trolls off of it!"

The horse, with an astonishing grasp of public relations, reared again as Moist pointed at the laboring masses.

"*That* is value! *That* is worth! What is the worth of a gold coin compared to the dexterity of the hand that holds it?" He replayed that line in his head and added, "That would make a good headline on page one, don't you think? And it's Lipwig with a G!"

Sacharissa laughed. "Page one is already crowded! What's going to happen to these things?"

"They'll stay here until cool heads decide what to do next!"

"And what are they guarding the city from right now, exactly?"

"Stupidity!"

"One last thing, Moist. You are the only one who knows the secret of the golems, yes?"

"Inexplicably, this seems to be the case!"

"Why is this?"

"I suppose I'm just a very persuasive person!" This got another laugh.

"Who just happens to command a huge, unstoppable army? What demands are you going to make?"

"None! No, on second thought, a coffee would be nice! I didn't have any breakfast!" That got a much bigger laugh from the crowd.

"And do you think the citizens should be glad it's you in the saddle, as it were?"

"Hell, yes! Trust me!" said Moist, dismounting and lifting a reluctant Mr. Fusspot down from his perch.

"Well, you should know about that, Mr. Lipwig." This got a round of applause. "You wouldn't care to tell us what happened to the gold from the bank, would you?"

"'Es wearin' it!" shouted a wag in the crowd, to cheering.

"Miss Cripslock, your cynicism is, as ever, a dagger to my heart!" said Moist. "I intended to get to the bottom of that today, but 'best-laid plans' and all that. I just don't seem to be able to clear my desk!"

Even this got a laugh, and it wasn't really very funny.

"Mr. Lipwig? I want you to come with me . . ."

Commander Vimes shoved his way through the crowd, with other watchmen materializing behind him.

"Am I under arrest?" said Moist.

"Hell, yes! You did leave the city!"

"I think he could successfully argue, Commander, that the city has come with him."

All heads turned. A path cleared itself for Lord Vetinari, as paths do for men known to have dungeons in their basement. And Adora Belle hobbled past him, threw herself at Moist, and started beating on his chest, shouting: "How did you get through to them? How did you make them understand? Tell me or I'll never promise to marry you again!"

"What are your intentions, Mr. Lipwig?" said Vetinari.

"I was planning to hand them over to the Golem Trust, sir," said Moist, fending off Adora Belle as gently as possible.

"You were?"

"But not the golem horses, sir. I'll bet they are faster than any flesh-and-blood creatures. There are nineteen of them, and if you'll take my advice, sir, you'll give one to the king of the dwarfs, because I imagine he's a bit angry right now. It's up to you what you do with the others. But I'd like to ask for half a dozen of them for the Post Offce. In the meantime, the rest of them will be safe under ground. I want them to be the basis of the currency, because—"

"Yes, I couldn't help overhearing," said Vetinari. "Well done, Mr. Lipwig, I can see you've been thinking about this. You have presented us with a sensible way forward, indeed. I have also been giving the situation much thought, and all that remains is for me—"

"Oh, no thanks are necessary—"

"—to say, 'Arrest this man, Commander.' Be so good as to handcuff him to a sturdy officer and put him in my coach."

"What?" said Moist.

"*What?*" screamed Adora Belle.

"The directors of the Royal Bank are pressing charges of embezzlement against you and the chairman, Mr. Lipwig." Vetinari reached down and picked up Mr. Fusspot by the scruff of his neck. The little dog swung gently back and forth in the Patrician's grasp, wide eyes open wider in terror, his toy vibrating apologetically in his mouth.

"You can't seriously blame him for anything," Moist protested.

"Alas, he *is* the chairman, Mr. Lipwig. His pawprints are on the documents."

"How can you do this to Moist after what's just happened?" said Adora Belle. "Hasn't he just saved the day?"

"Possibly, although I'm not sure whom he has saved it for. The law must be obeyed, Miss Dearheart. Even tyrants have to obey the law." He paused, looking thoughtful, and continued, "No, I tell a lie, tyrants do *not* have to obey the law, obviously, but they do have to observe the niceties. At least, I do."

"But he didn't take—" Adora Belle began.

"Nine o'clock tomorrow, in the Great Hall," said Vetinari. "I invite all interested parties to attend. We shall get to the bottom of this." He raised his voice. "Are there any directors of the Royal Bank here? Ah, Mr. Lavish. Are you well?"

Cosmo Lavish, walking unsteadily, pushed his way through the crowd, supported on one side by a young man in a brown robe.

"You have had him arrested?" said Cosmo.

"One uncontested fact is that Mr. Lipwig, on behalf of Mr. Fusspot, did formally take responsibility for the gold."

"Indeed he did," said Cosmo, glaring at Moist.

"But in the circumstances I feel I should look into all aspects of the situation."

"We are in agreement there," said Cosmo.

"And to that end I am arranging for my clerks to enter the bank tonight and examine its records," Vetinari went on.

"I cannot agree to your request," said Cosmo.

"Fortuitously, it was not a request." Lord Vetinari tucked Mr. Fusspot under his arm, and continued: "I have the chairman with me, you see. Commander Vimes, Mr. Lipwig into my coach, please. See that Miss Dearheart is escorted safely home, will you? We shall sort this out tomorrow."

Vetinari looked at the tower of dust that now enveloped the industrious golems, and added, "We've all had a very busy day."

O UT IN THE back alley behind the Pink Pussy-Cat Club the insistent, pumping music was muffled but still pervasive.

Dark figures lurked . . .

"Mr. Hicks, sir?"

The head of the Department of Postmortem Communications paused in the act of drawing a complicated rune among the rather less complex ev-

eryday graffiti and looked up at the concerned face
of his student.

"Yes? Barnsforth?"

"Is this exactly *legal* under college rules, sir?"

"Of course not! Think of what might happen if
this sort of thing fell into the wrong hands! Hold
the lantern higher, Goatly, we're losing the light."

"And whose hands would that be, sir?"

"Well, technically ours, as a matter of fact. But
it's perfectly all right if the council don't find out.
And they won't, of course. They know better than
to go around finding things out."

"So it *is* illegal, technically?"

"Well now," said Hicks, drawing a glyph which
flamed blue for a moment, "who among us, when
you get right down to it, can say what is right and
what is wrong?"

"The college council, sir?" said Barnsforth.

Hicks threw down the chalk and straightened up.

"Now listen to me, you four! We are going to in-
sorcise Flead, understand? To his eternal satisfaction
and the not-inconsiderable good of the department,
believe me! This is a difficult ritual but if you assist
me you'll be doctors of postmortem communication
by the end of the term, understand? Straight A's for
the lot of you and, of course, the skull ring! Since
you have so far managed to turn in one-third of an
essay between you, I would say that is a bargain,
wouldn't you, Barnsforth?"

The student blinked in the force of the question,
but natural talent came to his aid. He coughed in a
curiously academic way, and said, "I think I under-

stand you, sir. What we are doing here goes *beyond* mundane definitions of right and wrong, does it not? We serve a higher truth."

"Well done, Barnsforth, you will go a long way. Everyone got that? Higher truth. Good! Now let's decant the old bugger and get out of here before anyone catches us!"

A TROLL OFFICER in a coach is hard to ignore. He just looms. That was Vimes's little joke, perhaps. Sergeant Detritus sat beside Moist, effectively clamping him into his seat. Lord Vetinari and Drumknott sat opposite, his lordship with his hands crossed on the silver-tipped cane and his chin resting on his hands. He watched Moist intently. Under Vetinari's seat, Mr. Fusspot buzzed.

There was a rumor that the sword in the stick was made with the iron taken from the blood of a thousand men. It seemed a waste, thought Moist, when for a bit of extra work you could get enough to make a plowshare. Who made up these things, anyway?

But with Vetinari, it seemed possible, if a bit messy.

"Look, if you let Cosmo—" he began.

"*Pas devant le gendarme*," said Lord Vetinari.

"Dat mean no talkin' in front o' me," Sergeant Detritus supplied helpfully.

"Then can we talk about angels?" said Moist, after a period of silence.

"No we can't. Mr. Lipwig, you appear to be the only person able to command the biggest army since the days of the Empire. Do you think that is a good idea?"

"I didn't want to! I just worked out how to do it!"

"You know, Mr. Lipwig, killing you right now would solve an incredibly large number of problems."

"I didn't intend this! Well . . . not exactly like this."

"We didn't intend the Empire. It just became a bad habit. So, Mr. Lipwig, now that you have your golems, what else do you intend to do with them?"

"Put one in to power every clacks tower. The donkey treadmills have never worked properly. The other cities can't object to that. It will be a boon to ma— to peoplekind and the donkeys won't object, I expect."

"That will account for a few hundred, perhaps. And the rest?"

"I intend to turn them into gold, sir. And I think it will solve all our problems."

Lord Vetinari raised a quizzical eyebrow. "*All* our problems?"

T HE PAIN WAS breaking through again, but somehow reassuring. He was becoming Vetinari, certainly. The pain was good. It was a *good* pain, concentrated, it helped him think.

Right now, Cosmo was thinking that Pucci really should have been strangled at birth, which family folklore said he had been trying to do. Everything about her was annoying. She was selfish, arrogant, greedy, vain, headstrong, and totally lacking in tact and the slightest amount of introspection.

Those were not, within the clan, considered to be drawbacks in a person; one could hardly stay rich if one bothered all the time about whether what one was doing was wrong or right. But Pucci thought she was beautiful, and that grated on his nerves. She did have good hair, that was true, but those high heels! She looked like a tethered balloon! The only reason she had any figure at all was because of the wonders of corsetry. And, while he'd heard that fat girls had lovely personalities, she just had a lot, and all of it was Lavish.

On the other hand, she was his age and at least had ambition and a wonderful gift for hatred. She wasn't lazy like the rest of them. They spent their lives huddled around the money. They had no vision. Pucci was someone he could talk to. She saw things from a softer, female perspective.

"You should have Bent killed," she said. "I'm sure he knows something. Let's hang him from one of the bridges by his ankles. That's what Granddaddy used to do. Why are you still wearing that glove?"

"He's been a loyal servant of the bank," said Cosmo, ignoring the last remark.

"Well? What's that got to do with it? Is there still something wrong with your hand?"

"My hand is fine," said Cosmo, as another red rose of pain bloomed all the way to his shoulder. *I'm so close*, he thought. *So close! Vetinari thinks he has me, but I have him! Oh, yes!* Nevertheless . . . perhaps it was time to start tidying up.

"I will send Cranberry to see Mr. Bent tonight," he said. "The man is no further use now that I have Cribbins."

"Good. And then Lipsbig will go to prison and we'll get our bank back. You don't look well, you know. You are very pale."

"As pale as Vetinari?" said Cosmo, pointing at the painting.

"What? What are you talking about? Don't be silly," said Pucci. "And there's a funny smell in here, too. Has something died?"

"My thoughts are unclouded. Tomorrow will be Vetinari's last day as Patrician, I assure you."

"You're being silly again. And ever so sweaty, I might add," said Pucci. "Honestly, it's dripping off your chin. Pull yourself together!"

"I imagine the caterpillar feels it is dying when it begins to turn into a beautiful butterfly," said Cosmo dreamily.

"What? What? Who knows? What's that got to do with anything?" Pucci demanded. "That's not how it works in any case, because, listen, this is very interesting: the caterpillar dies, right, and goes all mushy, and then a tiny bit of it, like a kidney or something, suddenly wakes up and eats the caterpillar soup, and *that's* what comes out as the butterfly. It's a wonder of nature. *You've* just got a touch of flu. Don't be a big baby. I have a date. See you in the morning."

She flounced out, leaving Cosmo alone except for Cranberry, who was reading in the corner.

It occurred to Cosmo that he really knew very little about the man. As Vetinari, of course, he would soon know everything about everybody.

"You were at the Assassins' School, weren't you, Cranberry?" he said.

Cranberry took the little silver bookmark from his top pocket, placed it carefully on the page, and closed the book.

"Yes, sir. Scholarship boy."

"Oh, yes. I remember them, scuttling about all the time. They tended to get bullied."

"Yes, sir. Some of us survived."

"Never bullied you, did I?"

"No, sir. I would have remembered."

"That's good. That's good. What is your first name, Cranberry?"

"Don't know, sir. Foundling."

"How sad. Your life must have been very hard."

"Yes, sir."

"The world can be so very harsh at times."

"Yes, sir."

"Will you be so good as to kill Mr. Bent tonight?"

"I have made a mental note, sir. I will take an associate and undertake the task an hour before dawn. Most of Mrs. Cake's lodgers will be out at that time and the fog will be thickest. Fortuitously, Mrs. Cake is staying with her old friend Mrs. Harms-Beetle in Welcome Soap tonight. I checked earlier, having anticipated this eventuality."

"You are a craftsman, Cranberry. I salute you."

"Thank you, sir."

"Have you seen Heretofore anywhere?"

"No, sir."

"I wonder where he's got to? Now go off and have your supper, anyway. I will not be dining tonight.

"Tomorrow I will change," he said aloud, when the door had shut behind Cranberry.

He reached down and drew the sword. It was a thing of beauty.

In the picture opposite, Lord Vetinari raised an eyebrow and said: "Tomorrow you will be a beautiful butterfly."

Cosmo smiled. He was nearly there. Vetinari had gone completely mad.

Mr. Bent opened his eyes and stared at the ceiling.

After a few seconds, this uninspiring view was replaced by an enormous nose, with the rest of a worried face some distance beyond it.

"You're awake!"

Mr. Bent blinked and refocused and looked up at Miss Drapes, a shadow against the lamplight.

"You had a bit of a funny turn, Mr. Bent," she said in the slow, careful voice people use for talking to mental patients, the elderly, and the dangerously armed.

"A funny turn? I did something funny?" He raised his head from the pillow, and sniffed.

"You are wearing a necklace of garlic, Miss Drapes?" he said.

"It's . . . a precaution," said Miss Drapes, looking

guilty, "against . . . colds . . . yes, colds. You can't be too careful. How do you feel, in yourself?"

Mr. Bent hesitated. He wasn't certain how he felt. He wasn't certain who he was. There seemed to be a hole inside. There was no himself in himself.

"What has been happening, Miss Drapes?"

"Oh, you don't want to worry about all that," said Miss Drapes, with fragile cheerfulness.

"I believe I do, Miss Drapes."

"The doctor said you weren't to get excited, Mr. Bent."

"I, to the best of my knowledge, have never been excited in my life, Miss Drapes."

The woman nodded. Alas, the statement was so easy to believe.

"Well, you know Mr. Lipwig? They say he stole all the gold out of the vault! The—"

—story unfolded. It was, in many places, speculations, both new and secondhand, and because Miss Drapes was a regular reader of the *Tanty Bugle*, it was recounted in the style and language in which tales of 'orrible murder are discussed.

What shocked her was the way the man just lay there. Once or twice he asked her to go back over a detail, but his expression never changed. She tried to add excitement, she painted the walls with exclamation marks, and he did not budge.

"—and now he's banging up in the Tanty," Miss Drapes said. "They say he will be hangéd by the neck until dead. I think hangéd is worse than just being hanged."

"But they cannot find the gold . . ." whispered Mavolio Bent, leaning back against the pillow.

"That's right! Some say it has been spirited away by dire accomplices!" said Miss Drapes. "They say informations have been laid against him by Mr. Lavish."

"I am a damned man, Miss Drapes, judged and damned," said Mr. Bent, staring at the wall.

"You, Mr. Bent? That's no way to talk! You, who've never made a mistake?"

"But I have sinned. Oh, indeed I have! I have worshiped false idols!"

"Well, sometimes you can't get real ones," said Miss Drapes, patting his hand and wondering if she should call someone. "Look, if you want absolution, I understand the Ionians are doing two sins for one this week—"

"It's caught me," he whispered. "Oh dear, Miss Drapes. There is something rising inside that wants to get out!"

"Don't you worry, we've got a bucket," said Miss Drapes.

"No! You should go, now! This will be horrible!"

"I'm not going anywhere, Mr. Bent," said Miss Drapes, a study in determination. "You're just having a funny turn, that's all."

"Ha," said Mr. Bent. "Ha . . . ha . . . haha . . ." The laugh climbed up his throat like something from the crypt.

His skinny body went rigid and arced as if it was rising from the mattress. Miss Drapes flung herself across the bed, but she was too late. The man's hand rose, trembling, and extended a finger toward the wardrobe.

"Here we are again!" Bent screamed.

The lock clicked. The doors swung open.

In the cupboard was a pile of ledgers and something . . . shrouded. Mr. Bent opened his eyes and looked up into those of Miss Drapes.

"I brought it with me," he said, as if talking to himself. "I hated it so much but I brought it with me. Why? Who runs the circus?"

Miss Drapes was silent. All she knew was that she was going to follow this to the end. After all, she'd spent the night in a man's bedroom, and Lady Deirdre Waggon had a lot to say about that. She was technically a Ruined Woman, which seemed unfair given that, even more technically, she wasn't.

She watched as Mr. Bent . . . changed. He had the decency to do so with his back turned, but she closed her eyes anyway. Then she remembered that she was Ruined, and so there wasn't much point, was there?

She opened them again.

"Miss Drapes?" said Mr. Bent dreamily.

"Yes, Mr. Bent?" she said through chattering teeth.

"We need to find . . . a bakery."

Cranberry and his associate stepped into the room, and stopped dead. This was not according to the plan.

"And possibly a ladder," said Mr. Bent. He pulled a strip of pink rubber from his pocket, and bowed.

CHAPTER 12

THERE WAS CLEAN straw in Moist's cell and he was pretty certain no one had gobbed in the stirabout, which contained what, if you were forced to name it, you would have to concede was meat. News had somehow got around that Moist was the reason that Bellyster was no longer on the staff. Even his fellow screws had hated the bullying bastard, so Moist also got a second helping without asking, his shoes cleaned, and a complimentary copy of the *Times* in the morning.

The marching golems had forced the bank's troubles onto page five. The golems were all over the front page, and a lot of the inner pages were full of Vox Pops, which meant people in the street who didn't know anything told other people what they knew, and lengthy articles by people who also didn't know anything but could say it very elegantly in 2,500 words.

He was just staring at the crossword puzzle* when someone knocked very politely on the cell door. It was the warden, who hoped Mr. Lipwig had enjoyed his brief stay with them, would like to show him to his carriage, and looked forward to the pleasure of his custom again should there be any further temporary doubts about his honesty. In the meantime, he would be grateful if Mr. Lipwig would be kind enough to wear these lightweight manacles, for the look of the thing, and when they were taken off him, as they surely would be when his character was proved to be *spotless*, would he please remind the officer in charge that they were prison property, thank you very much.

There was a crowd outside the prison, but they were standing back from the large golem which, down on one knee and with fist thrust into the air, was waiting outside the gate. It had turned up last night and if Mr. Lipwig could see his way clear to getting it to move, said the warden, everyone would be most appreciative.

Moist tried to look as though he'd expected it. He had told Black Mustache to await further orders. He hadn't expected *this*.

In fact, it stomped after the coach all the way to

---

*1 down "Shaken players shift the lead." Nine letters. Lord Vetinari had sneered at it.

the palace. There were a lot of watchmen lining the route and there seemed to be a black-clad figure on every rooftop. It looked as though Vetinari was not taking any chances on him escaping. There were more guards waiting in the back courtyard—more than was efficient, Moist could tell, since it can be easier for a swift-thinking man to get away from twenty men than from five. But somebody was Making A Statement. It didn't matter what it was, so long as it looked impressive.

He was led by dark passages into the sudden light of the Great Hall, which was packed. There was a smattering of applause, one or two cheers, and a ringing series of "boo"s from Pucci, who was sitting next to her brother in the front row of the big block of seats. Moist was led to a small podium, which was going to serve as a dock, where he could look around at the guild leaders, senior wizards, important priests, and members of the Great and the Good, or at least the Big and the Noisy. There was Harry King, grinning at him, and the cloud of smoke that indicated the presence of Adora Belle, and—oh yes, the new high priestess of Anoia, her crown of bent spoons all shiny, her ceremonial ladle held stiffly, her face rigid with nerves and importance. *You owe me, girl*, Moist thought, *'cos a year ago you had to work in a bar in the evenings to make a living and Anoia was just one of half a dozen demigoddesses who shared an altar, which, let's face it, was your kitchen table with a cloth on it. What's one little miracle compared to that?*

There was a whisking of cloth and suddenly Lord Vetinari was in his seat, with Drumknott by his side. The buzz of conversation ceased, as the Patrician looked around the hall.

"Thank you for coming, ladies and gentlemen," he said. "Let us get on, shall we? This is not a court of law, as such. It is a court of inquiry, which I have convened to look into the circumstances surrounding the disappearance of ten tons of gold bullion from the Royal Bank of Ankh-Morpork. The good name of the bank has been called into question, and so we will consider all matters apparently pertaining to it—"

"No matter where they lead?"

"Indeed, Mr. Cosmo Lavish, no matter *where* they lead."

"We have your assurance on this?" Cosmo insisted.

"I believe I have already given it, Mr. Lavish. Can we proceed? I have appointed the Learned Mr. Slant, of Morecombe, Slant and Honeyplace, as counsel to the inquiry. He will examine and cross-examine as he sees fit. I think it is known to all that Mr. Slant commands the total respect of Ankh-Morpork's legal profession."

Mr. Slant bowed to Vetinari and let his steady gaze take in the rest of the room. It lingered a long time on the ranks of the Lavishes.

"First, the matter of the gold," said Vetinari. "I present Drumknott, my secretary and chief clerk, who overnight took a team of my senior clerks into the bank—"

"Am I in the dock here?" said Moist.

Vetinari glanced at him and looked down at his

paperwork. "I have here your signature on a receipt for some ten tons of gold," he said. "Do you dispute its authenticity?"

"No but I thought that was just a formality!" said Moist.

"Ten tons of gold is a formality, is it? And did you later break into the vault?"

"Well, yes, technically. I couldn't unlock it because Mr. Bent had fainted inside and left the key in the lock."

"Ah, yes, Mr. Bent, the chief cashier. Is he with us today?"

A quick survey found the room Bentless.

"I understood that he was in a somewhat distressed state but not seriously harmed," said Lord Vetinari. "Commander Vimes, please be so good as to send some men along to his lodgings, will you? I would like him to join us."

He turned back to Moist. "No, Mr. Lipwig, you are not on trial, as yet. Generally speaking, before someone is put on trial it helps to have some clear reason for doing so. It is considered neater. I must point out, though, that you took formal responsibility for the gold which, we must assume, was clearly gold and clearly in the vault at that time. In order to have a thorough understanding of the bank's disposition at *this* time I asked my secretary to audit the bank's affairs, which he and his team did last nigh—"

"If I'm not actually on trial at this moment can I get rid of these shackles? They do rather bias the case against me," said Moist.

"Yes, very well. Guards, see to it. Now Mr. Drumknott, if you please?"

I'm going to be hung out to dry, thought Moist, as Drumknott started speaking. *What is Vetinari playing at?*

He stared at the crowds as Drumknott went through the tedious litany of accountancy. Right in front, in a great black mass, was the Lavish family. From here, they looked like vultures. This was going to take a long time, by the sound of Drumknott's earnest drone. They were going to set him up, and Vetinari was—ah, yes, and then it would be, in some quiet room: "Mr. Lipwig, if you could see your way clear to telling me *how* you controlled those golems . . ."

A commotion near the door came as a welcome respite and now Sergeant Fred Colon, trailed by his inseparable associate Nobby Nobbs, was practically swimming through the crowd. Vimes pushed his way toward them, with Sacharissa drifting in his wake. There was a hurried conversation, and a ripple of horrified excitement rolled through the crowd.

Moist caught the word *murdered*!

Vetinari stood up and brought his stick down flat on the table, ending the noise like the punctuation of the gods.

"What has happened, Commander?" he said.

"Bodies, sir. In Mr. Bent's lodgings!"

"He's been murdered?"

"Nossir!" Vimes conferred briefly and urgently with his sergeant. "Body provisionally identified as

Professor Cranberry, sir, not a real professor, he's a nasty hired killer who likes reading. We thought he'd left the city. Sounds like the other one is Ribcage Jack, who was kicked to death"—there was another whispered briefing, but Commander Vimes tended to raise his voice when he was angry—"by a *what*? On the second floor? Don't be daft! So what got Cranberry? Eh? Did you just say what I thought you said?"

He straightened up. "Sorry, sir, I'm going to have to go and see this for myself. I think someone is having a jape."

"And poor Bent?" said Vetinari.

"No sign of him, sir."

"Thank you, Commander." Vetinari waved a hand. "Do hurry back when you know more. We cannot have japes. Thank you, Drumknott. I gather you found nothing untoward apart from the lack of gold. I'm sure that comes as a relief to us all. The floor is yours, Mr. Slant."

The lawyer arose with an air of dignity and mothballs.

"Tell me, Mr. Lipwig, what was your job before you came to Ankh-Morpork?" he said.

O . . . kay, thought Moist, looking at Vetinari, *I've worked it out. If I'm good and say the right things, I might live. At a price. Well, no thanks. All I wanted to do was make some money.*

"Your job, Mr. Lipwig?" Slant repeated.

Moist looked along the rows of watchers, and saw the face of Cribbins. The man winked.

"Hmm?" he said.

"I asked you what your job was before you arrived in this city!"

It was at this point that Moist became aware of a regrettably familiar whirring sound, and from his raised position he was the first to see the chairman of the Royal Bank appear from behind the curtains at the far end of the hall with his wonderful new toy clamped firmly in his mouth. Some trick of the vibrations was propelling Mr. Fusspot backward across the shiny marble.

People in the audience craned their necks as, with tail wagging, the little dog passed behind Vetinari's chair and disappeared behind the curtains on the opposite side.

I'm in a world where that just happened, Moist thought. *Nothing matters.* It was an insight of incredibly wonderful liberation.

"Mr. Lipwig, I asked you a question," Slant growled.

"Oh, sorry. I was a crook." . . . And he flew! This was it! This was better than hanging off some old building! Look at the expression on Cosmo's face! Look at Cribbins! They had it all planned out, and now it had got away from them. He had them all in his hand, and he was flying!

Slant hesitated.

"By 'crook' you mean—"

"Confidence trickster. Occasional forgery. I'd like to think I was more of a scallywag, to be frank."

Moist saw the looks that passed between Cosmo and Cribbins, and exulted within. No, this wasn't supposed to happen, was it? And now you're going to have to run to keep up . . .

Mr. Slant was certainly having trouble in that area.

"Can I be clear here? You broke the law for a living?"

"Mostly I took advantage of other people's greed, Mr. Slant. I think there was an element of education, too."

Mr. Slant shook his head in amazement, causing an earwig to fall, with a keen sense of the appropriate, out of his ear.

"Education?" he said.

"Yes. A lot of people learned that no one sells a real diamond ring for one-tenth of its value."

"And then you stepped into one of the highest public offices in the city?" said Mr. Slant, above the laughter. It was a release. People had been holding their breath for too long.

"I had to. It was that or be hanged," said Moist, and added, "again."

Mr. Slant looked flustered, and turned his eyes to Vetinari.

"Are you sure you wish me to continue, my lord?"

"Oh yes," said Vetinari. "To the death, Mr. Slant."

"Er . . . you have been hanged before?" Slant said to Moist.

"Oh, yes. I did not wish it to become a habit."

That got another laugh.

Mr. Slant turned again to Vetinari, who was smiling faintly.

"Is this true, my lord?"

"Indeed," said Vetinari calmly. "Mr. Lipwig was hanged last year under the name of Albert Spangler, but it turned out that he had a very tough neck, as was found when he was being placed in his coffin. You may be aware, Mr. Slant, of the ancient principle *quia ego sic dico*? A man who survives being hanged may have been selected by the gods for a different destiny, as yet unfulfilled? And since fortune had favored him, I resolved to put him on parole and charge him with resurrecting the Post Office, a task which had already taken the lives of four of my clerks. If he succeeded, well and good. If he failed, the city would have been spared the cost of another hanging. It was a cruel joke which, I am happy to say, rebounded to the general good. I don't think that anyone here would argue that the Post Office is now a veritable jewel of the city? Indeed, the leopard *can* change his shorts!"

Mr. Slant nodded automatically, remembered himself, and fumbled with his notes. He had lost his place.

"And now we come to, er, the matter of the bank—"

"Mrs. Lavish, a lady many of us were privileged to know, recently confided in me that she was dying," said Vetinari. "She asked me for advice on the future of the bank, given that her obvious heirs were, in her words, 'as nasty a bunch of weasels as you could ever hope not to meet—' "

All thirty-one of the Lavish lawyers stood up and spoke at once, incurring a total cost to their clients of $AM119.28p.

Mr. Slant glared at them.

Mr. Slant did not, despite what had been said,

have the respect of Ankh-Morpork's legal profession. He commanded its fear. Death had not diminished his encyclopedic memory, his guile, his talent for corkscrew reasoning, and the vitriol of his stare. Do not cross me this day, it advised the lawyers. Do not cross me, for if you do I will have the flesh from your very bones and the marrow therein. You know those leather-bound tomes you have on the wall behind your desk to impress your clients? I have read them all, and I wrote half of them. Do not try me. I am not in a good mood.

One by one, they sat down.*

"If I may continue?" said Vetinari. "I understand that Mrs. Lavish subsequently interviewed Mr. Lipwig and considered that he would be a superb chairman in the very best traditions of the Lavish family and the ideal guardian for the dog Mr. Fusspot, who is, by the custom of the bank, its chairman."

Cosmo rose slowly to his feet and stepped out into the center of the floor. "I object most strongly to the suggestion that this scoundrel is in the best traditions of my—" he began. Mr. Slant was on his feet as though propelled by a spring. Quick as he was, Moist was faster.

"I object!" he said.

"How do you dare object," Cosmo spat, "when you have *admitted* to being an arrogant scofflaw?"

"I object to Lord Vetinari's allegation that I have had anything to do with the fine traditions of the

---

*Total cost, including time and disbursements: $AM253.16p.

Lavish family," said Moist, staring into eyes that now seemed to be weeping green tears. "For example, I have never been a pirate or traded in slaves—"

There was a great rising of lawyers.

Mr. Slant glared. There was a great seating.

"They admit it," said Moist. "It's in the bank's own official history!"

"That is correct, Mr. Slant," said Vetinari. "I have read it. *Volenti non fit injuria* clearly applies."

The whirring started again. Mr. Fusspot was coming back the other way. Moist forced himself not to look.

"Oh, this is low indeed!" snarled Cosmo. "Whose history could withstand this type of malice!"

Moist raised a hand. "Oooh, oooh, I know this one!" he said. "Mine can. The worst I ever did was rob people who thought they were robbing me, but I never used violence and I gave it all back. Okay, I robbed a couple of banks, well, defrauded, really, but only because they made it so easy—"

"Gave it back?" said Slant, looking for some kind of response from Vetinari. But the Patrician was staring over the heads of the crowd, who were almost all engrossed in the transit of Mr. Fusspot, and merely raised a finger in either acknowledgment or dismissal.

"Yes, you may recall that I saw the error of my ways last year when the gods—" Moist began.

"'Robbed a couple of banks'?" said Cosmo. "Vetinari, are we to believe that you knowingly put the most important bank in the city into the charge of a known bank robber?"

The mass ranks of the Lavishes arose, united in the defense of the money. Vetinari still stared at the ceiling.

Moist looked up. A disc, something white, skimmed through the air near the ceiling, descended as it circled, and hit Cosmo between the eyes. A second one swooped on over the head of Moist and landed in the bosoms of the Lavishes.

"Should he have left it in the hands of *unknown* bank robbers?" a voice shouted, as collateral custard landed on every smart black suit. "Here we are again!"

A second wave of pies was already in the air, circling the room in trajectories that dropped them into the struggling Lavishes. And then a figure fought its way out of the crowd, to the groans and screams of those who'd temporarily been in its way; this was because those who managed to escape having their feet trodden on by the big shoes jumped back in time to be scythed down by the ladder the newcomer was carrying. Then it'd innocently turned to see what mayhem it had caused, and the swinging ladder felled anyone too slow to get away. There was a method to it, though; as Moist watched, the clown stepped away from the ladder, leaving four people trapped among the rungs in such a way that any attempt to get out would cause huge pain to the other three and, in the case of one of the watchmen, a serious impairment of marriage prospects.

Red-nosed and raggedy-hatted, it bounced into the arena in great, leaping strides, his enormous boots flapping on the floor with every *familiar* step.

"Mr. Bent?" said Moist. "Is that you?"

"My jolly good pal Mr. Lipwig!" shouted the clown. "You think the ringmaster runs the circus, do you? Only by the consent of the clowns, Mr. Lipwig! Only by the consent of the clowns!"

Bent drew back his arm and hurled a pie at Lord Vetinari, but Moist was already in full leap before the pie started its journey. His brain came a poor third, and delivered its thoughts all in one go, telling him what his legs had apparently worked out for themselves: that the dignity of the great could rarely survive a faceful of custard, that a picture of an encustarded Patrician on the front page of the *Times* would rock the power politics of the city, and most of all, that in a post-Vetinari world he, Moist, would not see tomorrow, which was one of his life-long ambitions.

As in a silent dream, he sailed toward the oncoming nemesis, reaching out with snail-pace fingers while the pie spun on to its date with history.

It hit him in the face.

The Patrician had not moved. Custard flew up and four hundred fascinated eyes watched as a glob of the stuff was thrown up by the collision and headed on toward Vetinari, who caught it in an up-raised hand.

The little smack as it landed in his palm was the only sound in the room.

Vetinari inspected the captured custard.

He dipped a finger into it, and tasted the blob thereon. He cast his eyes upward thoughtfully, while the room held its collective breath, and then said: "I do believe it is pineapple."

There was a thunder of applause. There had to be; even if you hated Vetinari, you had to admire the timing.

And now he was coming down the steps, advancing on a frozen and fearful clown.

"The clowns do not run *my* circus, sir," he said, grabbing the man by his big red nose and pulling it to the full extent of the elastic. "Is that understood?"

The clown produced a bulbous horn and gave a mournful honk.

"Good. I'm glad you agree. And now I want to talk to Mr. Bent, please."

There were two honks this time.

"Oh yes he is," said Vetinari. "Shall we get him out for the boys and girls? *What is 15.3 percent of 59.66?*"

"You leave him alone! Just you leave him alone!"

The battered crowd parted yet again, this time for a disheveled Miss Drapes, as outraged and indignant as a mother hen. She was clasping something heavy to her sparse bosom, and Moist realized that it was a stack of ledgers.

"This is what it's all about!" she announced triumphantly, flinging her arms wide. "It's not his fault! They took advantage of him!"

She pointed an accusatory finger at the dripping ranks of the Lavishes. If a battle goddess was allowed to have a respectable blouse and hair escaping rapidly from a tight bun, then Miss Drapes could have been deified. "It was them! They sold the gold years ago!" This caused a general and enthusiastic uproar on all sides not containing a Lavish.

"There will be silence!" shouted Vetinari.

The lawyers rose. Mr. Slant glared. The lawyers sank.

And Moist wiped pineapple custard from his eyes just in time.

"Look out! He's got a daisy!" he shouted, and then thought: *I just shouted "Look out! He's got a daisy," and I think I'm going to remember forever just how embarrassing this was.*

Lord Vetinari looked down at the improbably large flower in the clown's buttonhole. A tiny drop of water glistened in the almost-well-concealed nozzle.

"Yes," he said, "I know. Now, sir, I do indeed believe you are Mr. Bent. I recognize the walk, you see. If you are not, then all you have to do is squeeze, and all I have to do is let go. I repeat: I'd like to hear from Mr. Bent."

Sometimes the gods don't have the right sense of occasion, Moist thought. There should be thunder, a plangent tone, a chord of tension, some kind of celestial acknowledgment that here was the moment of tru—

"9.12798," said the clown.

Vetinari smiled and patted him on the shoulder.

"Welcome back," he said, and looked around the room until his gaze found Dr. Whiteface of the Fools' Guild.

"Doctor, would you take care of Mr. Bent, please? I think he needs to be among his own."

"It would be an honor, my lord. Seven pies in the air at once and a four-man ladder tie? Exemplary! Whoever you are brother, I offer you the joke handshake of welcome . . ."

"He's not going anywhere without me," said Miss Drapes grimly, as the white-faced clown stepped forward.

"Indeed, who could imagine how he would," said Vetinari. "And please extend the courtesy of your guild to Mr. Bent's young lady, Doctor," he added, to the surprise and delight of Miss Drapes, who clung on daily to the "lady" but had reluctantly said good-bye to the "young" years ago.

"And will somebody please release those people from that ladder? I think a saw will be required," Vetinari went on. "Drumknott, collect up these intriguing new ledgers that Mr. Bent's young lady has so kindly supplied. And I think Mr. Lavish needs medical attention—"

"I . . . do . . . not!" Cosmo, dripping custard, was trying to remain upright. It was painful to watch. He managed to point a furious but wavering finger at the tumbled books. "Those," he declared, "are the property of the bank!"

"Mr. Lavish, it is clear to us all that you are ill—" Vetinari began.

"Yes, you'd like everyone to believe that, wouldn't you—impostor!" Cosmo said, visibly swaying. In his head the crowd cheered.

"The Royal Bank of Ankh-Morpork," said Vetinari, without taking his eyes off Cosmo, "prides itself on its red-leather ledgers, which without fail are embossed with the seal of the city in gold leaf. Drumknott?"

"These are cheap cardboard-bound ones, sir. You can buy them anywhere. The writing within, however, is the unmistakable fine copperplate hand of Mr. Bent."

"You are sure?"

"Oh, yes. He does a wonderful cursive script."

"Fake," said Cosmo, as if his tongue was an inch thick, "all fake. Stolen!"

Moist looked at the watching people and saw the shared expression. Whatever you thought of him, it was not good to see a man fall to bits where he stood. A couple of watchmen were sidling carefully toward him.

"I never stole a thing in my life!" said Miss Drapes, bridling enough for gymkhana. "They were in his wardrobe—" she hesitated and decided she'd rather be scarlet than gray—"and I don't care what Lady Deirdre Waggon thinks! And I've taken a look inside them, too! Your father took the gold and sold it and forced him to hide it in the numbers! And that's not the half of it!"

". . . Beautiful but'fly," Cosmo slurred, blinking at Vetinari. "You not me any mo'. Walked mile in y'shoes!"

Moist also edged in his direction. Cosmo had the look of someone who might explode at any moment, or collapse, or just possibly fall on Moist's neck, mumbling things like "You're m'bestest pal, you are, it's you'n me 'gainst the worl' pal."

Greenish sweat was pouring down the man's face.

to focus on him.

down, Mr. Lavish," said

MAKING MONEY   431

"I . . .
Moist carefully. Cos

"'S a good pain," the
"Got 'li'l hat, got got sword o
with a whisper of steel, a gray bla
glitter to it, was pointing between
didn't waver. Behind it, Cosmo was tr
twitching, but the sword stayed rigid and u

The advancing watchmen slowed down a little. Their job had a pension.

"Will no one at all make any move, please? I think I can deal with this," said Moist, squinting along the blade. This was a time for delicacy . . .

"Oh, this is so silly," said Pucci, strutting forward with a clatter of heels. "We've got nothing to be ashamed of. It's our gold, isn't it? Who cares what he wrote down in his books?"

The phalanx of Lavish lawyers rose very cautiously to their feet, while the two employed by Pucci began to whisper urgently to her. She ignored them. Everyone was staring at *her* now, not her brother. Everyone was paying attention to *her*.

"Could you please be quiet, Miss Lavish?" said Moist. The stillness of the blade worried him. Some part of Cosmo was functioning very well indeed.

"Oh yes, I expect you just *would* like me to shut up, and I'm not going to!" said Pucci gleefully. Like Moist confronted by an open notebook, she triumphantly plunged on without a care: "We can't steal what already belongs to us, can we? So what if Father put the wretched gold to better use? It was just sitting there! Honestly, why are you all so

year. A...
was not go...
bankers in th...
Moist resisted...
as though anyone's go...
the gold still exists, yes? In i...
cares where it is?"
dense? Everybody does it. It's n...

...ot stealing. I mean,
...ings and things. It's not
...g to throw it away. Who

...ne impulse to look at the other
... room. Everyone does it, eh? Pucci
...ing to get many Hogswatch cards this
...nd her brother was staring at her in horror.
The rest of the clan, those who weren't still engrossed in decustarding themselves, were contriv-
ing to give the impression that they had never seen
Pucci before. Who is this madwoman? said their
faces. Who let her in? What is she talking about?

"I think your brother is very ill, miss," he said.

Pucci tossed her admittedly fine locks dismissively. "Don't worry about him, he's just being silly,"
she said. "He's only doing it to attract attention.
Silly boyish stuff about wanting to be Vetinari, as if
anyone in their right mind would—"

"He's dribbling green," said Moist, but nothing
cut through the barrage of chatter. He stared at
Cosmo's ravaged face, and everything made sense.
Beard. Cap. Sword stick, yes, with someone's tacky
idea of what a blade made from the iron in the blood
of a thousand men should look like. And what about
the murder of a man who made rings? And under
that stinking glove . . .

This is my world. I know how to do this.

"I beg your pardon! You are Lord Vetinari, aren't
you?" he said.

For a moment, Cosmo drew himself up and a
spark of imperiousness shone through.

"Indeed! Yes indeed," he said, raising one eyebrow. Then it sagged, and his puffy face sagged with it.

"Got ring. Vetin'ry ring," he mumbled. "'S mine really. *Good* pain . . ."

The sword dropped, too.

Moist grabbed the man's left hand and tore the glove off. It came away with a sucking sound and a smell that was unimaginably, nose-cakingly bad. The nearest guard threw up. *So many colors,* thought Moist. *So many . . . wiggling things . . .*

And there, still visible in the suppurating mass, was the unmistakable sullen gleam of stygium.

Moist grabbed Cosmo's other hand.

"I think you ought to come outside, my lord, now you are the Patrician," he said loudly. "You must meet the people . . ."

Once again, some inner Cosmo got a slippery grip, enough to cause the dribbling mouth to utter "Yes, this is very important . . ." before reverting to "Feel ill. Finger looks funny . . ."

"The sunshine will do it good," said Moist, taking him gently in tow. "Trust me."

CHAPTER 13

Gladys Is Doing It For Herself
❀ *To the House of Mirth* ❀ *The history of Mr. Bent*
❀ *Usefulness of clowns as nurses is questioned*
❀ *Owlswick gets an angel*
❀ *The golden secret (not exactly dragon magic)*
❀ *The return of the teeth* ❀ *Vetinari looks ahead*
❀ *The bank triumphant* ❀ *The Glooper's little gift*
❀ *How to spoil a perfect day*

ON THE FIRST day of the rest of his life Moist von Lipwig woke up, which was nice, given that on any particular day a number of people do not, but woke up alone, which was less pleasing.

It was six a.m., and the fog seemed glued to the windows, so thick that it should have contained croutons. But he liked these moments, before the fragments of yesterday reassembled themselves.

Hold on, this wasn't the suite, was it? This was his room in the Post Office, which had all the luxury and comfort that you would normally associate with the term "civil-service issue."

A piece of yesterday fell into place. Oh yes, Vetinari had ordered the bank shut while his clerks looked at *everything* this time. Moist wished them luck with the late Sir Joshua's special cupboard . . .

There was no Mr. Fusspot, which was a shame. You don't appreciate an early-morning slobber until it's gone. And there was no Gladys, either, which was worrying.

She didn't turn up while he was getting dressed, either, and there was no copy of the *Times* on his desk. His suit needed pressing, too.

He eventually found her pushing a trolley of mail in the sorting room. The blue dress was gone, to be replaced by a gray one which, by the nascent standards of golem dressmaking, looked quite smart.

"Good morning, Gladys," Moist ventured, "any chance of some pressed trouser?"

"There Is Always A Warm Iron In The Postmen's Locker Room, Mr. Lipwig."

"Oh? Ah. Right. And, er . . . the *Times*?"

"Four Copies Are Delivered To Mr. Groat's Office Every Morning, Mr. Lipwig."

"I suppose a sandwich is totally out of—"

"I Really Must Get On With My Duties, Mr. Lipwig," said the golem reproachfully.

"You know, Gladys, I can't help thinking that here's something different about you," said Moist.

"Yes! I Am Doing It For Myself," said Gladys, her eyes glowing.

"Doing what, exactly?"

"I Have Not Ascertained This Yet, But I Am Only Ten Pages Into The Book."

"Ah. You have been reading a new book? But not one by Lady Deirdre Waggon, I'll wager."

"No, Because She Is Out Of Touch With Modern Thought. I Laugh With Scorn."

"Yes, I imagine you would do," said Moist thoughtfully. "And I expect Miss Dearheart gave you said book?"

"Yes. It Is Entitled *Why Men Get Under Your Feet*, By Releventia Flout," said Gladys earnestly.

And we start out with the best of intentions, thought Moist, find 'em out, dig 'em up, make 'em free. But we don't know what we're doing, or what we're doing it to.

"Gladys, the thing about books . . . well, the thing . . . I mean just because it's written down, you don't have to . . . that is to say, it doesn't mean it's . . . what I'm getting at is that every book is—"

He stopped. They believe in words. Words give them life. I can't tell her that we just throw them around like jugglers, we change their meaning to suit ourselves—

He patted Gladys on the shoulder. "Well, read them all and make up your own mind, eh?"

"That Was Very Nearly Inappropriate Touching, Mr. Lipwig."

Moist started to laugh, and stopped at the sight of her grave expression.

"Er, only for Ms. Flout, I expect," he said, and went to grab a *Times* before they were all stolen.

It must have been another bittersweet day for the editor. After all, there can only be one front page. In the end he'd stuffed in everything—the "I do believe it is pineapple" line, with a picture showing the dripping Lavishes in the background and, oh yes, here was Pucci's speech, in detail. It was wonderful. And she'd gone on and on. It was all perfectly clear, from her point of view: she was right and everyone was silly. She was so in love with her own voice that the watchmen had to write down their official caution on a piece of paper and hold it up in front of her before they towed her away, still talking . . .

And someone had got a picture of Cosmo's ring catching the sunlight. It was near perfect surgery, they said down at the hospital, and had probably saved his life, they said, and how had Moist known what to do, they said, when the entirety of Moist's relevant medical knowledge was that a finger shouldn't have green mushrooms growing on it—

The paper was twitched out of his hands.

"What have you done with Professor Flead?" Adora Belle demanded. "I know you've done something! Don't lie."

"I haven't done anything!" Moist protested, and checked the wording. Yes, technically true.

"I've been to the Department of Postmortem Communications, you know!"

"And what did they say?"

"I don't know! There was a squid blocking the door! But you've done something, I know it! He told

you the secret of getting through to the golems,
didn't he!"

"No." Absolutely true.

"He didn't?"

"No. I got some extra vocabulary, but that's no
secret."

"Will it work for me?"

"No." Currently true.

"They'd only take orders from a man? I bet
that's it."

"I don't think so." True enough.

"So there is a secret?"

"It's not really a secret. Flead told us. He just
didn't know it was a secret." True.

"It's a word?"

"No." True.

"Look, why won't you tell me? You know you can
trust me!"

"Well, yes. Of course. But can I trust you if someone holds a knife to your throat?"

"Why should they do that?"

Moist sighed. "Because you'll know how to command the biggest army there has ever been! Didn't
you look around outside? Didn't you see all the coppers? They turned up right after the hearing!"

"What coppers?"

"Those trolls re-laying the cobbles? How often
do you see that happening? The line of cabs that
aren't interested in passengers? The battalion of
beggars? And the coach yard around the back is full
of hangers-on, lounging about and watching the

windows. *Those* coppers. It's called a stakeout, and I'm the meat—"

There was a knock at the door. Moist recognized it; it sought to alert without disturbing.

"Come in, Stanley," he said. The door opened.

"It's me, sir," said Stanley, who went through life with the care of a man reading a manual translated from a foreign language.

"Yes, Stanley."

"Head of stamps, sir," said Stanley.

"Yes, Stanley?"

"Lord Vetinari is in the coach yard, sir, inspecting the new automatic pick-up mechanism. He says there is no rush, sir."

"He says there is no rush," said Moist to Adora Belle.

"We'd better hurry, then?"

"Exactly."

"REMARKABLY LIKE A gibbet," said Lord Vetinari, while behind him coaches rumbled in and out of the fog.

"It will allow a fast coach to pick up mailbags without slowing," said Moist. "That means letters going from small country offices can travel express without slowing the coach. It could save a few minutes on a long run."

"And, of course, if I let you have some of the golem horses the coaches might travel at a hundred miles an hour, I'm told, and I wonder if those glowing eyes could see even through this murk."

"Possibly, sir. But, in fact, I already have *all* the golem horses," said Moist.

Vetinari gave him a cool look, and then said, "Hah! And you also have all your ears. What exchange rate are we discussing?"

"Look, it's not that I want to be Lord of the Golems—" Moist began.

"On the way, please. Do join me in my coach," said Vetinari.

"Where are we going?"

"Hardly any distance. We're going to see Mr. Bent."

THE CLOWN WHO opened the little sliding door in the Fools' Guild's forbidding gates looked from Vetinari to Moist to Adora Belle, and wasn't very happy about any of them.

"We are here to see Dr. Whiteface," said Vetinari. "I require you to let us in with the minimum of mirth."

The door snapped back. There was some hurried whispering and a clanking noise, and one half of the double doors opened a little way, just enough for people to walk through in single file. Moist stepped forward, but Vetinari put a restraining hand on his shoulder and pointed up with his stick.

"This is the Fools' Guild," he said. "Expect . . fun."

There was a bucket balanced on the door. He sighed, and gave it a push with his stick. There was a thud and a splash from the other side.

"I don't know why they persist in this, I really don't," he said, sweeping through. "It's not funny and it could hurt someone. Mind the custard." There was a groan from the dark behind the door.

"Mr. Bent was born Charlie Benito, according to Dr. Whiteface," said Vetinari, pushing his way through the tent that occupied the Guild's quadrangle. "And he was born a clown."

Dozens of clowns paused in their daily training to watch them pass. Pies remained unflung, trousers did not fill with whitewash, invisible dogs paused in mid-widdle.

"*Born* a clown?" said Moist.

"Indeed, Mr. Lipwig. A great clown, from a family of clowns, who have worn the Charlie Benito makeup for centuries. You saw him last night."

"I thought he'd gone mad!"

"Dr. Whiteface, on the other hand, thinks he has come to his senses. Young Bent had a terrible childhood, I gather. No one told him he was a clown until he was thirteen. And his mother, for reasons of her own, discouraged all clownishness in him."

"She must have liked clowns once," said Adora Belle. She looked around them. All the clowns hurriedly looked away.

"She loved clowns," said Vetinari. "Or should I say, one clown. And for one night."

"Oh. I see," said Moist. "And then the circus moved on?"

"As circuses do, alas. After which I suspect she rather went off men with red noses."

"How do you know all this?" said Moist.

"Some of it is informed conjecture, but Miss Drapes has got a lot out of him in the last couple of days. She is a lady of some depth and determination."

On the far side of the big tent there was another doorway, where the head of the Guild was waiting for them.

He was white all over—white hat, white boots, white costume, and white face—and on that face, delineated in thin lines of red greasepaint, was a smile belying the real face, which was as cold and proud as that of a prince of Hell.

Dr. Whiteface nodded at Vetinari.

"My lord . . ."

"Dr. Whiteface," said the Patrician. "And how is the patient?"

"Oh, if only he had come to us when he was young," said Whiteface, "what a clown he would have been! What timing! Oh, by the way, we do not normally allow women visitors into the Guild, but in these special circumstances we are waiving this rule."

"Oh, I'm so glad," said Adora Belle, acid etching every syllable.

"It is simply that, whatever the Jokes For Women group says, women are just not funny."

"It is a terrible affliction," Adora Belle agreed.

"An interesting dichotomy, in fact, since neither are clowns," said Vetinari.

"I've always thought so," said Adora Belle.

"They are tragic," said Vetinari, "and we laugh at their tragedy as we laugh at our own. The painted grin leers out at us from the darkness, mocking our insane belief in order, logic, status, the reality of reality. The mask knows that we are born on the banana skin that leads only to the open manhole cover of doom, and all we can hope for are the cheers of the crowd."

"Where do the squeaky balloon animals fit in?" said Moist.

"I have no idea. But I understand that when the would-be murderers broke in, Mr. Bent strangled one with quite a lifelike humorous pink elephant made out of balloons."

"Just imagine the noise," said Adora Belle cheerfully.

"Yes! What a turn! And without any training! And the business with the ladder? Pure battleclowning! Superb!" said Whiteface. "We know it all now, Havelock. After his mother died, his father came back and, of course, took him off to the circus. Any clown could see the boy had funny bones. Those feet! They should have sent him to us! A boy of that age, it can be very tricky! But no, he was bundled into his grandfather's old gear and shoved out into the ring in some tiny little town, and well, that's where clowning lost a king."

"Why? What happened?" said Moist.

"Why do you think? They laughed at him."

❋ ❋ ❋

T WAS RAINING, and wet branches lashed at him as he bounded through the woods, whitewash still dribbling from his baggy trousers. The pants themselves bounced up and down on their elastic braces, occasionally hitting him under the chin.

The boots were good. They were amazing boots. They were the only ones he'd had that fitted.

But Mother had brought him up properly. Clothes should be a respectable gray, mirth was indecent, and makeup was a sin.

Well, punishment had come fast enough!

At dawn he found a barn. He scraped off the dried custard and caked greasepaint and washed himself in a puddle. Oh, that face! The fat nose, the huge mouth, the white tear painted on—he would remember it in nightmares, he knew it.

At least he still had his own shirt and drawers, which covered all the important bits. He was about to throw everything else away when an inner voice stopped him. His mother was dead and he hadn't been able to stop the bailiffs taking everything, even the brass ring Mother polished every day; he'd never see his father again . . . he had to keep something, there had to be something, *something*, so that he might remember who and why he was and where he'd come from and even why he'd left. The barn yielded a sack full of holes; that was good enough. The hated suit was stuffed inside.

Later that day he'd come across some caravans parked under the trees, but they were not the garish carts of the circus. Probably they were religious, he thought, and Mother had approved of the quieter religions, provided the gods weren't foreign.

They gave him rabbit stew. And when he looked over the shoulder of a man sitting quietly at a small folding table, he saw a book full of numbers, all written down. He liked numbers. They'd always made sense in a world that didn't. And then he'd asked the man, very politely, what the number at the bottom was, and the answer had been, "It's what we call the total," and he'd replied, "No, that's not the total, that's three farthings short of the total." "How do you know?" said the man, and he'd said, "I can see it is," and the man had said, "But you only just glanced at it!" and he'd said, "Well, yes, isn't that why?"

And then more books were opened and the people gathered round and gave him sums to do, and they were all so, so easy . . .

It was all the fun the circus couldn't be, and involved no custard, ever.

H E OPENED HIS eyes and made out the indistinct figures.

"Am I going to be arrested?"

Moist glanced at Vetinari, who waved a hand vaguely.

"Not necessarily," said Moist carefully. "We know about the gold."

"Mr. Lavish said he would let it be known about my . . . family," said Mr. Bent.

"Yes, we know."

"People would laugh. I couldn't stand that. And then I think I . . . you know, I think I convinced myself that it was all a dream? That provided I never looked for it, it would still be there." He paused, as if random thoughts were queuing for the use of the mouth. "Mr. Whiteface has been kind enough to show me the history of the Charlie Benito face . . ." Another pause. "I hear I threw custard pies with considerable accuracy. Perhaps my ancestor will be proud."

"How do you feel now?" said Moist.

"Oh, quite well in myself," said Bent, "whoever that is."

"Good. Then I want to see you at work tomorrow, Mr. Bent."

"You can't ask him to go back so soon!" Miss Drapes protested.

Moist turned to Whiteface and Vetinari. "Could you please leave us, gentlemen?"

There was an affronted look on the chief clown's face, which was made worse by the permanent happy smile, but the door shut behind them.

"Listen, Mr. Bent," said Moist urgently. "We're in a mess—"

"I believed in the gold, you know," said Bent. "Didn't know where it was, but I believed."

"Good. And it probably still exists in Pucci's jewelry box," said Moist. "But I want to open the bank again tomorrow, and Vetinari's people have been through every piece of paper in the place, and you can guess what kind of mess *they* leave. And I want to launch the notes tomorrow, you know? The money that doesn't need gold? And the bank doesn't need gold. We know this. It worked for years with a vault full of junk! But the bank needs *you*, Mr. Bent. The Lavishes are in real trouble; Cosmo's locked up somewhere; Mr. Fusspot's in the palace; and to-morrow, Mr. Bent, the bank opens and you must be there. Please? Oh, and the chairman has graciously barked assent to putting you on a salary of sixty-five dollars a month. I know you are not a man to be influenced by money, but the raise might be worth considering by a man contemplating a, ah, change in his domestic arrangements?"

It wasn't a shot in the dark. It was a shot in the light—clear, blazing light. Miss Drapes was definitely a woman with a plan, and it had to be a better one than the rest of a life spent in a narrow room in Elm Street.

"It's your choice, of course," he said, standing up. "Are they treating him all right, Miss Drapes?"

"Only because I'm here," she said smartly. "This morning three clowns came in with a big rope and a small elephant and wanted to pull one of his poor teeth! And then I'd hardly got them out when two more came in and started to whitewash the room, very inefficiently, in my opinion! I got them out of here in very short order, I can tell you!"

"Well done, Miss Drapes!"

Vetinari was waiting outside the Guild with the coach door open and, Moist noted with relief, Mr. Fusspot asleep on the cushions.

"You will get in," Vetinari said. "You too, Miss Dearheart."

"Actually it's a very short walk to—"

"Get *in*, Mr. Lipwig. We will go the pretty way.

"I believe you think our relationship is a game," said Vetinari, as the coach pulled away. "You believe that all sins will be forgiven. So let me give you this."

He took up a black walking stick with a silver skull on the handle, and tugged at the handle.

"This curious thing was in the possession of Cosmo Lavish," he said, as the blade slid out.

"I know. Isn't it a replica of yours?" said Moist.

"Oh really," said Vetinari. "Am I a sword-made-of-the-blood-of-a-thousand-men kind of ruler? It'll be a crown of skulls next, I suppose. I believe Cosmo had it made."

"So it's a replica of a rumor?" said Adora Belle. Outside the coach, some gates were swung open.

"Indeed," said Vetinari. "A copy of something that does not exist. One can only assume that it is authentic in every respect."

The coach door was opened, and Moist and Adora Belle stepped down into the palace gardens.

They had the usual look of such places—neat, tidy, lots of gravel and pointy trees and no vegetables.

"Why are we here?" said Adora Belle. "It's about the golems, isn't it?"

"Miss Dearheart, what do our local golems think about this new army?"

"They don't like them. They think they will cause trouble. They have no chem that can be changed. They're worse than zombies."

"Thank you. A further question: Will they kill?"

"Historically, golem-makers have learned not to make golems that kill—"

"Is that a no?"

"I don't know!"

"We make progress. Is it possible to give them an order which cannot be countermanded by another person?"

"Well, er . . . Yes. If they don't know the wretched secret."

"Which is?" Vetinari turned back to Moist and drew the sword.

"It must be the way I give the orders, sir," said Moist, squinting downward at the blade for the second time. It really did glint.

He was braced for what happened, except that it happened in entirely the wrong way.

Vetinari handed him the sword and said, "Miss Dearheart, I really wish you would not leave the city for long periods. It makes this man seek danger. Tell us the secret, Mr. Lipwig."

"I think it could be too dangerous, sir."

"Mr. Lipwig, do I need a button that says TYRANT?"

"Can I make a bargain?"

"Of course. I am a reasonable man."

"Will you keep to it?"

"No. But *I* will make a different bargain," said Vetinari. "The Post Office can have six golem horses. The other golem warriors will be considered wards of the Golem Trust, but the use of four hundred of them to improve the operation of the clacks system will, I am sure, meet with international approval. We will replace gold with golems as a basis for our currency, as you have so eloquently pleaded. The two of you have made the international situation very . . . interesting—"

"Sorry, why is it me that's holding this sword?" said Moist.

"—and you tell us the secret and, best of all, you live," Vetinari finished, "and who is going to give you a better offer?"

"Oh, all right," said Moist. "I knew this would have to happen. The golems obey me be—"

"—because you wear a golden suit and therefore, in their eyes, must be an Umnian priest," said Vetinari, "because for an order to be fully realized the right person must say the right words to the right recipient. I used to be quite a scholar. It's a matter of reasoning. Do not continue to stand there with your mouth open."

"You already knew?"

"It wasn't exactly dragon magic."

"So why did you give me this horrible sword?"

"It *is* tasteless, isn't it," said Vetinari, taking it from him. "One might imagine it belonging to someone with a name like Krax the Mighty. I was just interested to see that you were more fearful when you were holding it. You really are not a violent man, are you . . ."

"That wasn't necessary!" said Moist. Adora Belle was grinning.

"Mr. Lipwig, Mr. Lipwig, Mr. Lipwig, will you never learn?" said Vetinari, sheathing the sword. "One of my predecessors used to have people torn apart by wild tortoises. It was not a quick death. He thought it was a hoot. Forgive me if my pleasures are a little more cerebral, will you? Let me see now, what was the other thing. Oh yes, I regret to tell you that a man called Owlswick Clamp has died."

There was something about the way he said it . . .

"Did an angel call him?" said Moist.

"Very likely, Mr. Lipwig. But should you find yourself in need of more designs, I'm sure I can find someone in the palace to assist."

"It was meant to be, I'm sure," said Moist. "I'm glad he's gone to a better place."

"Less damp, certainly. Go now. My coach is at your disposal. You have a bank to open! The world spins on, and this morning it is spinning on my desk. Follow me, Mr. Fusspot."

"Can I make a suggestion that might help?" said Moist, as Vetinari turned away.

"What is it?"

"Well, why don't you tell all the other Plains governments about the golden secret? That would mean no one could use them as soldiers. That would take the pressure off."

"Hmm, interesting. And would you agree with that, Miss Dearheart?"

"Yes! We don't want golem armies! It's a very good idea!"

Vetinari reached down and gave Mr. Fusspot a dog biscuit. When he straightened up, there was an almost imperceptible change in his expression.

"Last night," he said, "some traitor sent the golden secret to the rulers of every major city in the plains, via a clacks message the origin of which appears to be untraceable. It wasn't you, was it, Mr. Lipwig?"

"Me? No!"

"But you just suggested it, did you not? Some would call it treason, incidentally."

"I only just mentioned it," said Moist. "You can't pin it on me! Anyway, it was a *good* idea," he added, trying not to catch Adora Belle's eye. If you don't think of *not* using fifty-foot-high killer golems first, someone else *will*."

He heard her giggle, for the first time ever.

"You have found fifty-foot-high killer golems now, Miss Dearheart?" said Vetinari, looking stern, as though he might add, "Well, I hope you brought enough for everybody!"

"No, sir. There aren't any," said Adora Belle, trying to look serious and not succeeding.

"Well, never mind, I'm sure some ingenious person will devise one for you eventually. When they do, don't hesitate to refrain from bringing it home. In the meantime, we have this wretched fait accompli." Vetinari shook his head in what Moist was sure was genuinely contrived annoyance and went on: "An army that will obey anyone with a shiny jacket, a megaphone, and the Umnian words for 'Dig a hole and bury yourselves' would turn war into nothing but a rather entertaining farce. Rest assured, I'm putting together a committee of inquiry. It will not rest, apart from statutory tea and biscuit breaks, until it has found the culprit. I shall take a personal interest, of course."

Of course you will, Moist thought. And I know that lots of people heard me shout Umnian commands, but I'm betting on a man who thinks war is a wicked waste of customers. A man who's a better con artist than I'll ever be, who thinks committees are a kind of wastepaper basket, who can turn sizzle into sausage, every day . . .

Moist and Adora Belle looked at one another. Their glances agreed: It's him. Of course it's him. Downey and all the rest of them will know it's him. Things that live on damp walls will know it's him. And no one will ever prove it.

Moist's thoughts added: He's probably got our signed confessions in his pocket right now, just in case. Owlswick's probably as busy as a bee and as happy as a pig in muck. Still, it could be worse. Better the devil who knows you . . .

"You can trust us," he said.

"Yes. I know," said Vetinari. "Come, Mr. Fusspot. There may be cake."

Moist didn't fancy another ride in the coach. Coaches carried some unpleasant associations right now.

"He's won, hasn't he," said Adora Belle, as the fog billowed around them.

"Well, he's got the chairman eating out of his hand."

"Is he allowed to do that?"

"I think that comes under the *quia ego sic dico* rule."

"Yes, what did that mean?"

" 'Because I say so,' I think."

"That doesn't sound like much of a rule."

"Actually, it's the only one he needs. All in all he could be—"

"You owe me five grand, Mishter Shpangler!"

The figure was out of the gloom and behind Adora Belle in one movement.

"No tricks, miss, on account o' this knife," said Cribbins, and Moist heard Adora Belle's sharp intake of breath. "Your chum promised it to me for peaching you, and since you peached yourself and sent him to the loony house I reckon you owe me, right?"

Moist's slowly moving hand found his pocket, but it was bereft of aid; the Tanty didn't like you to bring blackjacks and lock picks in with you and expected you to buy such things from the wardens, like everyone else.

"Put the knife away and we can talk," he said.

"Oh yeah, talk! You like talkin', you do! You got a magic tongue, you have! I sheen you! You flap it about and you're the golden boy! You tell 'em you're goin' to rob them and they laugh! How d'you get away with that, eh?"

Cribbins was champing and spitting with rage. Angry people make mistakes, but that's no comfort when they're holding a knife a few inches from your girlfriend's kidneys. She'd gone pale, and Moist had to hope that she'd worked out that this was no time to stamp her foot. Above all, he had to stop himself from looking over Cribbins's shoulder, because in the edge of his vision he was sure someone was creeping up.

"This is no time for rash moves," he said loudly. The shadow in the fog appeared to halt.

"Cribbins, this is why you never made it," Moist went on. "I mean, do you expect me to have that much money on me?"

"Plenty of places round here for ush to be coshy while we wait, eh?"

Dumb, thought Moist. Dumb but dangerous. And a thought said: It's brain against brain. And a weapon he doesn't know how to use belongs to you. Push him.

"Just back away and we'll forget we saw you," he said. "That's the best offer you're going to get."

"You're going to try to talk your way out of thish, you shmarmy bashtard? I'm goin' to—"

There was a muffled twang, and Cribbins made a noise. It was the sound of someone trying to scream, except that even screaming was too painful. Moist grabbed Adora Belle as the man bent double, clutching at his mouth. There was another twang, and blood appeared on Cribbins's cheek, causing him to whimper and roll up into a ball.

Even then, there were more twangs as a dead man's dentures, mistreated and ill-used over the years, finally gave up the ghost, who made a determined effort to take the hated Cribbins with him. Later on, the doctor said one spring almost made it into a sinus.

Captain Carrot and Nobby Nobbs ran out of the fog, and stared down at the man who twitched now and again with a ping.

"Sorry, sir, we lost you in the muck," said Carrot. "What happened to him?"

Moist held Adora Belle tightly. "His dentures exploded," he said.

"How could that happen, sir?"

"I have no idea, Captain. Why not do a good deed and get him to the hospital?"

"Will you want to press charges, Mr. Lipwig?" Carrot said, lifting the whimpering Cribbins with some care.

"I'd prefer a brandy," said Moist. He thought: *Perhaps Anoia was just awaiting her moment. I'd better go to her temple and hang up a big, big ladle. It may not be a good idea to be ungrateful . . .*

SECRETARY DRUMKNOTT TIPTOED into Lord Vetinari's office on velvet-shod feet.

"Good morning," said his lordship, turning away from the window. "The fog has a very pleasing tint of yellow this morning. Any news about Heretofore?"

"The watch in Quirm are searching for him, sir," said Drumknott, putting the city edition of the *Times* in front of him.

"Why?"

"He bought a ticket for Quirm."

"But he will have bought another one from the

coachman for Genua. He will run as far as he can. Send a short clacks to our man there, will you?"

"I hope you are right, sir."

"Do you? I hope I am wrong. It will be good for me. Ah. Ahaha."

"Sir?"

"I see the *Times* has put color on the front page again. The front and back of the one-dollar note."

"Yes, sir. Very nice."

"Actual size, too," said Vetinari, still smiling. "I see here that this is to familiarize people with the look of the things. Even now, Drumknott, *even now*, honest citizens are carefully cutting out both sides of this note and gluing them together."

"Shall I have a word with the editor, sir?"

"Don't. It will be more entertaining to let things take their course."

Vetinari leaned back in his chair and shut his eyes with a sigh. "Very well, Drumknott, I feel strong enough now to hear what the political cartoon looks like."

There was a crackle of paper as Drumknott found the right page.

"Well, there is a very good likeness of Mr. Fusspot." Under Vetinari's chair the dog opened his eyes at the sound of his name. So did his new master, with more urgency.

"Surely he has nothing in his mouth?"

"No, sir, it is empty," said Drumknott calmly. "This *is* the *Times* of Ankh-Morpork, sir."

Vetinari relaxed again. "Continue."

"He is on a leash, sir, and looking unaccustomedly ferocious. You are holding the leash, sir. In front of him, and backing nervously into a corner, are a group of very fat cats. They are wearing top hats, sir."

"As cats do, yes." Vetinari nodded.

"And they have the words THE BANKS on them," Drumknott added.

"Subtle indeed!"

"While you, sir, are waving a handful of paper money at them and the speech bubble says—"

"Don't tell me. 'THIS does NOT taste of pineapple'?"

"Well done, sir. Incidentally, it does so happen that the chairmen of the rest of the city banks wish to see you, at your convenience."

"Good. This afternoon, then."

Vetinari got up and walked over to the window. The fog was thinning, but its drifting cloud still obscured the city.

"Mr. Lipwig is a very . . . *popular* young man, is he not, Drumknott?" said Vetinari, staring into the gloom.

"Oh yes, sir," said the secretary, folding up the newspaper. "Extremely so. The *Times* likes him. The people seem to like him. He is an entertainer, and much is forgiven of such people."

"And very confident in himself, I think."

"I would say so."

"And loyal?"

"He took a pie for you, sir."

"A tactical thinker at speed, then."

"Oh yes."

"Bearing in mind his own future was riding on the pie as well."

"He is certainly sensitive to political currents, no doubt about it," said Drumknott, picking up his bundle of files.

"And, as you say, popular," said Vetinari, still a gaunt outline against the fog.

Drumknott waited. Moist was not the only one sensitive to political currents.

"An asset to the city, indeed," said Vetinari, after a while. "And we should not waste him. Obviously, though, he should be at the Royal Bank long enough to bend it to his satisfaction," Vetinari mused. Drumknott said nothing, but arranged some of the files into a more pleasing order. A name struck him, and he shifted a file to the top.

"Of course, then he will get restless again and become a danger to others as well as himself . . ."

Drumknott smiled at his files. His hand hovered . . .

"Apropos of nothing, how old is Mr. Creaser?"

"The taxmaster? In his seventies, sir," said Drumknott, opening the file he had just selected. "Yes, seventy-four, it says here."

"We have recently pondered his methods, have we not?"

"Indeed we have, sir. Last week."

"Not a man with a flexible cast of mind, I feel. A little at sea in the modern world. Holding someone upside down over a bucket and giving them a good shaking is not the way forward. I won't blame him when he decides to take an honorable and well-earned retirement."

"Yes sir. When would you like him to decide that, sir?" said Drumknott.

"No rush," said Vetinari. "No rush."

"Have you given any thought to his successor? It's not a job that creates friends," said Drumknott. "It would need a special sort of person."

"I shall ponder it," said Vetinari. "No doubt a name will present itself."

THE BANK STAFF were at work early, pushing through the crowds who were filling the street because (a) this was another act in the wonderful street theater that was Ankh-Morpork and (b) there was going to be big trouble if *their* money had gone missing. There was, however, no sign of Mr. Bent or Miss Drapes.

Moist was in the Mint. Mr. Spools's men had, well, they'd done their best. It's an apologetic phrase, commonly used to mean that the result is just one step above mediocre, but *their* best was one leap above superb.

"I'm sure we can improve them," said Mr. Spools, as Moist gloated.

"They are perfect, Mr. Spools!"

"Anything but. But it's kind of you to say so. We've done seventy thousand so far."

"Nothing like enough!"

"With respect, we are not printing a newspaper here. But we're getting better. You have talked about other denominations . . . ?"

"Oh, yes. Two, five, and ten dollars to start with. And the fives and tens will talk."

Nothing like enough, he thought, as the colors of money flowed through his fingers. *People will queue up for this. They won't want the grubby, heavy coins, not when they see this! Backed by golems! What is a coin compared to the hand that holds it? That's worth! That's value! Hm, yes, that'd look good on the two-dollar note, too, I'd better remember that.*

"The money . . . will talk?" said Mr. Spools carefully.

"Imps," said Moist. "They're only a sort of intelligent spell. They don't even have to have a shape. We'll print them on the higher denominations."

"Do you think the university will agree to that?" said Spools.

"Yes, because I'm going to put Ridcully's head on the five-dollar note. I'll go and talk to Ponder Stibbons. This looks like a job for inadvisably applied magic if ever I saw one."

"And what would the money say?"

"Anything we want it to. 'Is your purchase really necessary?' perhaps, or 'Why not save me for a rainy day?' The possibilities are endless!"

"It usually says good-bye to me," said a printer, to ritual amusement.

"Well, maybe we can make it blow you a kiss as well," said Moist. He turned to the Men of the Sheds, who were beaming and gleaming with new-found importance. "Now, if some of you gentlemen will help me carry this lot into the bank . . ."

The hands of the clock were chasing one another to the top of the hour when Moist arrived at the head of the procession, and there was still no sign of Mr. Bent.

"Is that clock right?" said Moist, as the hands began the relaxing stroll to the half hour.

"Oh yes, sir," said a counter clerk. "Mr. Bent sets it twice a day."

"Maybe, but he hasn't been here for more than—"

The doors swung open, and there he was. Moist had, for some reason, expected the clown outfit, but this was the smooth and shiny, ironed-in-his-clothes Bent with the smart jacket and pinstripe trousers and—

—the red nose. And he was arm-in-arm with Miss Drapes.

The staff stared at it all, too shocked for a reaction.

"Ladies and gentlemen," said Bent, his voice echoing in the silence. "I owe so many apologies. I have made many mistakes. Indeed, my whole life has been a mistake. I believed that true worth lodged in lumps of metal, metal which I doubt we shall see again. Much of what I believed is worthless, in fact, but Mr. Lipwig believed in me and so I am here today. Let us make money based not on a trick of geology but on the ingenuity of hand and brain. And now—" he paused, because Miss Drapes had squeezed his arm.

"Oh, yes, how could I forget," Bent went on, "what I do now believe with all my heart is that Miss

Drapes will marry me in the Chapel of Fun in the Fools' Guild on Saturday, the ceremony to be conducted by the Reverend Brother 'Whacko' Whopply. You are all, of course, invited—"

"—but be careful what you wear because it's a whitewash wedding," said Miss Drapes coyly, or what she probably thought was coyly.

"And with that it only remains for me to—" Bent tried to continue, but the staff had realized what their ears had heard, and closed in on the couple, the women drawn to the soon-not-to-be-Miss Drapes by the legendarily high gravity of an engagement ring and the men intent on slapping Mr. Bent on the back and then doing the hitherto unthinkable, which involved picking him up and carrying him around the room on their shoulders.

Eventually, it was Moist who had to cup his hands and shout: "Look at the time, ladies and gentlemen! Our customers are *waiting*, ladies and gentlemen! Let us not stand in the way of making money! We mustn't be a dam in the economic flow!"

. . . and he wondered what Hubert was doing now . . .

WITH HIS TONGUE out in concentration, Igor removed a slim tube from the gurgling bowels of the Glooper.

A few bubbles zigzagged to the top of the central hydro unit and burst on the surface with a *gloop*.

Hubert breathed a deep sigh of relief.

"Well done, Igor, only one more to . . . Igor?"

"Right here, thur," said Igor, stepping out from behind him.

"It looks as though it's working, Igor. Good old hyphenated silicon! But you're sure it'll still work as an economic modeler afterward?"

"Yeth, thur. I am confident in the new valve array. The thity will affect the Glooper, if you withh, but not the other way around."

"Even so, it would be dreadful if it fell into the wrong hands, Igor. I wonder if I should present the Glooper to the government. What do you think?"

Igor gave this some thought. In his experience a prime definition of "the wrong hands" was "the government."

"I think you ought to take the opportunity to get out a bit more, thur," he said kindly.

"Yes, I suppose I have been overdoing it," said Hubert. "Um . . . about Mr. Lipwig . . ."

"Yeth?"

Hubert looked like a man who had been wrestling with his conscience and got a knee in his eye.

"I want to put the gold back in the vault. That'll stop all this trouble."

"But it wath thtolen away yearth ago, thur," Igor explained patiently. "It wathen't your fault. It wath not even there when the Glooper wath built."

"No, but they were blaming Mr. Lipwig, who's always been very kind to us."

"I think he got off on that one, thur."

"But we *could* put it back," Hubert insisted. "It

would come back from wherever it was taken to, wouldn't it?"

Igor scratched his head, causing a faint metallic noise. He had been following events with more care than Hubert employed, and as far as he could see, the missing gold had been disposed of by the Lavishes years ago. Mr. Lipwig had been in trouble, but it seemed to Igor that trouble hit Mr. Lipwig like a big wave hitting a flotilla of ducks. Afterward, there was no wave but there was still a lot of duck.

"It might," he conceded.

"So that would be a good thing, yes?" Hubert insisted. "And he's been very kind. We owe him that little favor."

"I don't think—"

"That is an order, Igor!"

Igor beamed. At last. All this politeness had been getting on his nerves. What an Igor expected was insane orders. That was what an Igor was born (and, to some extent, made) for. A shouted order to do something of dubious morality with an unpredictable outcome? Thweeet!

Of course, thunder and lightning would have been more appropriate. Instead there was nothing more than the bubbling of the Glooper and gentle glassy noises that always made Igor think he was in a wind-chime factory. But sometimes you just had to improvise.

He closed the little valve on the bottom of a funnel that drained into the Gold Reserve flask, and then filled it to the ten-tons marker, fiddled with the shiny valve array for a minute or two, and then stood back.

"When I turn thith wheel, marthter, the Glooper will depothit into the vault flathk an analogue of ten tonth of gold. Thith will cauth ten tonth of gold to gently appear in the vault, tho that reality ith in balance. Ath thoon ath thith ith done, the Glooper will then clothe the connection."

"Very good, Igor."

"Er, you wouldn't like to thtout thomthing, would you," Igor hinted.

"Like what?"

"Oh, I don't know . . . perhapth 'They said' . . . sorry, 'thaid' . . . thorry . . . 'I wath mad but thith will show them!!' "

"That's not really me."

"No?" said Igor. "Perhapth a laugh, then?"

"Would that help?"

"Yeth, thur," said Igor. "It will help me."

"Oh, very well, if you think it will help," said Hubert. He took a sip from the jug Igor had just used, and cleared his throat.

"Hah," he said. "Er, hahahh hah HA HA HA **HA HA HA** . . ."

What a waste of a wonderful gift, thought Igor, and turned the wheel.

Gloop!

EVEN FROM DOWN here in the vaults, you could hear the buzz of activity in the banking hall.

Moist walked slowly under the weight of a crate of bank notes, to Adora Belle's annoyance.

"Why can't you put them in a safe?"

"Because they're full of coins. Anyway, we'll have to keep them in here for now, until we get sorted out."

"It's really just a victory thing, isn't it? Your triumph over gold?"

"A bit, yes."

"You got away with it again."

"I wouldn't exactly put it like that. Gladys has applied to be my secretary."

"Here's a tip: don't let her sit on your lap."

"I'm being serious here! She's ferocious! She probably wants my job now! She believes everything she reads!"

"There's your answer, then. Good grief, she's the least of your problems!"

"Every problem is an opportunity," said Moist primly.

"Well, if you upset Vetinari again you will have a wonderful opportunity to never have to buy another hat."

"No, I think he likes a little opposition."

"And are you any good at knowing how much?"

"No, that's what I enjoy. You get a wonderful view from the point of no return."

Moist opened the vault and put the crate on a shelf. It looked a bit lost and alone, but he could just make out the thudding of the press in the Mint as they worked hard at providing it with company.

Adora Belle leaned on the door frame, watching him carefully.

"I keep hearing that while I was away you did all kinds of risky things. Is that true?"

"I like to flirt with risk. It's always been part of my life."

"But you don't do that kind of stuff while I'm around," said Adora Belle. "So I'm enough of a thrill, am I?"

She advanced. The heels helped, of course, but Spike could move like a snake trying to sashay, and the severe, tight, and ostensibly modest dresses she wore left everything to the imagination, which is *much* more inflammatory than leaving nothing. Speculation is always more interesting than facts.

"What are you thinking about right now?" she said. She dropped her cigarette stub and pinned it with a heel.

"Piggy banks," said Moist instantly.

"Piggy banks?"

"Yes, in the shape of not so much a pig as the bank and the Mint. To teach the kiddies the habits of thrift. The money could go in the slot where the Bad Penny is—"

"Are you *really* thinking about money boxes?"

"Er, no. I'm flirting with risk again."

"That's better!"

"Although you must admit that it's a pretty clev—"

Adora Belle grabbed Moist by the shoulders.

"Moist von Lipwig, if you don't give me a big wet kiss right now— Ow! Are there fleas down here?"

It felt like a hailstorm. The air in the vault had become a golden mist. It would have been pretty, if it wasn't so heavy. It stung where it touched.

Moist grabbed her hand and dragged her out as the teeming particles became a torrent. Outside, he took off his hat, which was already so heavy that it was endangering his ears, and tipped a small fortune in gold onto the floor. The vault was already half-full.

"Oh no," he moaned. "*Just* when it was going so well . . ."

Epilogue

WHITENESS, COOLNESS, the smell of starch.

"Good morning, my lord."

Cosmo opened his eyes. A female face, surrounded by a white cap, was looking down at him.

Ah, so it had worked. He had known it would.

"Would you like to get up?" said the woman, stepping back. There were a couple of heavily built men behind her, also in white. This was just as it should be.

He looked down at the place where a whole finger should be, and saw a stump covered in a bandage. He couldn't quite remember how this had happened, but that was fine. After all, in order to change, something had to be lost as well as gained. That was fine. So this was a hospital. That was fine.

"This *is* a hospital, yes?" he said, sitting up in the bed.

"Well done, Your Lordship. You are in the Lord Vetinari ward, as a matter of fact."

That is fine, Cosmo thought. *So I endowed a ward at some time. That was very forward-looking of me.*

"And those men are bodyguards?" he said, nodding at the men.

"Well, they are here to see that no harm comes to you," said the nurse, "so I suppose that's true."

There were a number of other patients in the long ward, all in white robes, some of them seated and playing board games, and a number of them standing at the big window, staring out. They stood in identical poses, their hands clasped behind their backs. Cosmo watched them for some time.

Then he stared at the small table where two men were sitting opposite each other, apparently taking turns to measure each other's foreheads. He had to pay careful attention for some time before he worked out what was going on. But Lord Vetinari was not a man to jump to conclusions.

"Excuse me, nurse," said Cosmo, and she hurried over. He beckoned her closer, and the two burly men drew nearer, too, not taking their eyes off him.

"I know those people are not entirely sane," he said. "They think *they* are Lord Vetinari, am I right? This is a ward for such people, yes? Those two are having an eyebrow-raising competition!"

"You are quite right," said the nurse. "Well done, my lord!"

"Doesn't it puzzle them when they see one another?"

"Not really, my lord. Each one thinks he's the real one."

"So they don't know that *I* am the real one?"

One of the guards leaned forward.

"No, my lord, we're keeping very quiet about it," he said, winking at his colleague.

Cosmo nodded. "Very good. This is a wonderful place to stay while I'm getting better. The perfect place to be incognito. Who would think of looking for me in this room of poor, sad madmen?"

"That's exactly the plan, sir. Well done!"

"You know, some sort of artificial skyline would make things more interesting for the poor souls at the window," he said.

"Ah, we can tell you're the real thing, sir," said the man, winking at his colleague.

Cosmo beamed. And two weeks later, when he won the eyebrow-raising competition, he was happier than he'd ever been before.

THE PINK PUSSYCAT Club was packed again tonight . . . except for seat seven (front row, center).

The record for anyone remaining in seat seven was nine seconds. The baffled management had replaced the cushions and the springs several times. It made no difference. On the other hand, everything else was going so inexplicably well lately. There seemed to be a good atmosphere in the club, especially among the dancers, who were working extra hard now that someone had invented a currency that could be stuck into a garter. Noisy drunks fell silent, disrespectful punters were hurrying frantically out of the door even before the bouncers got to them.

The whole place was running like a clock, the management concluded, and it somehow had to do with that empty seat. Well, a happy house was worth a seat, especially in view of what had happened when they tried to take the damn thing away . . .